Please visit the website to see a:

Topical Index of *A Perfect Finish*

To contact the author or learn more about riding the Alaska Highway, APF characters, Whitehorse adventures, the Dedication, all those moons, and the real story of writing A Perfect Finish please visit:

www.APerfectFinish.info

Scan to Read About the Story

If you like this book, please write a book review.

Why settle for an ordinary death?
when you can have . . .

A Perfect Finish

Christopher Lude

First Edition–Trade Paperback

The story, all names, characters, and incidents portrayed in this production are fictitious. No identification with actual persons (living or deceased) should be inferred.

Publisher: 5280 Scribblers, Inc.

www.aperfectfinish.info

ISBN: 979 | 8-9887845-1-7

Dedication

This book is lovingly dedicated to my indomitable grandmother, Jane. She carved her own path, with grit and determination, before Alzheimer's cast its shadows.

Acknowledgements

My wife Hanna, sister-in-law Emma, and friend Tony Robinson were gracious early readers. Their insightful suggestions were pivotal in shaping *A Perfect Finish* into the story it is today.

I extend my heartfelt thanks to the community of Whitehorse of the Yukon Territory, whose charm, wit, and hospitality have always kept me coming back for more. Special gratitude goes to Denise and Vernon, whose generosity and knowledge of the local flora, fauna, terrain, trails, and river enriched my experience beyond measure. Their enthusiastic support (coupled with Hanna paying my monthly credit card bills) allowed me to immerse myself in the writing process throughout a memorable summer in Canada's Wilderness City.

My nephew Brandon created the image for the cover, was a cold-blooded comma-zombie-killer, and proposed a plethora of ideas from outer space.

Julie G (@jgolden268) and Kaitlin S (@ksclafani) were incredibly generous and patient (Fiverr) editors. They combined constructive criticism with extensive detailed suggestions for improving the manuscript. Julie wielded an axe. Kaitlin polished tirelessly. Had I accepted more of their suggestions, we could have saved the cat and tamed the vixen.

Wael Wafik created the inside images, the book cover, and the website.

Finally, I thank Hanna, my love, for her balanced insight, tireless editing, unfailing patience, and supreme generosity in allowing me to write this book.

Table of Contents

Whitehorse YT

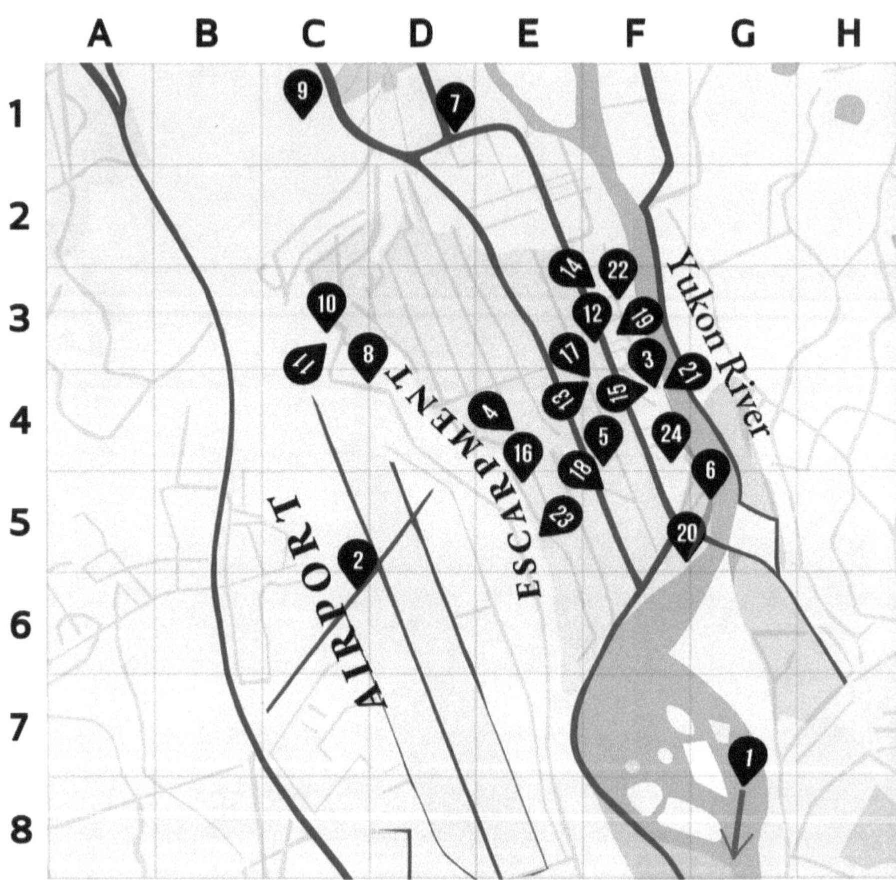

1: Miles Canyon Bridge (NA)
2: Whitehorse Int'l Airport (6-C)
3: Edgewater Hotel (4-F)
4: Gold Nugget Inn (4-E)
5: Meriwa's Apartment (4-F)
6: One Mile Riverwalk (5-G)
7: Three Mile Riverwalk (1-D)
8: Black Street Stairs (4-C)
9: Two-Mile Hill (1-C)
10: Confession Bench (3-C)
11: Kissing Tree (3-C)
12: Bullet Hole Bagels (3-F)

13: Klondike Rib & Salmon (4-F)
14: The 98 Hotel (3-F)
15: Sheep Camp (4-F)
16: Wayfarer Oysters (5-E)
17: Burnt Toast (4-F)
18: Kind Café (5-F)
19: MacBride Museum (3-F)
20: S.S. Klondike (5-F)
21: W & Y Route Depot (4-F)
22: Kwanlin Dün Cultural Ctr (3-F)
23: Secret Rope Trail (5-E)
24: Yukon Visitors Center (4-F)

Prologue: The Business Plan

The purpose of A Perfect Finish (APF) is to promote and advocate for new laws on assistance-in-dying. Our goal is to generate significant press coverage and internet traffic through our activities in the Yukon, spark public discourse and raise awareness on providing seniors the option of death with dignity.

APF provides a means for American women over seventy to exit with grace and style, rather than exposing their dignity to modern medicine and the whims of fate. For one million dollars, clients will experience two weeks of adventure in the Yukon Wilderness. They will traverse the rapids in historic Miles Canyon, hike the Klondike trails, soar over the peaks of Kluane Range, and sing around the campfires at Tagish Lake.

During this time, clients will have the opportunity to say their goodbyes. Our videographers will capture and document the final journeys in a series of private and public blog posts that can be revisited as a tribute. We will also offer our clients the opportunity to donate to the First Nations Business Accelerator of the Yukon Territory, if they so choose.

Recent medical advances have extended the lifespan of Americans by twelve years, leading to a surge in the number of nursing homes. This further exacerbates suffering, as science prolongs lives without adequately addressing the challenges of aging. The moment a retiree is admitted to a nursing home or ICU, she forfeits her autonomy to make decisions about the time and manner of her death.

Canada's Medical Assistance in Dying (MAID) law offers a viable alternative to Canadians. Since the enactment of these laws, more than two-and-a-half percent of deceased Canadians have chosen this option as their final choice.

In the USA, the following have enacted euthanasia laws with varying degrees of effectiveness: California, Colorado, Hawaii, Montana, Oregon, Vermont, Washington, and Washington DC.

Beyond broadening the public discourse and raising awareness, A Perfect Finish will provide a unique experience and enhanced legacy for those Americans who freely choose a dignified and painless end to their lives.

Alamea Grace Mumford

Seattle, Washington

1. Bump in The Road

Steve was not expecting a flat tire when he woke up at 5 am to pack his motorcycle. The replacement tire had to be flown in from Alaska, and the resulting delay put him in a bind.

He had originally planned to leave Whitehorse early and ride for ten-and-a-half hours to Fairbanks, where he would spend the night before picking up his thirteen-year-old stepdaughter Rachel. However, now he would have to ride through the half-light of the northern night on two hundred miles of the roughest stretch of the Alaska Highway to meet her flight on time. At 7 pm, Steve set the cruise control to fifty miles per hour and headed west in misty rain.

After an hour the rain subsided, and he was able to speed up a bit. Between Destruction Bay and Burwash Landing, road conditions worsened due to frost heaves that occur commonly during the winter months. Water seeps through the pavement, freezes, and expands, causing the asphalt to buckle. Although the damage is repaired each spring, this final patch of Canada's highway is clearly a low priority.

Steve rode across the White River and rounded a bend, where a full-grown grizzly bear was feeding on roadkill. He sped up and gave the bear a wide berth. The creature stood on its hind legs as Steve rode past.

A mixture of fear and delight at the sight distracted him from noticing the frost heave. He gripped the handlebars as he flew through the air and landed with a jarring thud on both wheels. His teeth clattered together as his helmet slammed into the fairing. He struggled to regain his balance on the running boards.

He pulled over, turned off the engine, and cursed himself for his carelessness and drowsiness. He inspected his bike for damage. His rolling sofa of a motorcycle was not designed for high-speed motocross jumps, but it survived unscathed. He took out his phone and checked the time. The signal strength indicator showed *No Service.*

As he finished relieving himself ten yards off the road, he recognized in the distance the distinctive rumble of a big twin engine. The headlights of a Harley-Davidson trike pulling a trailer barreled toward him and the frost heave. He ran uphill to the road, waved his arms, and pointed to the frost heave. The driver accelerated. As the vehicle hit the bump, it went up on two wheels and rolled sideways, dragging the trailer with it.

Steve gasped and grabbed clumps of hair as the Harley and its two riders careened off the road and tumbled down the embankment. The trailer broke loose and bounced like a beach ball, scattering its contents as it disintegrated.

As the chaos subsided, Steve stood dazed in a cloud of dust and listened to a choir of crickets, locusts, and katydids, their sing-song buzz continuing as though nothing unusual had occurred. Aside from the scars etched into the hillside, the only evidence of the crash was the trailer axle and tongue pitched against an aspen tree and a taillight glimmering faintly through the dust.

Steve pushed through the brush. The faint sound of coughing and wheezing led him to a woman lying on her back, her leg bent at an unnatural angle. She unbuckled her helmet and spilled her long chestnut hair onto the grass and fireweed. Steve recognized her face and caught his breath to suppress his surprise. "Does your leg hurt?"

"I can't feel it. It's hard to breathe," she wheezed.

"Can I carry you to the light?" he asked.

"Please don't," she responded.

Steve ran to his bike, turned on the headlights and flashers, took his knife and a bungee cord from the trunk, and retrieved his motorcycle cover from the bottom of his saddlebag. He spread the cover over the weeds. She cried in pain as he helped her straighten her leg and settled her on top. He grabbed the edges of the cover and dragged her out of the ditch. Once on the road's shoulder, he examined her in the headlights.

His breath came in short, sharp bursts as his adrenaline-fueled hands searched frantically for the source of blood. There was a small tear in her leather pants, halfway down her leg. He fumbled in his pocket for the knife. She breathed rapidly and coughed up blood. Her skin had taken on a pale grayish-green hue.

She's seriously injured—it's worse than just a mangled leg.

Beginning from the bottom, he cut his way up the outside of her pants leg until he revealed the gash on the inside of her knee. He took two towels from his trunk, handed her one, and with the bungee cord, bound the other around the wound. He looked at her expectantly.

"Nice work," she whispered through labored breaths and a forced smile. She wiped blood from her face and asked, "How's Evel Knievel?"

"Who?"

"Mark, my husband. Is he okay?"

Steve hesitated. "Oh. Oh, sure."

"Please go check."

He jogged through the fireweed toward the glimmering red light, wondering what he would find. "Mark?" he called out.

The brotherhood of Harley riders? What kind of jackass speeds up when he sees a fellow motorcyclist waving him down on a deserted highway?

When he reached the bloody mess, he inhaled sharply and staggered backwards. The man was lying in what should have been a face-down position with his arms outstretched in a touchdown pose, except for his head. It had been crushed, possibly by the trailer wheel. Brains and pieces of broken skull were scattered across the grass. Bitter bile stung the back of Steve's throat.

The Harley trike sat upright, with its front wheel twisted at a thirty-degree angle. Despite the gruesome scene, Steve could not help but notice the shoes–lots of fancy high-heeled shoes–scattered down the hill and around the trike. He turned on the trike's emergency flashers and shut off the ignition. As he headed back up the hill, he picked up a helmet and was not surprised to find the buckle undone. He dropped it and hurried back to the woman.

Her eyes were pinched shut and her teeth chattered. He removed his jacket, covered her with it, and knelt beside her. "Where does it hurt?"

"It's hard to breathe," she rasped. "How is Mark?"

Steve hesitated, leaned close and whispered, "I'm so sorry. He didn't make it."

She took a jagged breath, nodded, and bit her lower lip. "Not exactly a perfect finish, but he finally got what he wanted." Steve blinked and shook his head. She explained, "He had brain cancer."

He fidgeted and finessed a retreat by examining her wound. "I'm Steve." He offered a bottle of water. "Here, take a sip."

She shook her head, pushed the bottle away and whispered between breaths, "I'm Alamea."

"Alamea? Hawaiian, from Oahu," he remarked as he caught her eye.

She raised her eyebrows. "How did you know that?"

"I went to college in Hawaii. I saw you on TV. You do the weather."

"No, that was my mother," she replied in a broken whisper.

"I can take you to the hospital," he suggested. "I'll hold you in front of me on the motorcycle."

She did a combination cough-chuckle. "I'm an ER nurse. The bleeding is internal. Let's wait for someone to drive by."

Steve rubbed his hands on his pants and searched the road in the direction from which they had come. He wiped sweat from his brow and checked his phone for the time and cell reception. With no signal, one survivor, the damaged trike, and all the blood, they were stranded. He'd ridden no more than ten minutes past the grizzly. Considering the wind's direction, the bear would have already detected the scent. If it came, it could cover the distance within thirty minutes. Ignoring the danger would be foolish. He was obliged to warn her.

"Alamea, I passed a grizzly not far from here. I'm worried that he may come."

"We passed him too. Ride away now. You can bring help," she replied.

Is she trying to save me from encountering the bear?

The faint whining buzz interrupted his thoughts. A cloud of mosquitoes, thick as the rings of Saturn, swarmed his headlamps. "We're going to attract every insect in the Yukon," he said as he turned off the lights, leaving only the warning flashers. He took a jacket and a sweatshirt out of his saddlebag and brushed mosquitoes from her face and leg before covering her. He knelt beside her and checked the time on his phone again. It had been thirteen minutes since he had last checked. There remained seven or eight hours of travel time to Fairbanks and less than ten hours until Rachel's plane would land. He wiped his brow again and took a deep breath.

She whispered haltingly, "There's a gun. A black case. In the back."

He ran to the trike and found two black cases in the storage compartment. Upon his return, she pointed to one and Steve opened it to find a Glock 34 pistol with three magazines, each loaded with nine-millimeter full metal jacket rounds. The gun had an SRO sight and a custom trigger. Steve had the same model at home, though not as fancy.

Great gun for the shooting range, not bad for home defense, but really lousy for shooting a bear. Low velocity, no penetration. Even bear spray would be better. Definitely not legal for tourists entering Canada! Why would she have it?

She said, "Give me the gun."

Steve assured her he knew how to use it and was in a better position to shoot. "I'll stay with you. If the bear comes, I'll be ready."

She blinked and nodded. "Thank you."

Steve rose and surveyed the road. If it attacked, he'd have no opportunity for a side shot. He knew from shooting wild hogs in Oklahoma that without a rifle, a charging animal presented the most difficult target. Pistol-caliber bullets wouldn't easily penetrate a thick, angled skull. He could pepper it, punching tiny nine-millimeter holes in the shoulders and chest, which would eventually kill the animal, but such a tactic would not prevent the creature from attacking him first. Without considerable luck, he would be mauled by an enraged, eight hundred-pound, bleeding grizzly bear. Still, he hoped he could save the woman.

He turned on the SRO sight and, with both eyes open, crouched and aimed at a tree twenty-five yards away. The sight worked well in the dim light of the northern night. Steve chambered a round and inserted a full magazine. He would shoot eighteen rounds—nine double-taps in series—taking his time to adjust between each pair.

He wiped the sweat from his brow and secured the gun in the waistband at the small of his back before returning to kneel beside her. As the minutes ticked by, the sound of Alamea's troubled breathing penetrated the insects' melody in the otherwise still night.

It was just a shadow when it first caught his eye. Less than one hundred yards away, the shadow grew more ominous as it loped alongside the road. Steve leapt up, stood directly over her legs, and drew the pistol. "The bear is coming," he said calmly, keeping his eyes trained on the animal. "Stay still and it may ignore you."

She raised herself up onto her right elbow as Steve ran twenty yards toward the massive beast. He had no doubt about the bear's intent: it was hunting. He took two deep breaths and drew the pistol. He planted his feet and settled the sights on the bear. He took another deep breath, relaxed his shoulders, and squeezed the trigger twice. A high-pitched ringing filled his ears. The bear, forty yards away, roared and charged at full speed. Double-tap, the muzzle rose, reset, aim lower, double-tap–Steve repeated as he counted to nine. The bear faltered as Steve changed magazines, and before he could chamber a round, it collapsed to the ground, its head not more than five yards away.

Steve fired two more shots, once at a distance of a few yards as the bear continued to move, then another point-blank in its ear. Some of his shots had ricocheted off the skull and jaw. One fortunate shot had penetrated the right eye.

Gunpowder smoke hung heavily in the air. He took several steps back, returned the gun to his waistband, and leaned over, hands on his knees, gasping for air. His eyes stung from the acrid fumes. The ringing in his ears throbbed in tempo with his racing heart. He shook his head and sighed before returning.

She smiled, still propped on her right elbow. "Nobody's ever saved me from a bear before. That was the bravest thing I've ever seen."

He forced a smile. "First time for me, too."

She settled back with her eyes closed. He took a deep breath, checked the leg wound, and took hold of her hand. She was still coughing blood and her breathing had deteriorated to fast and shallow panting. As he considered his options, he let out a desperate sigh and looked skyward, searching for an answer in the constellations, but in the northern white night appeared only the waxing crescent of the Buck Moon.

Her whisper pierced his thoughts. "Do you have a pen and paper? Look for a notepad in Mark's bag."

"Are you serious?"

"As a motorcycle crash," she whispered with a cough.

He brought her a pen and notepad. She asked, "What's your full name?"

She rolled to her left side and in the dim blinking lights wrote:

Change to My Last Will & Testament

Steven Ward Hamilton saved me from the bear. I need his help in pursuing A Perfect Finish. Accordingly, being of sound mind, I do hereby alter my last will and testament and bequeath to him all that I have.

Alamea Grace Mumford

He read the page twice before she asked for the second case he had taken from the trike. "Inside is everything you need. If you like the business plan, use my funds to implement it."

He pinched his eyebrows together. "Really Alamea, don't worry, you are going to be fine."

She removed her gold Cartier Tank watch. "For Meriwa. Clyde will understand," she said as she handed it to him.

The watch was remarkably heavy and warm. A wave of sadness washed over him as he turned it, weighed it, felt its warmth, and considered the finality of the act. "Meriwa, Meriwa," he repeated. She took off her black pearl necklace and earrings and gave those to him as well. "These too."

He put the watch and jewelry in his pocket. She dug her nails into his flesh, as she grasped his forearm and pulled him in. Her breathing was shallow and rapid. She locked eyes with him and whispered, "Steve, if you leave my things behind, they will be lost. Promise me you'll take them with you."

Tears stung the back of his eyes and his throat was tight. His voice broke. "Okay, I promise. Look, Alamea, the danger of the bear is finished. I should run for help."

She gripped his arm tighter. Shaking, she said, "Stay with me. I need you." He nodded. She released his arm and directed, "In the other bag, there's a letter. Get it."

He found an envelope labeled *For Mark Jr.*

Her teeth chattered. "Tell Mark Jr this letter written by his father is my gift to him. Tell him, 'Love prospers when a fault is forgiven'."

"What?" He put his ear near her mouth.

Her words were barely audible. "Love prospers when a fault is forgiven."

He repeated the phrase, and said, "Okay, I'll do it. Please, Alamea, let me run for help."

"If you go, I'll die alone." Her voice was fading. "Stay with me, Steve. I'm so cold."

She's right. If I leave, she might die alone on this empty wilderness highway. It's her right to decide.

"Don't worry. I'm here." He lay down beside her and held her hand. Her coughing ceased and she shivered in waves. He breathed into her neck, close enough to smell her perfume, a delicate fragrance of roses. In a murmur, she asked him to sing her a song.

Steve sang softly, a timeless melody of love. The lyrics of *Beyond the Sea* floated through the air. He sang with his mouth close to her ear and at the end of the first verse, she gave a gentle squeeze of his hand. When Steve finished the third verse, he could no longer detect her breath. He checked for a pulse but found none. A wave of grief washed over him as he covered her face.

He had just witnessed the passing of a woman he barely knew, yet it was the memory of his late wife Emily, lying in their bed at home, that consumed his thoughts. Somehow, he blended both losses–the death of his wife and this woman, their last acts of bravery, their fearless smiles–into a tapestry of grief.

Pushing the shock of the moment aside, he opened Alamea's case and gasped at neat bundles of hundred-dollar bills. Inside was also a blue leather satchel and a small journal. The satchel held some gold pieces of jewelry. He added her pearls and watch and returned it to the Harley case. The journal was mostly empty, apart from the names of those Alamea had mentioned. On the first blank page of the journal, he wrote her words:

Love prospers when a fault is forgiven.

He put on his jacket and pocketed the will, Mark Jr's letter, and the journal. As he looked around at the scene of the accident, he contemplated the two black soft-sided Harley trike cases at his feet. Gun, money, jewelry– he was tempted to leave the entire mess and just ride away.

He could wait for another vehicle to arrive or go somewhere to report the accident and the shooting, but the nearest place to locate an official might be Burwash Landing or worse, Destruction Bay. Both were at least an hour's ride in the wrong direction, and they wouldn't open for hours. If he returned, he was certain to miss his rendezvous with Rachel. He would have to press toward Alaska, but what to take and what to leave behind?

A Perfect Finish

This scene can be misconstrued in unimaginable ways. Take just the jewelry, leave the gun and the money? Leave just the gun? Leave everything? Take everything?

If he mismanaged this, Mark's trike wreck could become Steve's train wreck. He could be blamed for fleeing the scene or accused of looting the site. He could be blamed for shooting the grizzly bear and not reporting the incident to the authorities. He could be arrested for possessing an illegal handgun in Canada. He could be busted for transiting undeclared cash into the US or taking a gun on the ferry. After he left, someone might happen by and raid the site, and Steve could be blamed for whatever crimes they commit.

I did all I could. She's gone, so what significance are her possessions now? What exactly did I promise? What about Rachel?

He looked at his watch and decided. Rachel would land at the airport in Fairbanks by noon and he would be there for her. Steve unloaded the gun, cleared the chamber, and recased it with the magazines. He took the blue leather jewelry satchel out of the Harley bag, put both bags in the top trunk of his own Harley, and placed the satchel of jewelry next to his wallet. After mounting the motorcycle, he stopped for a look back.

Poise. Presence. Style. Hers was an incredibly brave death.

He rode away, leaving the scene behind. He searched for a kilometer marker. The first was 1830 km.

Once he had decided to ditch the cases rather than risk transiting them across borders or on the ferry, it became a question of where. The tallest tree was located directly east of the 1832-kilometer marker. Steve put the two cases in plastic bags and, with some cord, climbed the black spruce and hung them ten feet above the ground. He returned to the road and looked back to make sure they were not visible. As he inspected the site, he wondered whether he would, or ever could, return and find the bags again. He took out Alamea's journal and scribbled:

1832 !!
*1830 ***

2. Cross the Same River Twice

The journey was a three thousand five hundred-mile road trip and fishing excursion from Denver, Colorado to Homer, Alaska on Steve's billiard red Harley-Davidson Road Glide Limited motorcycle. Two years prior, Steve and his stepson Michael had completed the Alaska Highway trip while Steve's wife Emily underwent treatment for breast cancer. They had shipped home one hundred-seventeen pounds of halibut and salmon. Michael had called it the trip of a lifetime and young Rachel was so impressed that she boasted to her friends about Steve's promise to take her fishing in Alaska when she turned thirteen.

During Thanksgiving break, four months before Emily's passing, Rachel had reminded Steve and Emily of the promise for the upcoming summer. Emily was concerned that Rachel's father might cancel the trip when the time finally arrived. So, she met with Steve and Rachel's father and secured their commitment to the plan. Looking back, Steve realized that Emily's insistence on planning and guaranteeing the trip may have been as much for his benefit as it was for Rachel's.

On the previous motorcycle trip with Michael, they had ridden the round-trip distance of more than eight thousand miles from Denver to Homer and back in just six weeks. The trip with Rachel would be different. No man ever steps in the same river twice, especially not with different passengers.

Rachel was not as patient as Michael when it came to motorcycle riding. She grew bored and fell asleep on longer trips, posing a safety risk. So, he would ride to Fairbanks alone and meet Rachel there. From Fairbanks, they planned to take a series of short motorcycle rides. They would visit Denali National Park, pet puppies at the Iditarod Racing Headquarters in Wasilla, and fish like maniacs in Homer. From there, they would take a puddle jumper to observe bears feasting on salmon at Brooks Falls in Katmai National Park, before returning to Homer. For the final Alaska leg, they would ride the short distance to Seward, where they would take the ferry to Bellingham. After leaving the ferry, they would ride the short distance to Seattle and, from there, Rachel would fly home, leaving Steve to ride solo to Denver.

The trip would last over six weeks for Steve and four weeks for Rachel. In theory, it was a motorcycle adventure comparable to the one Steve had taken with Michael. In reality, Rachel's trip would consist of a series of short motorcycle jaunts interspersed with fun activities and a long, scenic ferry ride.

✳ ✳ ✳

At the US Border Guard station, Steve reported the accident he had witnessed southeast of marker 1830. He informed the officer that he fled the scene when a bear appeared. This caused some confusion at the station as the US Customs and Border Control lacked jurisdiction over accidents that occurred in Canada. The officer held a phone to one ear and a shortwave radio to the other. Amidst the confusion, he motioned for Steve to proceed.

As Steve rode from the border to Fairbanks, he thought back on his time in Whitehorse. On the first morning, he had hiked for two hours to Miles Canyon where he stood on the bridge and looked down at the mighty Yukon River. Gazing at the swirling currents below, he contemplated the river's power to convey the passing of time and preserve his eternal bond with Emily. The river was the medium he sought. Standing alone on the bridge and looking down upon the water, he explained his situation, and she heard him.

✳ ✳ ✳

Over lunch, Steve told Rachel the story of Alamea. Rachel had a knack for cutting straight to the heart of a matter. "You saved the lady from the bear, but she still died. Kind of like with Mom. You saved her from her seizure, but later she died anyway." Rachel reached for the bottle and squeezed ketchup on her French fries.

Steve nodded and tried to hide his pain and admiration. Rachel was a slugger, like her mother. She put down the ketchup bottle, took a long sip of her milkshake and looked over the glass at him, before throwing the knockout punch. "So, are you going to keep your promise to the lady?"

✳ ✳ ✳

Steve and Rachel rode from Fairbanks to Denali National Park. After checking into their hotel, they took the shuttle to the puppy farm for two hours of serious puppy petting and to watch the show about the Iditarod racers. Instead of watching the show, Rachel spent her time playing with the little puppy sled-dog-racer-wannabes.

The next day, they rode to Wasilla, the location of the Iditarod Racing Center. They arrived at the hotel, dined, and while Rachel showered, Steve inspected Alamea's journal. It was empty except for the first three pages.

On the first page:

Alamea Grace Mumford
Gmail
Username: AGM_Estate_0117
Password: OutOfTh3Bl00!

Into the black . . .

On the second page in the same handwriting:

Step 1: Call Clyde Zenith (John Goodenough), Seattle WA
Step 2: Call Mark Mumford Jr, Seattle WA
Step 3: Call Akiko Saito, Haleiwa HI
Step 4: Call Meriwa Naqi, Whitehorse YT

Steve logged into the Gmail account and found it mostly empty. He checked the associated contact list and found phone numbers for the five individuals. Steve called the first person mentioned in the journal, Clyde, and left a message about Alamea and her journal. Within minutes, he received a return call. Clyde introduced himself as Alamea's godfather and asked questions to verify Steve's story. Steve offered his condolences and described the trip and the activities he had planned with Rachel. The two men agreed to meet once Steve and Rachel had completed their trip.

During the conversation Steve revealed, "I have something for you. It's a blue leather jewelry satchel."

Clyde caught his breath. "Oh my! We had wondered what had become of that. I suppose the fact that she wasn't robbed offers some small consolation."

Steve hesitated. He shouldn't have been surprised to learn that he was suspected of robbery. He wanted to offer a useless platitude like, "I wish I could have done more," but decided to hold off. He would have to clarify the situation once they met in person. He asked, "One more question, if I may. I see another name in the journal, John Goodenough?"

"He's my husband and Alamea's attorney. Or, I should say, her estate's attorney. We can include him in the meeting."

"Ummm . . . great," replied Steve.

Suspicion of robbery? And now I get to explain to an attorney how I skipped reporting the shooting of a bear, and why I hung Alamea's gun and money in a tree? What could be better?

"There is one other person who would be interested in meeting you," Clyde added. "Alamea's cousin, Ron. If you don't mind, we can include him too."

3. Postmortem

During breakfast, Steven Ward Hamilton had received an email from the coach of his alma mater announcing the schedule for the upcoming football season. As he rode the elevator to the fourteenth floor in Downtown Seattle, he reminisced about six years prior, when he had taken Emily to Oahu for homecoming. The trip had doubled as a honeymoon. After the game, they had met his friends, coaches, and ex-teammates, and he was never prouder than when he introduced the beautiful doctor as his wife.

At thirty-eight years old, Steve still looked like he could play a college scatback. With medium height and muscular physique, he could juke when possible, but bowl over a safety when necessary. When smiling, his chiseled jawline and intense blue eyes gave the impression he was game for anything. When serious, he resembled the restless dreamer, contemplating the meaning of life's transitions. Now, as he journeyed through a particularly transitional patch, Steve conveyed a persistent sense of happiness interrupted.

A secretary ushered him into a posh conference room. As it closed, the door emitted a soft click, leaving him with only the sound of his own breathing. He sat and twisted his wedding ring as he gazed out the window at Elliot Bay, taking in the view of the bustling harbor and sparkling blue water stretching westward across Puget Sound to the Olympic Peninsula.

His thoughts drifted to that fateful night. In terms of the cosmos, surely a small glint of a ripple occurring on the third rock from the sun did not register as an event. On the other hand, chaos theory rests on the notion that the cosmos is deeply interconnected and that one small occurrence in the corner of the solar system can impact the destiny of the galaxy. Its kernel is based on the idea that a small butterfly flapping its wings in Africa could cause a typhoon in Seattle. Imagine if one were able to discern today in this meeting the first hint of a breeze caused by the flapping of her wings in the Klondike.

His grandmother, who always kept both feet planted firmly on Oklahoma soil, had no patience for chaos theory or cosmic thought. She would have said, "This is your day to stand before Saint Peter's Gate," and so it was. In his estimation, he had much to be proud of and only a few technicalities about which to worry. Undoubtedly, she would have judged him more severely. An expression of apprehension was etched on his face.

The door opened and a man, old enough to be Steve's father, strolled in with a friendly smile. His long dark curls, threaded with silver, conveyed a seasoned intelligence, but his boyish good looks and devil-may-care demeanor belied his age. Dressed in a checked sports jacket, a neatly pressed blue button-down shirt, and suede loafers, he carried himself with the confidence of someone who had achieved enough and was now content to live life on his own terms.

"Hi Steve, thank you for coming," he said with a firm handshake. He set his briefcase on a chair and retrieved his business card, which indicated that he was an art dealer. Clyde motioned towards Steve's chair and took a seat himself before asking about the ferry, fishing, Katmai National Park, the Kluane Range and Rachel's flight. Steve gave short replies. Clyde slid into easy chatter about his own travels to Alaska, rambling on eloquently for so long about so little. His voice flowed effortlessly from nicety to inquiry without a pause. Clyde was the queen's champion sentinel of social charm sent to battle the forces of awkward silences.

Imagine if he met my grandmother and she introduced him to her pregnant pause? He would probably say it wasn't his.

Steve listened and nodded before opening his backpack and retrieving Alamea's blue leather satchel filled with jewelry, including the watch. Clyde's words trailed off as his gaze fell upon the satchel. Steve explained that Alamea had said it was for Meriwa.

Clyde nodded, before placing it in his briefcase. "Thank you, Steve. This will mean a lot to Meriwa."

Clyde proceeded to explain how he had known Alamea's parents and become her godfather. As he spoke, he placed a hand on his chest, took a deep breath, and exclaimed, "Looking back, it was one of the best days of my life."

And so it begins—a breeze.

Another man arrived and Clyde introduced him as Alamea's cousin, Ron. His handsome face and striking appearance complemented his dazzling smile. He was a few years younger than Steve. His broad shoulders and muscular build were those of a linebacker. He dressed casually in jeans and a button-down shirt and wore an easy *darn glad to know ya* on his sleeve, exuding the unmistakable relaxed charm of the rural heartland.

Ron smiled broadly as he extended his hand. "Nice to meet you Steve. Thank you for including me today."

As they sat, Clyde said, "Ah, and always last to enter, here is our grand attorney, John."

John shook Steve's hand and, with neither a smile nor hint of the heartland, offered his business card. He was John Goodenough, the Managing Partner of Goodenough, Arenberg & Halbrecht Law Firm in Seattle. Steve looked up from the card and surveyed the man. He was a black man dressed impeccably in a gray pinstripe suit, with the stripes matching the speckles of silver in his hair. Tall, slender, and imposing, he exuded an air of authority and confidence that subtly conveyed the message, "Don't mess with me." Steve gave the business card a second look before proceeding. "I'm Steve Hamilton. Thank-thank you for meeting me today. I've been admiring your view of the bay."

John nodded and flashed what was almost a smile. "View of the bay, yes, yes. Let me start by addressing the first question most people have when they meet me: this is not a billable meeting. I don't officially represent Clyde as his attorney or in his role as Alamea's executor, but I am available to him as an informal legal advisor. I also dry dishes, take out the trash, and do whatever chores he assigns me." He completed the introduction without a smile, shuffled some papers, placed his fancy pen on a blank notepad and turned his focus to Steve.

"Sometimes yes, sometimes no, not quite as one might hope," Clyde said with a chuckle. "I have a feeling John would be more consistent in completing his chores if he could find a way to bill for housework."

Everyone laughed, except John who gave Clyde a sideways glance. Clyde continued rambling with his persistent smile. "When John says 'informal,' he means he doesn't intend to bill any of us here or the estate, which is fortunate because not even Satan can afford the Managing Partner's billing rates. Can you imagine his bill for loading the dishwasher?" Steve and Ron laughed again.

John flashed a quick scowl at Clyde before resuming. "We're fortunate Ron's here today. He's in town to pick up the Ducati that Alamea gave him before she left town."

Ron stared studiously at his blank pad of paper. People who planned to return would not normally give away valuable stuff to their cousin right before departing on a trip. There was sufficient pause to allow Steve to either swallow the gristle in the assertion or inquire. It was not his business.

John asked to see the journal. Steve retrieved it from his backpack and handed it over. "Alamea gave it to me just before she died. Oh, and she also wrote this." From his backpack he extracted and unfolded the page–a stained, lined, handwritten note with a frayed edge.

John studied the document without expression. Ron sat up straight and traded glances with Clyde–as poker players, Ron and Clyde would be primary contributors. Steve stared out the window, allowing the attorney time to twice-frown his way through Alamea's final wishes.

John cleared his throat, adjusted his tie, and pointed his pen accusingly at the paper. "As a legal document, this leaves much to be desired. Alamea writing this while dying raises questions about its validity. Assuming she was of sound mind and body, and if its validity could be established, this document might represent a codicil to Alamea's last will and testament." John paused and looked directly at Steve, who matched his gaze. "However, since Alamea's death took place in Canada, a codicil must be witnessed by two people and notarized to be valid." He twirled his pen and stabbed it toward the page. "This document fails to meet those essential requirements."

Steve looked out across the bay. John was a real breeze-kill. Imagine becoming an attorney–investing one's entire life in the pursuit of dissecting rat shit–so you could dictate what's what to mere humans.

John droned on, casually dismembering what Alamea had written with her own hand. "Should Clyde, out of some sense of obligation to honor the deceased's dying request, decide otherwise, he'll discover that presenting this document in a court of law will be akin to carrying a cocktail umbrella in a hurricane."

John raised himself straight in his seat and gave his pen another twirl as he looked at Steve with piercing eyes. Steve nodded and rubbed his chin. Ron tapped his standard issue Goodenough, Arenberg & Halbrecht Law Firm blue click pen steadily on an empty pad of paper, as though auditioning for the band. Clyde held out his hand toward John. John handed the cocktail umbrella to Clyde and turned his attention to the drummer. "Speaking of Alamea's evil stepmother and rotten half-sisters, how are they doing nowadays?"

Ron dropped his blue click pen on the pad of paper and covered it with both hands to stop it from attracting any further attention. He glanced toward Clyde, as though he were in a tough spot and needed a lifeline, but Clyde was focused on the cocktail umbrella. Ron gulped and paused for two more abracadabras before venturing, "You're asking about my aunt and twin cousins?"

"Yes, Ron. They happen to be Alamea's closest living relatives. In terms of contestants to Alamea's will, her sisters and stepmother are potential contenders."

Ron nodded. "Oh. Oh yeah. They've all married quite well. One cousin married an investment banker and lives in Manhattan. The other married a Walton and lives in Bentonville. After Alamea's father died, her stepmother married again, an attorney in Carmel."

"What type of attorney?"

"What *type* of attorney? I don't know. The type that does law, I suppose. Does it matter?"

"It always matters. Can you find his name and give it to Clyde, please?" It wasn't really a question, but Ron nodded anyway.

John had the mightiest pen and the rest of them were screwed. He swiveled toward Steve and pointed like it was a sword. "I detect an accent?"

Steve shook his head. "I don't think so. Oklahoma?"

"Where were you born?" John persisted.

"Calgary?" queried Steve, as though he were a game show contestant taking another wild guess.

John swiveled toward Clyde, leaned back in his chair, and beat his pen on the table in a repetitive *rat-a-tat-tat*. For capturing the jury's attention, tapping the table was definitely more effective than Ron's pad whacking. Also, John's Montblanc had better resonance and tone than Ron's complementary click pen.

"Clyde, Steve was born in Calgary," John said without a frown. "Were you keeping that a secret, like your love for pecan ice cream?"

"John, not a big deal, eh? I speak Canadian too, eh? See, just add an 'eh' at the end. If you want to say 'no,' just say 'no, no' instead. It's not difficult, sweetie. If you do those two little things, you and Steve will communicate swimmingly. If that doesn't work, why not just ask Steve to speak American?" Clyde finished with a wink, earning a hearty laugh from Ron and a token smile from Steve.

"Clyde, you don't discover important information because you don't ask the appropriate questions." John enunciated each syllable as though he were lecturing a toddler. "If you're going to interview someone then do a proper job of it."

He aimed his frown and his pen at Steve. "How many passports do you have?"

"Am I being interviewed?" asked Steve as he stole a glance toward Clyde.

John turned slowly toward Clyde, again without a frown. "See, Clyde, that's what I'm talking about." He twirled his pen in circles three times before stabbing it in Clyde's direction. "Steve gets it."

Maybe a not-frown was John's version of a smile. As he turned toward Steve again, the frown reappeared. "This meeting is not an interview. It's an introduction."

"I have two passports," replied Steve. "I was born in Calgary where my mother and her family live. I was raised in Oklahoma, mostly by my father's parents. I have dual citizenship."

John leaned back in his chair again, swiveled toward Clyde, and beat out another victory *rat-a-tat-tat*. "See?"

Clyde pursed his lips and glared back. "Oh, excellent job Mr Border Patrol Agent. Just for that, you're going straight to your room when you get home. No supper." Ron laughed enough for everyone.

"Don't worry, we really do like each other," John said in a monotone.

Steve pondered the elements of a happy relationship. In terms of matches, there existed countless compatible combinations. A perpetual smile paired with a perennial frown? They obviously enjoyed each other's company. One foot in a bucket of ice water, the other in boiling oil—on average the perfect temperature for the perfect marriage?

John asked Steve if he intended to call Mark Jr, before offering a warning. "Mark Jr is also an attorney, and I know what type. Watch what you say to that man. In terms of potential contestants to Alamea's will, he may be our biggest threat."

Steve nodded as John swiveled toward Clyde with his non-frown. "Well, Chuckles, since I'll be doing cleanup, let's try not to make this executor business any more exciting than it has already become."

John gathered his papers and pointed his fancy drumstick at Steve. "You have my card." He twirled it and stabbed twice. "Do try to stay out of trouble." He shook his head, before saying, "Don't hesitate to contact me anytime."

"Except when I'm sleeping," Clyde chirped. Ron laughed.

Stay out of trouble?

Steve put his elbows on the table and rested his chin on his fists.

"And there he goes," said Clyde. He asked to see Alamea's journal, flipped to the third page, and read aloud, "*Step 2: Call Mark Mumford Jr, Seattle, WA.*"

"Mark Mumford Jr became Alamea's stepson when he was seventeen. I still remember him sulking through the wedding and romping through the reception. He is now a junior attorney in a reputable local law firm founded by his grandfather, Frank. I could say Junior is the black sheep of the family, but he's more like the black sheep in a flock of black sheep."

Clyde is incapable of impregnating. A pause.

"Frank recently kicked Mark and Alamea out of the mansion. The man is older than dirt and not long for this world, so when he learned about Mark's cancer, he drafted up the documents and got Alamea to sign away any matrimonial claims in exchange for two hundred thousand dollars in cash. Oh, and a bag of chips."

Steve replied, "Wow, what a mean offer."

"Yeah, well, Frank is a mean son of a bitch," Clyde responded in a louder agitated voice. "So, that's the story about Mark Jr. If I were you, I'd tell the prick as little as possible."

Clyde really hates the Mumfords. And I thought they were just crap motorcycle riders.

Clyde took a drink of water before referring to the journal again, reading aloud, "*Step 3: Call Akiko Saito, Haleiwa HI.*"

"To say I know Akiko well would be an understatement. She was married–for about ten minutes–to my father. That was before the joyful day when he walked into our kitchen and found her doing it on the table with the neighbor. Really, sometimes life can be funnier than fiction. Akiko was interested in playing an active role in Alamea's business. If you have questions about the business plan, she knows as much about it as anyone.

Enjoy the call. I can't wait to hear about it."

Clyde referred again to the journal. "*Step 4: Call Meriwa Naqi, Whitehorse YT. Meriwa is Alamea's best friend from college and now remains the dearest reminder I have of her.*"

Clyde put his head down and rubbed his forehead with both hands. Steve caught Ron's eye and they both looked down and waited. Clyde took a deep breath and continued. "Aside from you, Meriwa was the last of us to see Alamea. Her uncle, the Chief of Whitehorse's Royal Canadian Mounted Police, is responsible for investigating the accident." Clyde looked towards Steve and addressed him. "Since you were there, I'm sure Meriwa will be keen to speak with you."

"Her uncle is responsible for investigating the accident," repeated Steve. "Hmmm. Does Meriwa know about me?"

"Before today, there was nothing to tell," replied Clyde. "Which brings us around to the main point of our meeting. What we would like to hear from you now, Steve, is what exactly happened that night. Please tell us."

Steve was worried about not having reported his shooting of the grizzly bear and about his decision to hang a gun and money in a tree along a remote stretch of highway in the Yukon, so he asked Clyde and Ron to keep everything he told them confidential, with the exception that Clyde could discuss it with John if he wanted. Ron and Clyde listened intently as Steve recounted in their entirety the events of that fateful night.

When Steve finished, Clyde, in meticulous detail, interviewed him for another hour, asking the same questions over and over in different ways like a Mr Gumshoe, but eventually there was nothing more to ask or say. When they exhausted the topic, Clyde got up and served them water.

As Clyde poured, Steve told them that he had once visited the North Shore. "I graduated from Hawaii State University. I was a tailback. I went there on a football scholarship. In fact, when I saw Alamea, I mistook her for the weather lady."

Clyde took a deep breath before explaining that whenever Alamea visited Oahu, the locals often mistook her for her famous mother, Kahului. "They were identical in looks, but different in most other aspects. Alamea wanted to save the world. Aside from becoming the famous TV weather lady, Kahului liked to live life freely–the typical North Shore surfer."

Ron excused himself for a break, and Steve asked Clyde to help him arrange a meeting with Mark Jr. They made the call and left a message. Ron returned, and while they waited for Mark Jr to call back, their conversation meandered its way around to Steve's situation. He told them about coaching the debate team and his volunteer work at the planetarium in the Museum of Nature and Science.

"So, what is your profession?" asked Clyde.

"I'm a high school English teacher," replied Steve. "Until I sold it last November, I also owned an internet marketing company. It was my side-gig and my summer job. I had to sell because I needed the time . . . to care for Emily. That's why, since December, I also took a break from volunteering, coaching, and teaching."

Ron and Clyde exchanged glances. Clyde nodded and asked, "Emily?"

"Emily was my wife. She died in April, from cancer."

They both nodded and Clyde said, "I'm sorry, Steve. You have my condolences."

Mark Jr called and agreed to meet Steve the next morning at a cafe. As Steve was preparing to leave, Clyde suggested that they meet the following night for drinks.

4. Awfully Bad Week

The following morning, Steve arrived early at Caffè Umbria. Patrons stood in line, ordered, and staked out their claims to tables, some sitting, some standing as they listened to the barista grind, brew, and froth his way through the orders.

Steve looked around the shop and tried to profile customers to identify Mark Jr based on Clyde's only description, "a total asshole." He identified several candidates, but the results were inconclusive, so at 9:04 Steve called Mark Jr. A phone rang behind him and he turned toward the sound. One of the candidates, a tall young man in a tailored suit, answered the phone and looked in Steve's direction. Steve gave a short wave and approached Mark Jr, hanging up the phone and shaking his hand.

For no apparent reason, within the first five minutes, Mark Jr launched into a tirade, informing Steve that he was in the process of a divorce from his third wife who had red hair and was totally stacked but not so great in the sack. She had found someone else, an accountant, who was shorter than him. The wife was now not only leaving but also misappropriating the new orange BMW i8, which Mark Jr had just purchased for her as a birthday gift. Oddly enough, the gift had not fixed this otherwise perfect marriage. Aside from the monologue, Mark Jr also emitted a heavy aroma of aftershave.

Why would someone wear so much aftershave to a coffee shop in downtown Seattle to meet a stranger who is dressed in blue jeans and a wrinkled shirt? I wonder if the smell affects the taste of his coffee. Why am I here?

Mark Jr droned on. The car had a three hundred sixty-nine-horsepower engine, a six-speed transmission, and could go zero to sixty in four-point-two seconds. Now, Mark Jr's blonde girlfriend with long legs and a dragon tattoo on her thigh, whom he had met at the law firm sixteen months ago, and who had a six-year-old daughter, was leaving him too. It was a twenty-seven-minute monologue describing in excruciating detail Mark Jr's awfully bad week.

This candy cane twist could be a guest on Jerry Springer, *or maybe* Maury.

Finally, Mark Jr took a breath and Steve seized the opportunity to recount an astonishingly abbreviated version of the accident, figuring he would follow up with answers to whatever questions Mark Jr might ask. As Steve began talking, Mark Jr picked up his phone and scrolled through messages.

Steve didn't mention the bump, the bear, the gun, the touchdown pose, the crushed skull, the injured knee, the singing, the cash, or the codicil. He did say he had a letter and message for Mark Jr. As he recited the message, Mark Jr suddenly looked up from his phone.

"What was that last part?" he asked.

"Love prospers when a fault is forgiven."

Mark Jr pocketed his phone and snapped to attention. "Really, she said that at the end?"

"Yes. She said, 'Tell Mark Jr, love prospers when a fault is forgiven.' Those were her final instructions." As Steve repeated it again, he handed over the letter. Mark Jr placed it in the left breast pocket of his suit jacket.

The candy cane twist began another monologue, explaining that he had never been mean to Alamea and felt bad about his grandfather mistreating her. He described how his own mother had been a gold-digger and shaken his father down during the divorce. His grandfather had interceded so Alamea would not repeat the trick.

Mark Jr went on to explain how, just as they were departing for Alaska, he had met his father and Alamea outside the mansion and how she had opened the trailer and shown him her mother's shoes to prove she had not stolen anything. He said he did not stop her from taking the shoes because he had no use for them anyway.

Steve interrupted, "Why did Alamea take a trailer full of shoes to Canada?"

"She missed her parents. They died unexpectedly. Alamea never got over it. When she rode her Ducati, she thought of her father. When she missed her mother, she wore the shoes. I told the police that I didn't want the shoes, but now that she's gone, the Ducati should be mine–it's worth thirty thousand dollars. Also, the police sent me the wedding rings but what happened to the other jewelry and Alamea's cash?"

Steve shook his head. Mark Jr sprang from his seat and pasted on an easy smile. "Nice to meet you, Steve. Gotta dash."

5. The Contraband

Steve walked from Seattle's Edgewater Hotel to Elliot's Oyster House to meet Clyde and Ron. As he approached the restaurant, he passed Miner's Landing on Pier 57, where the first Klondike gold landed in 1897. Its arrival initiated the stampede that passed through Whitehorse via the Yukon River, resulting in idiotic prospectors floating through, or drowning by the boatloads in, the Whitehorse Rapids as they headed to the Klondike Gold Fields. Now Miner's Landing is an amusement park that peddles cotton candy to stroller pushers dressed in Lycra leisure wear.

The restaurant was bustling. Clyde had reserved seating during sunset with a view of the glimmering waters of Puget Sound. Over the din of the crowd and gulls squawking in the background, they ordered drinks and chatted about the pier. Their drinks arrived and Clyde began, "I discussed your story in depth with John. He thinks you are a bit of a nut to have hung the gun in a tree."

Steve exchanged smiles with Ron and took a sip of beer.

"Before we met you, John and I speculated about what had happened to the contraband: the cash, the jewelry, and the gun. In fact, John proposed having you arrested while you were still in Alaska. If you hadn't mentioned the jewelry satchel in your first call to me, I may not have been able to dissuade him from calling the police."

Clyde said it with a smile, but the weight of the word "arrested" hung in the air. Steve stared blankly at Clyde, wishing he had taken the seat facing the door.

"After meeting you and receiving the jewelry, it helped, but for John, the thing that tipped the scale in your favor was discovering you were Canadian. Despite that, you weren't out of the woods until yesterday when you disclosed what had become of the cash. Otherwise, John suggested having you served papers at Caffè Umbria this morning during your meeting with Mark Jr."

"You're kidding, right?"

Clyde replied, "Don't take it personally, Steve, but nobody jokes about two hundred thousand dollars."

Clyde dropped a manilla envelope on the table. "You might find this interesting."

With a furrowed brow, Steve removed eight stapled pages, and looked questioningly at Ron.

"It's the police report," said Ron. "I have my own copy, but you should read it. If you don't mind, I'll have a stroll on the pier."

Clyde stayed with Steve and scrolled through his phone messages as Steve studied the police report.

The report confirmed that both persons had died as a result of the motor vehicle accident and described the gruesome scene that developed after Steve had ridden away. A mother black bear and two cubs were found at the scene and could not be chased away. All three animals were shot by officers. What was not clear to the police was who shot and killed an adult male grizzly bear which was also there. Shooting the grizzly without reporting it was a felony.

The report included an attachment that cited the law and penalty:

> *"Firearms should only be used as a last resort in a life-threatening situation. If a bear is killed in defense of life or property, you are legally required to report the incident to a conservation officer as soon as possible.*
>
> *Failure to report the shooting of a grizzly bear is a violation of the Yukon Wildlife Act and carries a maximum fine of $50,000, one year imprisonment, or both."*

The report went on to speculate that the handgun used may have been possessed illegally. Officers extracted twelve nine-millimeter slugs from the boar for forensic analysis. The rear trunk of the trike had been opened and the vehicle ignition turned off. Police found fingerprints that did not belong to either victim and they were analyzing casings found at the accident scene. The report stated that the police were continuing to investigate the shooting and classified what transpired following the accident as a possible theft.

A witness who had been at the scene failed to report the accident to Canadian authorities but reported it to US authorities after leaving Canada. It was not yet clear whether the witness was the possible perpetrator. The incident remained under investigation by the Yukon Royal Canadian Mounted Police in Whitehorse, and the US Customs and Border Control were cooperating with the investigation.

After finishing reading the report, Steve sat up straight and blinked.

Clyde told Steve that he could keep the copy of the report and went on to explain, "Prior to her departure, John instructed Alamea to create a journal and strongly advised her against transiting the cash and gun through Canada to Alaska. Mark wanted to bring the cash to help start the business and cover trip expenses. Alamea agreed because she didn't really care about it anyway.

"Mark, the surgeon, decided to forgo traditional cancer treatment once Alamea, the nurse, told him that she would not be performing traditional nursing home services for his closing act. Their relationship was not a happy one. In fact, after Mark's diagnosis, I advised Alamea to leave him."

"Why did they even get married?" asked Steve.

"That's another story," said Clyde. "Theirs was not a traditional marriage. They attended high society events and looked great in pictures together, but they kept separate relationships on the side. It was a convenient arrangement, until Mark got sick."

To Steve's relief, Ron returned, and Clyde ordered another round of drinks. Clyde continued, "Mark begged Alamea to come with him to Alaska—he had decided to use the gun to solve his terminal brain cancer problem and chose Alaska to prevent the story from splashing across Seattle news. Alamea agreed to go along. She broke up with her friend and intended to quit Seattle altogether. That's why she took her things along."

"That's sad," replied Steve. "I can see why Mark needed a gun, but I don't see why Alamea would have agreed to go along on the trip, bring her money, or end a relationship for Mark."

"It was because Meriwa had just gotten a divorce and moved from Boston to Whitehorse, so Alamea was looking forward to relocating there. She would have done so even if Mark hadn't gotten sick. As for the money, it was always a nuisance to Alamea, and she particularly hated that pile of cash. She said it even smelled like Frank. Regarding her overall fortune, Alamea considered it accidental, even inconsequential."

"Would it be rude to ask how Alamea came to have a fortune?" asked Steve.

"At the time of her death, she had accumulated over five-and-a-half million dollars," Clyde replied.

Clyde liked to talk, and without buzz-kill John around, it must have been like he was on recess.

I wonder what he would say if I asked him for his identity details and passwords.

Clyde continued babbling like a brook. "The money came mostly from her mother's and father's life insurance policies, which both included double indemnity clauses for accidental death. Alamea called it blood money. Her grandmother had set aside child support payments paid voluntarily by Kyle, Alamea's father, throughout her childhood. Plus, Kahului had savings from her meteorologist career. Combine all that with earnings on investments, plus Alamea's own savings from working in the ER, and her fortune just kept growing. She wanted to find the perfect use for it."

"The perfect use for it," repeated Steve. "I wonder what would be the perfect use for two hundred thousand dollars hung in a tree."

"I'm sure you'll figure that out, once it's untreed," replied Clyde.

Steve drained his glass and Ron waved to the server.

Clyde continued, "According to John, the irony of Frank forcing Alamea to sign her rights away in return for two hundred thousand dollars is that the settlement agreement insulates Alamea's estate from any claims by Mark Jr."

"That's interesting," remarked Steve. "What about the Ducati?"

Ron snapped to attention. "Why do you ask about the Ducati?"

"Mark Jr told me he wants the Ducati. He said it's worth thirty thousand bucks."

Clyde shook his head, leaned forward, and slammed his hand on the table. "That smug little bastard. He doesn't even know how to ride a motorcycle! Alamea owned a Ducati before she married Mark. When she traded it in for the new one, she used her own earnings to pay the difference."

Steve raised his hands in surrender. "I'm just passing along what Mark Jr said."

"No, no, I know, and thanks for mentioning it," said Clyde, as he calmed down a bit. "I'll pass it on to John. Speaking of claims against Alamea's estate, after our meeting yesterday, John pointed out that the evil stepmother was bitter that Kyle's life insurance proceeds had been split evenly among the three daughters."

Ron nodded. "That's definitely true."

"He expects she might consider this a chance to nick her stepdaughter's share," continued Clyde. "Getting back to the matter at hand, have you decided what to do about pursuing Alamea's business plan?"

"I haven't seen it. I have no idea about it."

"Try using her login from the journal. I'm sure you'll find the business plan once you log in." Clyde motioned for the check. "And what about your two mystery bags hanging in a Christmas tree on the road to nowhere? Have you given any thought to those?"

"I dream of them every night, visions of sugar plums dancing in my head," Steve replied. "What do you suggest?"

Clyde's smile disappeared. "If you decide not to pursue the plan then maybe you should anonymously inform the police about the location of the bags. If you decide to report the stash, I'll do what I can to recover the assets for the benefit of the estate, but I doubt we will prevail once the RCMP sends the money to Mark Jr or seizes it as undeclared cash. Alternatively, if you decide to pursue the business plan, then maybe the cash can defer some startup costs."

Clyde's phone rang, and he excused himself, leaving the table. He returned several minutes later, rubbing the back of his neck. "The estate just received an affidavit from Mark Jr claiming two hundred thousand dollars in missing cash and the Ducati."

"What? No way!" exclaimed Steve.

"My Ducati?" asked Ron.

Clyde looked at Ron. "Yes, your Ducati," he said, before turning back to Steve. "It was sent same-day registered mail, which means Mark Jr wrote it this morning after meeting you."

Steve widened his eyes in surprise. Clyde waved his hand. "Don't worry. Nobody is blaming you. In fact, after I returned home last night, John predicted this would happen. I bet him a dollar it wouldn't. By the way, can I borrow a dollar?"

Clyde paid the bill and they said their farewells. Outside the bar, Ron surprised Steve with a hug. "Thank you. Thank you for shooting that bear. I love you, man. I love you for staying with her."

Clyde hailed a taxi and smiled. The two straight men, a former linebacker and a former running back, embraced awkwardly. The running back broke loose. Clyde and Ron crossed the street and hopped into the backseat. Steve stood alone on the sidewalk, as the taxi joined the traffic racing north on Alaska Way.

6. Let's Talk Trash

Once Steve returned to Denver, he found the business plan and read it before calling Akiko. She picked up on the third ring, "Saito Life Insurance. This is Akiko. How can I assist you?"

"Hi, this is Steve Hamilton. You are listed in Alamea's journal as one of the people to call."

Akiko added a teaspoon of honey to her voice. "Well, hello. Clyde told me you would be phoning me about the Munchkin. I'm glad you called."

"Thanks for your time," said Steve. "Clyde told me a little about you. He said you knew Alamea when she was little."

"We can discuss that, but before we talk trash, I'd like to ask you a question, sweetie. What kind of car do you drive?"

"Talk trash about my car? You're asking about my car? Well, umm. I mean, when I'm not driving my Harley, I drive a Ford F-150 pickup. Why do you ask?"

"You asked how I knew the Munchkin, and I'm explaining, so don't interrupt me. Hawaii sits just east of the Great Pacific Garbage Patch. As a result, plastic from all over the world washes up on our shorelines. That happens because you mainlanders can't be bothered to recycle. Meanwhile, I come to the beach every Saturday and pick up your fucking trash."

There was something about the way Akiko chucked her "fucking trash" sentence like a javelin that reminded Steve of his grandmother, who had mostly raised him. She was abrasive, loving, and a laugh a minute when he wasn't in the line of fire. She had passed away while he was at college, which was, at the time, the saddest event of his life. Although Akiko's rant about trash was different, her inclination to bless a total stranger with insightfully tailored insults and hostile vulgarities was eerily reminiscent.

As Akiko continued to rant, Steve thought back to a moment that took place during his final summer in Oklahoma. While Steve hid beside the truck and pumped gas, his grandmother stood on the other side of the flatbed farm truck in a house dress and slippers, holding her red plastic cup of Jack and Coke. With her free hand, she stabbed a finger towards the gas station attendant, who had played tight end with Steve in high school and told him in colorful language how she felt about his broken air hose.

Akiko was still talking. "I want you to think about that, the next time you're rolling around the heartland in your F-150, listening to some 'Jesus Take the Wheel' music, before tossing that Coke bottle out your pickup truck window."

"I can't say I've ever done that exactly," said Steve. "But I'll take your concerns into consideration. Regardless, I didn't call to talk trash. Can we get back on track? What does all this have to do with Alamea's business plan?"

"If you quit interrupting me, I could get to that part. I was friends with Alamea's grandmother. We met at a Greenpeace demonstration. She was head of nursing at an Alzheimer's ward."

"But the plan," he insisted.

"If you want to hear the plan, quit interrupting," she huffed. "Alamea used to tag along with her grandmother, first as a sort of off-the-books candy striper, and, once she became old enough, as a hospice assistant. That means she changed diapers for a bunch of old gits who had lost their marbles. Before she was twenty, the Munchkin changed enough diapers to break a landfill."

Akiko liked to invest in the setup which, for the listener, required sifting through heaps of extraneous information. He checked his email and let her run, offering an occasional "uh-huh."

"I don't blame the Munchkin," continued Akiko. "I blame her grandmother who, as a member of Greenpeace, was actually a real planet trasher. She claimed to give a shit about the environment, but for thirty years she managed over two hundred-fifty beds filled with wrinkled climate-deniers whose only remaining purpose was to fill four more diapers every day. Meanwhile, her only concern was saving the demented gits for six more Medicaid payments, so she could roll them to the polls for one more election cycle. Save the planet by stacking diapers to the moon so two hundred-fifty climate-deniers can vote one more time–it makes no sense at all–which brings me to the Munchkin's business plan."

"Yes, precisely, the business plan," Steve persisted.

"The Munchkin came up with the idea many years ago, probably when both of her grandmothers checked out early, or it could have been when her father did his Romeo and Juliet trick."

WTF. Don't even ask.

"Last year, when Mark was diagnosed with cancer, she came to visit me for two weeks. She told me that even after a decade of patching up injured and sick people in the ER, the thing that stuck with her the most was the tragedy that occurred routinely in nursing homes. She pitched her business idea as the solution, so I told her when she was ready to launch it, I would help, even if it's the last thing I do."

"The last thing you do. Did you ever discuss marketing and financial projections?" asked Steve.

"We discussed client profiles. I told Alamea that a new widow is the best target. Get her when she's sad. If she's sad she may be ready to die, and if she's ready to die, she won't mind paying because she can't take it with her, right?"

"I guess so," replied Steve.

"Clyde told me that you recently lost your wife to cancer. Is that true?"

"Well, yes, it . . . it is."

"Then you understand. At first a person is grief stricken, right? At the apex of sadness, that's when you've got to target these rich old widows. Timing is everything."

"Hmmm," replied Steve. "So, did Alamea create any projections or a marketing plan?"

"Don't be obtuse. I just told you the Munchkin's marketing plan. Projections? I don't know. Why do you care about the business?"

"I told Clyde I would look into Alamea's business idea," replied Steve, pronouncing each syllable distinctly. "I agreed to evaluate the concept."

"Yeah, right," sneered Akiko. "Alamea, your damsel in distress. Let me ask, do you have children?"

With a heavy sigh, he replied, "Yes, I have two."

"Do you have life insurance?"

7. Dynamic Marketing

Steve and Emily had been friends with Liz and her husband for years, and their kids had attended the same schools. The men often played chess together and shot traps, and the women had been tennis partners. Liz was a Certified Financial Planner for high-net-worth individuals.

Since the success of the business depended on whether there were enough rich old women interested in paying someone to orchestrate their perfect finish, Steve called Liz and asked if a Certified Financial Planner might have some ideas on the matter. At first, Liz laughed, but he insisted that he really wanted her help in profiling market segments for potential customers.

"That should be no problem," she joked. "I'll consult with the 'Rich Wives of Beverly Hills' book club on the matter."

✳ ✳ ✳

A week later, Liz called and suggested they meet for Mollusk Mondays at Angelo's Taverna on Sixth Avenue. Steve was second to arrive and interrupted Liz as she sat at the bar and chatted with the bartender about the stock market. Steve gave her a hug and ordered a beer. Liz asked about Rachel and mentioned that they wanted to invite her for a sleepover. Steve advised her to check with Rachel's stepmother.

"We've been worried about you," Liz said as she put her hand on his. "How have you been coping since your return from Alaska?"

"Well, I haven't been alone exactly," Steve replied, giving her hand a squeeze, before taking a sip of beer. "I've been teaching Michael to drive. He has his permit and needs to log fifty hours of drive time to get his license. Also, the kids have loaned me Cosmo while I'm in town."

"Golden Retrievers are great companions, but we're still worried about you. Why don't you come by for dinner one night? We'd love to have you."

"Sure, that would be nice," Steve replied as he fiddled with his wedding ring.

"Will you go back to teaching this fall?" Liz asked.

"Maybe next year," Steve said. "I'm heading back to Whitehorse. I really love the place. If you like rivers, it's got one to die for. But before I go, I would like to explore this business plan further, you know?"

"Yes, the plan." She nodded as she extracted papers from her briefcase. "You asked me to think about the marketing aspect."

"Yes, marketing. I was wondering if you think people in nursing homes would be potential clients?"

"Steve, when was the last time you visited a nursing home? I don't have a single client who lives in one. Most people in a typical nursing home are on Medicaid and aren't even allowed to have investment accounts. It would be harder to convince someone living in a nursing home to pay a hundred dollars than it would be to convince a super-rich person to pay ten million dollars. Which clientele would you rather have, one super rich woman or one hundred thousand poor bastards?"

He nodded. "Okay, so what do you see as the profile? Someone who is ready to die, who also has a million bucks?"

"No way! Imagine you find someone with eight grandkids and one million dollars, who pays you her only million to die in the Yukon wilderness. How many of the eight grandkids are going to bring a civil suit against you to recover their dead granny's million bucks? All eight, that's how many. The prospect must have a minimum of ten million dollars. Then her heirs will be happy to give up one million to get the remaining nine million sooner."

"Isn't that a rather crass way of looking at it?"

"Not crass, just realistic," replied Liz. "I know plenty of rich widows and every single one has heirs who are watching bank balances tick lower as they wait for granny to die. The key is to align our interests with those of the heirs."

"I see what you mean," replied Steve. "If heirs stand to gain an accelerated payout, they won't mind losing a million and a granny."

"Exactly," said Liz with a smile. "The problem is, we not only have to find a hyper-rich person who is still lucid and physically capable, she must also be up for an adventure and motivated to check out early. We're looking for a sad, sorry Humpty Dumpty before she falls off the wall, because once she falls, she'll go straight to the ICU and be hooked up to machines and institutionalized. At that point, she might still be a candidate for a garden variety assisted suicide, but she won't be our client. Are you familiar with the five stages of loss by Dr Elisabeth Kübler-Ross?"

"Are we still talking about marketing?"

"Of course. To close sales we're going to have to find women who have already progressed through the stages of denial, anger, bargaining, depression, and acceptance, and have decided to meet death on their own terms.

"Their reasons might vary–terminal illness, early dementia, the recent death of a spouse–something like that. In fact, I might have *one* such prospect. She's as rich as Croesus, a widow who has just spent three years caring for a spouse with Alzheimer's. When I first met her, she introduced me to her comatose husband and quoted the obituary of English author Iris Murdoch, 'Life with a demented spouse is like being chained to a corpse.' She's terrified that her own early signs of dementia will worsen and one day condemn her children to caring for her."

"You already found a rich widow ready to pay a million bucks for assistance–in–dying?" asked Steve.

"Maybe, but just one, and that's the problem. I'm not going to be able to find a single real estate agent, financial planner, doctor, or insurance agent who knows enough prospects to bring in the next dozen APF clients. However, I do have a solution."

"I'm listening."

"Think of Dr Kevorkian selling Amway."

Steve exclaimed, "Multi-level-marketing? MLM? I hate it already!"

"I know, I know." She waved for him to stop. "Hear me out. In order to motivate an agent to identify her very best prospect, we need to pay a huge referral fee. With these salespeople, anything less than a hundred grand isn't going to cut it. The second thing is, once an agent has identified and presented her single best candidate, that agent becomes your best prospect for finding the next professional to do the same. That, my friend, is, by definition, MLM.

"For example, tomorrow I solicit my best and only prospect. She signs up. I earn a hundred grand. My next step is do nothing, because that was it, or I could make a call to a colleague and try to get her to cough up her best prospect. If she does, then she earns a hundred grand and I get, let's say, fifty grand for recruiting her. Do you like it?"

Steve smiled. "You just became an Amway salesman, and this is your pitch to recruit me."

"Pretty much. By the way, how are you going to off them?"

"No idea. I'm not really involved in operational details. It's probably something like grannies drinking Kool-Aid around the campfire in the land of the midnight sun."

"Why wouldn't granny save a buck and visit the grandkids instead?" Liz countered. "She can sip Kool-Aid in the backyard during the barbecue for free."

"Yeah, you're right. We're going to need something more adventurous than Kool-Aid. I wonder how far Whitehorse is from the North Pole."

Liz started gathering papers and putting them in her briefcase. "I have one more question, why not men?"

"What do you mean?"

"Why is APF offering its services only to old women, not old men?"

8. Fork in the Road

Steve phoned Clyde, who was in New York City at an auction buying paintings for a client. Clyde asked Steve whether he had made any progress phoning the people in Alamea's journal.

"I spoke to Akiko, but the conversation wandered off track. She talked a lot about trash and tried to sell me life insurance."

"Trash talk? Life insurance? That definitely sounds like Akiko."

"She did mention a couple of things about Alamea which I was hoping you could clarify. She said both of her grandmothers had checked out early. She also said something about Alamea's father doing a Romeo and Juliet."

"All true. Alamea's grandmothers were more than just acquaintances with each other. I'd go so far as to say that with Akiko, the three of them were quite good friends. In fact, each of the grandmothers consulted me before their deaths."

"Consulted you?" asked Steve. "Why you?"

"The grandmothers understood that I was in a position to support and console Alamea afterwards. Anyway, in their own way, each of them told me that she had achieved her objectives on Earth, didn't want to lose her independence, and wouldn't risk being a burden to Alamea. In their own ways, they felt they were doing it for Alamea's benefit."

"You're telling me that Alamea's father and both grandmothers died by suicide?" asked Steve.

"I've never thought of it in quite those terms—I mean, it's not like it was a group event. The deaths occurred over a period of three years. First, Alamea's grandfather died of a heart attack while she was helping him with the milking. A couple of months later, her grandmother took pills with her morning coffee.

"As for the Romeo and Juliet part, right after Alamea graduated from college, it was in our dining room that Kyle asked Kahului to marry him. Alamea was over the moon about her parents finally marrying, but the following week, Kahului died in a freak helicopter accident. After hearing the news, Kyle rode his motorcycle off a cliff."

"Romeo and Juliet never abandoned a daughter," interrupted Steve.

"Precisely Alamea's sentiments, and that wasn't the end of it. Kahului's mother was also devastated. Alamea begged her to come live with her in Seattle, but she refused. Two months later, Akiko called Alamea to inform her that she had found her grandmother's sandals on the beach. The next day, Alamea received the letter."

"Poor Alamea," said Steve. "So, that's the genesis of A Perfect Finish?"

"Sure, that and her years working in the nursing home and the emergency room. Alamea witnessed more deaths than we can imagine."

"I had no idea," replied Steve. "Sorry to drag us so far off track. What I really phoned you for was to discuss the fourth item in Alamea's journal."

"Yes, the fourth item," said Clyde. "Calling Meriwa?"

"I was thinking, rather than calling her, I would just speak with her directly when I get to Whitehorse, but I have a question about that. Considering Meriwa is the niece of the Chief of Police, what have you told her?"

"You asked us to keep it confidential, so we've told her nothing about it. In fact, I've never mentioned anything about you to her. What you tell her is up to you, but don't underestimate her."

"Why is that?"

"If you meet her, you'll understand soon enough. But really, John says there is no good reason for you to go to Canada. Why not just call Meriwa instead?"

"I'm definitely going, but not necessarily to pursue Alamea's business. In fact, I have to say I'm pretty skeptical about the business."

"Pretty skeptical? Why?"

"Two reasons," replied Steve. "First, I can't say I'm personally excited about the death business. Really, I'm not a fan."

"Can you explain?" pressed Clyde.

"Look, it's not that I don't believe there is a place for assistance-in-dying. It's just that with my most recent experiences with Emily, the issue definitely touches a raw nerve. I'm just not ready to dive right in and embrace it."

"I see. And you said there is a second reason?"

"Oh, yes, the second reason: prison."

"Hmm. You said prison?"

"Yep. When the shit hits the fan, I don't see how whoever is in charge of the death camp will avoid prison."

"Well, John will be pleased to hear your decision," replied Clyde with a laugh. "But what is the point of the trip then?"

"I'm not teaching this fall and I'm dying to visit the Yukon River again. Aside from that, I've got a compelling personal reason . . . you know, some roadside litter to clean up."

"Aha. Right. John did inquire about that. He thinks you should have the RCMP pick it up. He doesn't want to be seen as advising you, but says picking up litter in the Yukon is too risky."

"Just because I'm not keen about her business concept doesn't mean I didn't make Alamea a promise. Not to be sentimental, but if the RCMP pick up those bags, they may seize them or send them to Mark Jr. Either way, it would be breaking my promise."

"I've always admired boy scouts," replied Clyde with a laugh. "But you can't ignore what you read in the police report. Whatever is in those bags is just not worth it. Nobody will blame you if you just let it go. John said if he were you, he would never step foot in Canada again."

"Yeah well, John isn't Canadian so that probably isn't very difficult for him, eh? Also, he's an attorney, so he doesn't think like a human."

"True. John doesn't like snow and quit thinking like a human when he was eight. Hearing that you haven't given up yet is going to make him even grumpier, considering Mark Jr just kicked his ass with the Ducati."

"Mark Jr won the Ducati?" asked Steve.

"Yesterday, I paid him forty grand from my own funds. John settled to avoid having to disclose anything further about Alamea's estate. He blames me, of course, for botching the title paperwork."

"But the Ducati wasn't even worth forty grand."

"In John's words, 'Give the prick what he asks for and move on.' So, you can see why John's been grumpy lately–that and the affidavit he received from the evil stepmother claiming two million dollars from Alamea's estate."

"Ouch. So far, everything John predicted has come true."

"Yeah, John the Fucking Baptist," said Clyde.

"Good luck at the auction."

"Thanks. Have a safe trip to the Yukon. Call me from jail when you get there."

9. Helping Hand

Steve phoned John's office and arranged a time to call. "I need John's help with a legal matter which has just come up," explained Steve.

That afternoon, he trimmed deadwood in Emily's rose garden while waiting for the call. He took off his gloves and caught it on the third ring. After some greetings, Steve said, "I hope you don't mind, but you did say to call if I need help."

"Sure, sure. Tell me about it," said John in a practiced priestly tone.

"Yesterday I was served papers, specifically a set of interrogatories and a summons. From what I can tell, I am being sued by the children's trust for the wrongful death of their mother, Emily."

"I see. When, where, and how did Emily die?" asked John.

"It started out as breast cancer, which progressed to brain cancer. About seven months ago, she gave herself an injection at home, in our bed."

"I'm sorry to hear that. You have my condolences. Were you present when she did so?"

"Yes, her sister and I were there, but she injected herself."

"Where was the syringe kept?"

"She prepared it in advance for herself. I kept it in the gun safe. When she was ready, she asked me for it."

"I see, a helping hand. Right-to-die. Colorado has laws for assisted suicide. Do you know if Emily filed any papers about that?"

"Emily was a pediatrician, so she managed it all herself. She chose hospice at home instead of dying in a hospital. Since she was a doctor, she didn't actually need assistance. That's why we skipped all that paperwork crap."

"Skipped all that paperwork crap," replied John.

"Yeah, it's no different than my great-grandfather who had Stage IV cancer. He shot himself behind the barn. That was in Oklahoma, and just in case you didn't know, people there don't need right-to-die laws. Everybody just understands."

"Everybody understands. I see. So, who is responsible for the children's trust?"

"Their father is the trustee, and that's what I still don't understand. I was at his house just last week for a barbecue. We drank beer in the backyard while his wife and the kids played in the swimming pool. Nothing seemed unusual."

"Well, that is a good sign. Maybe the kids aren't aware of the lawsuit."

"I agree. It must be just some legal ploy their father devised. Maybe that's why he asked questions about Emily's death."

"You're saying you discussed Emily's death with him at the barbecue?"

"Yeah, he said he admired my courage for helping Emily."

"I see. What can you tell me about the father?"

"He's an attorney. He owns his own law firm. His picture is on billboards around town."

"Billboards? So, he's an injury attorney in Colorado, a state with right-to-die laws, except that you skipped the paperwork crap? Looks like you've hit the jackpot, Steve, and this is the man you chatted with about Emily's death?"

"Yeah, in retrospect, it may have been a mistake, eh?"

"What's done is done. Don't speak to him about this matter again without consulting me. What can you tell me about Emily's estate? Are you overseeing that?"

"No, no, her husband, I mean the kids' father, is the administrator."

"Right. Emily, the pediatrician, chose an injury attorney ex-husband over her English teacher husband to manage her estate for the benefit of the children. Are you a beneficiary of the estate?"

"Not really. I keep the house and its contents, and everything else goes to the kids' trust. But the house is no big deal, because I'm just keeping it until the kids are old enough to take it over. They still have their childhood bedrooms here and their toys are in the attic."

"Generally, a beneficiary is precluded from assisting in a suicide, and as far as your provisional ownership of the house, no attorney will view it as being no big deal. Any idea how much the house is worth?"

"Yeah, about two-point-five million dollars, empty. According to Emily, the art in the house is worth another million. Some of the paintings were purchased by her ex-husband. When Emily divorced him, she fought for the house and its contents. She asked me to save it for the kids. Everything will just stay where it is until they get it."

"How do you feel about the house? Would you consider selling it and moving out of state, maybe to Florida, for example?"

"No, no, I have to stay here," replied Steve. "Also, I've gotta keep Emily's rose garden. The kids need it. The roses belonged to Emily."

"Emily's rose garden. Okay. The art and the roses will not matter once you end up in prison. Look, Steve, I don't want to present the worst-case scenario as your base case, but there have been situations where a defendant loses a civil case for wrongful death and then, immediately following a verdict, gets criminally charged and arrested for murder."

"Arrested for murder? No, no, I don't think so. It's been seven months. Emily's cause of death has been settled—she died of cancer."

"Still, it's a risk we can't ignore. That is why your objective in this matter should be to avoid going to court."

Steve tried to interrupt, but John said, "Hear me out. That may not be so difficult because if you're up against an injury attorney, we already know what he wants. That is why, if you are willing to give up the house, I would expect him to drop the lawsuit."

"Can I give up the house and keep the rose garden?" asked Steve.

"If you pay fifty thousand dollars as my up-front retainer, then I will certainly take your peculiar request under consideration. Maybe you can stay on as the gardener or something. For negotiations, I am your best option, but if the matter ends up going to court, you'll need to hire a local attorney. The retainer will not cover a court case."

"I see," said Steve. He would have to sell shares in his brokerage account to pay John, but he still had plenty left over from the sale of his business. As far as shysters go, John seemed meaner than Emily's ex-husband. "Let's do it. What is the next step?"

"My assistant will send you the wire details to pay my fee along with some other papers to sign. Make the payment and overnight the signed documents to us, along with the papers you were served. Keep a copy for yourself, of course."

As Steve tried to sign off, John interrupted him. "One more thing. Clyde told me you are heading to Whitehorse. Is that still true?"

"Yep. I've got an errand to run, plus I'm going to meet Alamea's friend, Meriwa. Oh, and I want to see the river."

"The river? I don't know what to say. I suppose leaving Denver for now is not such a bad idea, but going to Canada seems like jumping out of the fire into the frying pan. Have you considered going south for a while instead, until this whole deal blows over? Maybe Tijuana? You could visit the Rio Grande River."

10. The Fatalist

The Saturday before his departure, they had tickets to a Rockies game. Before the game, Steve took the kids to Tattered Cover Book Store on Colfax where he let each of them choose three items, with the qualification that only one could be a food item and at least one had to be an actual book. It was a rule that Emily used to enforce when they would visit as a family on Saturday mornings. As usual, Rachel spent the better part of an hour in the YA section and selected three books. Steve had planned to browse independently but instead spent the entire time with Michael, first buying him a scone, then listening to Michael's reviews on the store's assortment of games. After selecting a book of puzzles, Michael filibustered away the remaining time negotiating the definition of "book." They were out of time and Michael knew it. Steve relented and allowed him to select a graphic novel as his book item.

At the game, Rachel got the Rockies logo painted on her face, and together they all got their picture taken with purple dinosaur Dinger, the team mascot.

The following night, the kids' stepmother swung by his house to pick up Cosmo. She found Steve out back with the gardener discussing roses and care for the yard. She greeted him with a friendly hug, as though her husband had not just taken a wrecking ball to his world.

So it was in the autumn, following the spring of Emily's death, that Steve rode alone toward Whitehorse and the mighty Yukon River, his medium with sweet Emily.

Riding to the historic mile zero of the ALCAN is its own one thousand six hundred-mile adventure. Starting from Denver, it took days to ride through Wyoming, wander through Big Sky country, sneak past the Little Bighorn, zig around Yellowstone National Park, zag past Glacier National Park, traverse the border, romp northward through Alberta to Calgary, Edmonton and Whitecourt, and finally cross west into British Columbia to reach Dawson Creek, the gateway of the 1,387-mile Alaska Highway.

On the first day, Steve left his home in Denver's Country Club Neighborhood at 7 am. He made it to Billings, Montana before stopping for the night. Before dinner, he made a quick call to Michael and Rachel to say goodbye once more. When he explained he would be crossing into Canada the following day, Rachel informed him that she was painting her nails and, being thirteen, had no time for either national or international goodbyes. Michael was similarly bothered. "Steve, you do know your phone will still work once you're in Canada, right?"

The following morning at the Canadian border in Coutts, he showed his Canadian passport and rode north to Lethbridge, Alberta. On the third day, he considered stopping to see his mother at Sylvan Lake, north of Calgary, but decided against it. He had not seen her since the funeral, and he was not yet prepared to dissect Emily's final days. He also wasn't keen to explain the inexplicable purpose of his trip to Whitehorse.

As he rode by Innisfail, Alberta, Steve thought of his two younger half-siblings who lived nearby. He had not seen them since his stepfather's funeral many years ago. The old man had gotten rich by fracking the hell out of the family homestead, hundreds of acres situated just north of Calgary. His will had divided the fortune into three parts, with one for each of Steve's half-siblings and one in a trust for Steve's mother. Any remaining amount when his mother passed away would go to the half-siblings. Steve's mother explained that the will was structured to prevent Steve from benefiting from his stepfather's life. Thus far, it had unfolded exactly as intended. However, since his stepfather's death, the half-siblings had squandered their own shares of the money and now awaited Steve's mother's passing to inherit the remainder.

Steve had two other half-siblings in Bartlesville Oklahoma, where his father had left the entirety of a smaller fortune to Steve's stepmother. The half-siblings there were also waiting to inherit. In total there were four, now in their early- to mid-thirties, all bearing the curse-of-the-bequeathed, wasting their lives away as they waited to inherit a dwindling legacy. Steve alone had eluded their fate, and through the extra income from, and sale of, his internet marketing business, he managed to "squeeze together a couple of nickels," as his grandfather used to say.

Three hours north of Sylvan Lake, on two-lane Highway 20, the rain began. Steve pulled over, put on his rain gear, and continued riding. The rain intensified and the wind became fierce. The four cars ahead of him slowed to thirty miles per hour. Steve couldn't see the road through the torrential rain and he struggled to keep up with the taillights of the car ahead. If he fell behind, he would be forced to stop. Without visibility, he couldn't identify a safe place to pull over. If he stopped on the highway, he risked being hit from behind. The trees gave way, and a gust of wind almost blew him into an oncoming semi.

The near miss left him with a pounding heart and an adrenaline rush. Panic was followed by a familiar sense of relief for narrowly cheating death, before giving way to introspection. What *are* the rules for kicking the grim reaper in the balls? The same as for shooting a charging bear: don't miss.

The wind and rain abated, and he rode on in light rain. He arrived at Whitecourt, Alberta, tired and wet. In ideal conditions, the ride was no more difficult than sitting in an easy chair, but on days like these, he was lucky to have arrived alive.

From Whitecourt, it's a four-hour ride to Dawson Creek, which marked the beginning of the Alaska Highway and an altogether different adventure. The US Army built the Alaska Highway in the 1930s to defend Alaska against potential attacks by the Japanese. From Dawson Creek to Whitehorse in the Yukon Territory, nine hundred miles of highway snakes through some of the most majestic scenery in North America.

Steve's previous motorcycle rides on the ALCAN had always included some cold and wet conditions. However, early September proved to be remarkably frigid. On the final day, riding at high altitudes through the Northern Rockies was bone-chilling. Steve crossed paths with no other motorcycles, and all the motorhomes he encountered were heading south.

Through the Northern Rockies, the road traced a path beside magnificent rivers and crystalline lakes. The forests flaunted their autumnal wardrobe, a kaleidoscope of yellows, oranges, and reds. Dominating the horizon, the snow-capped peaks of the Cassiar Mountains rose with grandeur. A myriad of wildlife thrived in this splendid landscape of dense forests, towering mountains, and picturesque meadows.

Between Muncho Lake and Watson Lake, Steve spotted bears on five occasions: four black bears and one grizzly. He encountered three mule deer, one moose, two elk, and four herds of roaming buffalo. Prior to his first pass into the Yukon Territory, he slowed to a crawl to count the largest herd he had seen—forty-three buffalo, including seven calves. They lay and walked both alongside and on the highway. The mothers and calves eyed him warily, but the others paid him no heed as he wove through the herd.

North of Fort Nelson, the ALCAN turned and headed more west than north. The highway ran west-by-northwest, but its direction varied considerably as it followed winding rivers: Liard, Teslin, Swift, Tanana, and finally the mighty Yukon River. The route's demarcation was lyrical. As it followed the Liard River, it entered Yukon Territory from British Columbia twice, hopping north with a sign that read *Welcome to Yukon Territory! Plus Grand Que Nature* before doubling back at Watson Creek to return to *British*

Columbia, The Best Place on Earth! and then North at Swift River for a second entry to *Yukon, Larger than Life!* just before Teslin.

Among motorcycle riders can be found Posers and Fatalists, but on the Alaska Highway wander only Fatalists. The Fatalist accepts that riding a motorcycle comes with some risks. Naturally, precautions can mitigate the Law of Large Numbers, but the principles of probability, causation, and correlation dictate that doing something risky over and over will eventually lead to a negative outcome. It is only a matter of time before the Fatalist meets his fate. Some think the Fatalist is suicidal, but that misses the point. The Fatalist is not riding to meet destiny; he is riding despite destiny.

Most of the hundreds and hundreds of miles go by in a lull. Setting aside the disparity in risk, riding a Harley-Davidson Road Glide is not so dissimilar to sitting on a sofa, except for the wind, the sun, the bugs, the noise, the rain, the cold, and the heat. If one has the patience for such trivialities and can ride a sofa, then one can manage most of the ALCAN on a Harley. Of course, from time to time, destiny will devise a test, but between such tests, riding the ALCAN can be devilishly boring.

As Steve cruised down the empty highway, the hum of the big twin engine and the hypnotic rhythm of the asphalt beneath his wheels lulled him into a sense of detachment. With his feet on the highway pegs, he used them to steer the bike as if he were in a dream. At times, the world around him would blur into a simulation and the sirens of the forest would beckon. He would feel as though he could step off the bike and into the void. Each time, before he could take a step, reality would prevail. When bored, Steve performed slaloms, either tight with hands or looping with no hands. When the tedium became particularly oppressive, Steve moved back to the passenger portion of the seat and imagined Elon was driving.

Taking the backseat while Elon drove was not a foolproof method of riding. Since Elon was entirely dependent on cruise control, he didn't appreciate the subtleties of varying one's speed to cause the bike to naturally fall into and rise out of a turn as it swept through a curve. Intelligence in its most artificial pretend form wasn't programmed to watch for wildlife or guard against gusts of wind. With the vehicle controls so far out of reach, there were no provisions for corrective steering or emergency braking. No warning against the method was mentioned in the Harley-Davidson Owner's Manual, but an amendment should be considered. With all the weight distributed on the back wheel, sitting on the backseat transformed the Harley into a catapult. If you were Elon's passenger, no frost heave was required–a mere dip in the road could unseat you. While being launched from a motorcycle at seventy miles per hour wouldn't necessarily result in a crushed skull, it could definitely leave a Mark.

11. Riding Whitehorse

Steve checked into the Edgewater Hotel in Whitehorse, jogged the stairs to his second-floor room, dropped his bags and went straight to the window. He raised the blinds and there it was, just as he remembered: the Yukon River, running fast and deep. He gazed at the river and watched the pedestrians on the riverwalk.

"Nobody ever saved me from a bear before. That was the bravest thing I've ever seen."

Where did Alamea stay when she was in Whitehorse?

The spell was broken by a red fox darting across the path, courting his lucky date, a hoary marmot.

He showered and headed out of the hotel toward the riverwalk. The White Pass & Yukon Historic Train Station is located on the river, directly across from the Edgewater Hotel. Inside the station, there is also the office for the Yukon Quest, the world's second-most-famous dog sled race. Steve checked out the shop before stepping outside for a moment to call his favorite thirteen-year-old.

"Hello Rachel baby, it's Steve."

"I never would have guessed. Wassup, Steve?"

"Do you remember when we went to the Iditarod Headquarters in Wasilla, Alaska?"

"Whaaaaat?"

"Rachel, remember when we visited the Iditarod Racetrack, rode on the cart, and petted puppies?"

"Yeeaah . . ."

"I'm here in Whitehorse. They have another race headquarters here. They have t-shirts and sweatshirts. Do you want me to buy you one?"

"Get me a puppy." Her words reminded Steve of several years prior when Rachel had pleaded with Emily to take one of the neighbor's puppies. He had gone with her after school, and it was Rachel who had selected Cosmo from a litter of eight.

"I could try to get a puppy, but it's going to have to run very fast because I'll have to tie it to the motorcycle."

"Get a puppy."

"Rachel, do you want a t-shirt or sweatshirt?"

"Oooookaaaay."

"Which one?"

"Surprise me, Steve."

"What size?"

"Surpriiiiiise me."

Steve stopped by his room to drop the surprise baby-blue Yukon Quest size-medium sweatshirt. As he left the hotel, he checked his watch and decided he had plenty of time before his meeting, so he opted for the Three Mile River Walk.

Two years prior, during Steve's first visit to Whitehorse with Michael, he had checked the distances for the paved pedestrian path that stretched along the Yukon River. From the historic train station, it ran upriver, south to the SS Klondike River Boat Museum. Round trip, it was a one-mile walk. Heading north in the opposite direction, toward Two Mile Hill before the footbridge, past Quartz Road and back, was about a three-mile walk.

After lunch or dinner each day, Steve let Michael choose which walk they would do. Michael had dubbed these two walks, "The One Mile River Walk" and "The Three Mile River Walk." It was only three days before departing that they discovered the Black Street Stairs. After that, Michael chose the stairs every time.

The city of Whitehorse was nestled between the escarpment to the west and the Yukon River to the east. The Black Street Stairs, more than two hundred metal treads, scaled the steep slope to the back side of the airport, situated above the city. The stairs ascended to a path extending along a tall chain link fence, through which one could see the airport runway. Turning north on the path led one through the woods along the precipice, with snippets of the city far below peeking through the trees.

The path through the woods reached its pinnacle at a park bench nestled in a clearing along the upper rim of the escarpment. It offered a breathtaking view of Whitehorse, with the mighty Yukon River snaking through. Buildings of all shapes and sizes appeared as specks along the stripes of city streets. Magnificent Grey Mountain towered in the distance, providing a fitting backdrop to the hub of commerce and government that is the city itself. Amid the hustle and bustle of daily life, the natural beauty of the surrounding landscape persisted, reminding one of the serenity and majesty of the vast Klondike wilderness that enveloped the city.

As Steve trekked the riverwalk, he stepped toward the riverbank, closed his eyes, and emptied his mind. The river began as a trickle of snowmelt from the coastal mountains of Kluane Range. On its hundred-mile journey, it gathered power and magnitude and acquired its unique scent of earth and pine, which, to the discerning nose of a salmon, represented a powerful homing beacon.

The river's powerful, untamed beauty was extraordinary, but its gushing sound hinted at a history of death and mayhem. To stampeders floating from the Kluane Range to the Klondike Gold Fields, the rapids racing through the deep narrow channel of Whitehorse babbled promises of riches and adventure, masking the dangers lurking in the depths of its swift currents. Steve pondered the abundance of life given, and lives taken, by the mighty Yukon River. As always, his thoughts turned to sweet Emily. "I miss you," he said aloud, before resuming the walk.

At Shipyards Park, Steve turned away from the river and wandered across town to the Pioneer Cemetery, remembering the way Emily would drag him through these somber resting places hypothesizing about the various tombstone inscriptions.

From the dates carved in stones, he identified those who had died around the turn of the century and guessed which had been Klondike Stampeders–the successful ones, that is, the lucky few who managed to be buried in an actual graveyard. Not those who perished in the river or were deserted along Chilkoot Pass with the tuckered beasts of burden. On one gravestone were inscribed words which would have amused Emily:

Unknown - 1900

The Klondike Can't Forget

the Stampeder it Never Knew

Two rows away, he found an example of Emily's favorite–the classic *mystery of the missing lover* tombstone:

Together Forever in Paradise

Robert Hesselton & Sarah Hesselton

1890 – 1934   1901 -

Emily would have said, "Robert's forever was Sarah's yesterday."

The day before Emily died, he had pleaded with her not to go. When he had suggested joining her, she told him to care for her children. She told him to love again.

In accordance with Emily's request, Steve and the kids, upon the first blossoms in May, had spread her ashes in the rose garden. Now they risked losing it forever.

12. Meet the Niece

Steve headed toward the center of town to meet Meriwa at the Klondike Rib & Salmon restaurant. He tried to conjure an image of this person, the niece of his investigator–the Chief of the Royal Canadian Mounted Police in Whitehorse. According to Clyde, she was a First Nations local who had managed to gain admission to Mount Holyoke College in Massachusetts, one of the world's most prestigious all-women colleges. If Alamea had been Meriwa's classmate, then she must be younger than his own thirty-eight years, probably between thirty-two and thirty-four.

Steve arrived early and waited in front of the restaurant to watch for her. When they arranged the meeting, Meriwa had said, "I'll be wearing a green Eddie Bauer jacket and carrying a brown briefcase."

Whitehorse prides itself in looking scruffy. The tourists, the locals, even the homeless had that nutty, crunchy look, like they had just returned from a wilderness hike or were heading out to pan for gold.

He spotted her walking toward him on the sidewalk. Little Miss Metro definitely was not channeling wilderness. The jacket hinted at a slim figure with an ample bosom. She was slightly shorter than average. Her skin was a pale, creamy color, neither light nor dark. She had stunning features, including high cheekbones, a noble nose, and full lips. The shape of her face, with a widow's peak and a sharp chin, was reminiscent of a heart. Her long black hair hung loosely down her back. She was dressed in a silk blouse, wool slacks and fancy heels. As she came closer, he noticed her emerald-green eyes framed by long lashes. Her makeup, jewelry and all-around getup were ready for prime time. In Manhattan, she would have been considered well-dressed for business, but in Whitehorse, she was the most fashionable person in town.

What could a woman like this be doing, living Larger than Life in The Wilderness City?

As she approached, Steve offered the biggest Oklahoma smile he could muster and extended his hand. "Hi, I'm Steve."

Though her lips hid it, the dimple in her right cheek and her eyes suggested a smile. Was it amusement, anticipation, enthusiasm, or scorn?

By comparison, I'm dressed like a dork on laundry day.

She accepted his handshake and replied in a silky alto voice, "Hi Steve. I'm Meriwa. Welcome to my city."

The restaurant was built inside a temporary-looking tented structure attached to what could have been an old saloon from the gold rush era. The place was chock-a-block full of rustic outdoorsy tourists; they were lucky to get a table without waiting. They both opted for the local brew, Yukon Gold, and for their meals, Meriwa selected the Yukon Arctic Char and Steve the Wild Elk Stroganoff.

While they waited for their beer, Steve began with small talk. "While I was waiting, I visited your graveyard."

"Ah, the Pioneer Cemetery. Alamea spent hours strolling among the stones."

Steve blinked and tilted his head. "Really?"

"That's Alamea. Tell me, how did you know her?"

"Know her? I'm friends with her cousin Ron who once introduced us." Steve delivered the lie, just as he had rehearsed. "He asked me to look into her business plan."

With an intense and expressionless gaze, Meriwa exaggerated a pregnant pause, allowing Steve an opportunity to say more, to give a full explanation, say something real, something true. His grandmother used to do that when he was small. She once told him he was worse at lying than any twelve-year-old she had ever met. Coming up empty, Meriwa pressed on. "What kind of plan?"

"The name she had for it was *A Perfect Finish*," said Steve. "She had planned to locate it in Whitehorse. I assume she discussed it with you?"

"Sure. Alamea visited me here the week before she died. Her death was a horrible shock. It's still being investigated. There was someone else at the scene of the accident the night she died. My uncle, the Chief Superintendent for the Royal Canadian Mounted Police in Whitehorse, informed me that the witness is still considered a person of interest, a suspect in the shooting of a bear, or even robbery." She narrowed her eyes and stared unblinkingly at Steve.

"It's an incredibly sad situation," Steve replied without skipping a beat. "Ron is taking it awfully hard. Also, Alamea's godfather is still trying to come to terms with the loss. Have you met them?"

The beer came. Had he been in control of the pace, the dessert would already be arriving before they had gotten this far into the conversation.

"I've never met her cousin, but I've known Clyde for years," said Meriwa. "During college once, I traveled with Alamea to Seattle for Thanksgiving break. We stayed in Clyde and John's pool house. The trip was amazing. Alamea and I had such a wonderful time, possibly the best ever. Clyde and John were so kind and generous. John cooked a lovely Thanksgiving dinner."

"Yes, I can imagine. Ron introduced me to Clyde last week. We discussed the business idea," he lied.

To his relief, the food came. As the server walked away, he took a bite of elk.

"Why are you really here, Steve?" Meriwa asked as he was chewing.

She's driving this conversation as though she's double-parked. Is that even a thing in Whitehorse?

He tried to swallow the elk so he could reply. "Your name is in Alamea's journal as one of the people to contact in the event of her death," he replied with a gulp.

"Thank you for informing me about Alamea's death. I read the police report; I was the one at the morgue."

"I've been asked to look into the business plan and consider pursuing it on Alamea's behalf." Steve said it in a rush and a noticeably higher tone, finishing with, "Is there anything you can tell me about the plan?"

She hadn't touched her beer and was ignoring her food. She stared at him with unblinking emerald-green eyes. On the back forty acres, his grandfather had once cautioned, "Beware of the ones with exotic eyes." At the time, he seemed to be referring to a poisonous green tree snake, but he may have meant more.

"Asked by whom?" Meriwa probed.

Lying and improv were a bad combination, especially with a mouthful of elk. He hadn't rehearsed for an inquisition. He swallowed and gulped and, as he reached for his glass, managed to reply, "Asked by Clyde and Ron."

"Well, Steve, I haven't learned much from you tonight. Let me discuss it, and think about it," she said in her silky alto as she pursed her lips and glared mean green.

"Discuss it with whom?" asked Steve with a few extra blinks.

"With my mother. With Clyde. With the RCMP. With the mayor. With the Tribal Leaders. With my dog."

Steve forced a smile but was powerless to stop the temperature rising in his face and extending to his ear lobes. Grasping at straws, he asked, "What's your dog's name?"

"Juneau."

"You think it would help if we gave Juneau a couple pieces of elk?" He took two pieces of elk from his plate and placed it in his napkin and offered it to her.

Meriwa placed the gift in her briefcase. Without smiling, mentioning the check, or saying anything further whatsoever, she got up, gathered her jacket, and walked away, leaving her beer and arctic char perfectly untouched. She weaved and swayed her way through the tables, right out of Klondike Rib & Salmon.

Where did I go wrong? Could it have been the first lie? Maybe the second, or the third? Or was it the ultimate culminating lie that wove them all together into a truly pathetic rag of a half-assed story? If my grandmother were here, I would be headed straight to the woodshed.

13. Homeopathic Remedy

Her message proposed 8:15, so it was on the following morning that Steve arrived at Burnt Toast Café at 8:05 and ordered coffee. He claimed a seat facing the door and watched the waitress–Brittany, or Chloe, or Zoe maybe–serve the tables by the window. She walked in moccasins like a ballerina-girl, with feet pointing slightly out, heel to instep at right angles to pour coffee. She had ballerina legs and a ballerina ass. She wore a heavy sweater, of course, because she had nothing to hide and because ballerinas get cold.

"She's pretty, isn't she?" asked Meriwa as she took her seat.

Steve said, "Damn, I hate it when that happens."

"Her name is Tammy. Do you want to meet her?"

Steve could feel his cheeks and ears burning red, as though Meriwa had just flipped his face switch. "That would be inappropriate. Nice, but inappropriate," he replied.

"Why would that be, Steve? Maybe because you are wearing a wedding ring?" Meriwa grinned, openly enjoying the moment.

"Well, um, sort of," Steve stammered and ran his fingers through his hair.

"Sort of? What does that mean, Steve? Does that mean you are sort of married?"

"My wife died from cancer," he blurted out.

"Oh. I'm sorry." Her expression became serious. "Do you have children?"

"Yes, I do. I mean, my wife had two, Michael and Rachel."

"That's heartbreaking," Meriwa said as she put her hand over her heart and met his gaze.

Steve nodded and cleared his throat. "It's been difficult for them."

"And for you?" Meriwa asked.

"Well, yes. That's why I still wear a ring," Steve admitted.

How has this perfect stranger managed to extract a random confession from an experienced high school teacher?

"I see," Meriwa said, showing just a hint of a dimple. "I can see how staring at Tammy's ass might represent a sort of homeopathic remedy." She finished with a full mischievous grin.

Steve had clumsily led them to this dead end and now there was no obvious appropriate response. He kept his head down and read the menu, tapping his fork on the table. Tammy smiled sweetly as she served him coffee. Meriwa reveled in the moment and smirked openly, before ordering a latte with skim milk.

The beauty likes her latte with skim. I need to remember that.

Steve ordered huevos rancheros. They sat in silence and checked their phones until Tammy brought his eggs and her latte.

Meriwa broke the silence. "By the way, thanks for the elk pieces. Juneau loved them. How was the museum?"

"The museum?" he asked with a forkful of huevos suspended halfway to his mouth.

She tilted her head and with a smile said, "Yes, I heard you were at the Macbride Museum yesterday afternoon."

"True, but how do you know that?" Steve asked with his eggs still stranded in midair.

"It's my town. Have you forgotten? People know me."

"Sure, but they don't know me," he said before taking the bite.

"You might be surprised," Meriwa said. "And now I must go, but my uncle wants to meet you." She handed him a note. "It's in front of your hotel. Can I tell him you'll be there?"

A Perfect Finish

<u>Meet:</u>	<u>Where:</u>	<u>When:</u>
Simon Smith	Baked Café	Sat 17 Sept
	Horwood Mall	7:45 pm
	109 Main St	

For a summons, it didn't look very official. Rather, it reminded Steve of the birthday party invitations Emily used to make for the kids. He let out a sigh. "Your uncle? Of course. Tell him I'll be there."

Without touching her latte, she got up and swayed her way through the tables and out of the restaurant. Right before clobbering him with the Tammy schtick, she had taken just a sip of her water, leaving a lip-shaped red smudge on the brim of the glass. He finished eating alone, sitting with a black eye and bruised lip, staring at the brim.

What is the point of asking to meet if she has nothing to say? I'm the running back who mows down linebackers on the way to the end zone. How am I allowing this Klondike-flavored mini-dom to ride me like a wheel?

On the way back to the museum, Steve walked by the World's Largest Copper Nugget. His ticket was good until 2 pm, and he still had to see the Telegraph Office and Sam McGee's Cabin. He had seen them before but what was the point of buying a ticket to the MacBride Museum if he wasn't even going to take a look at Sam McGee's Cabin?

When he finished, he smiled, thinking of little Michael.

"Steve, let's do the Three Mile River Walk."

He headed past the Kwanlin Dun Cultural Center and decided to go in. As fortune would have it, the regalia display included vamps, beaded leather moccasin tops. As the narrative explained, the fireweed designs represented new life and beauty that springs up after a disaster, a metaphor for Indigenous resilience.

The self-guided tour included an explanation of the clan system that divided the First Nations in two—Wolf and Crow. It was based on the Creation Story, in which Crow created people and ordered half to follow Wolf and the other half to follow Crow. Crow then brought the sun and light to share among members of both clans. Each First Nations member inherited the clan from their mother and can only marry someone from the opposite clan. In this way, the clans were continuously woven together across generations.

After the tour, he resumed the Three Mile River Walk. He thought of Meriwa and their first meeting and asked aloud, "Are you a Crow or a Wolf?"

14. Ashes to Ashes

Steve returned to his hotel room and waited for the scheduled call with John to discuss the progress of the civil suit. Steve had helped two dying people in their final hours and was now at risk of arrest in the Yukon and Colorado.

The civil suit seemed like extortion. It had caught him by total surprise but, thinking back on the tense relationship he had always had with Emily's ex-husband, he should have suspected that it wouldn't be all smooth sailing once Emily's hand was no longer on the tiller.

His phone rang. After salutations, John began, "Over the past week, I've had numerous discussions with the plaintiff. As I suspected, he hopes to settle the matter out of court."

"Are you saying that I'm in the clear?" asked Steve.

"No, but I am saying that we have a clear path forward. The estate proposes to drop all claims if you immediately forfeit your rights to the house and its contents."

"We're losing the rose garden?" asked Steve.

"If I were you, I would consider the roses already gone. The estate intends to immediately liquidate the property for the benefit of the children's trust," replied John.

Steve stood at his hotel window and watched the Yukon River surge through Whitehorse. "I can't accept such an offer. I've done nothing wrong, and losing the roses means losing them for the children, too. That was never Emily's plan."

"Look, Steve, I'm sorry. I really am," consoled John. "I understand that you supported Emily in a decision she made, but the reality is that for whatever reasons, the circumstances of her death and your failure to comply with the requirements and mandated process of Colorado's End-of-Life Options Act puts you in a difficult spot."

John paused, giving Steve an opportunity to reply, before proceeding. "The estate's attorney has made it clear that he has gathered sufficient evidence to have you brought up on charges of second-degree murder if you refuse his offer. Even if you succeeded in your defense, and I have no reason to believe you could, your teaching career might be over, and the press coverage could severely impact the children and could even damage your relationship with them permanently."

Steve continued looking out the window. "When you say the estate's attorney, you're referring to Emily's ex-husband? You're saying he could cause the district attorney to initiate a criminal investigation?"

"Of course," confirmed John. "He says his private investigator already has all the evidence they need. All he has to do is turn it over to the district attorney, and I don't doubt he would do so. In my opinion, you have no choice but to accept the offer. Otherwise, you should expect to be charged with murder."

Don't attack the messenger, especially after you just paid him fifty grand.

Steve remained silent as he considered how discussions with Emily's ex would have gone if he had not hired John.

John continued, "There's an unexpected matter that arose during the discussions."

"What is it?" asked Steve.

John hesitated. Steve could hear John killing time with some table drumming.

How often does he have to replace his pen?

The drumming stopped. "He requests that you cease calling the children."

Steve closed his eyes and leaned forward, resting his forehead against the cold glass. In insufferable circumstances, denial always serves as the harbinger of false hope. "That's . . . that's just not possible. I've been teaching Michael how to drive, and I just bought Rachel a sweatshirt. What about Michael's rugby games and Rachel's debate team competitions? Has he discussed this with the children?"

"He intends to discuss your involvement in Emily's death with them himself," replied John. "Once he has done so, he'll leave it up to them to choose how or if they wish to proceed. In the meantime, he is ordering you to sever all communications with them."

"He's playing God now that Emily is gone," Steve protested. "What gives him the right to wreck my relationship with my stepchildren and overturn Emily's final decisions about her house?"

"I understand how you feel, Steve, and I'm sorry. As the children's father, guardian, trustee, and executor of the estate, he does have an incredible amount of leverage. He told me that if you do not voluntarily agree to comply with the request, he will file a restraining order against you. He does not want to do that."

"That's kind of him," retorted Steve.

"He also said that his promise to Emily about your trip with Rachel precluded him from bringing the lawsuit earlier, and that I should mention that to you. He said he waited until your return from Alaska out of respect for his promise. Tell me, did Emily ever discuss her end-of-life plans with the children?"

"I assumed she at least hinted at her plans when she spoke with them. I mean, she met with them individually the night before to say goodbye. I would be incredibly sad to learn they blamed me in any way for Emily's death."

15. Drop in the River

That evening Steve arrived early at the Baked Café, ordered a quadruple espresso, and chose a table outside on the sidewalk. He didn't know who he was looking for–Uncle Simon might be in uniform or maybe plain clothes–so he just sat and sipped for half an hour. He thought about the accident and rehearsed what he was going to say. He was considering simply coming clean about having shot the grizzly, but without an attorney, it seemed risky.

At ten past eight, a rather shabbily-dressed, homeless-looking Indigenous man stepped in front of him and said, "Hi, I'm Simon."

Steve suppressed his surprise and confusion, rose and offered his hand. "Hello, I'm Steve."

"I know," said Simon, as he ignored Steve's hand.

"Can I buy you a coffee?" asked Steve, but Simon was already walking away.

"This place is too fancy," muttered Simon. "Let's visit the river."

Steve binned his empty paper espresso cup and hurried to catch up.

Wow, this guy must be seriously undercover. Can that really be a thing in Whitehorse?

The two of them walked in silence across the street toward the viewing dock. It was not set up for loading the huge paddle wheel steam ships anymore. It had been redesigned with a railing to keep idiot tourists from tripping into the river. Simon sidled up to the railing and stared into the water. Steve joined him.

"My name is Simon Smith. Say it: Simon Smith."

"Simon Smith," parroted Steve.

"That's right and my grandfather was Chief Steven Smith. He negotiated agreements for the First Nations. Say it: Chief Steven Smith. Say it."

Steve, still surveying Simon to discover where he might be concealing an official weapon, obeyed. "Chief Steven Smith."

"That's right. That was my grandfather. They call me Animal. Do you know why?" asked Simon.

Steve shook his head.

"Because I'm a survivor. In prison, they tried to kill me. See this scar?" Simon pointed to a scar on his face that ran from below his ear to the corner of his mouth. "They cut me, but they can't kill me. I'm a survivor," he repeated, pausing for emphasis. Steve nodded.

"And the police broke my leg right here, and also right here. The police did that, and they broke my clavicle. But I survived. I'm a survivor. Say it: survivor. Say it."

"Survivor," repeated Steve, wondering how this game of *Simon Says* would end.

"That's right, I'm an animal. Say it, 'Animal.'"

"Animal," mimicked Steve.

There was a pause in the game. Steve rested his hands on the railing and gazed at the Yukon River. Simon reached into his grubby coat and extracted a can of Mike's Harder Blood Orange. He opened it and took a couple swigs before wiping his mouth and continuing. "What do you see? What do you see when you look at the river?"

Steve had contemplated precisely that the night before as he had stood near that very spot and stared at the Yukon River. So, for this question he was well prepared. "Before us roars the Yukon River, its waters flowing continually for centuries, day and night, week after week, year after year. I was in Denver last week, yet here flowed the Yukon River, pulsing through the heart of Whitehorse."

Simon set his Harder on the rail and stared expectantly at Steve. Steve paused to consider the river's source and destination, its magnificent depth, velocity, and sheer volume before continuing.

"Time flows like a river, bearing the spirits of those who have lived on this earth. Each drop of water in the river represents a soul, destined to be forgotten in the depths of the Bering Sea. Most lives fade into obscurity, etching not even a trace in the annals of history. How many souls are remembered two hundred years after their passing? In the end, what remains of any of us? A mere drop on this earth, and this earth itself? A trifling speck in the dustpan of the galaxy. Yet here we stand tonight, you and I, on this speck, observing the majestic spectacle of the mighty Yukon River ushering an eternity of souls to the Bering Sea."

They stood side-by-side in silence. Steve stared at the river, while Simon stared at Steve. Finally, Steve turned to Simon.

Simon rubbed his scruffy chin. "Very good, Steve. That was very good, indeed, and it's lucky for me you said that." An expression as dark as a moonless winter night descended on Simon's face. "My second wife died last week. She is one of those souls, a drop traveling to the Bering Sea. We are still alive. So, we stand here tonight, honoring her while we can."

Steve remained silent, sensing the gravity of the moment. Simon took a sip of his Harder. "She overdosed just like my first wife. I used to have a drug problem, but not anymore. I solved it, but she couldn't. She hid it from me. Then she died."

Simon took a long drink from his Harder, sat the can on the rail, and fished a one-foot-long spruce branch from his inside coat pocket.

What else does he have in there? Maybe he has just come from a ceremony because that branch hasn't been broken from a tree, it's a cutting. What's up with the Harder? Maybe he's not even a Mountie.

"This is for my lovely Clara Wolf," he said as he tore some evergreen needles from the spruce branch and threw them into the water. He paused before repeating the tear and toss. "And this is for my Mary Wolf. I love you, Mary. You take some," Simon said, as he presented the spruce branch to Steve.

A knot formed in Steve's throat and tears welled up in his eyes as an image of Emily floated to mind. He plucked a few needles from the spruce branch and released them into the Yukon River. His thoughts turned to Alamea, and he freed a few more needles. Simon watched and tilted his head as Steve wiped tears from his face. Simon resumed methodically unleashing needles from the spruce branch and offering them to the river, a few at a time, between sips of Harder. Steve watched the ritual in silence.

Once the spruce branch was barren, still looking at the river, Simon asked, "How long are you staying?"

"A few days, but I'll return," Steve replied.

"You need to return for the Rendezvous. It's before the equinox in late February. Say it: the Rendezvous."

Steve obeyed. "The Rendezvous during the spring equinox."

"No! It's in late February, before the equinox! Say it."

"The Rendezvous, in late February," Steve replied timidly.

"Right." Simon threw the stripped spruce branch into the river. They watched it sink out of sight.

"Look at that! It's heavy. It sank like a cheechako. Say it: it's heavy. Say it," Simon insisted.

"It's heavy, like a cheechako," Steve obeyed.

At that moment four other homeless-looking locals slunk by, casting sideways glances. Simon extended his hand. "Nice to meet you, Steve. See you at the Rendezvous."

Steve shook his hand. "Nice to meet you too, Simon."

Simon joined his friends and headed downriver in the direction of the drops. Steve crossed the street to his hotel.

"What is a cheechako?" he asked the night clerk.

"You are a cheechako. If you make it to spring, you'll be a sourdough. Most stampeders don't survive the Yukon winter. Tourists never do. Are you a tourist or a stampeder?"

"I don't know yet. Are those my only choices?" Steve quipped.

"You have a message from Meriwa." The clerk handed Steve an envelope with his first name handwritten on the front.

The night clerk knows Meriwa.

Steve removed his jacket and made himself a drink before opening it.

> *Hi Steve,*
>> *Thank you for meeting Simon. He's*
>> *been having a rough time lately. I'll*
>> *be having breakfast at Burnt Toast Café.*
>> *Tomorrow, 8 am, join me if you wish.*
>
> *Sincerely,*
> *Meriwa*

He tossed the note on the desk.

Again, the Burnt fucking Toast? Is she testing my patience? Is she secretly having me watched as I schlep around town like an idiot, waiting for our next meeting? Is she going to arrange for me to meet every rando relative she has? This must be a plot to string me along until the snow arrives so I freeze my cheechako ass off in the Klondike.

16. Clyde Guarantees You

Meriwa was already drinking coffee when he arrived—more business casual, maybe less casual, with a low-cut blouse. The makeup and hair were the same, but she looked different. Same eyes, definitely more smile, less scorn. It wasn't just the dimple this time; even her lips were smiling. She had swapped the Eddie Bauer for a snazzy blue designer jacket.

Clad alluringly in Neptune's blue. The blue is suffocating methane gas . . .

Steve smiled back and asked, "Hey beautiful, mind if I join you?"

"I'm waiting for someone . . . but he's late."

Steve sat and ordered coffee and a bagel with lox.

"How did it go with Simon?" she asked.

"I thought you said your uncle was a Mountie."

"Yeah, different uncle. Simon is on my mom's side. The Mountie is on my father's side."

Steve poured milk into his coffee and took a taste. "Hmmm, your mother's a Crow and your father's a Wolf."

The corners of Meriwa's lips curled up the slightest bit and she revealed a dimple, before blowing gently on her coffee and taking a gentle sip.

Steve sighed. "It went as well as it could have. I mean, Simon seems to be pretty down right now."

"Yeah, we're all worried about him," Meriwa replied. "By the way, he told my mother he likes you. He mentioned that you spoke of death and the river. He said you are plugged into our world. I introduced you two because I thought you might be able to use him for Alamea's business plan. Plus, my mother has to approve, and helping Simon could go a long way with her."

Steve sat his cup down and leaned forward. "Your mother has to approve? Are you serious?"

Meriwa scowled and her green eyes flashed a warning. "Yes, Steve, very serious."

Steve took refuge by fiddling with his bagel. "I spoke with Clyde yesterday," she continued. "He says you were a genuine friend to Alamea.

Clyde *guarantees* you. He assured me that you are trustworthy." She paused, giving him a chance to reply.

The petulant lass still hasn't learned that Grandmother's pregnant pause doesn't work on me.

"I'm sorry if I wasn't very friendly the other night. I just felt like you were not being straight with me. Clyde assured me that you will come around when you are ready. Is that true, Steve?" she asked, looking directly at him.

Steve weighed his words. "Someday, I hope to be able to tell you more." His voice was an octave higher than usual.

Leaning forward, she locked her intense gaze on him, like a teacher preparing a lying student for an admonishment. She pursed her lips, shook her head, and let out a sigh before softening her tone. "Well, until then, I suppose I cannot continue torturing you, or in Clyde's words, 'using a can opener on you.' Clyde thinks you represent our best shot at fulfilling Alamea's business plan. Personally, I don't agree, but my mother insists that I help you since you were a friend of Alamea's. So, now I'm offering my assistance. How can I help?"

Steve was startled by the sudden shift in sentiment.

Maybe she actually has been busy while I've been schlepping around town waiting to meet her.

"When you discussed it, what were the next steps?"

"Alamea wanted me to help set up the business, legally I mean, and hook her up operationally. We did a lot of leg work. For example, I introduced her to Harold, a bush pilot who owns some luxury outfitter cabins on Tagish Lake. He told her he would help, for the right price, of course."

"The bush pilot is another uncle?" asked Steve.

"No, he's a cousin on my father's side."

Steve nodded and focused on his coffee.

Meriwa continued, "Years ago, my parents met Alamea when she was here with her father. The elders remembered Alamea and appreciated that she was a native of Hawaii, so they endorsed her concept of offering a dignified death to the elderly and granted permission for her to operate the business in Whitehorse."

"You're kidding?" replied Steve, trying to suppress a smile. "The elders decide these things?"

"Steve, you're not in Denver anymore," Meriwa scolded.

"Yes, I know, and I'm a cheechako," said Steve, evoking a full smile from Meriwa.

"As I was saying," Meriwa continued, "Alamea was encouraged by the positive reception. However, she still had to deal with the matter of Mark's terminal illness. We agreed to put the idea on ice until Mark was on ice, so to speak. That is how we left it, and then Alamea and Mark headed to Alaska with her shoes."

"What?" Steve opened his mouth and the word just fell out.

"What is your question?" Meriwa, Esquire, interrogated.

"Why the shoes?" Steve asked defensively.

"You know about the shoes?" she pressed.

"You mentioned them, so I'm asking why they're important," Steve backpedaled.

Telling that first lie is like jumping off a high dive. The entire way down, you regret jumping. You plunge into cold, dark water. The consequences carry you deeper and deeper. You fear you'll never find your way back to the surface.

Meriwa narrowed her eyes. "They belonged to Alamea's mother. Why is that important to you, Steve?"

"It's not," he replied, before quickly changing the subject as smoothly as a washboard. "So, did you discuss any approximate dates?"

Meriwa shook her head and smirked, signaling that she was an attorney seasoned in Central Boston, not a guppy. "Conceptually we did. Alamea proposed that during the winter she would sign up clients for the summer, booking them months in advance. You will have to book them no later than March to be reserved for next summer."

Did she mean to substitute me into the picture?

"Did Alamea see the cabins?" he asked.

"Harold flew her out to see them. They toured the cabins, went for a hike, and returned in time for dinner. She liked the cabins and my cousin was impressed by her. They even discussed prices and terms. I helped them prepare a term sheet. I can send it to you if you want."

"Yes, please. What about operations and employees?" Steve asked.

"I introduced Alamea to one of my cousins who makes websites. Do you want to meet her?"

"Sure, why not?"

Meriwa took out her phone and dialed. "Angi, we're at Burnt Toast Café. Do you have ten minutes to spare?" There was a pause. "Sure, now is great." She ended the call. "Angi's on her way."

Steve nodded casually, as though he also summoned web developers at the drop of a hat.

Meriwa waved to Tammy for another latte. "We talked about adventure guides, offices, hotel rooms, charter flights, therapists, medical professionals, and outfitters," Meriwa continued. "I introduced her to my cousin, who would have been her assistant."

"Another cousin," Steve noted. "Did you discuss how you would be involved?"

"I agreed to hook her up locally and manage any legal aspects. Beyond that, I have a full-time job and plans of my own."

Steve cocked his head and waited.

"I am the community Justice Coordinator for the Indigenous Court Worker Program."

See, the pregnant pause still works on her.

"Is that like a public defender?" Steve asked.

"Sort of. In a way, I suppose."

"Meriwa returns to the Yukon to bring justice to the poor," Steve joked.

She smiled charmingly, offering a glimpse of herself. "Yes, on a good day, that's how I look at it."

"And I'd pegged you as the Devil Wears Prada kind of girl."

"I frequently do," Meriwa said with a laugh, before changing the subject. "What is your next step?"

Wow, she looks sweet when she laughs. I need to make her laugh more.

"Steve, hello, Steve? What's next, then?"

"Oh yes, sorry. I'd like to leave my motorcycle here for the winter. Do you know where I can stash it?"

"I was wondering how you were going to get back. You know it snowed last night in the Northern Rockies? I thought maybe you planned to spend the winter in the Yukon."

"Alas, no sourdough status for me. I'm afraid I'm destined to remain a cheechako for life."

"For life, really?" Meriwa's tone made it difficult to decipher whether her disappointment was genuine or sarcastic. "The safest place for your motorcycle would be my yard. It will be exposed to the weather, but it won't be touched. Nobody messes with the Justice Coordinator. Juneau will keep it company. When do you plan to leave?"

"I'm flying out the day after tomorrow," Steve answered as he twirled his wedding band on his finger.

"Where to?" Meriwa asked.

"Seattle."

She tilted her head. "Oh, Seattle? The day after tomorrow? Are you going to the baseball game?"

"What baseball game?" Steve was confused.

"Never mind. Let's discuss Angi. She's kind of intense. She holds Canada's high school record for high-hurdles. Don't be put off by her manner. She still sort of behaves like a sprinter," Meriwa said, as Angi appeared at the table. They both stood and the two women hugged, before Meriwa made the introduction. "Thank you for coming. This is our Steven I was telling you about."

Angi's big, round lenses hid an impish face. Despite her loose-fitting wool slacks and blouse with ruffles, she looked as though she might still win a sprint. She stacked her black hair atop her head in a strict bun which, combined with her glasses, completed the Marian look. She was slightly out of breath, as if she had just cleared a series of ten hurdles on her way from the library.

The Music Man's Madame Librarian: Marian the Librarian?

She turned toward Steve, extended her hand, and gave him a huge Marian smile. "Hi Steve, I'm sooo glad to meet you. I was worried there would be nobody to look at my website and all my work would be for nothing."

He smiled and shook her hand. "Hi Angi, it's my pleasure. Thank you for taking the time."

Angi was a fast talker. "No, no, it's nothing really," she said as they all continued standing. "And about my time, don't worry, you're paying for that."

Steve didn't miss a beat. "Sure, sure, of course. Meriwa says you hold the record for the hundred-meter high-hurdles."

"If you're talking about the Canadian high school record, I held it for five years, but it was broken last year by an amazing sprinter from Edmonton. Kudos to her. Let's discuss websites."

Meriwa interrupted Angi and hugged her again, guiding her to a chair. "Angi, are you going to eat something, or would you like some coffee?"

Angi continued talking at a sprinter's pace. "No, thank you. I have the website on my server at home on a subdomain. I saved screenshots on my phone. Do you want to see it?"

Double-parking is actually a thing in Whitehorse. Meriwa's entire family probably does it.

"*Absolutely*," Steve said with exaggerated enthusiasm, which elicited a cautionary scowl from Meriwa.

"Here it is," Angi said. "This is how it looks on a mobile of course." She pressed her phone toward Steve's face. He had to push her hand away from his eyelids a little to see it.

"Wow, this is a very professional-looking website. You did all this?" Steve asked.

"Uh-huh, and here is how you access the menu. The website's focus is marketing, not so much . . ."

On and on, Angi raced. Snippets sunk in—photography, videography, newspapers, publications, content, search engines. Finally, he found the break he had been waiting for and tried to launch his sentence as though it were a pace car. He spoke softly and slowly, "Very nice. Very nice. Who created the content for this website?"

Angi downshifted, zoomed past the pace car, shifted back into high gear and was off again. "Alamea wrote text for some pages and I took some from her business plan . . ." Angi continued, stringing together words without stopping, sentences and paragraphs without feedback. Steve watched her mouth move.

Whitehorse's Marian just might be the real deal.

Steve stole a glance at Meriwa who returned a stern look. Angi droned on at high speed about content, blog pages for clients, photos, messages to family and friends, all the time talking a mile a minute.

She never stops to breathe. I wonder if all sprinters talk this fast. Not having to breathe as much must have ancillary benefits. I should recruit sprinters for our debate team.

Steve listened as Angi explained her ideas for the client blog. "The public pages will be edited to highlight each client's finest moments in the Yukon, you know, to portray his or her Perfect Finish. The public will see those, of course, so we need to make sure the clients look super spiffy."

Of all the do-gooder ideas in the world, why the dying business? We could offer assistance-in-dying to a retired woman who would otherwise suffer a horrible death, or we could just donate a kidney to a stranger.

Steve hadn't realized she had paused. He looked at each of the women who were staring expectantly at him. "Are these your ideas or Alamea's?"

"Um, obviously, the general concept is Alamea's but capturing the individual stories and arranging the blog is mine."

His question was enough to confirm he was still listening. Angi cleared the hurdle and sprinted on. "Then, for traffic, we're going to get that mostly in the beginning by sending blog links to our clients' family members, friends, and associates, and we'll also include links in any published obituaries. Also, the sales team can send it to prospective clients . . ."

Angi's eyes sparkled as she described each concept. Her words flowed effortlessly and blended together. He nodded and glanced at Meriwa, who winked over the edge of her coffee cup.

What are they putting in the water at the Whitehorse library?

Angi looked at Steve and paused. "You are surprised? You didn't know about this website?" She looked toward Meriwa in alarm.

Meriwa sat her cup on the table, scrunched her eyebrows and looked serious again. "Angi, Steve has read the business plan," she said soothingly. "He knows all about the project. And look at him, he definitely cares about your website."

Looking like I care? Damn, how could I be so transparent? I'm going to have to be more careful around this Meriwa devil.

"What deal did you make with Alamea–before she went to Alaska?" Steve asked.

"Alamea showed me her business plan. I created a couple of screenshots so she could see my work. She told me she would have a look at the sample pages the moment she got settled in Alaska."

Fantastic discovery! There remains not one person in my entire family who still falls for the pregnant pause. Yet here is an entire village full of fresh quarry. It's like traveling to the Klondike and striking gold!

Angi concluded, ". . . I didn't hear from her and then I found out about the accident, but I was just so excited about the website and the whole video aspect of the project I couldn't stop working on it."

Of course, she never stopped working on it.

Meriwa filled the void. "It's really great work, don't you think, Steve? Steve?"

Steve aborted his trip to Mars. "I have to say, this looks very professional. I know an experienced web developer. If you don't mind, I would like to have him look at it, to get his views on the back end, structure, loading speed, and searchability."

"That's perfect," said Angi. "You know I went to college for this stuff, right? Those are the things I'm good at. Most of my website clients don't even appreciate those things. If you don't mind showing this to him, I would really appreciate it. I want to hear every single point of his feedback."

"Sure," said Steve. "He'll discuss it with me, and when he's done, I'll have him call you directly and tell you what he thinks."

Angi beamed like a full Buck Moon. She bounced up and down in her chair with excitement, like Rachel used to do when she was eight. Angi was about to get up then held herself down, about to get up then held herself down, then went straight to the real point. "So, do I get paid?"

Do you take cash? Maybe not the right question. What if it's more than Alamea's two hundred thousand dollars? That would suck too.

Steve managed a reply. "How much?"

"Well, we have only just begun of course and the key to success will be the ongoing work. You know, interviewing the clients, shooting the videos, the photos and editing and all that. When I discussed it with Alamea, she said maybe it could become a full-time job for me, but since there was no website, we never got a chance to discuss that part."

"Angi, circumstances have obviously changed," Meriwa broke in. "Let's not get ahead of ourselves. Steve is asking how much you wish to get paid for the work you have completed so far."

Without hesitation, Angi said, "Twenty-five hundred Canadian dollars."

"Done!" Steve exclaimed as he smacked his palm on the table. "I'm not sure how you'll be paid or to whom you'll send the invoice, but you have my personal guarantee that if you create an invoice for that amount and copy me on it today, you will be paid within one week. Is that satisfactory?"

Angi popped out of her seat. "YES! That rocks! Thank you, Steve. I'm so happy to have met you. If you want, I can send you the link so you can access the website on the subdomain."

"Angi, I'll send him the link," Meriwa said in a calming voice.

Steve looked at Angi as he said, "Meriwa, can you please send Angi my email address as well so she can copy me on the invoice?"

Meriwa pasted on a smile, sat up straight and gathered herself like a cat the second before it leapt in the air for the bird. She paused and took a breath before hissing, "Suuure."

Steve ignored Meriwa's display of insubordination. "Oh, and Angi, it's time to drop the pencils on this project."

Angi looked puzzled. "What do you mean?"

"Stop working on it," Steve replied. Angi looked disappointed. She paused. Steve said, "For now, I mean. You know, until you get paid, and we find the perfect direction."

Angi was happy again. "Sure, sure."

Damn, the librarian just kicked my ass with a pregnant pause.

Steve held up his hand as a signal that he wasn't finished. "I have just one more question for you. Are you a Wolf or a Crow?"

Angi beamed again. "Crow, of course."

Steve nodded. "Yes, of course."

As Angi departed, Meriwa picked up the conversation as though they were not in the middle of a pregnant pause contest. "Steve, I have to ask, to whom exactly do you imagine Angi will address that invoice if she's only to send you a copy?"

Steve paused. He paused some more.

Damn. Don't tell me it's over already.

"Any recommendations?" Steve asked with a grin.

Meriwa rolled her eyes as she stood and said, "I've got to go."

Steve asked for the bill, as Meriwa completed another Oscar-worthy exit.

She's good at this. I would like to drink a pint with her ex-husband. I could tell him about the time I trained Meriwa to poker face her way through a pregnant pause contest. Then I could listen to him tell me how he had taught Meriwa the Hollywood exit trick.

He heard his name and looked up just before blowing straight past the moon and becoming utterly lost in space. It was Tammy, the ballerina waitress. "Steve? Steeeve, did you want the machine now?"

He nodded and while signing, tried to avoid crashing the portable credit card reader into the moon.

How does ballerina-girl know my name?

17. Kicking the Can

Departing at 3 am he rode slowly up Two Mile Hill until he met the Alaska Highway and headed westward.

The ALCAN: Alaskan Canadian Highway, or if you are Canadian, The Alaska Highway. Of course, nobody in Canada would call it by its American name, the ALCAN. If you are already in Canada, it doesn't go to Canada, it goes to Alaska.

Steve stopped at Haines Junction for gas. He knew many of the gas stations would be closed at night but had done the calculations. A full tank in Haines Junction should get him to the international border at Beaver Creek, but since he was not going all the way to the border, he'd have to get fuel in Burwash Landing outbound then Destruction Bay upon his return.

In the dim light, he slowly headed out of Haines Junction, taking a hard right to continue on Highway 1 instead of continuing straight on Highway 3 toward Chilkoot Pass, over which the stampeders had ascended the coastal peaks to reach the Klondike Gold Fields.

In the predawn light of the northern night, he marveled at the silhouette of the towering peaks on the horizon, listened to the mesmerizing beat of the big twin engine, and reminisced about drinking morning coffee with Emily. He remembered the aroma of freshly ground coffee beans, the soft hum of the espresso machine, the gurgling noise as he steamed the milk, and the anticipation of joining her as he prepared the tray. The fragrance of roses filled the crisp morning air as he served her coffee in the garden. She removed her gloves and brushed back her long blonde hair. The memory of her voice echoed in his mind as she turned to reveal her sweet smile. "Angel, you've made coffee."

As dawn broke, Steve rode toward Kluane Lake on freshly laid chip seal gravel. The chips were slick beneath the tread of his highway tires, like riding on marbles. When he came around the lake and crossed the Slims River Bridge, the wind picked up, buffeting his bike toward the angled shoulder. He struggled to keep control, barely crawling across the bridge at twenty miles per hour as the wind transformed the ride on marbles from tedious to perilous.

It took Steve three-and-a-half hours to reach Burwash Landing, where he stopped for gas. He rode on for another hour before reaching the White River Bridge, where he slowed to forty-five miles per hour and began looking for the place where he had first spotted the bear. However, he rode past without recognizing it and suddenly found himself at the site of the accident. A small dash of yellow paint on the asphalt marked the spot where the police had been. He would not have noticed it if he hadn't been paying attention to the roadside kilometer markers. The scene looked so different now, with the fireweed gone and the frost heave repaired.

Along the roadside to and from the spot where the bear had dropped, he searched for debris or any sign of the accident. Except for the paint, he found nothing. As he searched through the cut fireweed, he thought of her chestnut hair spilling out of her helmet among the flowers. He found the place she had been, but there was not the slightest sign that anything bad had ever occurred there. Further down the hill, where the trailer had stopped, he found a bare spot where the trike had gouged the hillside, but still no debris. He examined the scar on the aspen made by the trailer axle. It was not until he was on his way back up the hill that he spotted the lonely left shoe. It was a black leather pump with a pointy toe, nestled in the cut fireweed, its three-inch heel aiming skyward. Steve picked it up and read on the inside: Prada, size seven.

He put the shoe into his trunk and opened the journal to confirm the next marker: *1832***

As he drove slowly on, he searched the surroundings for something familiar. A lake, sure, there were hundreds, but in the wilderness, none were labeled. Some were hidden in fog. Trees, sure, and even some he could recognize by variety.

What kind of moron looks for a tree among thousands of trees across from a lake among hundreds of lakes hidden in fog somewhere in the Yukon wilderness?

What if the marker is gone? What if the tall tree has fallen over? The spruce looked kind of sickly, with its tip stripped of branches four feet from the top.

He was almost shocked to find the bags exactly as he had left them. They had haunted him every day since he made the fateful decision. At the time, it seemed like the lesser of two evils, to leave them there so that he could meet Rachel. In retrospect, it seemed completely absurd to hang a gun and bag of money in a tree by the side of the road.

He stopped outside Haines Junction to switch the bags around and lock his saddlebags. He rode into the small town and bought gas before following his garden path back to Meriwa's apartment in Whitehorse.

This isn't collecting roadside litter. It is more like kicking the can down the road.

He imagined Princess Meriwa would be living in a castle, but instead she resided in a small apartment situated in a collection of grubby three-story buildings on Lambert Street. The residents were packed densely into small efficiency units. The front yards looked like backyards enclosed by four-foot chain-link fencing, with no outside entrances to the individual plots. Fortunately, Meriwa's apartment was located on the corner. Steve could just barely walk the motorcycle along the public walkway and negotiate the turn to get it into her fenced yard before parking it on the corner of her brick patio. Juneau announced his arrival. Meriwa helped him move four medium-sized planters to accommodate the motorcycle as Juneau, excited by the new yard ornament, barked, circled, and ran back and forth.

Steve had stowed the loot in the saddlebags under his rain gear. He removed his backpack and the motorcycle cover, locked his helmet in the top trunk, and locked the fork before checking the compartment locks. Meriwa watched his every move intently. He put the cover on and surveyed it.

"Your motorcycle cover looks brand new," Meriwa remarked.

"Yes, the service department was giving them away for free," he ad-libbed.

Why would she ask about the new cover? Does it look like a motorcycle full of guns and money? Oh yeah, and the shoe. The only thing missing is a brick of cocaine.

Is this going to be yet another decision I will worry over and regret? What options do I have? As long as I'm playing "Steve Pants on Fire," I am going to have to also play "Steve the Money Launderer" and "Steve the Gun Fence." Now I'm adding one more crime, "Steve the Stasher of Contraband," and with none other than Yukon's innocent Indigenous Court Worker.

Go to hell, go straight to hell, do not cross Chilkoot Pass, and do not collect two hundred thousand dollars.

"Steve? Oh, Steeeve? Do you have any plans tonight? Would you like to meet my cousin?"

"Another cousin? Sure, let's meet another cousin."

18. Lucky Punch

The place was difficult to find because it was situated on the edge of town and looked more like a warehouse than a restaurant. Steve was about to give up when he noticed the name barely legible in faded print on the half-open warehouse door: *Wayfarer Oyster House.*

He was ridiculously early, hoping to get a beer ahead before Meriwa arrived. From his seat at the bar, he could observe the kitchen staff and, if he turned around, could see everyone in the restaurant. Meriwa had told him that her cousin tended the bar, so he observed the two bartenders and tried to catch their names as they interacted with the servers.

The cousin is probably the thinner bartender named Jessie, the only one who is First Nations. A dagger tattoo on her right forearm? I wonder what that means. Black hair cut in a no-nonsense bob. Channeling capability, hard work, plus a dollop of charm applied sparingly for tipping patrons.

He had perused the reviews. The place had won awards. There were five cooks in the kitchen serving up dishes as fast as the waitstaff could order and deliver them. Jessie brought him the first beer, a Winterlong Haze Junction Ale. The "haze" word worried him, but he found it drinkable. The bartenders were shucking oysters in orders of six and twelve and mixing fancy drinks. Both were really moving to keep up with the drinks and the oyster orders. Still, whenever they had a few seconds' break, they would drop clever remarks to patrons at the bar.

The blonde bartender asked Steve how he had found the place and how long he was in town. She had him pegged as a tourist.

Maybe there are still a few whom Meriwa forgot to inform.

On the wall behind the bar, nestled between a plaque and a license plate, graced a ten-by-fourteen black and white photo set in the Yukon during the 1890s, or a little later. The photographer had captured the image of three miner's daughters, aged about eight to eleven, standing shoulder-to-shoulder in raggedy dresses with unkempt hair, glaring intensely at the camera. They looked as though they had just slaughtered the chickens and were waiting to skin the milkman.

As the blonde bartender stopped to fill his water glass, Steve pointed to the picture and said he'd like to meet the three girls, especially the mean one at the end. She laughed and said she had always wondered what had become of those three, before dashing off to shuck more oysters.

The mean one is what Meriwa would have looked like if she were born in 1892, except she would be wearing fancier clothes.

The devil herself tapped him on the shoulder. "Aha, caught me daydreaming!" he exclaimed with a smile.

"No doubt. Do you mind if we get a table?" Meriwa led him to one by the half-open warehouse door. She dressed in her own version of casual—dress slacks, sweater, and a fancy silk scarf, gold necklace, and bracelet—making him feel as underdressed as usual.

Jessie followed them with menus in hand. "Hi, Meriwa. Are you together?"

Meriwa hugged Jessie before sitting. "Yes, this is Steve. He's the one I told you about. Steve, this is my cousin, Jessie. Alamea was going to hire Jessie to work in the office."

Steve smiled at Jessie. "If you work as hard in an office as you do at the bar, I can see why Alamea chose you."

Jessie returned the smile. "Yes, I know how to run a bar, but Alamea said she could teach me other things."

"I'm sure she would have," replied Steve, without thinking. It was an awkward reply leading to an unfortunate pause.

Meriwa rescued them. "Jessie, Steve is considering pursuing Alamea's business plan. If he does, maybe you would be interested in working with him. You could help him in the office like you discussed with Alamea. It's just an idea at this point, but I thought you might be interested. Alamea's godfather has guaranteed Steve."

As Meriwa was giving her the recruitment spiel, Jessie smiled, nodded, and stole glances toward the bar. "Thank you," said Jessie. "That would be nice, of course. I need to get back to the bar, but I'm very glad to meet you, Steve. Meriwa can give you my phone number and you can call me anytime, whenever you are ready to discuss the matter. I mean, if you want me."

"Nice to meet you, too," replied Steve. "I'm leaving tomorrow. I look forward to seeing you again when I return. I just have one question for you, are you a Crow or a Wolf?"

"Wolf, of course."

"Yes, of course. Wolf."

As Jessie walked away, Meriwa asked, "When you return? Does that mean you are returning?"

"Did you think I planned to abandon my motorcycle in your yard forever?"

Meriwa looked at Steve sternly. "Jessie is my baby cousin, you know. Don't forget that."

"Sure. You can count on me."

Meriwa gave an exaggerated nod and a smirk. "That's what Clyde says. We'll see."

The fancy drinks came, then oysters, and Meriwa relaxed, all ivory and dimples through the main course, then fancy after-dinner drinks. At the end of the meal, Meriwa not only ordered coffee, but she even drank it. They were actually having a good time together, almost like a new couple getting to know one another. It was a feeling Steve had not felt for over seven years, when he had first courted Emily in San Francisco.

Without mentioning the civil suit, Steve told Meriwa about not speaking with Rachel and Michael lately and how their father had forbidden him from contacting them.

With a look of concern, Meriwa asked, "Can he do that? I mean does he have the authority to do so?"

"According to John, yes. He is their father. He can do as he pleases."

"From what you've told me, I can tell they mean a lot to you. I'm really sorry, Steve."

Her kindness filled his heart with warmth. Before his emotions could get the best of him, he shifted the focus to her. "Tell me about Alamea. How did you come to know her?"

Meriwa regaled him with stories of their time at Mount Holyoke College. "We were two brown peasants from the West amidst a sea of refined white sugar city girls from the East. They mocked us for wearing sandals and moccasins. The second weekend, there was a so-called 'secret' party that was to take place off-campus. Everyone in the hall was invited to meet students from nearby colleges. Alamea and I went shopping in town. We bought four pairs of shoes to share.

"That night at the party, there were about twenty students in the basement playing beer pong. Some boy from Amherst College asked me to get him another beer, like I was a waitress. I ignored him, but he persisted with a squeeze of my ass. Alamea appeared, stepping in front of me without a word. The boy asked, 'Who are you, her mother?' Alamea punched him hard, just once on the side of his face. He hit the floor and didn't get up for several minutes. We heard that he wore a black eye to class for a week.

"Two of the girls from our hall saw the whole thing. We went from being outcasts to popular. Alamea called it a lucky punch. My mother still refers to her as Wonder Woman.

"The summer before graduation, Alamea and her father rode their motorcycles on the Alaska Highway to visit me. My mother introduced them to the elders and Kyle even repaired Uncle Simon's truck. My little sister had a major crush on him. Aside from him being so damn charming and good looking, my mother liked Kyle because he was, as she called him, a doer, not just a dreamer."

Meriwa paused and picked up her coffee cup. "Alamea's more recent visit took us back to our college days." A glint of tears appeared in Meriwa's left eye as she drained the cup and looked directly at him. "She was the only girl I ever loved."

What was that last part?

She turned away and, with a gesture to Jessie, requested the bill. "Clyde said I could have some of Alamea's things. You know, stuff from the scene of the accident. Also, I have her ashes."

Alamea's things? Minus one three-inch size 7 black Prada shoe? No mention of jewelry?

"Steve. Oh, Steve? Are you listening to me?"

"Huh?"

"What time do you want to go to the airport tomorrow? I can have Simon swing by and pick you up."

"Really? That would be swell. How about 6:30?"

"Done. Wait for him in the lobby. Don't be late," Meriwa warned.

Steve walked back to the hotel alone, pondering the conversation. How could he have been so consumed with his own grief not to have recognized her pain? Some obvious clues were ignored: Clyde had mentioned that she had gone to the morgue; and she was listed in the journal. She projected a tough exterior, but maybe they had more in common than he could have imagined. She seemed to genuinely relate to his loss. Perhaps that was why she had been willing to keep meeting him.

In the morning, Steve arrived early in the lobby with his bags and waited five minutes. Simon rushed in. "Let's go." He grabbed Steve's two saddlebag inserts and walked out.

Steve grabbed his other bag and backpack and spoke to Simon's back as he followed him out the door. "Good morning, Simon. Thanks for picking me up. I could have gotten a taxi, but this is nice. Thanks."

As he approached the car, he was surprised to find Meriwa sitting in the front passenger seat. Simon opened the back door and motioned for him to get in. He shoved the two saddlebag inserts onto Steve's lap before closing the car door.

With thin morning traffic on a Saturday, the airport was only ten minutes away. Steve and Meriwa exchanged greetings and she filled the air with morning drizzle: weather, small talk about coffee, and then something about a conversation with her sister.

Oh yeah, when am I going to meet Meriwa's baby Crow sister who had a crush on Kyle?

They arrived. Simon and Meriwa got out of the car and opened the trunk. By the time Steve got his own bags out, Simon was handing Meriwa a rolling bag.

Simon drove away without even a nod to Steve, who was left standing alone on the airport curb beside his bags. Meriwa was already halfway to the entrance, rolling away. He was slow on the uptake and had to two-step it to catch up with her.

"So, you're flying too? Where to?" he asked, out of breath, still chasing her from several steps back.

"Seattle." She kept walking, like they were crossing midtown.

"Really, with me?"

Without looking back, she replied, "Whoa, cowboy. We're both going to Seattle but I'm not going with you, right?"

He was still talking to her back but now he had almost caught up. "Oh yeah, sure. There is no way you could be going with me because I had no idea you were going. When were you planning on telling me we're going to the same place on the same day on the same flight? You don't think that was worth mentioning?"

"Sure, it's worth mentioning. That's why I just mentioned it. I wanted to *wait* to tell you, but then I thought, no, I better tell Steve now, before it becomes awkward."

He was still chasing her. He could see her grin, but he wasn't ready for jokes. "Don't you think that's a little off?"

Meriwa stopped, wheeled, and faced him. Steve had to pull hard on the emergency brake just to avoid ramming into her C-cups. "Okay, Steve, which part is off? Is it the part where Simon and I swing by your hotel and give you a free lift to the airport, which doesn't look so great for me? Or the part where we're not actually going to the same place because I'm staying in a friend's pool house outside Seattle while you're staying in a downtown hotel, and in order for me to convince Simon to pick you up I actually have to sell that to him? Is it the part where I have a number of things to do in Seattle that do not involve you? Or the part where we leave Seattle on different days heading to different destinations? Or is it the part where it's really none of your damn business, but you seem to think so strongly that it is that you're actually angry? Really? You're acting like a teenager."

She turned and wheeled away, and of course Steve followed her, not just for the view, but because they were both simultaneously heading for the same Northern Air ticketing desk to check in for the exact same flight to the same destination.

19. Four Suitcases

Steve flew Whitehorse to Seattle, sitting eight rows behind Meriwa. She departed the plane well ahead of him, and by the time he made his way to immigration and customs, there was no sign of her. He caught a cab and checked into the Edgewater Hotel.

How did she clear passport control so fast? Two passports?

During check-in he inquired, "I just stayed at the Edgewater Hotel in Whitehorse. Are your hotels connected?"

"What do you think? The elevator is there to your right. Take it to the third floor. You're in room 372, with a view of the bay."

Steve rubbed his jaw before grabbing his bags and catching an elevator. He proceeded to his room and opened the blinds: Elliot Bay.

Helluva view. Maybe the desk clerk isn't such a bad guy, after all.

Steve arrived at John's office ten minutes early and was shown to the conference room. John entered and placed two stacks of paper on the table, un-pocketed his pen, and set it beside the stacks.

"Clyde wants to meet with you once we have finished our business, if that's not inconvenient," began John.

"Sure," agreed Steve.

John took a breath and picked up his pen. He gave it a couple of baton spins before proceeding. "As we previously discussed, the father has warned you to have no contact with the children. He says the children may, after some time, reach out to you if they so choose."

"He's a bastard," said Steve as he clenched his fists. "What about the rose garden?"

"Since we last spoke, I discussed that with him," said John. "He told me that it would be between you and whoever purchases the property. Of course, since the roses are located along the perimeter of the property, you can visit them whenever you please just by walking by on the sidewalk. Is that good enough for you?"

"There really isn't anything else you can do?"

John sat across from Steve and every rough edge softened as he spoke. "Steve, believe me, if there was something I could do I would. This guy makes my skin crawl and I think what he's doing is positively evil and vindictive."

"Vindictive of what though?"

"Maybe he's jealous that you had with Emily what he never could. Maybe he's jealous of your relationship with the kids. Maybe he doesn't like that you have an original Kandinsky that should have gone to him in their divorce. Maybe he doesn't like the color of your eyes. Bottom line is, the *why* doesn't really matter."

"I understand. You did what you could. So, how long do I have?"

"The proposed timetable would require you to remove only your personal belongings and hand over the keys to the property by a week from Saturday. If you're ready, I can walk you through the agreements and we can settle the matter now."

He gave the table a *rat-a-tat-tat* gaveling, indicating that it was time to focus and settle the matter, or maybe it was a signal to the secretary, because shortly afterwards she came in and offered them coffee.

They reviewed the paperwork for half an hour. After using one of the firm's click pens to sign half a dozen agreements, Steve pocketed it. For fifty thousand dollars, he should at least get a pen out of the deal.

They discussed Steve's next steps. Once he returned to Denver, Steve planned to look for a place he could rent month-to-month. When he had first moved in with Emily years ago, he had relocated from San Francisco. Aside from his truck, motorcycle, and the camping gear which he stored in the truck, all his personal items had fit in just four suitcases. He still had the suitcases in the garage and hadn't accumulated much in the interim. John asked if Steve was worried about meeting the move-out deadline. Steve assured him that it wouldn't take him more than an hour to pack his bags.

As John was leaving, Steve asked, "Do you think I should tell Clyde about any of this?"

"That's your decision," replied John. "We don't talk shop around the house."

"Okay. I'll mention it to him, but if you don't mind, you can fill him in on the details."

"If he asks me about it, I'll keep that in mind," replied John before saying farewell and exiting.

Clyde entered. Steve took a deep breath and resolved to shift his mood and refocus on something less grim. Clyde's smile was infectious. "Welcome. I'm so glad you've come to brief us. How was Whitehorse, did you enjoy the trip?"

"It was great, except I left my motorcycle there," replied Steve. "I miss it already."

"Oh, sorry to hear that." Clyde feigned serious concern. "How will you get it back?"

"I'll have to fly back in the summer for it. I have my truck for the winter, so I'll survive without it. When I'm not volunteering at the planetarium, I plan to do some hunting and camping in Colorado. Hopefully the children will call me soon and I can go camping with them."

"Camping with children? That sounds grand," Clyde said, bleeding sarcasm.

"Except that I've been forbidden to contact them," said Steve. "I guess you didn't know about any of that?"

"Well, no, I wasn't aware. You just took Rachel to Alaska. Is everything alright?"

"Not really, I mean, not at all. The children's father has requested that I wait for them to contact me, so that's what I'll be doing."

"I see. Is there anything I can do to help?"

"Not really. My next step is to head back to Denver to, you know, move out of the house. Everything will be fine. I discussed it with John and told him that it's okay to update you about it. He can fill you in."

Clyde replied, "Okay then, I'll discuss it with him. Let me know if I can help with anything."

Steve could see why Alamea's parents would have chosen Clyde as a godfather. Also, he was lucky to have hired John. Had he tried to manage the situation himself, he likely would have lost his cool about the children and landed himself in even more trouble.

Clyde poured Steve some water before adjusting the blinds and returning to the table with a jovial smile. It was difficult not to be jolly around Clyde.

"So, how about a baseball game?" asked Clyde. "Have you heard that the Rockies are in town? The game is tomorrow. T-Mobile Park. John has box seats. You're invited. Are you in?"

"Baseball? Box seats? The Rockies? Of course, I'm in!" exclaimed Steve.

Clyde seemed pleased to finally get a smile out of him.

Steve asked, "Is Meriwa going to be at the game?"

"The whole APF team will be there, sort of a pre-company outing," Clyde replied with a wink.

"We have a team? We have a company? Clyde, don't tell me this deal is already a go."

"Well, not exactly, but the pieces do seem to be falling into place, don't you think?"

"I think it still depends on marketing," said Steve. "Liz has leads, but she hasn't landed even one yet."

"Don't worry, tomorrow is just informal introductions. We can discuss it further the following day. We plan to meet for breakfast at my place. Also, Angi will be phoning in with some ideas about FunBite. You've heard of that, right?"

"It is mentioned in the business plan, but I have no idea what it could be."

"Angi will explain it tomorrow. John wants to hold the meeting before he goes to the office. The early hour will be a problem for Eddie, of course."

"Problem for Eddie?" asked Steve.

"Eddie is a surfer I've known for many years who has only recently taken up temporary residence in our pool house," Clyde explained as he shook his head. "He sometimes refers to himself as my brother, but let's be clear, he is not actually related to me. Eddie is Akiko's son from a teenage fling she had with a US Naval officer. She gifted Eddie to my dad and me when she split. That's how he came to dwell in our basement on the North Shore throughout what would have been his high school years had he not quit school. Eddie introduced me to Kahului, and they taught me to surf. That was before Eddie went to India and became a guru. Now he grows mushrooms and has four Little Eddies back in Hawaii, two of whom I used to pay child support for. I could say more, but my blood pressure is rising, so let's leave it at that for now."

"He's your ex-stepbrother?" Steve confirmed.

"If only it were so simple. If you ask him, he'll say he's the next Dalai Lama. Meanwhile, John calls him our five-foot-ten-inch tapeworm from Calcutta."

20. Heavenly Match

The next day, Steve and Ron walked to T-Mobile Park together, arriving just before the national anthem. The box overlooked the first baseline. Steve knew everyone in the box, except for two people, who could only be Eddie and Akiko.

Eddie was half-Japanese and half-Black. His curly hair was jet black, streaked generously with gray, and worn in long, loose curls. He had a ruggedly handsome face and was in great shape for a fifty-seven-year-old, but if he were actively trying to channel the next Dalai Lama, his North Shore surfer-dude getup wasn't convincing. Aside from his Dodgers hat and sandals, he sported a faded Ramones concert tee and cargo shorts with a frayed hole in the pocket. He dressed to not impress and wore the look with serene confidence.

As the music began, they stood, and Eddie removed his hat. After the anthem, Clyde made introductions as Meriwa and John conferenced by the rail.

Akiko was thin and elegantly turned out in business attire and gold jewelry, not exactly dressed for a baseball game. She was in her seventies, had retained a nice figure, and wore her long black hair with dyed white streaks in a bun at the back of her head. She carried herself with the confidence of a woman who had once been the belle of the ball.

"Nice to meet you, ma'am. You too, Eddie," said Ron.

"Clyde, did you hear that?" exclaimed Akiko. "You need to learn some manners like Baby Kyle."

Clyde edged backwards, plotting his escape.

"Hi, I'm Steve," he said to both of them, but Eddie was already heading toward the refrigerator.

"Nice to meet you too, sweet cheeks," Akiko said as she took Steve's hand and held it hostage.

"Can I get anyone something?" Clyde offered, as he continued taking baby steps backwards.

Steve retrieved his hand from Akiko. "Thanks, we can have a look ourselves," he said as he headed for the fridge. He was halfway there before he noticed Clyde leading Ron in the opposite direction toward the rail to join Meriwa and John. Akiko followed Clyde, leaving Steve alone with Eddie.

"Sorry bro, what was your name?" asked Eddie.

"I'm Steve."

"Steve? Yo, Stevo, my man. I'm Eddie."

"Nice to meet you, Eddie. Can I get you a beer?"

"No alcohol for me today, Stevo, I'm tripping balls. It's a rad wave, know what I mean? Water for me, bro."

Steve reached into the fridge and grabbed a bottle of water and a Stella. Eddie looked over Steve's shoulder. "Yo Stevo, check it out, Hoosier Boy strikes again. Who's the score?"

Stevo turned around and saw Meriwa, all dimples and pearly whites, posing as though she were being introduced to Brad Pitt. Akiko had a front-row view, positioned between Clyde and John.

Wheels within wheels—Eddie and Stevo on the outside looking in.

"That, my friend, is the introduction of Hoosier Boy to Meriwa, Queen of the Yukon."

21. MAID Tsunami

John greeted Akiko, Ron, and Steve at the grand oak front door as they arrived for breakfast. "Welcome to our humble abode."

Akiko led the way into the oversized modern kitchen where Meriwa and Clyde were laughing. Meriwa was setting the breakfast table and Clyde was standing at his fancy stainless steel stove, fussing over his quiche. John made his way to the head of the table, and they all sat except for Akiko, who arranged the napkins.

Meriwa flaunted her dimples and pearly teeth and fidgeted with her hair. She grabbed a piece and wrapped it around her finger repeatedly, as if it were a small man. She sat beside Steve and looked across at Ron, who smiled adoringly back at her. While the rest approached the breakfast as a business meeting, the preening couple acted as if it were a second date.

Akiko served coffee and quiche, and John took charge of the meeting. "We can begin by allowing Steve a few moments to reflect on his discoveries so far in terms of the prospect of pursuing Alamea's business plan for A Perfect Finish."

Steve described the meetings he'd had in Whitehorse and the candidates he had met. "The website went live yesterday," he said. "If any of you have not seen it, please take a look, as it describes the APF business proposition rather succinctly."

"Steve, what can you tell us about your efforts so far in terms of marketing?" asked John.

"Liz and her contacts have identified half a dozen prospective clients. If we were to proceed, I suggest we do so on a test basis," continued Steve, earning a scowl from Meriwa. "We could sign up four to six clients for the first season and then reevaluate the business' prospects based on what we learn. This would require a shoestring budget, without committing ourselves to any course of action beyond the first season. If all goes well, we could deploy additional resources in the next season and plan for a full schedule in the second year."

"Is there anyone who thinks we should not proceed?" asked John.

Steve looked around the table before raising his hand.

The fucking deathcamp business? Nobody else thinks this is ludicrous?

"Well Steve, I know you have expressed some doubts about the nature of the business. Would you care to share those now?" prompted John.

"This business is doomed to fail," said Steve. "The heart of the matter is that it involves assisting clients in dying. While the practice is gaining acceptance in Canada, it remains a lightning rod issue in the United States. Bringing retired folks to Canada to die involves logistical and legal challenges and potential points of failure, including compliance with end-of-life care laws, caring for clients throughout the process, coping with heirs, and managing local sentiment toward our company."

John nodded. "Those are all important considerations. Meriwa, you have spoken to Clyde about some of these issues. Would you like to comment?"

"Thank you, Steve, for sharing your thoughts," began Meriwa, as she darted a wicked glare toward Steve. "While we may not agree on everything, I share your reservations about this business plan. I want to remind you all that this was not my vision. The true passion for this business died with Alamea on the Alaska Highway. A Perfect Finish, as a business, is fundamentally flawed and doomed to fail. In fact, I told Alamea precisely that. Her reply was that the purpose of this business wasn't to succeed as an enterprise, but rather to provoke a tsunami, which will in turn provoke the United States to enact legislation similar to Canada's MAID law to provide seniors with end-of-life care options. As long as we stay true to that vision, we can honor Alamea's wishes."

John continued, "Thank you both. So, let's try that again. If, as a group, we decide to proceed with A Perfect Finish, who here is committed to executing Steve's proposal that it be launched on a test basis?"

Everyone raised their hands except for Meriwa. John frowned. "I see, first Steve, now Meriwa. Meriwa, would you care to explain?"

Meriwa took a deep breath and placed her fork on her plate. "Implementing the business plan will require leasing physical space, initiating contracts with vendors, and hiring employees, all of which has the potential to leave behind a trail of pain and broken promises should APF subsequently decide to abandon the business."

She sat up straight, faced Steve, and caught his eye. "Steve, you propose that APF retain an option to proceed or withdraw after a year. There are two sides to every option. When APF is long the option, everyone in Whitehorse who supports the endeavor will be short the option." Steve blinked as she lectured him.

Meriwa turned her attention back to the group, focusing primarily on John and Clyde. "The lack of commitment associated with launching this business on a test basis has a familiar, bitter taste in Whitehorse. We have a history of outsiders coming through our city on the way to the Klondike Gold Fields, laying waste to it as they pass through. We call them stampeders. So, let me be clear: my first obligation is to my people, in my city."

Meriwa surveyed her audience. Clyde nodded encouragingly, John held his cards close, Ron smiled politely, Akiko refilled coffee cups, and Steve stared sullenly down at his blank notepad. She directed her conclusion primarily at Clyde and John. "I've already discussed this matter with my family. My mother has two conditions: first, you must commit no less than one million dollars; second, you must compensate employees and suppliers in a manner that leaves them richer, not poorer, for the experience."

Meriwa turned to Steve. "So, you see, Steve, the idea that this business will be launched on a shoestring has already been rejected by the city of Whitehorse."

Clyde spoke in a calm and soothing voice. "Meriwa, I promise we can satisfy your mother's requirements. If we decide to proceed, pony up the million bucks, and put you in the driver's seat in terms of structure and contracts, are you willing to support the endeavor?"

Meriwa's tone softened, and her dimples reappeared as she looked at Clyde. "Yes, of course, because I love Alamea and it was her vision. On my terms, I will support it."

Clyde caught Steve's eye and asked him if he was interested in leading the endeavor. Until his experience with Emily, he hadn't given assistance-in-dying much thought. As compared to global warming, for example, the issue just didn't seem to have the potential to impact the future of the planet, and it certainly didn't register on a cosmic scale. His experience with Emily's death was formative, but still too painfully fresh to think about. It was difficult to assess how his position on the issue had evolved.

"I remain skeptical about the marketing aspect, and my heart isn't bleeding for the social issue of assistance-in-dying, but if I thought the enterprise had a reasonable chance of achieving its objectives, I might consider it," Steve replied.

John stood, put his hands on his hips, and glared. "Well, there you are, Clyde. You seem to have gotten your wish. The entire lot of you seem committed to launching your Frankenstein of a company on the basis that it is doomed to fail and will evoke a damaging storm. After setting the bar so low, what could possibly go wrong?"

Clyde made no effort to contain his amusement. "Thank you, John, for that vote of confidence."

John slipped on his suit jacket. "Easy for you to say, Chuckles. You're not going to be the lucky fellow who has to clean up the mess caused by provoking a tsunami. I've got to go. Do you mind finishing?" he asked, before heading to the door.

"The cat went away with a sad kind of look," Clyde said with a grin. "Now that he's gone, it's time to play." He clapped his hands and rubbed them together. "Let's take a break. Meriwa, when are we expecting a call from Angi?"

"Thirty minutes," she replied.

They rose from the table and began milling about the kitchen. Meriwa approached Steve and gave his shoulder a nudge. "By the way, I thought you would be amused to hear that last week Angi asked why you call her Marian the Librarian."

"Did you mention the glasses, the hair, the ruffles, and the plaid?" Steve asked as he smiled and poured himself more coffee.

"No, I told her she should ask you directly. Has she?"

"Not yet, but it'll be fun when she does," replied Steve as Clyde approached.

Clyde asked, "Am I interrupting?"

"Not at all," replied Meriwa. "We were just discussing the librarian qualities of our marketing wizard."

"I'm looking forward to meeting Angi in person," replied Clyde. "I couldn't help but notice some tension during our meeting. Are you two even capable of working effectively together? How would you feel about discussing it in private while we wait for Angi's call?"

"Sure," responded Meriwa.

"Working together? For me, this is not work," replied Steve. "I've agreed to come to Seattle to close a chapter."

Clyde said, "And I thank you for making the trip. Still, I wonder if you two wouldn't mind discussing Alamea's business plan while we wait for Angi?"

Clyde and Meriwa exchanged glances. Meriwa nodded and said, "For you Clyde, anything. Is John's office free?"

Clyde replied, "Of course. Steve, do you mind?"

Meriwa's response seemed prepared, but Steve went along with it. "Sure, why not?"

"This way," replied Clyde as he led them down the hall to John's office.

22. Co-authors

They settled into their seats at opposing ends of John's brown leather sofa situated in front of shelves of leather-bound law journals. Across the room, a majestic oak desk stood as a sentinel against a backdrop of floor-to-ceiling windows, framing a view of fancy dwarf willows and maples adorned in hues of yellow, red, and orange.

Meriwa began, "I realize this is not really your project, and I wouldn't blame you if you walked away."

"Clyde asked me to look into Alamea's business plan and I've done that," said Steve. "I have no further obligation."

"I understand. What are your plans now?" asked Meriwa.

"Do you really care to know?" asked Steve.

"Actually, I do," replied Meriwa. "After all, I am holding your motorcycle hostage, so it's only a matter of time before you turn up on my doorstep. I think there may be a story there, don't you?"

"A story?" asked Steve. "What kind of story?"

"Everyone thinks this is a story about the business of assistance-in-dying, but you and I know better. This story is about two sad people who have just lost the most important person in their lives. It's about two people who could use a friend. It's a story about resilience and renewal. It's a story about you and me."

"That does sound like us. A story like that would definitely be more fun than all this buzzkill dying rot."

"See, we do think alike. I was impressed by your river speech with Simon and I enjoyed the time we shared the other night at the Wayfarer. We talked like I haven't with anyone since Alamea." With a playful glint in her eyes, Meriwa tilted her head. A mischievous grin crept across her face. "Maybe, in the end, we'll discover that the key to our redemption is hidden somewhere between your fascination with the Yukon River and your fascination with me. So, my offer is that you and I become co-authors of a better story."

"Co-authors? Fascinating. That would involve collaboration, a skill you may not possess and with, no less, someone who refuses to follow rules."

"What rules exactly?" she asked with a shake of her head.

"As co-authors, we could follow our own rules," said Steve. "Just don't break my balls and then expect me to engage in sappy descriptions about how I feel. I'll leave that for you to infer. Is that asking too much?"

"Allow me to summarize," said Meriwa as she rubbed her chin. "I offer that we become co-authors of a better story. You question my ability to collaborate, suggest that we break all the rules, accuse me of being an insensitive ball-breaker, and then make excuses for your own inability to communicate your feelings. Should I take that as a yes?"

"Interesting," replied Steve. "Clyde puts us in a room to discuss Alamea's business plan, and this is what you come up with?"

"Clyde suggested that we explore whether we could find a basis for working together, and this is the best I have to offer you. If you're stuck on the assistance-in-dying story, then we are definitely not going to be co-authors. That story is already destined to write itself."

"I had fun the other night, too. Unless I get hit by a meteor, I'm definitely returning to Whitehorse next summer to get my motorcycle, but I prefer to come as a tourist, do some hiking, spend some time on the river. If their father allows it, I might even bring the kids."

"What will you do until then?" asked Meriwa as she rose, took two glasses from John's cabinet, poured water, handed a glass to Steve and retook her seat.

"I'm not teaching high school this year, but I have some gigs set up at the planetarium in Denver. Also, there's an astronomy professor I know from university who is teaching an after-school course for middle-school kids in San Francisco. He has invited me out for a couple of weeks to do a show about Uranus and its twenty-seven moons, including the history of Miranda." Steve took a drink of water and placed the glass on the table. "Did you hear about the house?"

"What house?" inquired Meriwa.

"The house is being sold for the benefit of the kids' trust. It was a big responsibility, with the rose garden and all, but not anymore."

"I see," Meriwa encouraged, with a nod.

"Anyway, I'll make the most of being homeless for a while, travel around, and visit some national parks."

"You don't need to work?" inquired Meriwa.

"I have savings from selling my internet business," replied Steve. "When the time comes, I'll go back to teaching."

"That sounds like a pretty good plan." An awkward silence ensued, as they nodded and looked around the room. Meriwa placed her glass on the table. "Look Steve, I know we haven't hit it off perfectly so far, and there are several reasons for that. Part of it is that if Clyde really decides to fund Alamea's business then I've already chosen three people to help me implement the plan. Now, out of nowhere, Angi, my mother, John, and Clyde all want to include you."

"That's news to me. Why would they choose me?" asked Steve.

"First of all, we can't ignore your potential benefit to the company in terms of marketing. Angi says that if you and Liz bring clients who can pay a million dollars, the business is automatically a go. My mother, on the other hand, doesn't think the death business will be good for my career. She thinks you would make the perfect buffer. John likes that you're Canadian, which means you don't need a work permit. That makes you plug-and-play for signing contracts and managing the Canadian and US press. Clyde thinks you're the sort of character who is comfortable coloring outside the lines. He believes, when the time comes, you can manage the tsunami–a designated fall guy. Is it true that you coach the debate team? Can you really manage a press interview?"

"I used to be the debate team coach, and I'm generally not easily intimidated. I suppose I could manage the press, but that doesn't mean I'm crazy about the idea. What about you? How do you feel about involving me?"

"We don't need you to launch or manage the business," replied Meriwa, flashing a menacing glare. "You are more likely to get in my way than to be useful."

"Wow, tell me how you really feel," replied Steve with a laugh.

Meriwa narrowed her eyes. "If we proceed and were to include you, are you going to get in my way?"

"It's unclear what role I would play. How would you define it?"

"If you and Liz can find clients, that would be useful. It would also be helpful to have someone besides me sign the contracts. Once the tsunami hits, I would rather not be the one doing press interviews. Otherwise, I would expect you to stay entirely out of my way. Do you think you could manage that?"

"Sign contracts, which you will draft, and wait for the press to call. Otherwise, I'll be just another tourist in Whitehorse?"

"That sounds about right," said Meriwa.

"Well, the business is seasonal, sort of like a summer job. It might even complement my teaching schedule someday. I could come for a few months per year, kayak on the Yukon River, and hike the trails until somebody needs me?"

"Maybe I could join you from time to time," replied Meriwa with a smile.

23. FunBite Nibble

From Whitehorse, Angi's lyrical staccato voice filled the kitchen's lofty ceilings. "Let me begin by introducing our new business incubator, *First Nations Business Accelerator of the Yukon Territory*, which we call FunBite. This company has already been established, and we're in the process of reviewing applications for the program."

Steve scanned the faces of the others, noting their apparent familiarity with FunBite.

They're treating me like a mushroom, keeping me in the dark and feeding me a steady diet of horseshit. What am I doing here?

"FunBite proposes to become a partner with A Perfect Finish," continued Angi. "My proposal is for FunBite to help facilitate the launch of APF to ensure the availability of services that it needs to execute its business plan. In return, FunBite will be permitted to pursue any fundraising opportunities that may arise with respect to APF clients."

"Angi, maybe we should open the floor to discussion," replied Clyde.

"Hello, Angi. It's Steve. How is APF even remotely related to any type of fundraising? Also, what is your projected donation potential?"

Angi described the APF proposition, which involved capturing clients' final moments and recording their final messages to loved ones. "As you can see, we are in a unique position to manage our clients' final messaging to their family and friends. Given the level of fees, we anticipate that APF clients will be affluent. We expect that those closest to them, particularly any grateful beneficiaries, may also be affluent. In their final messages, clients may encourage their loved ones to make donations to a designated charity instead of sending flowers or other traditional tributes," Angi explained.

"What makes you think clients would designate FunBite?" asked Steve, as he glared at the phone like it was Angi herself sitting in the middle of the table.

"Obviously they'll designate whichever charity they prefer," Angi responded, pausing for a moment. "Steve, I'm not asking to present FunBite as the exclusive designee for APF. I'm requesting to present FunBite as an option and let clients decide. In return, FunBite will support the launch of APF."

"What makes you think APF requires the assistance of FunBite to launch its business plan?" asked Steve.

Meriwa raised her hand. "Angi, I can answer that, if you wish."

Somehow, during the break, they had shuffled seats. Ron had taken Steve's seat beside Meriwa and Steve was now sitting directly across from her. She took a sip of water and looked around the table before tilting her head. "Steve, let me state this in the simplest of terms: without FunBite's explicit support, the APF MAID business in Whitehorse would be dead on arrival."

Steve stole a glance toward Clyde, who paused and surveyed the room, allowing Meriwa's cannon shot to clear the bow. Only Steve was shell shocked. Clyde took it in stride, and the other two seemed totally preoccupied–Ron with his dream girl, and Akiko with clearing dishes. Clyde rubbed his chin and said, "Go on then, Angi. Steve asked about your projections for potential donations."

"Sure, okay, about our projections. Think of it this way. Every client's blog post will include a short video of the client endorsing a charity of their choice. We are the final service providers to the client, and we have a wonderful cause–to support the advancement of First Nations businesses in the Yukon. Throughout each client's experience with us, we aim to provide exceptional service, and our support and kind hearts will win us appreciation. As a result, some of those clients may select FunBite as their specific designated charity.

"Now, put yourself in the shoes of an heir who has inherited two million dollars. You have just watched up to eight hours of exquisitely edited videos of your loved one's final adventures, including a personalized message to you. In the deceased's final message, they invite family and friends to donate to a designated charity in their honor. How much would you donate, Steve?"

"Probably ten bucks," Steve replied with a scowl.

"So, what we are asking is for FunBite to be allowed the chance to receive those ten dollars."

"Have you discussed any of this with John?" asked Steve.

"Of course," replied Clyde. "But you seem skeptical. Do you have any *specific* objections to FunBite?"

"Objections?" remarked Steve as he placed both palms on the table. "Let's just say I find the idea of panhandling at funerals to be rather unconventional and in poor taste. I'm not on board with introducing unnecessary noise into APF's operations and website, and I doubt the idea has the potential to generate any meaningful amount of donations."

Meriwa addressed Clyde directly, speaking slowly and deliberately. "Clyde, Angi is seeking permission to put a FunBite fundraising form on the APF website today, and in the event APF launches, the explicit permission to recognize FunBite as APF's preferred recipient for charitable contributions. She is requesting official approval."

"Ron, Steve, Akiko, are all of you onboard?" asked Clyde.

Akiko had been cleaning the table. She stopped and hovered over Clyde, pointing her index-finger and glaring first at him, then in turn at the other two men. "Clyde, quit acting like an ass. Meriwa just made a my-way-or-the-highway proposal to you third-grade morons. Here we have Baby Kyle, in love, biting his nails. Here sits our whiner from outer space, presenting an entire bouquet of stupid questions. Finally, there's you, Clyde, playing Chairman of the fucking Board and pretending you have even an ounce of negotiating power."

Clyde blinked and looked at each of the men before replying, "Well Madam Ambassador, I wouldn't have put it quite that way. Ron, Steve?"

Ron shrugged and nodded. Steve scowled and looked down at his empty pad. Meriwa suppressed a smile and raised her eyebrows before gazing sweetly toward Clyde.

"Okay Angi, you have the greenlight to add the FunBite form to the APF website," replied Clyde. "I'll discuss the matter with John and draft an email giving you permission to designate FunBite as APF's preferred recipient of charitable donations."

Meriwa pursed her lips before covering her mouth, but her dimples and twinkling eyes betrayed her grin.

How can Meriwa so naturally control the room? Jupiter's mass is more than two-and-a-half times the combined mass of the other planets, yet Meriwa, who weighs a mere one hundred twenty pounds, conveys the force of Jupiter.

"What else do you have for us?" Clyde asked.

"I want to discuss the tsunami," said Angi. "It's a matter of importance which Alamea and I spent considerable time discussing. As we launch APF, we are setting in motion forces we cannot control."

A butterfly flaps her wings in the Yukon and creates a tsunami. Are they actually going to do this?

Angi continued, "The tsunami may hit at an inconvenient moment and could arise from a direction we cannot anticipate."

"Thank you for that storm warning but is there a point to your anti-forecast?" chided Clyde.

"Of course. Preparation is the key to success. We should over-engineer the website and add resources to handle heavy traffic. We should anticipate the storm and develop a plan to capitalize on it financially, strategically, and politically. We need to develop the means to lobby local governments, prepare press releases in advance, and rehearse our responses. These level-two concepts are not mentioned in the business plan, so I'm bringing them to your attention today."

24. FSD Offer

That evening at the Edgewater Hotel in Seattle, Steve had just finished his room service meal and was laying on the king-sized bed, drinking wine and reading a newspaper, when Clyde called.

"I wanted to speak with you before you flew back to Denver. In terms of funding, I've decided to invest one million dollars of my own funds for an eighty percent stake in A Perfect Finish."

Clyde demonstrated a perfect pause, proving that he actually could, before continuing, "As compensation for becoming the Chief Executive Officer, APF offers you ten percent in sweat equity plus ten thousand US dollars per month. If you accept, the contract will be year-to-year, effective retroactively to the first of August. What do you think?"

"In terms of company shares, eighty plus ten is ninety percent. What about the other ten percent?" asked Steve.

"It's Meriwa's carry for her services and support. She won't be employed; she'll be a passive owner."

"I see, but she will be drafting the contracts, so not exactly passive, right?"

"Well, you'll be signing the contracts, but yes, we have agreed that she'll be drafting them."

"Who else will be involved?" asked Steve.

"Akiko has volunteered to be a seasonal employee in Whitehorse, without compensation."

"Do you think Akiko can add any real value?" asked Steve.

"I've seen her in her prime, kicking some Greenpeace ass. Will she be valuable to you? I guarantee it!" Clyde continued, "And then there's Eddie."

"No way," interrupted Steve. "No Eddie. Why would you even consider it?"

"Well, it's somewhat of a proposition with a reverse competitive advantage," replied Clyde. "I can't imagine Eddie being more helpful in any other role. After all, he has experience providing therapy, massage, and guru services to retired folks. In that sense, this may be the perfect job for him, don't you think? Anyway, it beats the hell out of him tripping in our pool house for the rest of his life."

"Is Eddie negotiable?" asked Steve.

"Akiko asked me to include him," replied Clyde in a soothing voice. "I'll personally pay his wages, so APF doesn't have to fund or actually employ him."

Clyde continued, smoothly assuming Steve's agreement to employ Eddie. "You'll have absolute authority. John, Meriwa, and I will assist you. I'll control the bank accounts, but you'll sign the contracts and be the public face of the company. John forbids me to act as an agent or even step foot in Canada and I have agreed to that stipulation as a condition precedent to his support when we need it. Also, Meriwa's mother forbids her to be directly involved. That's why, if you agree today, APF will be your baby effective immediately."

Apparently, "absolute authority" did not involve managing the money, which somewhat made sense since the money being invested to fund the business belonged to Clyde. On the other hand, if Steve did not have to manage money, then he would not be obligated to account for it either. The job also did not include any actual negotiations or hiring. Skipping these responsibilities would definitely lighten the workload.

The position didn't sound like the typical CEO job. It would be like sitting in a fully self-driving (FSD) car. Meriwa would control the steering and Clyde would control the pedals. Of course, even a car with FSD needed someone to occupy the driver's seat. Otherwise, when it crashed, Elon would have nobody to blame.

Steve asked, "Most of the work I would do could be done from anywhere, and I wouldn't actually ever meet clients–I mean, to assist them or anything, right?"

Clyde confirmed that Steve would be the face of the company and on the ground in Whitehorse when clients were there, but otherwise he would not be directly involved in marketing, finance, or operations–especially the therapy, spa, or medical assistance-in-dying aspects of the business. "After all," concluded Clyde, "the whole point of including FunBite as a partner is to manage the operational and medical aspects."

Steve agreed to give Clyde his answer by Saturday after he returned home and moved out of the house.

25. MAID for the Wilderness

Steve flew into Whitehorse the third Sunday of March, missing the Rendezvous by a month. Conditions were dreary, drizzly, icy, and bleak. The Rendezvous must have really sucked. He caught a cab and checked into the Edgewater Hotel, scoring his favorite room with a view. He dropped his bags and headed directly to the window. With each exhale, his breath formed a ring of fog, as he marveled at the river flowing swiftly to the Bering Sea. It was a frigid day to be a drop in the Yukon River, but the riverwalk was clear of snow and full of pedestrians.

"She was the only girl I ever loved."

What if Alamea had helped Mark with his perfect finish and returned from Alaska? Would she have lived in Whitehorse and become a sourdough instead of a drop in the river? I never would have met Alamea or Meriwa.

Steve had arranged with Meriwa to meet the nurse practitioners, Daisy and Lily, at the Miner's Daughter. The restaurant was crowded with hungry and thirsty tourists, but the three women were easy to find, seated at a table near the open fireplace.

They rose and Steve shook their hands before ordering a drink and perusing the menu. The women carried on with their conversation, something about Daisy's daughter. Lily compulsively tucked her fluorescent red hair behind her ear. Her denim shirt was wrinkled, and her makeup looked like it may have been applied during a stop at a red light. Daisy, on the other hand, exuded confidence. In a pressed button-down denim shirt and khaki skirt, she portrayed a no-nonsense demeanor, reminding Steve of his favorite aunt. Compared to Lily, Daisy was older, a little heavier, and considerably more refined.

Daisy is the nurse you would choose, regardless of whether you wished to live or die.

Meriwa leaned in close to Steve and whispered, "I saw your motorcycle this morning, still leaning upright on its kickstand. Do you plan to take it home with you when you leave?"

"I have been missing it, but no, I'm not dressed for riding a motorcycle in March in the Yukon, but I might come by and just give it a pat."

The server returned with Steve's drink and took the food orders.

"John and I have been working on the residency aspect of the MAID law," began Meriwa. "We have some solutions for qualifying clients for the first requirement, which is that they must be eligible for government-funded health insurance. The key will be getting them visas to work in the Territory. It's not trivial, but since our clients are still ambulatory and have money to invest, we'll manage. We've already applied for visas for this season's clients, and I expect all four to be completed this week. The second hurdle is meeting the requirements for evaluation by two independent health-care professionals."

"This is where you two come in?" asked Steve as he looked at Lily and Daisy.

Daisy smiled and nodded slightly. "Yes and no. We're both here today because, in principle, we could each be one of the two."

Lily nodded. "I plan to get my Nurse Practitioner qualification this year, so I won't be able to sign off on a MAID form until the second season."

"And even after she gets it, we'll never sign off on a MAID form together. It will be one of us," said Daisy, as she wagged her finger between her and Lily, "plus Dr Nahu, who is the physician chair of the MAID team at Whitehorse General Hospital. He has agreed to assist us in applying the law. On Friday he'll travel with me on the initial visits, just to make sure everything is set up properly. For future cases, he'll appoint someone else from his team to travel with us, to provide an independent second professional opinion."

Lily took the baton. "Dr Nahu really gets it. He believes MAID will benefit not just individuals but society in general. It used to be that the MAID law only applied to persons who were terminally ill, but that requirement has been eliminated. Now, anyone who has a legal status in Canada can request medical assistance-in-dying. The key requirement is that the person must have the mental capacity to make the decision."

"There's a ninety-day waiting period to qualify," cut in Meriwa. "I've prepared the MAID forms for the first four clients. Daisy and Dr Nahu will visit each of them next week and complete the applications. We'll ask for someone close to the client to act as a witness, but that person cannot be an heir. I've reviewed the proposed witnesses for each of the four to make sure they qualify. Dr Nahu's direct involvement will ensure that everything is done correctly and professionally."

"Who would be independent?" Steve interrupted.

"Anyone who does not stand to benefit from the death," replied Meriwa. "One of the clients proposed a notary, which is perfect. Really, just any adult with capacity who is not a beneficiary and can be reached for verification, if necessary."

The server returned with their food.

Daisy resumed, "Just before dying, clients are given the opportunity to confirm or withdraw consent. I will be the one who documents that final decision."

"Okay, then what?" Steve asked.

Daisy hesitated and looked toward Meriwa, who offered a nod. She looked at Lily, who immediately looked away. So, Daisy proceeded, "Are you aware of Harold's proposal to use his CASA C-212 Aviocar for the final flights?"

"The final flights?" Steve blinked and looked expectantly at Meriwa, who excused herself and weaved her way around tables in the direction of the restroom.

"Wait," Daisy said to Meriwa's back. Daisy took a deep breath before continuing. "Based on Harold's plan, I'll be there on the final plane ride to document clients' choices and consent. After takeoff, I'll recount the options with the client. These include the default option, which is to take a scenic plane ride out and back, as any tourist would. We call this the blue pill option. The red pill option includes skydiving. For jumpers, parachutes are optional, although we expect most clients will choose one, even if they don't pull the cord. Those who plan to jump can do so after taking a red pill. The red pill is a barbiturate which will put the client to sleep within five-to-ten minutes, and result in death within sixty-to-ninety minutes. The blue pill is a placebo and choosing it is an indication that the client has changed their mind about dying."

Steve looked around the restaurant for Meriwa. Lily sipped her drink as though everything was going great and Daisy hadn't just suggested anything preposterous. Maybe Lily was a cosmic thinker like Steve or maybe she wasn't even listening.

"Those choosing to jump will be offered a parachute," continued Daisy. "If she wants one, we'll suit her up and instruct her how to activate it. She'll take the red pill and, within a couple minutes, be assisted to the jump door. She can jump, if she wishes. See, it's always her choice, it's her adventure, right to the end. I'll be there. I'll document the choice at every step."

"That sounds kind of sketchy," replied Steve. He rubbed his forehead and searched for Meriwa. "Is there any precedent for this adventure form of MAID?"

"It's groundbreaking, MAID for the wilderness," replied Lily. "According to Uncle Harold, that's the whole point. It's what the clients are paying for, right? An adventure death in the wilderness."

Steve pressed on. "Right. So, a client jumps from the plane. What happens next?"

Daisy replied with a pained expression, "She will die from the medication, or if she chooses not to activate the parachute, she'll die upon impact."

Steve choked on a swig of beer, but Lily didn't miss a beat. "My uncle says he has a spot where he'll guarantee they won't land in the trees. He uses it for adventure skydiving drops. It's beyond his cabins, near Tagish Lake. It's remote, and our trips will not take place during the hunting season. Harold says he'll check the clearing first, just to make sure we don't risk more than one casualty per drop. Usually, skydivers drop into the area and then hike to the lake where Harold's men pick them up with a Zodiac launch."

Meriwa returned and Daisy handed some dirty plates to the server. Lily explained about delivering the body bag to the morgue. "Of course, according to MAID law, the death certificate will state that the person died of their stated condition, which, for many of our clients, will be old age. That's how they will be recorded legally by the coroner. However, for announcements in the client's hometown newspaper, her death can be reported in whatever manner the heirs choose."

"All of this for an adventure death? Really? How is hopping off a plane better than popping a handful of pills at home?"

"Don't be cheeky," admonished Meriwa. "This end-of-life option isn't for everyone, but those who have chosen it obviously believe the final experience and the death report, together, are an upgrade to the alternatives. According to Liz, for some prospects, the fact that their deaths won't be reported in their hometown newspapers as suicides, combined with the stories documented in the adventure blogs, represent compelling selling points. Particularly for those who are religious, it can be the difference of how a ceremony is presented. For family members who believe that suicide is a sin, believing that their loved ones are in heaven can mitigate their grief."

"It all just sounds so morbid," Steve said as he wiped his hands on his napkin.

"Honestly, Steve." Meriwa flashed menacing green eyes at him. "Are you just now coming to terms with the fact that our work is going to end with people actually dying?"

"I hate to say it, but yes. It's really starting to sink in, just now, with the mention of the words body bag and morgue."

Meriwa intensified her glare. "Let's not get off track. The bottom line is we are applying MAID for the benefit of clients, and for our own protection. We're relying on Canada's MAID Law to keep us out of prison. So, we have to comply with the letter of the law."

Steve raised his hands in surrender. "Okay, okay, I get it. What about those who choose not to jump?"

Daisy replied, "Those who don't jump will return home and their adventure will end. Speaking of which, I really have to get back. I promised the sitter I would be home by nine."

Once Daisy and Meriwa were out of earshot, Meriwa whipped her head around to Steve. "Body bags and morgue? Really? Are you trying to scare them off? Who do you think we're going to find to complete the MAID documents after you drive these two away?"

"Yeah, you're right. That was thoughtless."

"Harold will be going with us when we see the office space tomorrow," resumed Meriwa.

"I look forward to finally meeting Harold."

"Yeah, there's a reason I delayed the introduction until I was certain this whole thing was a go. Harold is difficult to control. Not even my mother can control him. Harold's mother can, to some extent. She is half-Irish, you know, like my father."

"Harold's mother is half-Irish, a Wolf? That means there were three siblings: Harold's mother, your father, and the Mountie. All half-Irish? Harold and you are both a quarter-Irish?"

"Sure, and our Irish grandfather was also a Mountie. Harold's a few years older than me. Not many kids make it out of Whitehorse for college, but he did, even if it was for just a few semesters before coming back to get his pilot's license and work for his father. After his father died, he inherited the company, including two planes, a boat, and a number of cabins. He also took over his father's contract with the forestry department and RCMP since he has the only CASA transport plane in the Yukon. The rear door makes it ideal for air drops and skydiving."

Steve asked if it was a done deal with Harold.

"No, not at all. Harold's proposal is his alone. Tomorrow you will evaluate it and decide how APF will proceed. It's an arms-length negotiation."

"Does he really need our business?" asked Steve.

"He does. His father never taught him how to find clients. When he heard about the accident, he was pretty disappointed about the deal falling through. Keep that in mind tomorrow when you negotiate with him. The four APF bookings may be the only ones Harold has for this year."

"I see," said Steve as he straightened the items on the table and placed his napkin on an empty chair. "Is this Adventure MAID concept going to be copasetic with the coroner, the police, the mayor, the *Whitehorse Daily Star*, and the general public?"

Meriwa nodded. "Harold has already discussed the proposal with our RCMP uncle. The two of them are managing the coroner."

"Who is your . . . ?"

"The coroner is married to my mother's sister. Don't worry, the death certificates are not going to be a problem."

"That's handy. I wonder why I never thought of asking that question before. How about the mayor and the newspaper?"

"No blood relation but if the coroner completes the cause of death as MAID and natural causes, there's no reason for the death to be reported as an accident or for it to provoke an investigation or autopsy. As long as it's not reported as an accident, Yukon's Department of Tourism doesn't have to include it in their accident statistics, which is the critical point for them. As for the *Whitehorse Daily Star*, random cheechakos dying of natural causes is a tradition in the Klondike and has never been worth inking."

"Are we paying any bribes to officials?" asked Steve with a chuckle.

"Steve, why do you ask such things?" replied Meriwa with a glare.

"I'm starting to see why Clyde chose me for this job," said Steve as he flipped his wedding ring between his middle and ring finger.

She shook her head. "Do you really think it was Clyde who chose you?" Meriwa began collecting her things and stood. "I've got to go."

She placed her hands on her hips, leaned toward him, and with amazing emerald-green eyes, delivered a menacing glare. He grinned in amusement. She tossed her hair, wheeled around, grabbed her jacket and satchel and strode out.

Wow, the girl has style.

"Steve. Oh Steeeeve . . . are you ready for the check now?

Damn, how does everyone know my name?

Why would anyone pay a million bucks for assistance-in-dying?
Let's learn about that from June, an actual customer, as she makes
the decision herself, at a moment we shall refer to as June One.

26. June One

Mother, with the saddest eyes, stood in the bathroom at Lorenzo's Pizza &
Pasta, holding the sink with one hand and lifting her dress with the other,
while I performed damage control. "Poor June," she said. "There's nothing
worse than helping your mother powder her nose during a ladies' luncheon."

Mother was sixty-one when I first noticed her looping a story from the
day before. After diagnosing her with early-stage Alzheimer's, the doctor
advised me to never smoke, eat plenty of blueberries, and take extra vitamin
B12 because having a parent with the disease increases one's risk of
developing it as well. I went home and tossed out a full case of Virginia
Slims. The following week I had the gardener replace half the rose bushes
with blueberry bushes.

At sixty-three years old, Mother had served on the Scottsdale, Arizona
city council for twenty years. Like her own mother, she was well-educated
and highly connected, with natural good looks and impeccable fashion
sense. Even as her mind began to betray her, she still turned heads and
captivated the hearts of younger men. Alzheimer's was a sneaky malady,
beginning slowly before progressing ferociously. It was the period in
between that was the most painful. Her memory slipped away while she still
retained enough awareness to recognize people's responses–pity, surprise,
or even ridicule–and reflect on what she had lost.

Aside from her funeral, the last time I saw Mother bedecked with
jewels, fancy clothes, and accessories was that day at Lorenzo's. The
following week, I helped her resign from our Executive Committee of the
Board of Visitors, Arizona's oldest women's charitable organization.

A year later, Mother's story loop had collapsed to an hour. She moved
in with us. By that time, Little Larry was long gone to live with his father in
Virginia. Initially, my daughter Beth and I took care of her. After Beth left
for college, Mother's condition worsened. She became hostile, chasing away
every nurse and aide we hired. After Beth's freshman year, she returned
home for summer break, and the two of us checked Mother into Scottsdale's
finest memory care facility.

I remember the lady who organized the paperwork asking us about
Mother's abilities. While checking the boxes and without looking up, she
nodded when I told her that I had only recently convinced Mother to wear
diapers. The lady informed me that in terms of making the decision to admit

someone to a facility, a patient's deterioration of toileting abilities was a significant crossroads. Even for the most exhausted caretaker, it felt like such a shallow reason for condemning someone you love.

During the first month, I visited Mother every day. Once, I even ran into one of her friends who had dropped by to check in on her.

I remember the first time, being accosted by the eye-watering reek of soiled sheets mixed with antiseptic on the walk down the hall to her room. To facilitate the cleaning of the rooms and changing of the beds, the patients were fed, zonked, and shuttled out to a large activity room at the end of the hall where an oversized television blared *The Price is Right*. Sadly, Mother fit right in among the patients who were slumped over tables. Within the group it was impossible to distinguish the cognitively impaired from the pharmaceutically constrained. Visiting was a downer. Working there must have been a perpetual downer. Living there would be unthinkable, and that made me sad because the day before we checked her in, Mother sometimes still masqueraded as a thinker.

After a month, I reduced my visits to every Saturday for breakfast. She no longer recognized me, perhaps due to the medication, so I began visiting every month or two.

Two years later, I asked the doctor about Mother's health, and he informed me that it had actually improved. Mother had always been a smoker and social drinker, but both habits were long forgotten. Her liver and lungs had healed and the prognosis was that, with proper care (implying sufficient funds), she could live a good, long time in the memory care facility. And that's what she did. She woke up each morning, was told her name during breakfast, and had forgotten it before the dishes were cleared. She watched reruns of *The Price is Right* for nearly ten years without ever remembering a price or recognizing the face of a caretaker, let alone a visitor. Eventually, she fell in the shower and broke a hip. Like flipping a light switch, she was pronounced dead within a week.

I was fifty-five when my mother died. On my sixty-first birthday, Beth accused me of repeating stories, like Mother. Two weeks later, in a moment of déjà vu as I stared at an MRI, the doctor pointed to white splotches on the round gray shape of my brain and said the word "amygdala." It was a term I had heard during Mother's diagnosis twenty years prior.

I told Beth of the prognosis. "Don't ever allow me to wander aimlessly into oblivion like your grandmother."

She asked me what I intended to do.

I replied, "Something different. I don't know yet."

A few weeks later, I consulted my financial planner, and it was then that I first learned about A Perfect Finish.

27. Fairchase Ambush

The next morning was a pull day in the Gold Rush Inn gym. Since the hotel was a sister property to the Edgewater Hotel, Steve's guest room key opened the gym door. While the gym wasn't a great place to work out, it was free and had a decent set of dumbbells and a pull-down machine, along with mirrors. It also had two treadmills, three generations of stationary bikes, and a 1970's style vibrating belt, which could have been used for shaking fat, if it weren't broken.

The best part of the gym was that it was a desert–Steve had never once observed another person using it. Anyone serious about lifting weights would find it unsuitable, and anyone serious about aerobics during the summer would just venture outdoors with a bike, kayak, or hiking shoes and head straight into the Yukon wilderness.

After the workout, Steve returned and showered before meeting Jessie and Meriwa in the lobby of the Edgewater Hotel. Jessie dressed in black slacks and a long-sleeved silk blouse, along with loafers and small pearl earrings. She carried an oversized brown briefcase, the sort that a mafia accountant would haul around. Her only flaws were a price tag hanging from the back of her blouse and a smudge in her lipstick on one corner of her mouth.

Who has Jessie been kissing, and what could she possibly be hauling around in her brand-new briefcase?

Meriwa introduced Steve to the hotel manager and inquired about the ten percent discount for booking weekly. While Steve struggled to get a better look at Jessie's price tag, she opened the briefcase and handed over a schedule with the dates and names of the guests. Jessie reserved rooms for four clients plus an additional one for Steve. The price of the blouse had been forty-two-ninety-nine, and the quote for two hundred thirty-six room nights was fifty-five thousand two hundred thirty-four dollars. Steve signed the reservation while Jessie took notes.

It was a three-minute walk to Bullet Hole Bagels. The pilot and real estate agent had arrived first. Harold, the not-so-tall fifty-year-old pilot cousin, was wearing aviator glasses on top of his head. His hair was thick with silver streaks in the front and he had a coarser version of Meriwa's gorgeous face. He wore a finely tailored sports-coat and dress pants, giving the impression he was dressed for a business brunch at a midtown café, rather than a casual Bullet Hole Bagels adventure in the Wilderness City.

Meriwa led the way, hugged Harold, and introduced Steve to the two men. Harold and the realtor both handed Steve business cards. "Nice to finally meet you," Harold said in a remarkable baritone voice.

"Thank you," Steve's voice deepened slightly in response as he held a business card in each hand and tried to read them both at once.

"Have you ordered yet?" Meriwa asked as she squeezed Harold's arm.

"Yes, in fact here is ours now." Harold grabbed two brown bags off the Bullet Hole counter and handed one to the realtor. Steve offered some Bullet Holes, but Meriwa and Jessie declined. Then, to Steve's disappointment, Meriwa and the realtor made their excuses and escaped.

Steve and Harold engaged in small talk as Jessie led them down the hall and up the stairs.

"We've been looking at this space for weeks," said Harold. "We're close to signing an agreement."

Jessie unlocked the door and they entered an open area two-thirds as long as a basketball court and a little narrower. It had two windows facing the parking lot and looked as though it had never been finished, with open ceiling joists, a plywood floor, and unfinished drywall for the outside walls. Jessie handed Steve her sketch. "If you approve, we'll provide this to the architect."

A Perfect Finish

Therapy & Spa Center

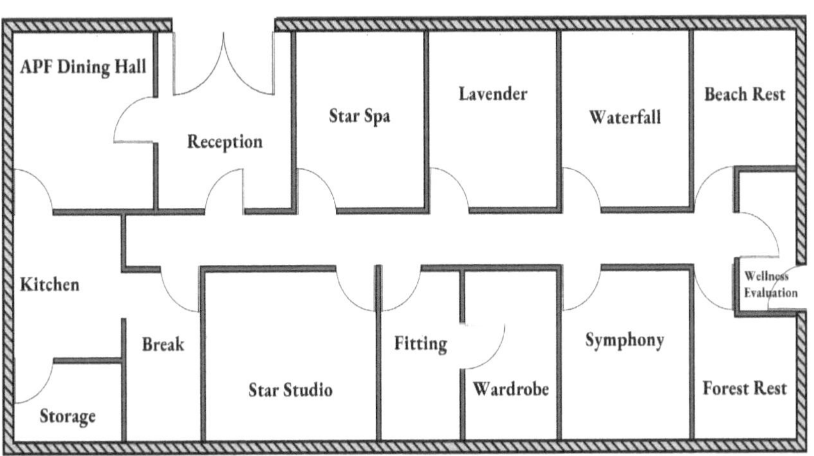

They discussed prices, the architect, and dimensions. Steve annoyed Harold by inquiring about the lease term.

"We've already agreed on a three-year term," Harold snapped. "We can't build these spaces out to use for only one season. Let's look at the spaces first, then we can talk about prices."

Jessie led the way to the executive suite. She opened the door to what had once been an open-concept office space for salespeople or customer service representatives. The space had four large windows, each with a spectacular view of the river. Jessie handed Steve the sketch and left the two men alone.

Fairchase Outfitters

Executive Suite

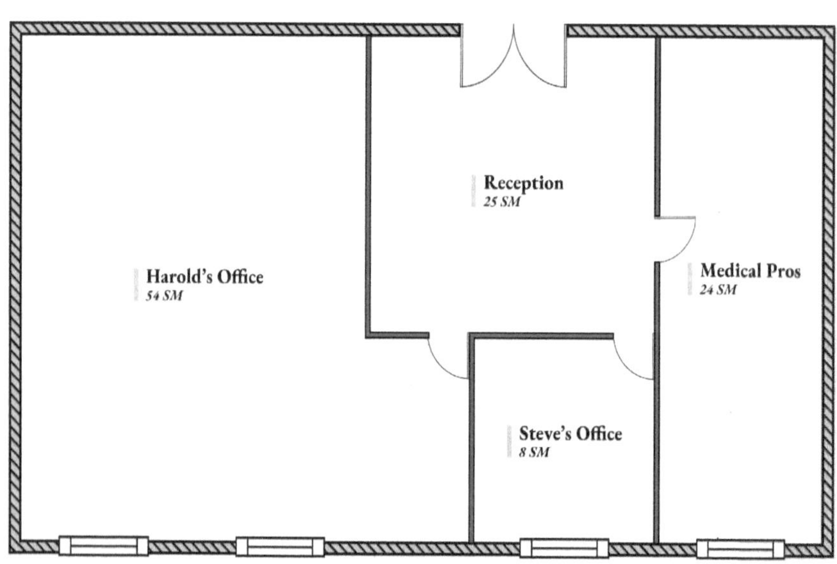

"This will be the Fairchase Outfitters executive suite," Harold explained. He proceeded to illustrate how his own office would be huge, while Steve would occupy the smallest conceivable space. He waited, offering Steve an opportunity to object, before proceeding to explain how APF would be paying the rent for the entire space.

Finally, Steve spoke up. "Okay, maybe it's best if we discuss lease terms later. I'll talk it over with Meriwa and I'm sure we can come to an agreement about the details."

"The matter has already been settled," Harold replied, as his booming voice echoed off the naked walls. "All that is needed now is for you to agree to the layout of the executive suite. I'm meeting with the realtor tomorrow to sign the lease agreements, but not until you pay me for three years at two hundred percent of the total lease rate. I need the money now for the first year."

Harold is fit enough to chase a moose. He would need different shoes. He has nice teeth and just enough silver hair to make him look seasoned. He can probably shoot, and he's a pilot. Still, no clients? No surprise: who would want to sit around a campfire and drink beer with a douchebag like him after a day in the bush?

"Steve, are you listening to me?"

"Oh yeah. Sorry. Why are we subletting?" Steve asked.

Harold's face took on a shade of raw steak. He scrunched up his eyebrows and his upper lip twitched. He spewed micro-bubbles of spittle as he insulted Steve and his half-baked business idea, saying that nobody in Whitehorse would even consider leasing property to him.

Steve stepped backward to avoid the misty ire and turned toward the window which Harold had designated as being located in his future closet of an office. His thoughts wandered to drops racing to the Bering Sea as he half-listened to Harold fill the air with drivel and drizzle. "I need you to build out this office space, furnish it, and I'll rent your portion of the finished space back to you."

Steve turned to face Harold. "You're telling me this area right here will be my office? With this window?"

"Yes."

"Can I tell you to get out of my office right now then? You're ruining the ambience."

Harold paused like he'd been thwacked on the nose with a rolled newspaper, then burst out laughing. "I'm glad we're on the same page!"

Steve was grateful for the cessation of geyser activity, as he ventured a half-chuckle. "What about renting your cabins?"

"My luxury cabins are the nicest on Tagish Lake," Harold began, spraying spittle again.

If I'm going to share an office suite with this lunatic, I'm going to need noise canceling headphones and a dehumidifier.

Steve turned back to the window, vaguely listening to Harold complain about the impact of APF clients on his business and his need to charge exorbitant fees, three times the normal, for the cabins, the flights with his float plane, and the river tours.

Thousands of dollars for flights and cabins? Should I ask about the cost of condiments and paper products?

"As for skydiving trips and the Kluane National Park glacial air tours, we will be using my CASA C-212 Aviocar. Boarding for those flights will be via the VIP terminal at Whitehorse Airport. Each trip with the CASA will cost eighty thousand dollars."

Harold paused, giving Steve a chance to object. Steve turned around to face Harold, leaned back against the windowsill, and crossed his arms. "Go on."

"Now, as for the recovery, there is no equivalent. For that I'm going to need to buy a new Zodiac, and that is not negotiable." Harold slipped his hands into his pants pockets and rocked back and forth on his heels. "The boat we will need for the recoveries is a twenty-one-foot Zodiac Medline with a Yamaha 300 outboard. I need an immediate advance payment of one hundred thousand dollars for that."

"What's a Zodiac?" asked Steve.

"Are you fucking serious?" Harold boomed as his red face spewed spit bubbles. "It's a boat, Steve, an inflatable rigid hull boat with a shallow draft. We use it for hauling hunters around rivers and lakes. We can land it without a dock."

"I see, I see," Steve said. "No need to get all worked up."

Harold pointed at Steve and raised the volume to describe his penultimate swindle. "The requirements for the recovery are unusual, and I'm going to have to pay my men a considerable sum for the task. I want one hundred thousand dollars for each recovery."

Steve gave him his best poker face. "Recovery? What do you envision a recovery will involve?"

Jessie hopped back into the room just in time to explain. "Three of Harold's men will wait until the drop zone is safe, then board the Zodiac at the cabins and proceed across the lake before landing at an inlet on the wilderness side. Once the men find the deceased, they will fill the body bag, boat back across the lake to the cabin, transfer the body bag into the SUV, and drive to Whitehorse General Hospital. Daisy or one of her professionals will be waiting there with the Chief Coroner."

Is my assistant eavesdropping right outside the door, hopping in and out just to avoid Harold?

Steve sidled sideways along the wall to move further out of spitting range and nodded as though the plan made perfect sense.

Harold continued, "One concern I have is that it may be difficult to locate the deceased. We plan to make the drop in a clearing which is accessible, but still quite a distance from the Zodiac landing point. Wind and any skydiving aerial maneuvers can significantly affect where clients land, so we shall have to see."

Jessie left the room again. Harold said, "About Jessie, she's my employee and she'll be on my payroll, but you have to pay for her. I want her salary paid to Fairchase Outfitters, the first year in advance including salary taxes."

Steve felt a wave of frustration and confusion wash over him. This meeting felt more like an ambush than a negotiation. "This is the first time I've heard that. Why should Jessie be employed by you?"

"Steve, nobody wants to be employed by your stupid fucking company. As soon as the shit hits the fan they'll be out of a job and have a stain on their resume for life."

Steve sidled sideways a couple more steps and stood on his back foot. Harold grabbed his Bullet Hole bag and stated that he'd been waiting weeks and wanted an immediate reply. Steve followed along as Harold ranted his way out the door, spewing bubbles all the way down the hall, without a goodbye or look back. "None of my terms are negotiable. You'll either accept them as offered or you can count Fairchase Outfitters out for all services. I have no interest in being involved if I'm not going to be fairly compensated and I can't afford to waste five more fucking minutes pursuing this contract if you're not ready to sign. I need an office now and I'm tired of waiting. You'll accept my offer at once or suffer the consequences."

Consequences? What consequences? What an asshole.

28. Show Me the Money

Jessie said they would see Angi next, and that it should be more fun. Steve said he'd settle for less tortuous. Jessie laughed. "She's waiting for us in the WWM offices."

Steve asked about WWM. Angi explained that it stood for Whitehorse Web Marketing, Angi's new company, which was the first FunBite company. Steve expressed his surprise that not only was FunBite active, but that Angi already had her own offices.

"They are sort of squatting in them," explained Jessie. "They've been waiting for you in order to complete the lease. Follow me."

The door, located next to the executive suite, was ajar. The space featured an open floor plan, just like the executive suite, except there were only two windows instead of four. Five people, including Angi, were seated at makeshift workstations consisting of plastic folding chairs and tables with laptop computers. Some boxes and two broken chairs were abandoned in the corner and cords and cables were strung across the floor.

Angi sprung up and gave him her sweetest librarian smile. "Steve! I'm so happy you've come." She rushed to him, hugged him, and giggled with delight. "Meriwa said you were coming. We've been waiting for you. Have you seen the changes to the website?"

"I have," Steve replied. "They are impressive."

Angi introduced her brother and gave him credit for the Miles Canyon page.

Steve inquired, "What's the story on this office space?"

"Well, it's not formally ours yet," Angi said, as she swept her arm across the room. "As you can see, we don't need to make any improvements. We can stay here one more week for free because Meriwa knows the landlord. After that we have to either sign a lease or get out. That's why we need you to pay us."

They discussed FunBite and its investments. "Meriwa is making FunBite operational faster so we can be employed through our own companies instead of through APF. It also applies to Daisy."

"Harold said nobody wants to be employed by APF. Is that true?" asked Steve.

"Remember Alamea's plan for a MAID tsunami?" asked Angi. "In the end, the company goes viral when everyone hears that its purpose is to help elderly women die. Think about it, how will being employed by APF help our careers? So, Meriwa advised us against it."

"She hasn't advised me against it."

"That's because you're the Managing Director, the one who has been hired to manage the storm."

"Do they sell raincoats in Whitehorse?" joked Steve.

Angi was talking about money, so she wasn't in a joking mood. She positioned herself in front of Steve and administered a reality infusion, informing him that she needed to be paid in advance for payroll and lease payments. Steve suggested that they relocate the conversation to the empty executive suite.

They entered and Steve walked to his window as Angi continued talking to the back of his head. "We need twenty thousand dollars for furnishings and computers, too, because the tables and chairs belong to my mother and the developers are using their own computers. We're borrowing the Wi-Fi from Bullet Hole Bagels. It's not sustainable, see? Our only project is the APF content and website right now, and none of these people have been paid."

Steve turned around and said, "Wow, sounds desperate."

"Oh, it is. It's really desperate, and for Daisy and Jessie too. That's our problem; nobody has been paid yet."

"But Clyde controls the money," replied Steve. "Why not just ask him for it?"

"He says you have to approve it. You need to sign our contracts," Angi exhorted. "That's why we've been waiting for you to arrive."

Jessie stepped forward and handed Steve a thick manilla envelope. "Steve, I've printed the contracts for your review. Daisy will be here in a minute if you have questions for her."

Steve tucked the envelope under his arm, turned, and studied the river while they waited for Daisy. A young boy carrying a black classical guitar case strolled upriver toward the SS Klondike in the opposite direction of the drops.

Maybe he is a busker. I wonder what he sings.

"Steve. Steve? Steeeeve, Daisy's here," announced Jessie.

"Daisy! Nice to see you again. Jessie tells me you've started your own company."

Daisy smiled like a new mother. "Yes, we have. Can you believe it?" She was off and running, explaining about the new FunBite company she had created with Lily, their shared ownership stakes, and how it would provide health services to retired folks living throughout the Yukon.

"How will you find clients?" interrupted Steve.

"You're already our client–I mean–once you start paying us. One of Meriwa's cousins is a doctor who serves First Nations communities located throughout the Yukon, and he is going to refer more clients. Also, Angi is going to find clients through the internet." Angi nodded in agreement.

"It sounds like you are on your way."

Daisy raised her voice and assumed a blocking stance with her hands on her hips. "We are, but we need to get paid. Lily and I have not been paid at all, and I'm just about ready to fly out of town. Are you here to pay us?"

"Yes, it's becoming clear that I've come to pay."

✶ ✶ ✶

Simon chatted and laughed with a friend on the dock beside the riverwalk. From a few yards away, Steve hollered, "Simon! Good to see you."

Simon smiled and raised both hands. "Hello, Steve. I missed you at the Rendezvous."

"I missed you too, Simon. How was it?"

"Totally rowdy. We drank some serious Mike's."

"Sorry I missed that. Next year for sure," Steve assured him, falsely. He had no intention of ever freezing his ass off at a fucking Klondike Sourdough Rendezvous.

"Meet my friend, Isaac. He spent time with me in the big house."

Isaac was a little taller and thinner than Simon. While he was likely no more than a decade older than Steve, the lines and pockmarks on his face made him look much older. He needed a haircut, but he was cleanly shaven and smelled faintly of soap. With the sleeves a little too short, Steve wondered if Isaac's button-down shirt might have been a better fit for

Simon. His shoes were shabby blue Nike sneakers. His jeans were worn but clean.

"Nice to meet you, Isaac. Do you mind if we go for a walk?"

"Nice to meet you, Steve. Where to?" asked Isaac.

"I've been jonesing for a peek at the SS Klondike," suggested Steve.

They began the One Mile River Walk, heading toward the old steamship which had been converted into a museum, with Isaac and Steve side-by-side and Simon a step behind. It was clear and cold, but with the midday sun and no wind, the temperature was comfortable for walking.

"Tell me about your experience, Isaac."

"That would be a lot to tell. I used to do some drugs, right, Simon?"

Simon kept his head down and trailed along.

"I went to prison for dealing cocaine." He paused and studied Steve, allowing time for his disclosure to ferment. Steve nodded slightly as he watched the river.

"My mother came to visit and told me it was time to decide whether I would live or die. She told me I couldn't just hang out on the planet and fuck up everybody's life."

Simon cleared his throat loudly.

"Oh, sorry for swearing," said Isaac. "Anyway, she told me, no more coasting in the middle, make a choice, live or die, decide NOW. I told her I wanted to live. She said, then clean up your life, go straight, make your mother proud. Since that day, that's what I've been doing, right, Simon?"

"Yep, that's true. On that day, Isaac set himself on a new path," confirmed Simon.

Steve nodded. "Isaac, I would like to do some role playing. Imagine you had to take a retired woman from the Edgewater Hotel to Henry's boat launch on Schwatka Lake. How would you do it?"

"My first concern would be about her falling. I would stand by the limo parked outside her hotel. As she approached, I would go to the hotel door and open it for her. 'Hello, ma'am.' I would offer her my arm. 'Allow me, ma'am.' We would walk to the car arm-in-arm. 'This way, ma'am.' I would open the car door for her. 'Careful with your head, ma'am.'"

They stepped off the path for a moment to allow a mother with a jogging stroller and a biker to pass. Steve and Isaac continued, with Simon just behind.

"I would drive to the launch at five miles per hour under the speed limit. 'Would you like some water, ma'am?' When we arrive at the launch, 'Please wait one moment, ma'am. Allow me to check they're prepared for us.' I would make sure Henry is ready, before opening her door. 'They are ready for us, ma'am.' I would help her out of the car. 'Allow me, ma'am.' I would offer her my arm. 'This way, ma'am,' and walk her to the launch."

Steve looked back at Simon who was grinning.

"Henry and I would help her into the plane and make sure she is buckled safely in her seat. I would wish her the best and wave goodbye. How's that?"

"Simon, where did you find this man? I like your answers, Isaac. I love your honesty. It's a pleasure to meet you. Simon, if you have more like this one let me know. It's time to buy Isaac a uniform."

Isaac's smile could melt a mother's heart. "It's nice to meet you, Steve. Thank you for the opportunity."

"You guys want a ticket to tour the SS Klondike or am I on my own here?"

29. FunBite Secret

Although Sheep Camp Lounge had been open for only an hour, it was already half full. Patrons generated a steady hum, competing with Prince's *Little Red Corvette* emanating from the speakers. The sweet smell of rigatoni pasta sauce wafted from plates Kurt had just served to a couple of young tourists. Steve ordered a drink. Just as the refrain began anew, Meriwa arrived wearing a lovely smile. They hugged, took their seats, and placed their drink orders.

In her silky, sweet alto voice Meriwa described her day. "I met with the Territory Commissioner about financing for FunBite before spending most of the day in court, where I totally kicked ass, just in case you're curious. How was your day?"

"I feel pretty good . . . for having just been run over by a FunBite train," Steve said without a smile.

"Just one train? You look like you've been hit by three," she replied with a big smile, dimples, and ivory.

"You've made some amazing progress while I've been away," he continued. "I thought there was a labor shortage in Whitehorse. How did you manage to add so much *unpaid* help so fast?"

"We've been busy. As for recruitment, that's a FunBite secret but I can tell you, since we're friends."

Are we?

Meriwa leaned forward, as if letting a cat out of the bag. "The FunBite secret is in the name—the real name, not just the acronym. Maybe you noticed all the new employees are First Nations. One thing that may not be clear to tourists and stampeders like you is that our ancestors roamed for centuries, not just the Yukon, but also all contiguous areas. We have relatives throughout Traditional Territory, which you now label Alaska, British Columbia, and the Northwest Territories."

Their drinks came and Kurt engaged in chit-chat with Meriwa about someone who was out of town, evidently in Toronto. Kurt made a joke and she offered a polite laugh as he left, allowing her to resume her cudgeling of Steve.

"To you, those lines on a map mean something, but to us, it's all land on which we've hunted and foraged for centuries. The people you met today have been brought to Whitehorse specifically to work for FunBite companies. They are literally sleeping on floors at their relatives' homes in Whitehorse. Angi, Jessie, Lily, Daisy, Simon, all have relatives camping in their homes. That's the FunBite secret. All the restaurants in town struggle to find people to hire. For FunBite, when we need to hire, we can bring people from anywhere and train them as necessary."

"Train them?" asked Steve.

"Sure, FunBite is all about development and that includes training. These people aren't here permanently. They are hungry to learn. We teach them skills that they take home with them. It's vocational training for our people living in the hinterlands and it's seasonal employees on-demand for us here in Whitehorse."

"So, it's all about FunBite?" asked Steve.

"Always, but it also benefits APF. Did you encounter any promising offers today?"

"Fistfuls, and when I added them all up, I discovered that nearly all of APF's net revenue for the first year will be used to fund the startup of FunBite companies. Why is that, and why do all the offers seem to have your fingerprints on them?"

"I've seen all their proposals. The incubator is a shareholder in each FunBite company, so I definitely have a degree of influence on their proposals. Harold's company is not affiliated with FunBite. He set his own course. I told him he would have to clear his overall proposal and details with you."

"Did you advise these people not to work directly for APF?"

"Sure, and I don't see why that should come as a surprise to you, Steve," Meriwa said in her spanking voice. "As Angi proposed months ago, one of the purposes of creating APF is to generate a MAID tsunami. You're the only one who signed up for hazard pay to manage the storm, right?"

Steve swiveled the olive in his glass as Meriwa smiled and tried to catch his eye. He couldn't argue the point but wasn't about to smile along with any type of spanking.

"FunBite is all about launching new businesses," continued Meriwa. "Daisy, Angi, and Simon all have legitimate business plans. Launching them into their own independent businesses allows them to solve the seasonality problem of working for APF, a company that, for this year, will only operate for five weeks. You do see how that makes sense, right?"

"Sure, from their point of view it makes sense," Steve said. "But please explain how it makes sense for APF to fund the startup costs for a bunch of FunBite companies?"

"Steve, what were you expecting to do with these people? Employ them for a few months, then head back to Denver like a cheechako for the winter? In the meantime, they just pine away all winter, waiting for your return? We know what happened when the stampeders arrived. We know how that worked out for our people. So, let me be perfectly clear about this: my loyalty lies first with my people. If you want to win our support, you'll have to demonstrate that you feel the same way."

"So, you're saying you agree with all the proposals, even Harold's?" asked Steve.

"Harold's proposal is insane, his prices are ludicrous, and his terms are heinously offensive," conceded Meriwa in a half-whisper. "I've told him so. Since Alamea's death and your takeover, he has expressed only marginal interest in the venture. I think it might have to do with him wanting a new Zodiac and needing clients to pay for maintaining his fancy planes. Of course, what he's offering to do isn't easy. He'll have to pay people quite a lot to recover dead bodies from the wilderness while being attacked by bears, and then somehow have the mangled corpses classified as typical MAID deaths before they are reduced to ashes."

Steve leaned back and took a long gulp of his drink. Meriwa studied his face and took a sip before resuming in her normal voice. "Anyway, Harold doesn't seem inclined to negotiate, and there is only so much I can do to help you out with that. I hate to say it, but at this point, your only options are to either accept Harold's offer, or skedaddle your ass out of the Territory."

Steve placed his glass on the table and rocked his chair back on two legs. "Have you discussed these things with Clyde?"

"Daily, but you should speak with him yourself." Meriwa checked her watch.

"Why didn't you ever discuss them with me?"

"I invited you to Whitehorse weeks ago. You arrived yesterday and discovered everything today. What, exactly, is your complaint?"

"I couldn't come earlier," replied Steve.

"Touché. I need to go. Call me tomorrow." Meriwa collected her things and left the restaurant without glancing back.

30. Hit the Beaches, Burn the Ships

From his hotel room, Steve called Clyde, who asked if he'd been having fun. "Yes, actually, I kind of missed the place," replied Steve.

"How is Meriwa doing?" asked Clyde.

"Totally hot. Totally busy. The usual."

"Busy doing what?"

"I don't know exactly," replied Steve. "It seems like work, volunteering at Yukon University, FunBite stuff. Her mother is on the City Council or the Mayor's Advisory Board or some such thing."

"Has she decided to run for mayor yet?" asked Clyde.

"I've never heard anything about that. How come you know more about what is going on in Whitehorse than I do?" asked Steve.

"Simple. I read the *Whitehorse Daily Star.* Meriwa is in the news every week. This week there was a picture of her on the front page standing in front of the World's Largest Copper Nugget with the president of the United Mine Workers of America. When I showed John the picture, he reminded me of something she once told us about her grandmother's plan. She said it was her grandmother's generation that had opened the door, and it was Meriwa's and her sister's obligation to walk through it. You know, her mother is on the City Council, so the next steps are Whitehorse Mayor and House of Representatives for the Territory. After that, the children of Meriwa and her sister will be elected to Ottawa. Meriwa told us this years ago while she was still in college."

"At this point, nothing about Meriwa would surprise me," said Steve. "Which brings me to my real question. Did you know FunBite has created all these companies and I'm going to be the only employee of APF?"

"Yeah, that's something the shysters came up with."

"Meriwa and John?" asked Steve.

"Yeah. I think it actually makes sense, don't you?"

"In a way, yes, but it appears to be having a significant impact on your cash flow. Did you see the proposals from the FunBite companies?" Steve asked, speaking slightly louder.

"Yep, Jessie sent me three of them. I've been waiting to discuss them with you."

"That's good, because I got an earful today from contractors who have been working without pay."

Clyde said, "The first is from Angi. She's requesting immediate payment of one year of salaries plus payroll taxes for five persons billed at cost-times-two, plus two hundred percent rent, twenty thousand dollars setup for computers and furnishings, plus fifty thousand dollars in working capital and contingencies, for a total of just over one million, Canadian. Do you agree with that?"

Steve raised his voice even higher. "Look, Clyde, I realize that you are the founder of the company and that Meriwa has been given free rein to draft contracts. And, of course, it's your dough, so it may not be my place to complain, but I thought we were running this first year on a shoestring. Somehow, we've moved way past laces. Today I learned that Simon is hiring a new driver, and Angi has hired a room full of web developers. Angi's proposed annual budget seems excessive. It smells like something a shyster came up with. Since when did we decide APF needed a full-time web development company? That's not shoestring."

Clyde spoke slowly in a calming voice. "It's not like I'm just giving my money away. Setting up a business requires an investment. Meriwa says Angi is a prize and if we want her services, we're going to have to set her up."

"No doubt Angi is a get, but saying that APF should fund the startup is a very convenient FunBite point of view. Simply hiring Angi directly would have been the affordable alternative. APF can't afford to employ the whole damn First Nations community of Whitehorse. I voiced my concerns to Meriwa today, just before she hopped on her FunBite pony and went on an APF rant about Klondike stampeders."

Clyde continued soothingly, "According to Meriwa, Alamea had already agreed to FunBite. It was always part of the plan."

"Come on, Clyde! Do you really believe that?"

"I don't believe it or disbelieve it." Clyde's words were smooth and reassuring. "Regardless of whether the discussion actually occurred or not is irrelevant, but the stampeder argument is valid. We can't just employ these people for a five-week test period, leave for the winter, then hope to return in the summer and find them available at our beck-and-call. That was Meriwa's point when we met in Seattle. I agreed to it, and since then, nothing has changed."

Steve sighed heavily. "What about the other invoices?"

"Same sort of deal from Daisy, for a total of five hundred and thirty-two thousand dollars. For Simon, the total is three hundred eighty-eight thousand dollars. Oh, and Meriwa says Simon wants to use my Benz as well."

"Use it?" asked Steve. "Are you giving your car to Simon's company?"

"I'm doing it to support my goddaughter's dream. It's a hazard of being APF's Chairman of the Board and my penance for not stepping foot in Canada. Also, I've already bought another car. Since we're on the topic, how would you feel about driving it to Whitehorse for me?"

"You're asking me to fly one-way to Seattle and drive your Mercedes-Benz back to Whitehorse?"

"Do you mind?" asked Clyde. "Eddie can help with the driving."

"Wait, Eddie? Are you kidding? Me in a car with Eddie, like a road trip?"

"Sure, why not?" Clyde pressed on. "And now for the invoice we've all been waiting for, Whitehorse Flights."

"Whitehorse Flights? What's that?" asked Steve.

"Whitehorse Flights is a special purpose vehicle for Harold's work with APF. It's a burner company. Meriwa is worried Harold might get a one-star review for dropping grannies out of his airplane, or maybe a ticket for littering the wilderness landscape with hospital scrubs, or bad press for feeding the bears."

"Are you serious? Meriwa said the words, 'feeding the bears?'"

"Yeah. Harold's worried about it. His biggest concern is having to shoot one. Turns out, it's bad luck in the First Nations culture to pop a bear. I suppose that makes you quite the bad boy in the Klondike, yeah?"

"Really? First Nations people don't eat bear meat?" asked Steve.

"No, everybody knows that. Meriwa says she has an associate at Yukon University, a professor who has a research grant to study bears in the Yukon. He wants to tag along with our team and if they encounter a grizzly or black bear while recovering sojourners, the professor will tranquilize and put a tracking collar on it."

"Now you're calling our clients 'sojourners?'" Steve chuckled.

"Yeah, that's what Simon is calling them," Clyde said before continuing to explain the invoice. "Harold not only wants a new boat, he also wants to be paid in advance for bookings. He has glacier tours, cabins, cabin transfers, skydiving, canyon boat trips, all times-five trips, four for skydiving, totaling two hundred twenty-five thousand Canadian. Then he has Jessie's salary and rental for the executive suite with a markup, totaling three hundred-and-two thousand. Then he has four hundred thousand in recovery fees. Altogether, it's just over a million, Canadian. What do you think?"

"Say no to the boat and don't pay the recovery fees in advance," replied Steve. "What if there is no recovery? The rates are absurd, but conceptually I can see paying in advance for the cabins and use of the planes on the basis of an advance booking concept, like the hotel. As Harold put it, for the recoveries, there is no equivalent. They require payment on a success-fee basis because success depends on a number of factors. Did granny jump? Did his men come out of the woods with a corpse? If you pay in advance for recoveries, it is not going to enhance Harold's probability of success."

"Yeah, good point, we need the recoveries to be successful. We can change that, but do you think the rest is reasonable?"

"No. The entire kit-and-kaboodle is totally unreasonable particularly as it relates to Jessie, the office situation, and the fucking Zodiac. Damn, we should just shop the contract."

"Are you willing to do that, Steve? Because if you are, great. But think about it–tomorrow you pick up the phone and say, 'Hi, you don't know me, but I was hoping you'd be willing to drop four of our grannies from your plane this season, I mean if you're not already booked up doing less interesting work.' Is that a call you're willing to make?"

Crickets.

Clyde continued, "Keep in mind, we've already taken the first payment from four actual customers. At this point if you spend a month shopping Harold's proposal, we risk forfeiting this entire first season, don't you think?"

Steve closed his eyes and took a deep breath. "Fine, but still, it's galling. Under the circumstances, we have no other options. For the test period, I recommend we buy Harold a fucking boat and pay him what he wants minus the recovery fees, which we remit on a success-fee basis. We can reevaluate the contract after the season is over and repeal his most unreasonable requests."

"I'll tell John that's your recommendation. He'll be pleased to hear it."

"Have you run the numbers?" asked Steve. "By my calculations, our fees to FunBite companies and Harold plus renovation and furnishings will chew through the better part of our three-point-six million in net revenue for the first season."

"Yes, but we'll get a little help from the exchange rate. Even with our US costs, we could come out ahead for the first year, and if not, we still have the million I put in as capital to fall back on, right?"

"I just can't believe you're going to let the locals take us for a ride."

"For a ride? I think of it as more of a win-win scenario. We get to execute the business plan while also helping the community. And now Meriwa says it's time for us to hit the beaches and burn the ships. Put up the dough or get the fuck out of Whitehorse."

"Those were her words?"

"'Beaches and ships' was Meriwa. 'Dough and fuck' was John. The duo makes a compelling artistic collaboration, wouldn't you say?"

Steve paused. "Maybe I shouldn't complain; imagine what it would cost if we had to pay shyster fees."

"Yeah, John mentioned that yesterday, something about motherfucking freeloaders. He said, 'Tell Steve thanks a lot.' He says if you hadn't crawled out of the woodwork at the last second, he'd be on a beach on Bermuda instead of doing pro bono work for MAID murders."

"I love shysters," replied Steve.

"Me too, they make me giggle," Clyde said with a laugh, before discussing hotel bookings. They agreed to put Akiko in the Gold Rush Inn and Eddie in The 98 Hotel, as recommended by Meriwa. After discussing money transfers, Steve inquired, "I've been meaning to ask you, for clients, how come we target only women, not men?"

"Meriwa told me she thought that was something you and Liz came up with," replied Clyde.

"No, it was in the business plan. Liz asked me, so that's why I'm inquiring."

Clyde paused. "I don't know."

"Hmm. So, what is the plan for Seattle?" asked Steve.

"Akiko, Eddie and I will meet you for breakfast at the Edgewater Hotel on Tuesday morning at 8 am. It's gonna be Eddie handover day. John wants that son of a bitch and his fucking mushrooms out of the motherfucking pool house."

31. River Styx

Steve timed his arrival in Whitehorse to precede the one-year anniversary of Emily's death. So it was on the morning of April 1 that he hiked alone to Miles Canyon.

From the heart of the Miles Canyon Bridge, Steve gazed down upon the surging, frigid currents and explained to Emily about Rachel and Michael, how they no longer spoke to him, how he missed them, how he still waited for them, how he had lost her rose garden, how he missed her more than ever, how he longed to join her, and she heard him.

Suspended alone above the historic rapids, Steve's reflections led him to the River Styx, where he envisioned himself poised between the blue and the black.

32. Eddie Launch

"So that's why I didn't go professional, Stevo. It all happened that day on the North Shore. After that, I started taking my business seriously. You know, really focusing on my special touch, building up my client base, and . . ."

On and fucking on. What fifty-seven-year-old man calls himself Eddie?

How did I ever allow myself to get roped into hiring Eddie? What was I thinking when I got into the car with this bonehead?

Why isn't Eddie flying to Whitehorse with his wiseass mother?

How can I ditch this douchebag?

"And that's how you make the perfect pancake, Stevo."

Steve had met Akiko, Clyde, and Eddie for breakfast before driving away with Eddie in Clyde's almost-new black Mercedes-Benz S Class, leaving Akiko and Clyde, smiling and waving, standing on the sidewalk together in front of Seattle's Edgewater Hotel.

As Steve and Eddie crossed the border, the Canadian Border Patrol asked the usual questions: guns, drugs, fruits, and vegetables. It hadn't occurred to Steve earlier that Eddie might be a security risk.

At the hotel, Steve had opened the trunk and found it absolutely packed with boxes and bags. So, he put his own bag in the backseat. He didn't have a clue how Eddie could have accumulated so much stuff since he had just flown in from Hawaii a couple weeks earlier with his mother. Surely, he hadn't brought all that crap to Seattle by plane.

Once they were underway, Steve asked, "Hey Eddie, what do we have in the trunk?"

"What do you think, Stevo? It's pictures and stuff. It's things we're gonna need for therapy. That's my whole life packed in one trunk. Think about it, bro, if you had to fit your whole life in the trunk, what would you bring?"

Four suitcases.

Steve kept driving.

"Stevo, have you ever heard of Kahului?"

Steve let out a noncommittal sound, something between a grunt and a sigh.

"I've been in love with her since I was eight. Rippin' surfer. You'd have loved her. Everybody does, Hoosier Boy, even the governor. She was the weather babe who surfs."

"Really, the weather lady?"

"Yep, selected as the hottest weather babe on the planet by the UK Sun. I framed the newspaper page, with a picture of me and her catching a gnarly party wave on the North Shore. It's in the trunk. When we get to Whitehorse, I'll show it to you."

"She's not still alive though, right?" Steve asked.

"No, she did a crash-and-burn in a helicopter, but I'm still in love with her. She's the only girl I've ever loved."

"Didn't Alamea and Kahului look alike?"

"They weren't alike at all. Alamea wasn't even a surfer. If she tried to catch a wave, like in that photo, she would have fallen on her face. They are totally different."

"I see," Steve muttered as he kept his eyes on the road. Eddie hadn't quite answered his question.

"Stevo, if you keep interrupting me, I'm not going to be able to finish my story before we get to the shop. We gotta make a quick stop in Vancouver. Do you mind?"

Oh no, what for? Don't ask. Less is more.

How did Michael do in his rugby game yesterday? Maybe Liz will know.

Once they reached Vancouver, Eddie directed him, "Left, right, no, the next left, there, it's there, yeah park, park here. Gnarly. Way to parallel park like a pro, Stevo. I'll be just a few minutes. You need any gardening supplies or anything?"

"From The Shroom Shop?" asked Steve.

Eddie went in alone and returned twenty minutes later. As they were driving away, Steve said, "You didn't buy anything illegal, right?" It was a mistake, of course, because for the next half-hour Eddie talked about his third favorite topic, magic mushrooms.

Steve listened to Eddie rattle on.

Eddie is like the fucking Energizer Bunny; he just keeps going and going. He doesn't need a feedback loop. Words just keep falling out of his fucking face. He is pure, unfiltered Id.

Mushrooms and spores and syringes and prints and light and dark and substrate and spawn and humidifiers and . . . on and on. They had almost thirty hours of driving in front of them.

How is Whitehorse going to cope with Eddie tripping on his fucking mushrooms?

"The important thing to remember, Stevo, is never, ever, ever trip with a golden-ager. They've got waaaay too much baggage, bro. When they start unloading, you don't wanna be around. Even a trained, experienced professional guru like me can't control all that baggage. For golden-agers the key is microdosing. That's my specialty, microdosing."

"You microdose your therapy clients with mushrooms?" Steve asked.

"Yo bro, that's me, the Shrooms Guru. Q one, do you ovulate? Q two, are you looking for a new outlook? Q three, can you afford me? Pass the entry test and start begging, sweetie, because I'm the guru of your dreams."

Can he drive and talk at the same time?

"Eddie, I thought you said you were a one-woman kind of man and you're in love with Kahului. How does that square with being a sex guru and having four Little Eddies on the side?"

"Yo, yo, Stevo, you got the whole thing twisted. First of all, I'm not a sex guru, just a guru, and sometimes a trip guide, right? Second of all, about the four Little Eddies, everyone always assumes I planned them but that's untrue. Think about it, who would plan something like that? And another thing, one of them is named Michael Edward so he's technically not even an Eddie.

"I'll start from the beginning, when I was still in high school. I ALWAYS used a condom on every first date but after I busted a few I changed it up. I made the girl agree she was in charge of birth control, otherwise no dice. You want to ride the Jolt, you gotta take the pledge, you know what I mean, Stevo?"

Steve stared straight ahead, watching the white dashes flash by.

"I would spring it on them like, 'Hey, you know, if you're already using birth control, we can just skip the condom. What do you think?' She would be like, 'Sure,' in which case we had a date, or she would be like, 'Noooo,' in which case no dice. Then I would say, 'Great, but if you get pregnant don't blame me,' right? And she would be like, 'Don't worry Eddie, I just wanna get Jolted.' I would say, 'How would I even know if it were mine anyway?' Right? 'If the kid's not named Eddie, there's no way it could be mine, agreed?' It started out, like, a sort of a Jolt joke, right?"

Maybe if I just clipped the guard rail lightly, I could distract him without killing him.

"The whole system seemed bullet-proof but guess what? Little Eddies started cropping up everywhere, like mushrooms. It all started with just one of those ovulating mamas showing up with her new Little Eddie, cute as a button. She said to me, 'Just like we agreed, his name is Eddie. I'm back for more.' After that, I gave her a Jolt whenever she wanted and sent her packing with fresh shrooms. From there, it kind of got out of hand. Some other girls started showing up with Little Eddies, and one of them didn't even look like me, you know what I mean, Stevo?

"After that they just started taking me for granted, you know? Like they could just swing by for a Jolt and some free shrooms whenever they got bored. It became really stressful."

Thirty-two miles until the next rest area. Maybe I can ditch him there . . .

"Yo Stevo, are you even listening? By then, I had already started my business. I needed to focus all my shrooms, energy, and talent on my paying clients. Of course, that's precisely when the Eddie-moms started getting unreasonable. Imagine four ovulators totally forgetting about the Eddie pledge, all at the same time. They started serving legal papers, literally chasing me right off the island. I had to get away, go find myself, you know what I mean, Stevo? And, of course, when things go really badly, that's when people let you down. My brother quit paying child support for the Little Eddies the same week my mom quit babysitting. It was like the perfect Little Eddie storm.

"Looking back on it now, it's definitely the best thing that ever happened to me. I went to India and found myself. I discovered the key to life and became a guru. It changed everything. After two years in India, I returned. Good thing because the wife of my guru got pregnant, and I was done with my training anyway."

There could be a reward for turning him in somewhere.

"When I returned, I was a changed man. No more ovulators, that was the key. After that it was nothing but golden-agers for me. Women of distinction and accomplishment. No more social climbers using Eddie's head as a foot peg. No more new Little Eddies. No more free Jolts. That's when I started raking it with my guru business.

"I'm not bragging, you know, but those golden-agers need therapy, they've got the dough, and they come to me. They love their guru, you know what I mean, Stevo? And that's how I honed my guru skills and discovered the power of begging. If they want shrooms, I make them beg. If they want a Jolt, they have to get on their knees and beg."

I wonder if Rachel liked her sweatshirt.

"That's the key to my success because if they beg, they can never come back later and say they didn't want it. When those golden-agers look me in the eye, they know they were the ones who wanted it. So that's pretty much my system in a nutshell. No tripping, just microdosing. Beg, beg, beg. That's all there is to it, my secret guru sauce. And that's what we're going to be using on your sojourners, Stevo."

Steve silently counted the center line dashes: ". . . nine-hundred ninety-two, nine-hundred ninety-three . . ."

"I guarantee it, Stevo. Ask ten people to hop out the back of a plane, and ten-outta-ten would rather do it tripping on shrooms, right? What I'm saying, Stevo, is you got my personal Eddie guarantee that those sojourners are going to die happy."

"Well, Eddie, you sound pretty confident."

"Damn right, Stevo. That's why the first thing we're going to do in Whitehorse is recruit two other therapists. Every single therapy session will begin with a beauty contest. Each time, it'll be me versus two ladies. If clients want a piece of the Eddie guru, they'll have to choose me over the others. You know what I mean, Stevo? It's all about freedom of choice. Let's just see how many choose Eddie versus how many unchoose Eddie. We're going to track that, Stevo. If they all choose me and none unchoose me, then you'll have to phone up my brother and get me a raise, right? You're going to do that for me, right Stevo?"

"What do you mean?"

"I mean, you're not actually my boss, right? My brother is paying me, and he is my boss. You know that, right? Stevo, you and me, we're like colleagues, bro, like two surfers in the lineup. I'm not your boss, you're not my boss. We both work for the big man in Seattle, right?"

"Well, I never thought of it that way. I am kind of the boss, you know, the CEO, the Chief Executive Officer."

"Whoa, whoa, Stevo! Slow down. Who's paying you? Just tell me that. It's my bro, right? And my bro is paying me too, right? Follow the money, dude! We're both working for the man, know what I mean?"

"I see what you mean."

"One more thing, Stevo. I'm a massage therapist, but I don't rub dudes. Clyde told you that, right? No dudes. That's Clyde's department."

"No dudes."

"There's a reason for that, Stevo."

"It's okay, I believe you."

"No, you gotta know this. When I rub golden-agers, I got a system, you know. It all comes back to the pictures. In the therapy rooms, we're going to hang Kahului pictures. It's important, you know? Because those pictures are inspiring. And getting inspired is the key to the golden-agers begging. Bottom line for you Stevo: I rub dames, not dudes. It's a rule, right Stevo?"

"Well, Eddie, I don't know what to say. It's a lot of information to process. We have four clients this year and, as luck would have it, it's one hundred percent dames. So, at least for this year, we don't have to worry."

"Way to go, Stevo! Now you're trippin' without shrooms."

"Hey, Eddie, do you want to drive?"

"Sure, I was hoping you would ask."

Steve found a spot to pull over and they switched seats. That's when Steve discovered Eddie couldn't talk while driving.

I wonder if he can chew gum and talk at the same time.

A few hours later, they stopped for gas. Steve went inside and bought a pack of gum while Eddie filled up.

Steve and Eddie took bar stools at Sheep Camp Lounge in Whitehorse and waited for their drinks. Eddie high-fived the bartender and said, "Yeah dude! Kurt, my man! Sure, it's with a 'K' not a 'C' because Kurt with a 'C' wouldn't be a good name for a bartender." Kurt was sort of on board with the joke but was taking extra care to avoid encouraging this particular customer.

"Sheep Camp is, like, a fancy-drinks place, yeah Stevo?"

"Yeah, fancy," said Steve as he swirled his drink in his glass.

"Good thing it's on the second floor, right, Stevo? Never put a fancy-drinks place in the cellar. Put it on the second floor. That way, you can just roll people down the stairs at the end of night, after they're broke. Put a fancy-drinks place in the cellar, every night you'd be stranded with fat deadbeats."

Stevo was still at least two fancy-drinks too sober to be impressed by Eddie's unique insights into gravity and the fancy-drinks business. Kurt-with-a-K continued to offer no encouragement, but since Eddie was playing to himself, an audience of one, the lack of feedback was no problemo. Eddie insisted on swapping fancy drink secrets with Kurt.

Kurt's drink was: <u>Kimono Remover</u>

> Sake
> Gin
> Lime
> Basil
> Simple syrup

Shake and pour neat into a 9-ounce glass.

Eddie's drink was: <u>Feelin Yo Oats</u>

Equal parts:

> Cold rolled oats
>
> Patron Silver Tequila
>
> Cranberry juice
>
> ¼ green apple

Microwave for two minutes, stir,

Microwave for two more minutes,

Add chopped green apple,

Stir and serve with a spoon in a coffee cup.

Kurt was like an artist with his drink board. Eddie tried to convince Kurt to add his invention to the board. Kurt resisted.

Eddie implored, "It's for when you expand your hours. You know, for your breakfast menu."

"You do know Sheep Camp stays open until 4 am, right?" replied Kurt with a pained expression. "I can't see us ever becoming a breakfast place."

"I guarantee it's the healthiest item on your drinks menu," insisted Eddie. "You can offer Feelin Yo Oats as a special menu item, you know, your go-to, to go after 2 am. Put a sign for it on the counter. You don't even have to tell your boss."

Kurt wiped down the bar as he moved away from Eddie.

"Kurt, are you listening? You could become the only super-early-morning breakfast place in Whitehorse. By then, all the kitchens are closed, and all the stoners are famished. I'd definitely be in for a nightcap. You would have me every morning."

Kurt continued wiping. "That's a start."

Eddie as a comedian was laying an egg.

He's joking, right?

Eddie continued as though Steve and Kurt were listening. "I could bring some friends. Stoned people always wake up broke because, for them, when the bars close, whatever cash they still have turns to Monopoly money. Make it a cash-only item. When they walk in and order a Feelin Yo Oats to go and ask, 'How much?' you just say, 'How much you got?' You'll be doing them a favor because stoners just keep going until they run out of dough."

Joke's definitely going to be on us when Eddie shows up on Good Morning America as the CEO of Feelin Yo Oats.

The next evening, Steve fetched Eddie from The 98 Hotel and escorted him to the Baked Café. They claimed a sidewalk table and ordered espressos. Meriwa and Simon strolled toward them, arm-in-arm, Meriwa laughing and impersonating the perfect niece, Simon the perfect uncle.

Steve rose and met them. "Simon, who is this happy tagalong?"

"Good to see you," said Simon. "You brought the guru?"

"The one and only," Steve said with raised eyebrows. "Hello, Meriwa, you look lovely as always."

Meriwa offered Steve her hand. "Thank you, Steve. Have you been going to the gym? It doesn't show yet, but don't give up."

"Meriwa, this is Eddie. Eddie, this is Simon."

Simon extended his hand. Meriwa did not. Steve offered to get them coffee, but before they could reply, Eddie said, "Yo, Stevo, it's Hoosier Boy's hot babe from the ball game."

"Eddie, please, be polite. This is Meriwa. She does legal work for the company."

Eddie grinned. "Sure she does."

Meriwa took a seat beside Steve, turned her head and looked directly at Eddie. "Never refer to me as babe. Is that clear?"

Eddie said, "Yo Stevo, get a grip on yo uptight mama."

Meriwa looked Eddie in the eye and said, "Simon?"

Simon stood and looked directly down at Eddie. "Eddie, I want to love you. After all, we are a kind people. However, we have a long history of ignorant fools blundering into our world, insensitive, unprepared, and unaware. Today, I am warning you: history has proven that the Yukon is no place for imprudence. Here, we dangle fools by their feet from the bridge in Miles Canyon to peer down at the lost souls of stampeders who died in the swirly currents below."

Eddie stared at the scar extending from Simon's left ear to the corner of his mouth.

"Clyde may have sent you here, but I will decide how long you linger. My rules are not unreasonable, but they are uncompromising. Let me explain them to you, today. With respect to my niece, you may never speak to her unless she first speaks to you. In reply, your options are limited to: 'Yes, ma'am,' 'No, ma'am,' or 'As you wish, ma'am.' Is that clear?"

Eddie blinked twice.

"Meriwa?"

"Eddie, is that clear?" Meriwa barked.

Eddie looked at Simon as he said, "Yes, ma'am."

"The second rule is, for as long as you remain in the Yukon Territory, you shall never cross the line with a person of the First Nations. As long as you follow these two rules, you will continue to thrive and be happy in the Yukon. Are these terms clear to you, Eddie?"

There was no reply.

"Meriwa?" prompted Simon.

"Eddie, is that clear?" repeated Meriwa.

"Yes, ma'am."

Simon took a step closer to Eddie. "Stand up."

Eddie stood.

I sure could have used Simon on our road trip.

Simon hugged Eddie and released him. Meriwa stood, accepted Simon's arm, and they walked up Main Street as though nothing had just happened.

✳ ✳ ✳

Two weeks and a day-and-a-half later, at 2 am, walking in misty rain as a cure for white night insomnia, Steve happened upon Eddie standing beside the Hot Diggity Dog food stand.

"Yo Stevo, sup?"

"Hi Eddie, how's it going? Is this your food truck?"

"Dude, check it out! My new business! The trailer is not mine, but I know the babe who closes. She gives me the key and I take care of her with snacks. Know what I mean, Stevo? Hey, I got a freebie for you bro. Here you go, a Feelin Yo Oats. It's a bestseller, Stevo, an after-2-am bestseller. Average *how much you got* price is thirty-two-sixty-eight, but for you, it's on the house."

"Wow, thanks Eddie. Can I ask what's in the cup?"

"Stevo, it's in a cup, but it's not a drink. See bro, you can't sell drinks in Whitehorse after 4 am. Plus, no drinks from the hotdog stand. Hot Diggity Dog is not licensed for drinks, bro. That's why Feelin Yo Oats is a breakfast item. Yo Stevo, you know the recipe already, right? I don't need to repeat it?"

"No, no, I remember. Well thanks, Eddie, this is great."

"Yo, yo Stevo, don't forget your plastic spoon, bro."

33. Turned to Stone

Ron called every few days, during breakfast right after milking cows. For Steve, it was during his morning workout.

The construction had been delayed due to permitting and inspection issues and because, on some days, the contractors just didn't bother showing up. Pushing the general contractor, Edward Pelly, was like pushing on a rope.

Steve had just completed a set of dumbbell military presses when the phone rang. "Steve, good morning, it's Ron."

Steve looked at himself in the mirror, nodding and smiling in an exaggerated manner as he greeted Ron. "Hi, Ron. What's up?"

"I've been talking to Clyde about the facilities project. How is it coming?" asked Ron.

Steve took a deep breath. "Not bad, not bad. We're behind schedule, but the general contractor assured me that we'll finish on time."

"That's why I'm calling," said Ron. "I was thinking maybe you could use a little help with some stuff. How about if I fly in on Thursday?"

"The day after tomorrow? Wow, really? That would be great. What kind of stuff would you help with?"

"You know, construction stuff, to keep the project on schedule. What do you think?"

"Well, I hadn't considered it but I'm sure it would be great. Should we run it past Meriwa? I mean, to make sure it will be okay with the general contractor?"

"I think Meriwa already knows. When I discussed the matter with Clyde, he said it's your call, you have the final say."

"Great, do you have a place to stay?"

"I haven't booked anything but if you give me the greenlight, I'll buy the plane ticket and book the hotel."

"Greenlight from me? Sure, you've got it. You do know it's the high season for tourists though, right? Anyway, if it works out that would be great. I look forward to seeing you. It'll give me a break from hanging out with Eddie."

"Great, I'll send you the details once I know them. Can you say hello to Meriwa for me, and let her know it's a go?"

"Sure, I'll tell her," said Steve.

"One more thing, if I bring a helmet, do you think there is any chance I could borrow your Harley while I'm there?"

Steve squeezed his eyes shut and looked down. "Yeah, sure, no problem. I need to wash it anyway. It'll be ready whenever you need it."

"Thanks, pal. I owe you one," said Ron.

Steve hung up and said to his reflection, "Hey Beaver, what do you plan to do with those two black soft-sided Harley trike cases you're hiding in your saddlebags?"

Then he changed his tone, higher this time. "Golly Gee, Wally, I never thoughta that."

* * *

It was a cold and rainy day in Whitehorse and the bumper crowd at Burnt Toast Café attested to the fact that it wasn't going to be a great day for Larger-Than-Life adventures. The kitchen was jamming and the place smelled distinctly of fried eggs and coffee.

Despite the rush, Tammy took the time to chat with Steve. The impact of her dawdling was reflected on the faces of the foursome at the window.

"Really, you have two jobs?" Steve asked.

Meriwa arrived and removed her jacket. "Hi Tammy. Latte skim for me?"

"It's already here. Steve ordered it for you," she replied as the women exchanged smiles.

Steve flashed his eyebrows at Meriwa. "Good morning, beautiful."

Meriwa smiled coyly as she took her seat. "Do I know you? Am I interrupting anything?"

"You'll never believe who I talked to this morning while at the gym," said Steve.

Meriwa took a drink and smiled over the top of her cup. "Why don't you just tell him to stop calling while you're working out?"

"I don't mind really. It gives me a chance to look at myself in the mirror," Steve said as his lox and bagel arrived.

"Sounds like a waste of workout time," said Meriwa as she warmed her hands on her cup.

"I'm supposed to tell you Clark Kent is coming to town," said Steve as he ate a caper.

"Yeah, Clyde told me. He asked me to call the Edgewater to get Ron a room since they told him they had no vacancies."

Steve put down his cup. "You got Ron a room when they were all booked up? How does that work?"

"Simple, Steve. Some tourists are going to arrive the day after tomorrow, and the desk clerk is going to send them packing to the Gold Rush Inn, maybe give them a free night or something. Or maybe there will be a cancellation. These things work themselves out," said Meriwa as she sipped her latte. "Simon and I are picking up Ron at the airport tomorrow at four o'clock. Do you want to ride along?"

"No thanks," said Steve. "I'll meet you for drinks though after he arrives. How about Sheep Camp at seven?"

"It's a date," said Meriwa. "You got the check?"

"For your latte? You're not eating?" asked Steve.

She swerved around the tables and swayed her way out of Burnt Toast Café before climbing into the back of the waiting Benz.

Meriwa could win the Miss Canada Walk-Away Contest.

Tammy said, "Steve. Earth-to-Steve. Do you want a refill?"

Steve and Eddie were milking their first drink when Meriwa and Ron came up the stairs. Steve felt a pang of disappointment when he saw Ron's hand on the small of Meriwa's back.

They really are a couple. My worst fears have come true.

Eddie jumped from his seat and hugged Ron. "Yo, Hoosier Boy! Welcome to the Yukon!" exclaimed Eddie as though they were still kids surfing on the North Shore. Ron looked confused but went with it.

Now Eddie's welcoming stampeders like he's a sourdough?

Steve extended his hand. "Hey, Ron, so glad you made it. How was the flight?"

"Great. They were all great. Nailed the landings, four-out-of-four," replied Ron with a convincing smile.

"Yeah, dude, Simon was really impressed by your luggage. He said it barely fit in the Benz," remarked Eddie.

"I didn't know which tools I would need," replied Ron, defensively. "Steve, how do you feel about excess baggage charges? Do you approve them?"

"Not generally. We can arm wrestle for it if you want," joked Steve.

Ron grinned. "That's what I was hoping to hear."

Without acknowledging Meriwa, Eddie said, "Well nice to see you again, Hoosier Boy. Sorry I have to run, but Simon is waiting for me."

Simon? Eddie and Simon? What could they possibly be doing tonight . . . besides mushrooms?

They remained standing until Eddie left. Meriwa sat close to Ron.

Whatever is happening isn't a secret.

"Meriwa, I've never seen you this happy," said Steve. "What's changed?"

Meriwa looked at Ron, who shrugged. She giggled and blushed. "You don't understand. Alamea told me she had a cousin I would like and that she would introduce me. At the same time, she told Ron she had a friend he should meet."

Ron nodded.

A guy would have said it in four words: we like each other.

"So, when we met at the Mariner's game, it wasn't really an accident. Clyde set that up," continued Meriwa.

"Aha!" exclaimed Steve. "I thought the ballgame visit was an ambush, but it was actually a setup."

Meriwa giggled again. "It's not always about you, Steve."

"The ambush had a business purpose, but it also involved some personal time," added Ron.

"Did you just take that straight from Clyde's expense report policies?"

Ron grinned. "How did you know?"

Steve looked at Ron solemnly. "How much have you told Meriwa?"

Ron's smile vanished. "It's not mine to tell."

They were silent until Steve called for another round. While Kurt made the drinks, Meriwa filled the air. "I've discussed the construction plan with Edward. He's agreed to meet us at the offices tomorrow. Simon and Eddie are dropping off Ron's tools there tonight. I'm taking the day off from work, and Simon and I are going to help Ron in case he needs materials or anything."

"Hold it, you're actually going to be there tomorrow? That sounds great," Steve remarked as Kurt brought the drinks. Silence resumed. Meriwa and Ron looked at him expectantly.

They're just pregnant pausing the shit out of me.

I had planned to tell her but not with Ron. Well, I did expect to do it with Ron, but not with them as a couple. The fact they're together doesn't actually change anything.

Meriwa cocked her head and caught his eye.

I wonder if Ron has the dough to bail me out of jail if they arrest me.

Kurt had gone to the kitchen. Steve took a deep breath, looked around the empty bar, and began speaking in barely more than a whisper. "Meriwa, I have a question for you. Do you ever represent clients, you know, legally?"

Meriwa leaned forward and replied in a whisper, "Well, yes and no. I am the Justice Coordinator, so while I can represent clients directly outside my job, I wouldn't normally do so."

"When you represent clients, is there some kind of client confidentiality system in Canada?"

"Are you planning to knock off a convenience store?"

"Seriously, what if I were your client? Could I be?"

"Well, if you needed me for legal help in the Yukon Territory and you requested it, then naturally I would help."

"Great. I am presently in the Yukon Territory, and I definitely need legal help. Will you help me?"

She smiled and looked at Ron. Ron stone-faced it. In this particular vignette, Ron was playing the role of the potted plant.

"Steve, I don't know what you need, but if it's important, I'm happy to be your legal advisor in the Yukon."

"It's just that simple?" he whispered.

"Yes, Steve, it's always been just that simple."

He looked around the empty bar. Kurt had returned from the kitchen but disappeared down the stairs. Steve leaned across the table closer to her and whispered, "I was there. On the night of the accident, I was there. That's where I met Alamea. I held her hand while she died."

Ron remained still, blending perfectly into his bar stool like a stone-faced chameleon. Meriwa waited. She reached across the table and placed her hand on Steve's forearm.

She is taking this pregnant pause thing to a whole new level: twins.

"I didn't want to tell you because I did some things that night that weren't, you know, perfect," he whispered.

"I know, Steve," she whispered.

Steve looked at Stone Face. No help.

Meriwa made a show of looking around CIA style, except more smirky. Savoring the moment, she leaned toward him and whispered, "I know this from my uncle. He found a thumb print on a shell casing and he wants to match it to *your* thumb. He thinks your fingers might match prints he's taken from the trike trunk and ignition. He blames you for not reporting the shooting of a grizzly bear. He has your fuel purchase timestamps and video footage of you purchasing gas in Haines Junction before the accident. He's already traced your identity through your credit card. He knows your check-out time from the Edgewater Hotel and the time of the tire repair. He has a matching tire print from the accident scene. He knows it all. I've known it even before I met you. I'm the one who sent Clyde the accident report."

Steve looked stunned, as though he had just been kicked in the stomach by a small First Nations woman from the Klondike.

"My uncle wants to ask you what became of a few missing items," continued Meriwa. "He's dying to learn the whereabouts of a Glock nine-millimeter pistol, for example, and he is especially interested in recovering a bag of money."

She stopped and looked over her shoulder. Still no Kurt. She whispered, "My uncle's nickname for you is *The Felon*. The only reason the investigation is on ice is because my uncle put it on ice because my mother asked my uncle to put it on ice because my mother loves Alamea and Kyle and because Alamea chose you."

She took her hand away from his forearm and took a sip of her drink. Stone Face had a sip too. Steve took the cue and had a sip.

Kurt returned. "How are the drinks?"

Mount Rushmore finally spoke. "They are great, thank you! Really great!"

Once Kurt left, Steve whispered, "Really, you've known all along?"

She whispered, "Yeeeeees, Steeeve. We've all known. On a good day, I could see why she chose you and I would admire you. Then you would say something dumb and remind me that you're a lying sack of shit. Then you would do something to redeem yourself and Clyde would remind me again that we needed you and that's how it has been for me. We could have been friends this whole time, but instead you chose to play charades."

Steve was silent for a moment. Finally, resuming a normal voice, he said, "Wow, I've been a total idiot, haven't I?"

Stone Face Ronned it up some more.

"Yep," said Meriwa with a nod.

"Well, obviously I've been living in a different dimension, but there is something I would like to know. How do you feel, Meriwa? Do you think I'm a felon?"

Meriwa smiled and got up from her seat. Steve stood as she rounded the table. "You were Alamea's angel," she replied as she hugged him.

Steve looked over her shoulder as he was being squeezed. "Meriwa is hugging me," Steve said loudly. "Look, Meriwa is hugging Steve. Kurt, Kurt, more drinks at this table please!" Ron's face broke into his most endearing *aw shucks* smile.

As they retook their seats, Steve said, "I have something I was hoping you could solve."

"Sure, anything," she replied.

Steve reached under the table and pulled out his weathered tan Hartman soft leather briefcase. He set it on his lap, unzipped the top and extracted a freshly polished, three-inch, black leather, size-seven Prada left shoe.

Meriwa gasped. She took Alamea's Prada pump, turned it over, and ran her hands over the toe, the heel, the sole. Her eyes filled with tears. "I-I can't tell you how much this means to me," she stammered. "This shoe belonged to Alamea's mother. Kahului did the weather in this shoe. I've sat holding a lonely right shoe so many nights, crying about this missing left shoe."

Ron got up and hugged Meriwa. He kissed her head, and she hugged him back. They stayed and ordered food and more drinks and talked and laughed like old friends.

At dinner that night, it should have occurred to Steve they wouldn't actually be meeting regularly, the three of them. In fact, that was the only time during Ron's visit to Whitehorse that the three of them dined together.

Once Ron and Meriwa left, Steve returned to his hotel room. He opened the room safe and found it stuffed full: the cash and Glock slide and barrel, exactly as he had left them.

34. Clark Kent Saves the Day

The following morning Steve entered the APF Therapy & Spa Center that was still posing as a construction site. Everyone else was already there. Well, everybody except Eddie and the general contractor, Edward. The Eds were missing, of course, but the rest were there.

Simon sat at the reception desk on a pile of sheetrock, drinking coffee with Akiko who was sitting on the opposite side of the desk on some boxes, and leaning in close.

Hmmm, how did we get from 'don't speak to my niece or I'll drown you in Miles Canyon' to 'I'm bopping your mom'?

I really have to start paying better attention. Is this how old age feels? Failing memory, vision, hearing? Walking around in oblivion, the last to know everything, swinging continuously from bliss to bewilderment?

At least the elderly have an excuse. I have vision, but fail to see, hearing, but fail to hear. Maybe it's not age; maybe I'm going biblically insane.

Steve stopped himself from drifting past the point of no return and turned to assess the rest of the facilities. Standing beside the coffee machine in the reception area were Harold, Lily, Jessie, and Angi, chatting with Daisy.

Three wolves and two crows. I bet even Daisy is related somehow. One of the great things about the Yukon is family sizes are limitless.

Last week Simon bragged about how he was the middle kid of nine. 'Exactly the middle. Say it: nine. Exactly the middle. Say it!'

Fucking pedantic. I wonder if he does the same to Akiko.

Steve turned and looked past the open metal studs, through the Star Spa to the Lavender Therapy Room. Meriwa was talking to Ron as she gestured through the open studded wall toward the Waterfall Therapy Room and beyond that, the Beach Rest Room, then toward the Wellness Evaluation Room. Ron followed as she wove her way through the framing.

Ron saw Steve and touched Meriwa's arm to get her attention. Meriwa turned, smiled, and waved. Wearing black Prada three-inch heels, she hopped and bounced like a gazelle over an electrical wire strung through the framing. She was wearing Alamea's gold Cartier Tank watch. "Good morning, Steve!" she said loudly as she approached, as an announcement. "Can I get you some coffee?"

She moves better in the Pradas than I do in loafers.

"Yes, please," he said as he stared at her watch. She walked toward the coffee setup arranged on a makeshift counter. Steve followed.

When did she get the watch? Does she have all the jewelry? Clyde must have given it to her when she was in Seattle.

Everyone stopped talking and made their way toward the reception area as a group, facing Steve and Meriwa. Steve turned toward the group and just as he was about to speak, Meriwa introduced him. "Thank you all for coming today and for being on time. You've met Ron; now for the primary reason we've invited you here today: Steve has some announcements."

Steve assumed his lecturing pose. "Yes, thank you. As I hope all of you are aware by now, we have the first four clients for APF arriving in just over three weeks. We're asking all of you to help in any way you can to turn this construction site into the nicest Therapy & Spa Center in the Yukon.

"In about ten days the carpet will be installed, and the furniture will be quick to follow. So, we have a lot of work to complete this week. As you all know, Ron is now part of our team. I'll let him speak about his role in the project."

Ron stepped forward as Meriwa handed Steve coffee. "Nice to meet all of you. This project has experienced a few hiccups, but with Meriwa's help, we can solve the permitting, inspection, and licensing issues. So now, I would like each of you to pledge the time you can commit to working over the next two weeks. Jessie, can you please create a schedule for each person here showing the working hours?"

Jessie took out a notepad and began scribbling.

Steve concluded, "Thank you, Ron. Are there any questions or suggestions?"

Harold raised his hand and boomed in his distinctive baritone voice, "What about Edward?"

"I look forward to meeting Edward, hopefully today," replied Ron. "Edward told Meriwa he would be here this morning, but as you can see, we're not waiting for anyone."

Harold scowled. "Just so you know, I have my own business and cannot help with your construction." He began texting as he spoke.

Meriwa interceded, "Harold, we invited you here today to keep you apprised of the progress and give you the chance to survey your office. We're not going to distract you with construction. Thank you for coming, by the way."

Harold seemed satisfied with his own special thank you plus an exclusive get-out-of-work pass. He pursed his lips, nodded, and continued texting.

"Any more questions?" asked Ron.

Jessie headed for the door, just to make sure nobody escaped without pledging work hours. Meriwa joined her, to whip any slackers.

Steve intercepted Harold, and Ron joined them. "Harold, have you shown Ron the executive suite?" asked Steve.

"No, but we can show him now," replied Harold.

They squeezed past Jessie's roadblock at the door and overheard Meriwa informing Lily that she would be helping Angi and her brother with painting. They walked a short distance down the hall and opened the door to the executive suite. It looked the same, no walls, four vertical windows, with a bonny view of the river.

"What is your plan for this space?" asked Ron.

Harold led them to the middle of the open space, where someone had suspended a broken flat-screen TV between two boxes to create a rickety and inconveniently low coffee table. On top of the TV lay Harold's three thousand dollar blueprints, which resembled the original sketch of the executive suite. Ron studied the blueprints and asked, "Do these offices need to be done before the clients arrive?"

"Absolutely!" exclaimed Harold. "I need this office finished now. I have to meet real clients, you know."

Steve ignored Harold and addressed Ron directly. "The APF Therapy & Spa Center is the primary priority. If it's possible to make progress here without impeding progress there, that's fine, but please keep in mind that there is no hard deadline for finishing this area."

"That's not true. I need my office now," Harold protested.

"Harold, I know you need an office," consoled Steve. "We've agreed to complete it and you have my word we will do so. But you do know why it isn't done yet, right? Edward is your relative. Do you need me to spell it out for you?"

Harold pressed his lips together and resumed texting, faking disinterest.

"Harold, you mentioned some electrical upgrades for the cabins," said Steve. "When we're done with the Therapy & Spa Center, maybe Ron can help with those?"

This brought Harold's head up. He pocketed his phone. "That's right. Ron, what do you know about electrical panels?"

Steve guided the two out as they conversed about voltage and amperage and wire gauges and appliances and heating systems and electrical loads.

In their absence, the sheetrockers had arrived and started working. Ron and Meriwa reviewed the work plan with Jessie, before Meriwa and Angi went to pick up doors.

Edward arrived. "Hey, it looks good, right?"

"Edward, this is Ron," said Steve. "He's here to help us get the project back on schedule. He has experience in construction and he is an engineer too."

"That might be fine for working in America," said Edward. "But if you don't have a Canadian work permit, I can't hire you."

Steve took a step toward Edward. "Nobody's asking you to hire Ron. He's going to help us, and if you have any questions, please direct them to Meriwa."

"Okay, fine," said Edward with a sneer. "What are you going to do for me, Ron?"

"I don't think you understand," interjected Steve. "The question is: what are you going to do for Ron? He's in charge now. Effective immediately, you and all your guys are working for him. Is that clear?"

"No, I don't think so," stammered Edward.

"Call Meriwa now. We'll wait," said Steve.

Edward walked out and returned after ten minutes. "So, Ron, what's the plan?"

That was it. That was how Ron managed to transform the APF Therapy & Spa Center and the executive suite from being a balled-up, delayed construction mess to a finished project in under three weeks.

35. Larger Than Life

Once the construction project was complete, Meriwa took the staff of four women, plus Simon and Isaac, to Vancouver to buy clothes. Clyde had agreed to a budget of three thousand dollars per person but they overspent it. Meriwa charged one hundred percent of the purchases to her APF credit card, personally approving every item down to underwear and socks, even for Simon and Isaac. Simon had been to Vancouver before, but for the others, it was their first visit to British Columbia. On Clyde's dime, Meriwa wined and dined the entire group in downtown Vancouver. They loved it.

With Meriwa out of town, the long days of the northern summer offered endless opportunities for adventure. Yukon is *Larger Than Life* and Steve and Ron rung every bit of adventure out of each day. Before departing, Simon loaned Ron his truck and connected him with a nephew who helped organize kayaking and mountain biking. In addition to renting the kayaks and gear for two days, the nephew also helped with the put-ins and moved the truck to the take-out points.

On the first day, they spent several hours kayaking the waves in the Whitehorse rapids below the dam and downtown. The temperature was sixty-two degrees, and the water was fifty-nine degrees. They ended the day in wetsuits, with Ron instructing Steve on technique as they practiced wet exits and T-rescues in Schwatka Lake. It was Steve's idea, an excuse to get into the water and taste it.

The second day, with Simon's nephew, they drove forty minutes upstream and put in the kayaks just below the locks at Marsh Lake dam. It was chilly on the water even with no wind and they were thankful they had worn the wetsuits.

The kayaking brought back memories for Steve of when he and Emily had taken the children on a four-day flatwater float and camping trip from the town of Green River down to Mineral Bottom, Utah. They had just married and he was still getting to know the children. It was their first real family experience, and the kids were still young enough to find it fun and fabulous, despite the sand in the sleeping bags, the biting flies, and the mosquitoes that snuck through unzipped tent flaps. He was in a two-person kayak and Emily, with the camping gear, was in the canoe. The children alternated between them. Both children had really opened up to him during those days on the Green River.

He told Ron about the trip. They discussed Emily's death, the civil suit, the restrictions contacting the kids, and how he missed speaking with them. Ron listened, consoled, and asked questions throughout their discussion.

Toward the day's end, they moored the kayaks on the riverbank at Historical Canyon City, just before Miles Canyon. They hiked around and about and through the ghost town, a relic of the Klondike Gold Rush. The town was built on the site of a First Nations camp. It had never been a big area and now it was partially overgrown with aspen and evergreens and smelled distinctly of pine resin.

It was at this site that stampeders were forced by law to disembark for routine fleecing. They paid five dollars to designated members of the Mounties to pilot their rickety barges through the dangerous waters of Miles Canyon and the Whitehorse rapids. Before this system was established, the first stampeders wrecked nearly three hundred floating contraptions trying to navigate the perilous waters, drowning countless early-bird gold-digger wannabes. After disembarking, stampeders portaged their goods four-and-a-half miles from Canyon City to downtown Whitehorse. Most hired horse-drawn tram cars for three cents per pound.

There remained indentations in the earth where reusable building material had once rested. The historical site was richly populated with insects—descendants of the very same biting flies, ticks and clouds of mosquitoes which had once famously regaled patrons of the original town. A few precious relics from the gold rush era remained, including rusty tin cans and an old tram car on log rails that someone had forgotten to steal.

While Steve and Ron explored the ghost town and fed the bugs, it began raining lightly, providing a cool relief as they were still wearing their wetsuits. By the time they returned to the river, it was raining steadily.

Steve copied Ron's technique and followed him through the turbulent currents of Miles Canyon. The dams had partially subdued the rapids and the kayaks were the perfect craft for the canyon. Still, the currents were spooky enough to cause a capsize. Despite the intensity of the moment, as Steve crossed under the Miles Canyon Bridge, he couldn't resist stealing a glance upward, half-expecting to see Eddie swinging upside-down.

After Miles Canyon, they crossed Schwatka Lake to Riverdale near the fish ladder, where Simon's nephew had parked the truck above the Whitehorse dam.

Steve and Ron ascended Grey Mountain twice, once on rented mountain bikes and once on foot.

For the bike trip, they parked Simon's truck at the Grey Mountain Road parking lot and unloaded the bikes before heading out on Dream Trail. Ron led the way, occasionally waiting for Steve to catch up.

On the ascent, they spotted a teenage black bear trampling a stand of young aspen trees and stripping them of leaves. The bear paused to glare at them before continuing its foraging.

Too early for berries. Waiting for wild soapberries, cranberries, blackberries, bearberries, and blueberries. Until then he's making do, living in the moment, angry as a vandal, hungry enough to eat a tree.

The weather was chilly and drizzly when they began the ride. By the time they reached Grey Mountain Summit, the rain had quit, but it remained overcast. They could see the trail, but the view from the mountaintop was obscured.

The next day, to hike Grey Mountain, they passed where they had parked for the bike rides and kept driving the logging road all the way to the communication towers. They hopped out of the truck and were greeted by a wedding party of ravenous mosquitoes.

Who would these biters have eaten today if we had skipped the hike?

They applied extra mosquito repellent and began the three-mile hike to climb eight hundred feet. In the beginning, there were a few bits where they scrambled along limestone slabs and ledges, but otherwise it was an easy hike. As they gained elevation to the ridge, the breeze picked up, and they left the mosquitoes behind. The day was clear, and the light was perfect, so they stopped every few minutes to consult their booklet and take photos of alpine wildflowers. In bloom were northern goldenrod, pink blueberries, kinnikinnick, white wild strawberries, and cut-leaf anemone. Ron also snapped some shots of the poisonous purple sweetvetch, or maybe it was edible bear root—they kind of looked the same. Steve tried to convince Ron to sample it, so they could know.

During the hike Steve identified a rock ptarmigan in flight by its distinctive, low, guttural call. They took the wrong path several times and had to double back as they headed toward the third summit. Once they reached the top, they could see all the way from where they had put the kayaks in at Marsh Lake to where they had taken them out at the fish ladder on Schwatka Lake.

From the highest summit of Grey Mountain, Steve looked down over the city and tried to gauge the location of the Confession Bench on the escarpment. In the opposite direction loomed Mount Lorne. They had chosen the perfect day for the hike. Except for a few wispy cirrus clouds, the sky was clear, and they could see all the way to the coastal snow-covered peaks of Kluane National Park.

As Ron took two Yukon Golds out of the backpack, Steve regaled him with a story of when the children were young and would get a scratch or a cut, how he would tell them the story about Mimas, the most badass moon in our universe, and how Michael had recently brought it up.

The last thing Steve had done with Michael was take a road trip to Saguaro National Park where they had camped and seen the nation's largest cactus. The primary purpose of the trip had been to give Michael practice driving on the highway in preparation for his driver's license test. On their return to Denver, Steve drove some when Michael wanted a break.

Out of the blue, Michael had asked, "Do you remember your owie story when we were little? The one you used to tell us about Mimas?"

The story had gone like this: wounds, whether of the flesh or the heart, heal with time and become scars. In the history of our own solar system, we can observe scars attesting to cosmic events of gargantuan proportions. The biggest is worn by a relatively small moon of Saturn called Mimas, which has a crater one hundred-thirty kilometers across. Whatever hit Mimas came close to shattering it to dust. If Mimas had not survived, the scar wouldn't exist and today its remnants would be indistinguishable from the chunks of comets, asteroids, and shattered moons that form the rings of Saturn. Just over four billion years ago, Mimas really took one for the team, and today the little moon bears the scar to prove it.

"Sure," Steve had replied. "The Herschel crater on Mimas, our solar system's biggest scar."

"You told us that the important thing is that Mimas survived," said Michael. "Do you think we'll survive Mom's death?"

The fact that Michael defined "we" to include him meant the world to Steve. After recounting the story, Steve took Ron's bottle and zipped both empties inside the backpack before they descended the mountain in silence.

Most days, they returned from their activities exhausted. On the days when they still had energy, they would scale the escarpment via the Secret Rope Trail at the north end. Steve never did the trail alone because of his bear nightmares.

After their activities, they would return to the hotel for a break before investing the remains of each day precipitously, alternating between Sheep Camp Lounge, Dirty Northern Bastard, and The 98 Hotel, where they would yuk it up over dinner and beers as though they were on college spring break.

36. Romeo and Juliet

Steve weaved his way through the smokers loitering outside the front door of The 98 Hotel. Ron held court at the crowded bar with three attractive American women in their mid-twenties. Two were sitting and one standing with her hand on his arm. A band was playing, and they were all leaning close to hear him over the music and the din of the crowd. Ron caught sight of Steve and waved him over.

"Hey Ron, are these ladies waiting for me?"

"Ladies, say hello to Steve. He's the old married guy with kids, the one from Denver I've been telling you about."

They laughed and played along. "Hi, married Steve." "Nice ring, Steve." "Hi, old Steve."

Steve smiled. "Yeah, very funny. I'm obviously a few beers behind." He raised his hand to catch Barney's attention.

The smiley redhead said, "You can have my seat. We're just leaving." She gathered her jacket and dropped a napkin with scribbles on it in front of Ron before they left.

"What's up with them?"

"They just flew in from Wisconsin for an adventure tour. They're in town for a couple of nights. Can I get you a drink?"

"Sure, what are you drinking, Yukon Gold?"

"Yeah, it's on me," offered Ron. Barney brought them the beer. Ron scrunched up the napkin with scribbles and handed it to him. Barney took it with a smirk.

"Cheers," said Ron as he raised his glass.

"Cheers," replied Steve. "By the way, why does Akiko call you Baby Kyle?"

"Baby Kyle? You do know Kyle was my uncle, right?" replied Ron.

"Yeah, I guess I do."

"Akiko says I look like him. She's not the only one. Even Meriwa's mother calls me Baby Kyle," explained Ron.

"So, you two really did look alike?"

"Yeah, but Kyle also taught me how to fix stuff and ride motocross. So, we had common interests. Kyle was a hell of a motocross rider."

"I thought he rode over a cliff."

"He didn't exactly just ride his Harley over a cliff. My father called him in the evening and told him about Kahului's accident. The next morning, he put his Harley sideways after skidding the back tire and putting it into a two-wheel slide. He raked all the parts off the left side. He stood on it and rode it like a surfboard right off the cliff. He did all that for the insurance company, for double indemnity, to prove it was an accident. My brother and I call him the six-million-dollar-man. Each of his three daughters got an extra buck for his final stunt. It was a six-million-dollar surfboard motocross Romeo-and-Juliet trick, just the sort of thing Uncle Kyle could pull off."

"You liked Kyle?" asked Steve.

"When my brother and I were little, Kyle was our hero. He fixed our dirt bikes. He gave us our first Ducati. He married my aunt, who my mother called the most beautiful woman in Indiana. When our family went to meet Alamea in Hawaii for the first time, we met Kahului, who was actually the hottest woman in Hawaii. Somehow Kyle, for all those years, managed to juggle Miss Indiana and Miss Hawaii–until, of course, one divorced him and the other died."

"It sounds complicated. It also sounds tragic." They ordered another round, before Steve asked, "What about Eddie? Why does he call you Hoosier Boy?"

"I've been wondering that myself. What are the chances that Eddie believes I really am Kyle?"

"I'd say it might depend on the time of day. If you ever managed to catch him in the morning, he might call you Ron."

There was a pause while they both drank Yukon Gold.

"When's the last time you saw Eddie in the morning?" asked Ron.

"Yeah, you're right. Eddie thinks you're Kyle."

37. Blackhat Whitehorse

The last morning before Meriwa and the gang returned, on their way to the Gold Rush Inn's desert gym, an RCMP vehicle passed by and slowed down. The officer locked eyes with Steve and a shiver of paranoia skittered up his spine. After the squad passed, Steve, in jest, referred to himself as a Blackhat in Whitehorse.

"Maybe so," replied Ron. "But Meriwa seems to be quite fond of you."

"Oh yeah?" responded Steve. "Well, Meriwa seems to be quite fond of you. For some reason, she called you capable."

"She said you're cut from a different cloth," retorted Ron.

"When she described the cloth did she use the word felon?" asked Steve, with a laugh.

"I think the word she used was courageous," answered Ron with a grin.

"Tell you what, how about we arm wrestle for her?" Steve proposed, with a laugh.

"That's a brilliant idea!" exclaimed Ron. "Let's do it tonight at The 98 Hotel."

"Okay," said Steve. "I have just one stipulation: you have to inform her about the results."

Ron laughed. "No way. The loser delivers the news. Just imagining her reaction is almost worth doing it."

As the persistent summer sun of the north began its descent, Ron and Steve climbed the Black Street Stairs. Ron ran the entire length, taking two steps at a time. Steve started jogging at a slow, steady pace for the first half before slowing to a walk. By the time Steve reached the top, Ron had caught his breath. They paused for several minutes to give Steve the chance to scan the airfield for any signs of alien spacecraft.

Once Steve had caught his breath, he led them north on Michael's favorite path. They reached the Confession Bench and Steve sat while Ron stood at the escarpment's edge and gazed across the city at Grey Mountain Summit before joining him.

"I was here last week with Meriwa," said Ron. "Do you know this bench is the place where Alamea first told Meriwa about me?"

Steve shook his head.

"Alamea showed Meriwa a picture of me and said the two of us would make great babies together."

Steve gazed at the city and listened to a pair of crows cawing to each other.

"Do you know I went to see Alamea in Seattle after her parents died?"

Steve shook his head.

"Alamea was reeling from losing both parents. That's when she still lived with Clyde, in Seattle. On the weekend, we rode down the Pacific Coast Highway, me on a rented Harley and her on her Ducati. We spent a couple of nights in Carmel-by-the-Sea. We brought the ashes of her parents and, from the Big Sur cliff where Uncle Kyle died, we scattered them on the sea."

Clouds crawled across Grey Mountain, stealing pieces of blue sky and cloaking the evening sun.

"We returned and my brother flew in to join us. Alamea took two days off work and it was just like old times. We walked the sidewalks of Seattle, arm-in-arm, just like the Three Musketeers."

Steve remained silent, as the river fell over the dams, skirted its way around the city, and flowed out of sight.

"I thought we would ride like that every summer," Ron continued. "Like she used to ride with her father, but we never did it again. She got married, and so on, and life went by."

Ron stood and looked toward the horizon, at the snow on Mount Lorne. He continued, "Before leaving Seattle, Alamea invited me to meet her in Alaska. She said I could come get her Ducati from Clyde's house and ride it to meet her there. A couple of weeks later, she called to discuss Meriwa. I asked, 'Is she like you?' Alamea said, 'We're different, but we are very good friends.' She described Meriwa as double tough and super sweet. She said, 'You know I wouldn't set up my favorite cousin with someone who wasn't a prize, right?' That's when I said, 'Yes,' and that was the last time I ever spoke with Alamea. That was the end."

Ron began walking. Steve followed him back along the trail, down the stairs, across town, and straight to Sheep Camp. They took a table before Steve broke the silence. "Kurt, two Vespers, please."

Meriwa and the crew made it back alive from Vancouver.

Just before 9 am on Thursday, July 28, Steve made his way up the stairs beside Bullet Hole Bagels. Upon entering, Angi rose from her desk in Reception and said, "Welcome to APF Therapy & Spa Center. May I offer you some coffee, sir?"

Steve played along. "Yes please, my lady. Cream, no sugar."

Angi looks fabulous. Still has librarian glasses, but the pantsuit is all Saks 5th Avenue.

Angi struck a pose and beamed like a full Sturgeon Moon when Steve complimented her hair and shoes. He accepted his coffee with a thank you and headed across the hall.

Akiko met him in the hall and walked alongside him. "Good morning, Captain Kirk."

"Lieutenant."

"I was wondering if you might know the time?"

"How would I know that?"

"Well, since you don't wear a watch, I thought you might refer to your phone, which leads me to my second question. Where is my little Mars Bar keeping his phone today?"

"Probably in my hotel room."

Akiko handed him his phone. "Oh really, that's why I found this ringing away in the reception area this morning? Do you think that might also explain why Meriwa just called my phone again and asked you to call her? I can't speak for Meriwa, but I, personally, find this particular foible of yours rather annoying. It's a recurring problem, perhaps because your women have done a shabby job of training you. So, tell you what I'm gonna do, Space Case. Tonight, I'll steal a fork from the hotel restaurant. The next time you forget your phone, I will stab you with it."

Akiko stopped but Steve kept walking as he chuckled nervously.

Akiko raised her voice and spoke to his back as he continued down the hall. "Please mention the training plan to Meriwa. I'm sure she'll appreciate the visual, next time she has to call me."

Steve smiled as he opened the door to the executive suite.

Snazzy Old Witch Stabs English Teacher with Fork.

In the reception area, Jessie, Lily, and Daisy giggled like girls at a slumber party. Same deal–they all looked like they'd just been hit with Meriwa's fashion wand. He complimented their professional attire and for several minutes traded banter. They soaked it in and regaled him with fascinating details about the shopping trip. Steve faded into his office, closed the door, set his coffee on the desk, took off his jacket, and hung it behind the door before surveying his office.

Finished, furnished, all mine . . . and finally, my own safe. Massive upgrade from the black spruce.

The night before, he had transferred two black soft-sided Harley trike cases from his hotel. They had been shabbily hidden and shuffled about for a year. Finally, they sat securely in a real safe. Coffee in hand, he sipped and watched the Yukon River flow to the Bering Sea.

The phone vibrated on his desk. "Congratulations on your new office," boomed Clyde.

"Thanks, and you were right about sending the crew to Vancouver. The entire lot is in the office today looking like they belong in Manhattan. Angi looks like the photographer from outer space. Daisy looks like she belongs onstage. Simon looks like he's ready to drive Miss Daisy. Jessie looks like she belongs on the cover of *Cosmo*. Massive upgrade."

"Can you get Angi to send me some photos?" Clyde requested.

"She's already taking them," assured Steve. "The entire team is in the office, dressed, polished, and queued up for picture day. Check the website later today. You'll see them all posted there."

38. Faded Poor Souvenirs

Meriwa appeared in Steve's office and found him speaking on the phone, peering out the window at afternoon raindrops splashing on the river. He turned and waved, holding up one finger. She hopped onto his desk, ankles crossed, wearing blue heels and a navy-blue suit as if she had just come from court. Steve finished his call. "Okay, Clyde, we'll speak tomorrow."

"Feeding the gossip machine?" she asked.

"Yep. When I say it's the least I can do, I mean it is *literally* the very least I can do."

She gave a slight nod and a quick smile and proceeded to recount her introduction of Ron to her parents. "Last night my mother told me it's time for me to make some babies."

"Sounds like they approve."

"Sure, but it's annoying as hell. I'd like to think the decision of who I make babies with and when I make them is mine."

"Is it?" Steve asked.

"Maybe," replied Meriwa as she examined her fingernails. "She does point out that Ron resembles his Uncle Kyle in more than just looks and that his genes are entirely recessive to mine."

Steve laughed. "That is truly an insight into her soul."

"Indeed," Meriwa said with a nod. "Speaking of my mother, she sends a message: 'Tell Steve he doesn't have to worry about anything. The spirits are with him.'"

"That's great."

Meriwa squinted her eyes, "Are you serious or are you being sarcastic?"

"Totally serious, and with the arrival of our first client this week, the timing couldn't be better. We can use all the help we can get. Tell your mother I said thank you."

"I will, and she will be pleased to hear that from you. She has supported you ever since Simon gave her a report about your extraordinary river speech."

Steve looked perplexed. "Really? I didn't know that."

Meriwa smiled playfully. "Absolutely. If Simon hadn't given my mother a positive report, the following morning at Burnt Toast Café, Tammy and I would have sat sipping lattes, watching my uncle arrest you."

"Wow, that would have sucked . . . for me, I mean."

"Yeah, and then we wouldn't have become friends. And then, who would have saved you from the river?" She flashed him a fetching smile with dimples.

Steve jutted out his chin and narrowed his eyes. "So that's what you think you're up to, saving me?"

Meriwa hopped off the desk and looked up at him. "In a way maybe. After all, you do find me attractive, right? And let's face it, Steve, at some point, you'll have to decide, will grief augment or stunt your heart?"

"Jane Hirshfield, the poet," said Steve. "I'm impressed. You tell me, Meriwa, how is grief working out for you?" He retreated a step and leaned against the windowsill.

Meriwa advanced. "It's easier for me. I will always love Alamea. I have no need to displace my love for her with another. I keep an indelible picture of her in my heart."

Steve said, "TS Eliot calls our recollections of those we love *the faded poor souvenirs of passionate moments*, but somehow you think your memories can last?"

"Souvenirs, yes; faded and poor, no," replied Meriwa as she looked up at him. "I'll treasure the memories of our moments forever. I don't need to displace them." She reached for his hand and pulled him toward her. "Pain is inevitable. Suffering is optional. Happiness is a choice. I choose to grieve Alamea's death while actively pursuing happiness. When you're ready, you can do the same."

Steve pulled his hand away and retreated. She inched closer. "What makes me sad is that I never got the chance to say goodbye to Alamea. At least with Emily, you were able to say goodbye."

"Goodbyes might not be all you imagine," Steve replied as he turned toward the window. "Emily had planned to die at noon on a Monday. Her pain was relentless, but she refused the morphine. The children were with her, and she wanted to be awake to say goodbye. The next morning, she said goodbye to her sister and me. I can't argue with her decision, but for me, the goodbye was not an experience I can recommend."

Meriwa slipped her arms around him from behind. He wiped his face with his sleeve and slid over to accommodate her. She stood beside him with her arm around him and her head pressed against his arm. They watched raindrops splash onto the surface of the Yukon River and flow to the Bering Sea.

39. Cosmic Butterflies

It was a clear, cool day in Whitehorse. Steve had gone for a hike in the morning and returned to his office mid-afternoon. In reply to a text, Clyde called. "We received final payment from client number four. Altogether, that is a total of four million dollars. I have paid out the sales commissions on the previous remittances, and here in front of me I have the commission check for the final remittance."

"I guess that's it," Steve replied with a sigh. "It's a go. We're on the hook."

"Most definitely. Are we ready?"

"We'll soon find out," replied Steve. "Tomorrow morning Akiko and Daisy are flying to Phoenix to pick up June, our first test bunny."

"Okay, and how is it going with our guru?"

"He usually rolls in mid-afternoon. I see him every day but not for long. I'm not actually sure what he does with his time. He says everything is ready, but I must admit, I'm kinda worried."

"We've never understood what Eddie does with his time, but this is the sort of thing he's actually good at. How is his mother doing? Still annoying as hell?"

Steve laughed. "Indeed, but you were right, she is surprisingly useful. Angi had her painting window trims last week."

"A surprisingly capable royal pain in the ass," Clyde said with a laugh. "Amazing for seventy-two, right?"

"Simon thinks so."

"Really? Simon and Akiko? Well, it has to be somebody, might as well be Simon."

"She has made a lot of friends," said Steve. "She started attending the Filipino Association. In fact, I met her new best friend, Ivonne."

"Let me guess, Ivonne's not married," replied Clyde with a laugh.

"How do you know that?"

"Akiko can never be friends with anyone who has a husband. Within a week she will have bagged him. Has she started the new Greenpeace chapter in Whitehorse yet?"

"She does seem to be hatching something with Ivonne. I'll have to inquire."

"How did you meet Ivonne?" asked Clyde.

"They were picking up trash early one morning on the riverwalk by Eddie's food trailer. Does that sound familiar?"

"Of course she's picking up trash in her free time," said Clyde. "Wait until I tell John. He'll laugh his ass off."

Steve hung up and returned to his window. On the riverwalk, a young mother jogged behind a stroller with an Alaskan Husky on a lead, heading downriver in the direction of the drops.

Gandhi's life was like the flapping of butterfly wings. It was a noble achievement to change the world, but changing the cosmos is a feat of an entirely different magnitude. Can the ripple effect of Gandhi's actions grow strong enough to spread like a solar wind and have a lasting impact on the cosmos?

Akiko's entrance shattered the moment, like a searing meteor bursting into the atmosphere. "Hey Space Case, what have you been up to today, besides looking out your porthole?"

"A little hiking, pondering the meaning of the universe, you know, the usual. Up to now, it's been a great day."

"Yoda, oh Yoda, do tell. What is the meaning of the universe?" asked Akiko with a snicker.

"I'm glad you asked. You may not know this, but our solar system is in a bit of a pickle and it's our job to save it. That's why we're here, you know, to do our part."

"Hocus fucking pocus. Go on, this should be good." Akiko sat in Steve's desk chair. She wore the smug smile of a twelve-year-old bully, as she swiveled back and forth.

Steve continued, "In just five-point-eight billion years, roughly six cosmic heartbeats, the sun will become a red giant. During the ensuing billion years it will vaporize Mercury, Venus and our own moon. Life will be wiped from Earth, but could flourish on other planets and moons, particularly Europa–the icy moon of Jupiter. Then, our sun will transform into a white dwarf and lose enough mass to possibly free some of its remaining planets, such as Jupiter and all her moons into outer space. As Elon has stated, for human survival, we must become interplanetary in a hurry. A lot could happen in the next six heartbeats.”

“Very interesting, Chewy,” said Akiko with her mischievous grin. “It does sound like quite the emergency, but you haven’t explained your own pivotal role in our quest to rescue mankind.”

“Since childhood, we dreamed of encountering spacemen, but reality is, life in the universe is rare. It’s quite possible that we will become spacemen before any spacemen discover us. If that’s the case, then it’s up to us to ensure that the spacemen we become are virtuous, not evil. That’s how the course of human history on Earth will potentially influence the course of the universe. It’s our job to ensure that our race is virtuous, so when the time comes, we will project virtue into space.”

“Very deep, Captain Kirk. I see why you require so much time to ponder these things. What would we possibly do without you?” She made a point of acting as though she were going to get up and hand him a note. “Have you considered what you are going to do when Mercury delivers the notice that your reality check has bounced?” She mockingly put her hand on her mouth in fake surprise, before settling back in Steve’s chair. “All this brings me to my real question: what do you think of this death camp business? I mean, since we’re actually doing it now, how do you really feel about helping these grannies hop off a plane?”

“I’m not sure their hop-offs are going to make the news in the *Galaxy Gazette*. Of course, there is the butterfly effect. I mean, Gandhi may not have become the force he was without the influence of his grandmothers. So, even though they are past the age of procreation, conceptually, the women could still have a lasting meaningful impact on the development of their grandkids.”

“Butterfly effect?” She laughed. “What is this, Marvin the fucking Martian? You don’t know shit about grandkids. The last things they need are grandparents. They have TikTok and volume controls on their earbuds. I can show you a video of one of the little darlings smashing an entire bucketful of your cosmic fucking butterflies. A grandma decides to hop off the planet ten seconds early. We help her. Yada, yada, gold star for us. There's nothing cosmic about it, Moonpie."

"Lucky you," said Steve, as he put on his jacket. "It doesn't sound like you'll be suffering any psychological damage from the granny deaths."

"Moonpie, you don't know how funny that is."

40. Sun Tzu Wants You

Steve invited Meriwa on the Three Mile River Walk. She suggested the Black Street Stairs.

"Sure. How about I swing by your place at 6 pm?" suggested Steve.

He was ten minutes early and sat in the front-back-yard playing with Juneau while waiting. He petted the slobbering, jumping, crazy dog, and threw sticks.

How will she climb the stairs in three-inch heels?

Meriwa appeared, looking for the first time as though she actually lived in Whitehorse. She wore two long black braids, gray running shoes instead of heels, black Lycra pants, a green sweatshirt, and no jewelry.

"Hello, Angel. I'm ready."

"Hello, Devil. You do look ready, but no watch?"

"No, why?"

"May I see it?"

Meriwa smiled, disappeared into the apartment and returned. She handed over Alamea's watch with a somber expression. He held it, weighed it, squeezed it, flipped it over, read the inscription: *Happy Graduation, Mea Pie. Love, Clyde.*

After holding it in his hand for a moment longer, he tilted his head and looked soberly at her. "I know this watch."

He handed it back to her and she held it for a moment before saying, "I know this watch too." She hesitated and then surprised him by swinging her arms over his shoulders, giving him a kiss on the cheek, and hugging him again hard. "Thank you, Steve," she whispered in his ear.

Steve squeezed her for an extra moment. "What's that smell? Your perfume?"

As she pulled away, she smiled sweetly. "Roses. It was in Alamea's things. I started wearing it. You recognize it?"

"Somehow, yes."

Meriwa squeezed Steve's hand as she walked past him, went inside, and returned without the watch.

"Does Juneau come too?" asked Steve.

"On the escarpment? Never! He'll go nuts and pull us right over the edge."

Meriwa led the way through city streets, west-by-southwest, away from the river. At the bottom of the Secret Rope Trail, they turned north, skirting along the path at the foot of the escarpment. After a stint of walking in silence, Steve asked, "Have I ever told you about my recurring nightmare?"

"You mentioned Emily dreams, but never nightmares."

"When I walk along the escarpment," Steve explained as he motioned toward the trees, "I always imagine that a grizzly will charge and attack from one of these little forest paths. You know, a vengeful cousin."

The pace was leisurely. Meriwa was uncharacteristically quiet.

"Really, it's the reason I don't walk this way very much. Ever since, you know . . . and twice I've dreamt about it."

They strode silently side-by-side along the escarpment, north toward Black Street, until Steve continued, "She was so brave right to the end. She was more concerned about my safety than her own. Last week when I saw her watch on your wrist, it took me back to the moment she handed it to me and made me promise to take it for you. It was a very heavy promise."

Meriwa slipped her hand into his and held his tricep with the other, pressing tight against him as they walked, causing him to shudder and squeeze her hand.

She smiled and looked up at him. "You know, Steve, there are four things I like about you. First, you were with Alamea that night and you sang to her. You were her angel. That was so sweet, and it means more to me than you can imagine."

Steve squeezed her hand. She pressed tighter against him. "Second, you shot the bear. Alamea was a powerful woman, yet she chose you for your courage. For all of us who knew her, that was one hell of an endorsement. It's the reason you are here with us today."

Steve squeezed her hand again.

"Third, you think I'm attractive, but you don't actually chase me. I find that rather amusing."

Why would the dog chase a bus? What if he caught it? What would he do with it?

Steve offered no confirmation of having heard "third."

"Fourth, you are a good listener."

She's using urban warfare tactics–lob a grenade, wait for the explosion, advance quickly.

Steve looked straight ahead and squeezed her hand again–he had heard "fourth."

As they walked, he could feel her breast against his arm, but on the outside, he was doing his best to channel fuzz, the kind you wake up to at 3 am when you fall asleep watching TV.

Meriwa continued to amuse herself, like a cat that has cornered a mouse. "Alamea wasn't prone to thoughtless acts. We have to assume she acted purposefully," she said, looking up at him and catching his eye. "Have you ever considered that she sent you to me? That the reason she chose you was so you would come here and meet me, you know, like as my plan B? Or maybe she wanted a belt-and-suspenders approach applied to the implementation of her business plan. Maybe you were sent to be the suspenders."

Steve looked away.

Run? Hide? Definitely duck.

"Or maybe she was offering me as a prize to the man who saved her from the bear," Meriwa said, smiling coyly and clearly enjoying the moment.

Steve tried to derail the conversation. "Maybe she wanted me to help with her business."

"Don't be naive, Steve," she said as she pinched the inside of his bicep.

No response goes unpunished.

She looked up quizzically at him, trying to catch his eye. "Alamea and I used to discuss the matter of assigning roles. Sun Tzu said, 'A skillful woman knows how to choose the perfect man for the perfect role.' What's the perfect role for you, Steve? For what shall I use you?"

He looked straight ahead.

The quote is a twist. The question is surely rhetorical.

"Welcome to my swamp, right this way, wade right in."

She smiled with satisfaction, squeezed his hand, and nudged his shoulder with her braid, goading him. Still, he ignored the question. In silence, they walked hand-in-hand, with Meriwa pressing against Steve's arm, all the way to the Black Street Stairs. At the bottom of the stairs Steve said, "Girls first, except for stairs, revolving doors, and sometimes bar entrances." He headed up the stairs ahead of her, and she paced herself politely behind.

At the top, Steve paused for a full minute to catch his breath while Meriwa peered through the chain link fence, pretending to watch planes land even though none were. Without a word, he led until they reached a clearing on the path, three-quarters of the way to the Confession Bench.

She stopped and exclaimed, "This is the tree!"

He retraced the path back to her. The tree was a lone white pine, mature and stately, scarred along the back side. It stood alone with the most remarkable view of just a piece of the city below, like one was peering through a small window framed by black spruce and aspen, a window with a view created just for this white pine.

Meriwa leaned against the Kissing Tree with a hand on it. The scent of pine and spruce was heavy in the still warm air.

"Years ago, when Alamea and her father visited, my mother made fresh cinnamon buns with raisins for us. I remember the smell of saffron and raisins as she served them hot, right out of the oven. Alamea called them Honey Bunnies. I don't know how she came to that exactly, but my mother loved the name.

"On the first morning of her recent visit, we met at my apartment. I had a picnic breakfast in my backpack. It was early and we made the hike. When we got to this spot, I stopped her. I took her by both hands. Alamea smiled at me, you know, that sweet smile. I kissed her. I kissed her like we used to kiss. She kissed me back and pulled me into her arms. She was so powerful and strong. She hugged me like she could save me from a hurricane."

Meriwa led the way to the Confession Bench. "My mother always supported my relationship with Alamea. She told me that if I wanted to marry her, I should do it, but to carry on the tradition of our family, children were required. That was the issue. Alamea did not want children, you know?"

"No, I had no idea about that," replied Steve.

Meriwa sat on the near side of the bench and motioned for Steve to sit to her left. "Alamea felt abandoned when her father died and didn't want to do the same to anyone. She wanted to be free to leave whenever she pleased."

Leave?

"On that morning, we sat here with the backpack between us. I served her warm Honey Bunnies and coffee. She told me she had always loved me, and I was still her choice. She said there was someone she wanted me to meet, *a solution*, she called it. You know, to satisfy my desire for a family. She told me about Ron and showed me a picture.

I asked her, 'what about you?' She told me, 'I can be your side dish.'"

Steve looked across Grey Mountain far above the city, checking for cracks in the sky above Mount Lorne.

"I almost cried. I told her, yes. Yes, to everything. I told her she was never my side dish, she was my love, my confidante. It's true. We told each other everything . . . everything except goodbye."

Meriwa's breathing was heavy and deliberate.

"The last time I saw Alamea, the night before she left, we sat on this bench again."

Meriwa stopped. She looked directly at Steve. A tear ran down her cheek as she said, "I mean, the second-to-last time, you know, because I identified her, after . . ."

Steve took her hand and gave it a squeeze.

"On her last night, Alamea told me that she had said goodbye to her grandparents, but never to either of her parents. She told me both of her parents' deaths were tragic, but her father's was the most painful because he chose to leave her without saying goodbye. She told me the business idea was her plan for fixing it, for others, so they would have a way to say goodbye. I promised her I would help when she returned."

He held her hand and watched a tear trickle slowly down her face, while she watched the river. As far as sad faces go, hers was painfully beautiful. She stood, released his hand, and he followed. As they made their way past the Kissing Tree, Meriwa zigged off the path, pressed her hand on the tree, and zagged back. They descended the stairs and, with a cool breeze in their faces, walked toward the city center.

When they arrived, they took a seat across from one another. Steve was the first to break the silence. "Kurt, two Vespers, please."

189

41. The Abduction

Daisy and Akiko traveled to Phoenix to meet June. They drove up a long, paved driveway to the mansion on the hill. At the door, they were greeted by the housekeeper, who led them to the back garden where they found June, her daughter Beth, and a friend of Beth's sitting under a canopy at a poolside table.

Daisy introduced Akiko, who explained the itinerary. "Don't worry about what you will wear, or toiletries and makeup. When you arrive, gorgeous clothes will be waiting for you. You'll be changing outfits throughout each day–for the video productions, of course. If you have any requests, your personal assistant will be ready to serve you."

"Each day with us will include three things," continued Akiko. "Adventure, spa treatments, and therapy sessions. You'll be dressed, fed, served, and treated like royalty. You'll feel amazing and look spectacular. It's going to be the trip of your lifetime, June. You'll love it, and then you'll leave it. Are you ready for that?"

"Mom, she's asking if you want to go on this trip?"

"Quit treating me like an invalid, Beth. Of course I'm going. I didn't pay a million dollars to back out now."

Daisy opened her tablet and placed it on the table in front of them. "Let's go over the legacy blog. Yesterday I sent this link to each person listed in the introduction survey. As I explained in the email, this is the blog that will document the most fascinating moments of June's Wilderness Adventure. Every adventure is unique. Some of the possible activities include rafting the Yukon River, flying over the peaks of Mount Logan, and hiking in the forests and along the Yukon River near Whitehorse. We'll also roast marshmallows around a campfire at luxury cabins on Tagish Lake."

Daisy paused and took a drink of water before continuing. Leaning forward, she addressed June directly. "Whitehorse is a popular destination. The restaurants are great, and every day you can decide where you want to eat. Our state-of-the-art Therapy & Spa Center, including our team of therapists and spa experts, will cater to your every need. Photos and videos of all these experiences will be uploaded to your personal Wilderness Adventure Legacy Blog. Tonight, our team will meet us at the airport in Whitehorse, and you will be taken to the hotel by private limousine." Daisy turned toward Beth. "You should be able to see the first blog post tonight before 7 pm." Beth gave a small nod of agreement.

"What about my Facebook followers?" asked June. "We need extra photos at the cabins and of the catered food, you know like the ones on the adventure page."

"We'll handle that for you," explained Daisy. "We'll help you update your Facebook and Instagram accounts several times each day. Your followers will enjoy reading about your adventure, and each of your social media posts will refer to your Legacy Blog. It will generate a mountain of likes."

June smiled and looked at Beth, who was nodding reassuringly. Beth touched Daisy's hand and said, "June wants her friends to remember her for her charity work and gala dresses. That's why we need to make sure we publish an article about her Wilderness Adventure in the *Arizona Republic* newspaper. I have a contact there. Can you arrange that for her?"

"Sure," replied Daisy. "If you already have a contact, maybe we can score two consecutive newspaper articles. The first can be about June's Wilderness Adventure and explain her Perfect Finish choice and the second can be the obituary, presented as a follow-up story. For both, we can insert links to June's Legacy Blog. Why not discuss it tomorrow with Angi, our Public Relations expert? If you're available at 10 am, we could call you."

Beth and June were smiling like the cameras were already flashing. "I'll contact my friend today to check," said Beth.

Daisy continued speaking to June. "About your Legacy Blog, there are two parts: a public section and a private section. Each invitee you designated has been sent a unique password. Throughout every day, you will have opportunities to record as many private messages as you wish."

"June, do you remember when we discussed Canada's MAID law?" asked Daisy.

"You explained it to me last time," June replied.

"I'm mentioning it now because I want to emphasize that it's my job to ensure we comply right up to the end," explained Daisy. "Throughout your adventure, I will continue to present you with a choice about whether you wish to proceed. If you change your mind at any point, we will immediately arrange your return and escort you home, where Beth will meet us. Do you understand the system, June?"

"Yes, I do," June replied with a nod.

"Beth, do you understand the system and are you committed to meeting us here upon our return, if necessary?" asked Daisy.

"I understand, and of course I will meet you here, because I'll be living here. We're moving in this weekend," she said as she exchanged glances with her friend.

"Oh, okay then," continued Daisy, skipping just one beat, before continuing. "Here is the document certifying that I have explained these terms to you today." She laid out the documents and June and Beth's friend signed them. June thanked the friend and looked expectantly at Daisy.

"Are you ready?" asked Daisy.

June stood, smiled, and held out her arms. "TTFN, Beth."

Beth and June hugged, and exchanged cheek kisses, as if it were just a weekend getaway. June turned to leave. "Come on, Daisy Flower."

As Daisy and Akiko departed with June, Beth asked the housekeeper for a pitcher of skinny palomas, causing Daisy to look twice. The women walked back to the table together. They were definitely holding hands.

Moving in this weekend? Holding hands? The witness has nothing to gain? Test case one, and already a pang of doubt.

✳ ✳ ✳

That morning, Steve had spoken to Emily while kayaking the river in town. The children had not called him. He explained his concerns and she listened.

He stood at his office window, watching the river. In the distance, his phone rang. He dashed to his jacket hanging behind the door, fumbled through a pocket, and found it just in time to answer.

"How's it going with Daisy and Akiko?" asked Clyde. "Have they completed their first induction meeting?"

"Great. Daisy just returned with the package. Akiko coined the meeting *the Abduction*," Steve replied.

"That's kind of funny. I mean funny to you, me, and Akiko, but let's not use that term around John."

"No," said Steve. "I try to avoid saying anything funny around John."

"Is the team ready?" asked Clyde.

"You know, amazingly so," said Steve. "The Therapy & Spa Center might not qualify as prime-time in Paris, but it has definitely become the nicest spa in the Yukon. Marian has been flashing her cameras like a paparazzi pro. The therapists and makeup team just can't wait to put Hollywood smiles on clients. Daisy is dying to do her very first MAID death. Eddie is looking forward to rubbing some new people the wrong way. I would say they're ready to launch some real stars. It's almost as though nobody got the memo mentioning the word death."

"You didn't mention Harold," Clyde prodded.

"I see Harold in his office every day," replied Steve, "but we don't talk much. If he could figure out how to get clients himself, he wouldn't need me. Good thing he has never met Liz."

"Have you spoken to Liz lately?" asked Clyde.

"Yeah, I spoke to her today. She gave me the low-down on Michael's rugby game and sent me the schedule for Rachel's debates. Michael scored a try and they won."

"That's great news, glad to hear it. So, they still haven't called you?"

"No, but that's not unusual. They are teenagers, you know. They are busy."

"Well, I'm sure they'll call you soon," said Clyde in his soothing manner.

"Thanks. You asked about Liz. She's already thinking ahead to next season. She has six salespeople to sign up under master agreements before we've even managed to test the first rat. If we agree to the new structure, she can blow the organization out to three multi-level-marketing tiers within a month. She wants to double the sales commission, so it pays a total of three hundred thousand dollars per sale. The first level commission will be one hundred fifty thousand, the second level will be one hundred thousand, and the third level will be fifty thousand."

"That wrecks our margins though, right?" cut in Clyde.

"Liz suggests that we double our fee to two million dollars to accommodate the increase," replied Steve. "She thinks that the more we charge, the less backlash we'll suffer during the tsunami, because the public never sympathizes with the rich. She also thinks that anyone who can afford to pay a million to jump out of a plane would die to pay double."

"Tell her to do it now so we can sign up the sales team and start booking clients for next year," said Clyde.

"What ever happened to doing the first year on a trial basis?"

"Don't worry, John will draft the sales agent and client agreements to include an escape clause. We'll make sure everyone can run for the Alaskan hills if things go south."

42. June Twenty-Nine

I've always been a bad flyer. I remember accompanying my little children, Beth and Larry, after the divorce to visit their father in Virginia. Before takeoff, I took three doses of Xanax, and upon arrival my ex found us wandering around looking for the luggage carousel. Of course, he never missed an opportunity to remind me of my finest moments. He was a real bastard and, it pains me to say, his son is no better–a real chip off the old block. A year later, I dropped little Larry off at the airport with a one-way ticket to Virginia. His father had found him a spot at one of the finest military schools in the country.

So, it's odd that I somehow overlooked the not-so-perfect flying aspect of A Perfect Finish. For that first flight to the cabins, the mushrooms definitely helped. I had never tried them before. When Eddie first offered, I refused. That was before the first massage.

He was a dark, handsome man with the body of Adonis, strong hands, and streaks of gray in his long black hair. He claimed to be a guru and spoke in surfer boy cliches, yet he gave a massage as though he knew his way around a woman's body. As he rubbed my shoulders, he put it in front of my face, and I touched it. I took it out and sucked it. It became impossibly huge. That first day, Eddie fucked me long and hard, and every morning thereafter–except when we were at the cabins-he gave me a daily dose. At the cabins, I kept hoping he would come, wondering where he was, who he was rubbing. Sex was an unpromised, over-delivered aspect of the service that was not documented on the company's website. I wondered if I should suggest updating Eddie's profile to Angi.

Before I made the trip, I had quit dating because it seemed like every date was about my money. The pool boys had been an easy solution, but I hadn't hired one since my diagnosis. There was definitely a hollow place inside me that needed filling. Eddie was no ordinary pool boy. The shrooms were transformative, and combined with sex, they were literally out of this world. During the second week, while getting our nails done, I discussed the service with another customer. She felt the same about Eddie. With a laugh, she suggested the company revise not just Eddie's bio, but also his picture. Later that day, I asked Daisy Flower what kind of vitamins Eddie was taking, and she pretended not to understand.

As a passenger, the mushrooms were definitely more effective than Xanax. Still, in a little bush plane, the water takeoffs and landings were terrifying. While at the cabins, I shared my fear with Akiko. She even suggested, for the kids' benefit, to make it look like an accident. "The beauty of purchasing a Wilderness Adventure is that you'll have plenty of opportunities to die. Choose the one that's best for you," she advised.

In high school, I was captain of my swim team and had always been like a fish in water. Looking at the schedule, I noticed a river tour with a write-up that described Miles Canyon as a breathtaking location with a rich history. When we hiked over the bridge, I looked down and found my perfect place.

43. Bird on the Wire

As the first Sojourner, June was almost perfect. She was remarkably photogenic; the makeup, hair and wardrobe team had her looking like Jane Fonda. Collectively, the action shots, combined with the photos from the Therapy & Spa Center generated enough content to support the first special interest piece that Beth and Angi created for the *Arizona Republic* newspaper article.

Steve walked into the WWM offices and found Angi working at her desk. "Hello Angi, got a minute?"

Angi smiled at Steve, beaming like a full Harvest Moon. "Sure, Steve, always for you. Did you see the blog posts and the article in today's *Arizona Republic*?"

"Great stuff. Did Daisy purposely choose June as the first client based on her looks?" asked Steve.

"We discussed the matter in advance," replied Angi. "Daisy said that June would make the best model of the four."

"Well done, and how did it go at the cabins?" asked Steve.

"Pretty well," replied Angi, "except June didn't like the flight much."

"Really? Is that going to be a problem, I mean, in the end?"

"Daisy spoke with her about it this evening. June assured Daisy it's not going to be a problem."

Steve asked about tomorrow's agenda and Angi explained they would be touring Miles Canyon, and that Harold would lead the water tour because his son was unavailable.

Angi changed the subject. "Did you see the login rate for June's blog?" Angi went on to explain that it was huge; there had been five hundred twenty-three visitors, including family, friends, college and high school classmates, and wealthy donors from June's fancy charity work.

"If I made an invitation list it would be like . . . ten people," replied Steve.

"Yeah, but our clients are not like you and me," explained Angi. "They've spent their entire lives trying to outdo their glamorous friends. They are here to prove that conspicuous consumption is not just for the living. Have you seen June's Facebook profile? She has over eight thousand followers."

"I thought we were using the Legacy Blog. Why are you mentioning her Facebook?"

"Are you kidding? What do you think we're doing all day while June is frolicking about the Klondike and lounging around the Therapy & Spa Center? We're preparing a continuous stream of Facebook posts to drive traffic to the APF public blog. We give her a tablet ten times a day, and she continuously posts to her profile. Have you seen the amazing shots of her hiking Miles Canyon today? Her reaction to the stunning scenery is priceless."

"Sure, nice nature shots, but why such a huge interest?" Steve asked as he leaned against her desk.

"Because what we're doing is insane," Angi said with a grin. "Think about it, Steve. Who among us would not log in to see the hottest, most successful, rich bitch from their high school prepare to drop out of a plane? In Phoenix, June is a public figure, and now she's become a public spectacle—the bird on the wire—and this story has legs. Remember the tsunami?"

"Yeah. You think we're going to blow ourselves up before we even get started?"

"It's possible. The comments are spilling over to the public part of the site already. Since the campfire at Tagish Lake on Sunday, we've gained over three thousand new active users."

Steve looked over Angi's shoulder to see her computer screen. "Really? From where?"

"The website has no search recognition," explained Angi. "The only possible sources at this point are personal references from June's original list, her Facebook, plus referrals from the newspaper article. Aside from that, we are now receiving referral visits from TikTok and YouTube. I'm not saying this is going viral yet, but it is beginning to attract a high level of interest, especially considering we started from zero."

"What are we doing to funnel leads to Liz?" asked Steve.

"I brought the new APF lead form live yesterday. Liz already called me. In just one day, she already has two qualified leads from the form. That's just from three days of blog posts for a single client."

Steve sat. "Really?"

"Yep," said Angi, as she swiveled away from her monitor to face Steve. "And can you imagine the impact of this traffic and referrals on our search rankings?"

"What do you think?" asked Steve.

Angi beamed like a full Hunter's Moon. "Remember I told you we shouldn't count on search rankings for the first year? Well, if we get similar login and referral rates for the next three clients, we will likely hit the first page of organic listings in a month. That's my prediction."

"Which search terms?"

"Death with dignity. MAID. Assistance-in-Dying. Yukon adventures. Miles Canyon."

"Are you serious? You think we can achieve search recognition for search terms not directly related to assistance-in-dying?"

"We will, not because we deserve them, but because all the other non-FunBite companies in the Yukon really suck when it comes to search marketing. We're going to kick their asses right off page-one search results. Pretty soon, anyone looking for a plumber in the Yukon is going to find *A Perfect Finish* listed first in the organic listings."

"Go, Angi, go!"

As Steve left Angi's office, Akiko was waiting for him. She followed him as he walked toward his own office. "Hi Han Solo, baby, how's it hanging?"

"Akiko, that's unprofessional."

"No Han, unprofessional is losing your fucking phone every day and turning me into your little telephone bitch. You're lucky someone snatched the fork out of my desk drawer."

Steve entered his office and started looking around, patting his pockets.

"I have a message from your praying mantis," continued Akiko with a smirk.

"Who?"

"Who do you think? Princess Fucking Leia. She says she'll meet you at 5 pm at Kind Café."

44. Mighty Jupiter

Steve arrived at Kind Café just before 5 pm to find Meriwa already there, sitting in the corner among the floral pillows, wearing a short skirt, a low cut teal sweater, and the watch. She was reading a legal file and already halfway through a latte.

"Hello, Devil. You look ravishing," Steve greeted her with a smile.

"Hello, Angel. How was your day?" Meriwa asked in her sweet alto voice.

"According to Marian, things are going swell," Steve said as he took the seat across from her.

"As long as Angi is in charge, I'm sure they are," Meriwa said, pointing to the counter. "That's yours. Double espresso, right?"

"Meriwa buys Steve coffee. That's a first!" Steve exclaimed, his smile growing as he made his way to the counter. On the way back, he brought the cup to his nose and inhaled the rich aroma. Meriwa stacked her papers and slid them into her bag.

"Tell me, Devil," inquired Steve. "What are your plans for tonight?"

She smiled coyly. "Is that an offer? Did you have something special in mind?"

"Well, no, but I could have. I mean, you are always so busy, but if you're free, we could do something."

"That's sweet," she said as she patted his hand. "But since you asked, I'm dining with my mother this evening. What about you?"

"Same old boring. I'll eat alone, go for a walk, do some reading, and go to bed early."

"Why not give Tammy a call? You obviously like her ass, and she's plainly keen."

"Calling Tammy is not something I've considered, exactly."

Meriwa smiled wickedly at him. "Poor Steve. Your blue balls say go, and your head says no. What are you going to do?"

"For now, umm, I'm going with no."

"Angel, so decisive. You know Alamea and I had an open relationship. Boys would come and boys would go, it didn't matter, no jealousy. Why would the main course be jealous of the appetizer, right?"

Steve bit his lower lip and smiled a little. "Or the dessert."

"Is that what you see yourself as, Steve, the dessert?"

"Well, no," he backtracked as his face flushed.

She tilted her head and nodded, before taking a sip and placing the cup on the table. "I suppose we shall see."

Steve drained his espresso cup as a ruse to avoid replying.

"Tell you what I'm going to do, Steve. I'm going to offer you a safe word. Would you like that?"

"I don't know. I can't say I've ever needed one. For what?"

"Never needed one? And you imagine, around me, precedence applies?" Meriwa laughed. "Let's say, it's for . . . for banter. If you want me to stop or even just go a little easier on you, just say the word: *Uncle*. Go ahead, say it."

"No."

"I see. We're on then. Would you like to walk?" she invited as she stood and gathered her things.

"Sure," he said as he rubbed both eyes. He stood, took the empty cups hostage, and fled with them to the dish cart.

Oh, my God. What if I just make a run for it?

Meriwa took Steve's hand as they left the café and walked toward the river. A cool breeze and a slight mist enveloped them as they waited for the light at First Avenue. The threatening sky made her shiver. He wrapped his arm around her and nuzzled her neck. She tilted her head and offered her ear. He whispered, "You smell like a rose."

She caught his eye and smiled sweetly. "I wore it for you. I knew you would notice."

The light changed and they walked hand-in-hand toward the river in silence. As they passed the Whitehorse Visitor Center, he savored the warmth of her grip and craved another whiff of her perfume.

Meriwa began, "Alamea was all about schools. The world was her ocean. When we went to a bar together, she called the men sand sharks, behaving as though we were their prey. By morning snack time, they would learn: orcas school sand sharks for sport."

Steve smiled but kept his head down as they headed toward the water. The river sirens, cloaked in a mantle of mist, exuded a musky aroma of pine and echoed a steady tempo of the rapids, enticing those with a discerning spirit.

Meriwa continued, "Alamea slept eleven nights in Whitehorse–the last ten with me."

Mighty Jupiter still orbits Alamea, yet herself commands eighty moons, the four Galileans as large as small planets.

Meriwa paused and tugged on Steve's hand, leading them to the river's edge, where they gazed into the dangerous current and listened to the mesmerizing beat. "On her final night, Alamea checked the weather to see how it would be for their ride. She undressed except for the pearls. She put on a pair of her mother's three-inch gray Gucci heels with straps and, pointing to an imaginary map, mimicked Kahului's routine as she presented the Whitehorse weather report."

Meriwa smiled in amusement, reminiscing as though Steve were not there. She fiddled with her phone before taking Steve's hand and leading him north along the river in misty rain. They walked in silence–like a couple–toward his hotel in the direction of the drops. Steve listened to the throbbing of his racing heart and tried to breathe normally, but his hands were sweating.

Who could blame Europa for feeling dizzy, circling Jupiter four-times faster than Callisto?

Her voice softened to fine worn silk. "She had intended to leave in the morning. Instead, they wasted the day in a pointless quarrel. At 8 pm, Alamea called to say goodbye. I begged her not to ride at night. I warned her against traveling with Mark. I invited her to stay with me instead, to be mine forever."

Steve squeezed her hand, pretending not to see the tears she wiped away. Maybe she was the fragile one–it was hard to know, with all her antics. They walked on until they reached his hotel where Simon was waiting with the Benz.

Meriwa faced Steve, rose up on her toes, and put her arms around his neck. As she kissed his cheek, she whispered, "Thank you, Angel."

Simon opened the back door for her. Steve could feel her tears on his cheek and a pain in his stomach as he watched Simon drive her away, up Main Street and south on Second Avenue.

45. Gumption and Guile

On Wednesday, Simon drove Angi and June to the boat launch on Schwatka Lake. During the fifteen-minute drive, June told Angi about her daughter's engagement. Upon arrival, Simon removed Angi's equipment from the trunk and escorted them to the dock.

Harold started the Zodiac. Simon assisted the women with their life jackets and gave Angi a hand getting into the boat. The three of them assisted June to the front, where she perched on the seat at the bow. Angi took a seat at the stern and Harold manned the captain's seat. Angi unpacked her cameras as Simon pushed the Zodiac away from the dock. Simon waved and smiled as the Zodiac turned and headed upriver toward Miles Canyon.

✳ ✳ ✳

Akiko found Steve in his office at his window, studying the drops and the pedestrians on the riverwalk.

"You're not going to find June that way, Moonshine, on account of the dams," Akiko informed him, as she stood in his doorway with her hands on her hips.

"Hello, Akiko. To what do I owe the pleasure?"

"You haven't even heard about it yet, have you?"

"Heard what?" inquired Steve as he turned to face her.

"June did a header," replied Akiko with a smirk.

"June where? Header how? Akiko, say whatever it is you are trying to say."

"Okay, I'll slow down for you, Moonbeam," Akiko replied with a carnival clown grin. "June, our very first client, remember her? She's the one scheduled for our little Wednesday boat ride photoshoot. Today during the return ride, under the bridge at Miles Canyon, she removed her life jacket, stood up on her seat, put her hands over her head, and flipped over backwards into the swirly currents. She sank to the bottom of the Yukon River and has not been seen since.

"Is that specific enough for you or do we need to show you the video? Because if you want to see the video, that's not going to be a problem. Angi captured the whole damn scene. She even has the sound effects with our very own Captain Kangaroo booming away, 'June, please sit down. What are you doing? June, don't do it. You're going to wreck my business. You stupid cunt, how could you fucking do this to me?' I've just watched the entire video. Harold's opera voice in the background, pleading like Othello, is the icing on the cake. Angi said she can add some background music. If you want a video that could knock it out of the awards-park on YouTube, this could be the one."

Steve rested his hands on his desk for balance. "Have they found the body? Is she dead? Are they searching?"

"The RCMP are there now with search and rescue and a Canadian Broadcasting Corporation camera team. The story is going to be on this evening's news. Daisy says they won't find the body until it begins to decompose. Then it will rise to the surface, hopefully above the damn dam."

Steve ran his hands through his hair. "Oh no. How long will that take?"

"Given the temperature of the water, Daisy predicts three days. Until then, our esteemed company will be the number one story in the Yukon. We're probably even going to earn a mention on Canada's national news."

"That sounds distinctly bad." He lowered himself into his chair.

"Distinctly bad? That's the sort of reply I'd expect to get from C-3PO. Distinctly bad? In terms of what? In terms of going zero-for-one on our execution of granny executions? Or in terms of having just distinguished our fine company in the press with the reporting of a horrific accident in the Yukon wilderness? Or in terms of pissing off the local government by trashing their accident ratings? Or in terms of the entire June Legacy Blog turning into a raging fire tornado?"

"Yeah, distinctly bad, in terms of all those things."

"Comet Cutie, you're killing me," Akiko said with a sardonic smile. "I wish we could get this entire conversation on video. The look on your English teacher's face is priceless, and somehow, I'm the only one here who is not surprised. I mean, Simon and me. We could have told you this was going to happen."

"Hold it. What are you saying?" asked Steve.

"Yeah, we knew it," explained Akiko as she raised her left hand and examined the dark red paint on her nails. "June told me at the cabins she hates flying and doesn't want to jump out of a plane. When she learned that I sell life insurance, she told me she has a double indemnity clause on her policy."

Akiko examined the nails of her other hand as she continued. "She told me it would be much better if her death was an accident, not a suicide. All I had to do from there was look at the next opportunity."

Satisfied with the state of her nail polish, Akiko looked up, smiled sweetly at Steve, and placed her hands on her hips again. "When she returned from the hike without hopping over a cliff, Simon paid me a dollar. When she did the header from the Zodiac, Simon paid me another dollar."

"Akiko, are you fucking kidding me? Are you telling me you knew this was going to happen and never told me?"

Akiko had just won two bucks but after seeing Steve's response, she grinned like she had won the lottery. "It was just a hunch. If Simon and I thought your uptight Jabberwocky ass were interested in betting, we would have cut you in on the action. The fact is, June paid good money to die in any manner she pleased. If she's scared of flying, why should she fly?"

Steve tried to interrupt, but Akiko raised her hand and continued, "And if I had told you, you probably would have made me go along with her on the hike *and* the boat ride. Then it would be me in the video, looking like a Japanese Charlie Chaplin with June dragging my skinny ass with her into the cold river, and today you would have double the trouble."

"Akiko, please stop. Find Angi. Bring her here."

"Sure, but then how will you see the news coverage? Your Space Mountain window isn't a computer screen. Wouldn't it be better to just moonwalk next door?"

Clyde let out a deep sigh. "Meriwa already filled me in on the details. She sent me the link to the live video. She's been busier than a hen in a foxhole, speaking with the mayor, the county commissioner, and the Mounties."

"Yeah, I haven't been able to get a hold of Meriwa because I had a little mishap with my phone," Steve replied with a nervous chuckle. "But I have been hanging out with Angi. She combined footage of June doing various adventure activities with another video of June's farewell message, explaining how APF is the best choice she could have made for a dignified death. In the blog, Angi is presenting June's improvisation as a mission accomplished."

This piqued Clyde's interest. "Really? So, how has the response been?"

"Surprisingly positive," replied Steve. "The thing I hadn't expected was the donation pitch that Angi cut in at the end of the farewell video. Instead of sending flowers, June asked people to contribute to FunBite. Amazingly, it's working like a charm."

"Angi created the donation video in advance?" asked Clyde in disbelief. "I thought she scheduled that for the end of the second week."

"I thought so too," replied Steve, "but it turns out our cunning Marian the Librarian captured the footage on June's very first day. June now has over a thousand unique active users logging into her private blog and over eight thousand logging into the public site. From those, FunBite already has over fourteen-hundred donations exceeding a total of one hundred thousand dollars."

"That's way more than ten dollars," Clyde said with a lilt.

"I knew that was coming," replied Steve with a fake laugh. "At our original meeting, I wrote off this fundraising idea as a complete waste of time. But in just four hours, Angi has ramped it into six figures. She thinks donations could grow by a factor of four-to-six times by next week after Beth hosts all June's fancy society friends at a remembrance ceremony in Phoenix."

"Unbelievable!" exclaimed Clyde. "What does Harold say about the dunk-a-granny SNAFU?"

"He's been trying to coerce Daisy into documenting it as a MAID death, but she's having none of it," said Steve. "Daisy says if she wasn't actually there, no assistance was given, and Harold is going to have to deal with his own stupid mess."

"Prizes like these two don't grow on trees," concluded Clyde. "Our nurse has gumption, and our librarian has guile."

46. Granny Dunker

After the Miles Canyon mishap, Harold quit entering the Therapy & Spa Center to avoid Akiko, who often guarded the reception area. Whenever Akiko saw Harold, she would make annoying remarks about him, such as:

"Hey girls, this is the sexy little granny dunker I was telling you about."

"How's our little Sandman doing? Still no clients?"

"Hey, girls, who wants to go on a plane ride with our little lady killer?"

Harold complained to Meriwa about it first. She listened diplomatically and remained expressionless throughout the conversation. When Harold finished, Meriwa changed the subject, so Harold turned to his backup plan–Steve.

"Her behavior is unprofessional," began Harold as he sat with his feet propped up on his desk.

"If you'd like, I can ask her to stop," Steve offered as he examined the worn leather soles of Harold's shoes. Rubber would be better suited for Whitehorse.

"That's precisely my point. This situation is entirely your fault." Harold stabbed his finger and spewed micro-bubbles of spit in Steve's direction. "Instead of actively managing your people like a real manager, you hide in your office like an oblivious fucking English teacher. Meanwhile, your pet witch is making all of us look bad."

Before lunch the next day, Steve searched for Akiko in the Therapy & Spa Center and found her organizing jackets in the wardrobe room. He spoke to her back as she worked. "Hey Akiko, um, Harold wants me to tell you, uh, all those little quips you've been lobbing at him are unprofessional." He stood with his hands behind his back as he completed the reprimand. "Also, the profanity. Yeah, he wants you to stop."

Akiko stopped shuffling jackets and turned to face Steve. She wore stark dark lipstick. The dim lights in the room made her look a little spookier than usual. She placed her hands on her hips and smiled in an exaggerated manner, rounding out the whole Addams Family vibe. Steve leaned backward stoically and clasped his hands in front, like he was playing soccer and was about to block a free kick.

"Moonpie, it's time for you to get your head out of your galaxy."

Grammatically, the sentence was correct, but it seemed rhetorical and lacked a question mark. Akiko took a deep breath and sighed. Her smile vanished. She stepped toward him. Steve froze, waiting for the kick.

"Let me explain this in a way that even you can understand." Akiko leaned toward him. "We don't need that motherfucking arrogant little prick hanging out in the Therapy & Spa Center. Have you noticed he doesn't come around very often? Why do you think that is?"

Steve remained motionless, except for the blinks.

"Can you imagine if he did come around? Pretty soon, every skirt you got would be at the beck-and-call of that little Mussolini motherfucker. Meanwhile the Munchkin would be paying their fucking salaries. Have you seen how that little douchebag treats Jessie? She's like his slave, right?"

Steve recalled the days when he moderated for the debate team. He reshuffled his position, stood straight, and placed his hands behind his back as though he were now simply evaluating Akiko's presentation. He listened and nodded in acknowledgement as she continued her debate, which was artfully camouflaged as an accusatory rant.

"While you're lost in space, Mini Dick Fly Boy is trying to do you with a Mars Bar. Guess what, sprinkles? If it weren't for me, he would have already succeeded. No wonder he wants me to quit making inconvenient remarks. In that little shit's pea brain, I'm the only force standing between him and world domination."

She placed her hands on her hips. "So, Captain Kirk, what was it you wanted to tell me?"

"Carry on, Lieutenant," Steve said with a nod.

Akiko led him by the elbow to the door. As they walked, she said, "Don't look so sad, my little Padawan. You're still learning. Even Darth Vader started out sucking on a binkie."

She sent him on his way with two pats on the ass. Steve smiled as he headed back to Space Mountain.

It's hard to believe anyone could have ever married that woman, yet she has had five husbands so far . . . a lot more if you count her friends' husbands.

He walked to his window and watched the river flowing past. A woman was walking her dog on the riverwalk. It was a husky mix of some type, of course.

Wouldn't it be something to be invited to the Exes of Akiko reunion? One could stand around the bar and listen to them reminisce. Imagine the things she must have taught those men.

Clyde called for a status update.

"Except for just the one drowning, not bad. Had a nice talk with your mom today. I told her she had to quit torturing Sandman. Somehow, she flipped the script and turned it into a business coaching session."

"Sandman? You mean the police, from *Logan's Run*? That's kind of funny."

"Yeah, that's something your mom came up with."

"My mom? Why do you keep saying that? I can only imagine the conversation. Have I ever told you about Akiko at our wedding reception? You should ask John about it someday. He has a name for it: *The Witch's I've Got a Gay Son Rant.*"

47. Three Out of Four Ain't Bad

Sojourners Two and Three were serviced exactly as planned. WWM did their glamor thing, decking them out in adventure duds from Main Street shops and capturing loads of videos: spa sessions, last-minute messages to loved (and hated) ones, campfire, hike, boat, glacier tour, eating at the nicest restaurants in Whitehorse. The MAID documentation was perfect, with requests for FunBite donations at the end. They followed the template perfectly, with the coroner signing off on their deaths as "died of old age" and appending a MAID notation. Since Americans didn't have a clue about MAID, the events were recorded eloquently by the sojourners' local newspapers. The Legacy Blog interactions were fabulous, and the donations went to the moon.

For client four, Molly, it went mostly the same, until Molly chose the blue pill on the plane. Upon her return, Akiko gave her a hug and dressed her in her original clothes. Lily accompanied her on the flight back home. This marked the end of Molly's participation in the APF program, except for the fact that Angi was able to finesse a FunBite donations page that generated an extra forty-two thousand dollars from family and friends.

After a gorgeous sunny morning of kayaking on Schwatka Lake, Steve strolled into Harold's office, with his infectious Oklahoma smile and convivial English teacher's charm. "Hi, Harold. Jessie said you were looking for me."

As he entered, Harold took his feet off his desk and sat up straight. "Steve, why did you book a client for a skydiving excursion who boarded my plane but failed to jump?" Harold bellowed. "I budgeted four recoveries this year and we've had only two. That wasn't what we agreed on."

Steve's Okie smile evaporated into a plume of steam. "Look Harold, you're the idiot who lost one recovery in the Yukon River. I can't change that. As far as the last one choosing not to jump, that's the whole point of the service, right? We help clients who want to be helped. If they choose death, it's our job to assist. If they choose life, it's our job to honor their choice. Molly had a great wilderness experience and now she is returning home to her family with a new zest for life. Angi has already posted from the APF team online congratulations and a lifetime of best wishes. It's really our best-case scenario, as it demonstrates to future clients that anything is possible and shows that the client remains in the driver's seat throughout the entire APF process. Surely you see the value in that?"

Spit bubbles appeared on his quivering bottom lip as Harold stood. Steve remembered the time he had visited Niagara Falls with Emily and how they had worn raincoats on the boat at the foot of the falls. He instinctively stepped back just in time to avoid the spray spouting from Harold's magenta-colored face. "Fuck you, Steve. You're an asshole. I'm out a hundred thousand dollars and you're spewing shit about some woolly fucking marketing benefits. You robbed that woman of a million dollars, returned her home, and paid me a token joy-ride fee. Do you really think she got her money's worth? Let me tell you what I'm going to do. From now on, my recovery fee is two hundred thousand dollars. How do you like that, Mr English Teacher imbecile? Also, I don't want that Daisy bitch on my airplane again. From now on, we're taking my niece along. Lily will be certified by next season, and she can sign off on the MAID documents."

"Let's not say something we're going to regret. We can put this conversation on ice and revisit it later with Meriwa."

Harold leaned closer and pointed up at Steve's nose. Shaking with rage and spraying spit, he boomed, "You are a cheechako moron. You still don't get it do you? Meriwa is Crow. I'm Wolf. She has no authority over me."

"Okay, okay, calm down," replied Steve as he retreated another step. "We can discuss this tomorrow."

Harold sat. "Great, Steve. Now get the fuck out of my office."

Steve walked past Jessie who was shuffling papers at her desk and pretending not to have heard. When he entered his own office, he found Akiko propped against his own window with her arms crossed, looking as happy as a five-year-old who had just run downstairs and found her Easter basket. "Good job, Darth."

"Akiko, this isn't a good time. What do you need?"

"Good time? That's funny. Wait until you hear this, Moonbeam. Close your door."

"Oh, please no. What is it?" After closing the door, he sat in his desk chair, rested his elbows on the desk, and hid his face in his hands.

Another Akiko entertainment opportunity.

"I've just got off the phone with Colonel Lawrence G Martin. He claims to be a retired US Army Ranger and the son of our recently recovered and reduced-to-ashes June Nelson. You know, the tight little package I just airmailed to the colonel's sister Beth in Phoenix?"

Steve swiveled to face her. The Cheshire Cat paused for effect. Steve waited for it.

"Colonel Larry says he wants to speak to the man responsible for murdering his mother."

Steve bolted out of the chair. "What did you tell him?"

"He actually sounded kinda spooky. I told him that Harold Pelly, the CEO of Whitehorse Flights, was in a meeting and to call back later."

48. The Game

Every time he entered The 98 Hotel, Steve looked for Eddie sitting in the corner by the fireplace, but today the corner was empty. Steve took a seat along the wall under the wolverine skin.

Barney swung past, carrying some empties. "Whataya have, matey?"

"Hey, Barney. A pint of Gold please."

It was Thursday, so Joe was playing the fiddle and a First Nations couple was dancing by the bar. It was 5 pm and the place was already half-full, excluding the dozen smokers loitering outside. At the bar sat four well-served patrons who looked like they had been regaling each other for several hours.

Meriwa arrived and ordered a beer. She wore a brown skirt cut well above the knee, tan pumps with three-inch heels, Kahului's pearls, a green silk blouse, and Alamea's watch. Barney served the beer and engaged her in small talk as she snagged a seat at the bar.

Steve approached from behind, reached around, and placed his hand on the watch. In the mirror behind the bar, she smiled at him. He hugged her, kissed her cheek, and caught a scent of roses before taking a seat beside her. "Hi, Devil. They know you here."

"Hi, Angel, they also knew my father. When he was a driver, he came here for his morning beer. Of course, that was before he married my mother."

"Ah, quite the history. Morning beer?" asked Steve with a laugh.

"Yes, this is Whitehorse's favorite for locals," replied Meriwa with a smile and nod. "It's the first to open. If you need a beer for breakfast, this is the place."

"Most bars offer beer before breakfast if you stay late enough," joked Steve.

Meriwa smiled. "I'll take your word for that. So, you're leaving tomorrow?"

"Yep, just in time. I hear you are in for your first snow this weekend."

"So that's it, Steve, you're leaving early to avoid the snow?"

"Basically, yes. You don't know of a place where I can store my bike, do you? I mean a place where a dog isn't going to lift its leg on it?"

"My backyard is home to Juneau. If you want to negotiate with him, be my guest. So, when will I see you again?"

"I'm going first to Denver, then Seattle."

"Great, I'll see you there. I'm meeting Ron in San Francisco and we're heading to Redwood National Park. He's going to give me a ride on Alamea's Ducati up the Pacific Coast Highway."

"Great ride through the redwoods. So, this is a real thing now, you and Ron?"

"I haven't decided."

"What does Ron think, doesn't he get to decide too?"

"That's not how it works. Men don't decide; women decide. You make a lot of mistakes, Steve, and you don't understand women so well. However, you're not a bad listener and I have a thing or two to say. Have you forgotten your safe word?"

Steve straightened his stance. "I remember."

She stepped closer and looked up at him. "Say it now."

Steve replied, "No."

Barney, with impeccable timing, wiped the counter between them. Steve took a sip and peeked over his glass at her before taking a full, long drink.

Meriwa took a sip and waited for Barney to move away. "Let's talk about something important."

"You mean Harold?" asked Steve.

"Don't be ridiculous," she scolded. "Something *important*. Alamea said she was coming back, but she never did, and she never said goodbye."

Steve watched bubbles rising from the bottom of the glass.

When the sun dies, it becomes a red giant and melts the ice of Jupiter's Galilean moon, Europa.

"Steve? Oh Steve? Do you want to play a game with me?"

"No."

"Don't say no when you mean yes. Listen to the rules, then you can say yes. The name of the game is *Alamea Says Goodbye to Meriwa*."

"It sounds far too complicated for me."

They both took a drink and before Steve could set his glass on the counter, Meriwa handed him hers, grabbed her bag, took him by the elbow, and led him toward the corner table.

As he followed, she said, "Girls like compliments, but then you already know that don't you, Steve?"

He took a seat with his back to the door as she struck a pose in front of the fireplace. "So, do you like it?"

He looked at her face. "I like your shoes. They are very nice shoes."

"She used to watch me like you watch me. When I stood like this, she would lick her lips. Then she would call me Honey Pie. You try it."

Steve started with her face and slowly panned down. He licked his lips. "I like your shoes, Honey Pie."

Meriwa giggled. "See, I knew you'd like this game."

"It seems dangerous. Why don't you play this game with Ron instead?"

"Steve, you say the dumbest things. Ron is a squeaky-clean from a long line of squeaky-cleans. He could never play this game."

Steve took another sip and hid behind the glass.

"For this game, I need a felon. You were with Alamea at the end. I need you. Don't you get it, Steve?"

"Uh, sort of. So then, um, when does Alamea say goodbye? Tomorrow?"

"Don't be absurd. We haven't even played yet." Meriwa gathered her bag. "Alamea will say goodbye when I'm ready. I'm not ready."

"You're not going to finish your beer?"

She leaned toward him and bit him a little on the left side of his chin. "Biter," Steve said as she walked away. He took a long drink of her beer as he watched her leave.

Once bitten twice shy . . .

49. Three Musketeers

The meeting took place in the conference room in Seattle at the end of John's workday. Angi and Meriwa faced the window, directly across from Ron and Steve. Clyde sat at the far end of the table.

"How was the Pacific Coast Highway?" asked Clyde.

"Truly epic," replied Meriwa. "Riding through the red giants on the back of a Ducati is the only way to go. Ron watched the road while I admired the trees."

John entered and said in Canadian, "No, no, don't get up. How is everyone? Thank you for coming today. I've been waiting to see you all and get some information first-hand. I mean, without Clyde's smart aleck embellishments."

"For thirty years I've been trying to make John laugh," quipped Clyde. "It has been like trying to get a smile out of a taxidermied raccoon."

They all laughed, except John, who rolled his eyes before turning his attention to Steve. "So, was it two-out-of-four or three-out-of-four?"

"Four-out-of-four paid us. That is a one hundred percent success rate," replied Steve with an apprehensive smile.

Clyde chuckled.

"What are the plans for next year?" asked John. "Double the danger and triple the lawsuits?"

"We'll double the price," replied Steve. "Then we'll pay double commissions and contractor fees and sign up three times as many clients."

"So, you think this business can actually scale?" asked John.

"Absolutely," replied Steve. "In fact, Harold wants to increase the number of skydiving trips to two per week. I told him we might consider it after next year. If we extend the season and double the volume per week, we could potentially generate one hundred million dollars in revenue."

"Do you really imagine the company will last that long?" asked Clyde.

John stole a glance toward Meriwa, who focused on her doodle masterpiece.

"Why not?" asked Steve.

John interjected, "Well, for starters, one of our clients' heirs is suing us. That translates to a twenty-five percent lawsuit ratio, which is unsustainable for any type of business, don't you agree?"

"Really? I thought our contracts included a no-sue policy," said Steve without a hint of cynicism.

"Yeah, right," said John, dismissively. "It's a civil suit in Phoenix court for the wrongful death of June Nelson."

"A colonel can serenely bear the loss of his mother, but the loss of his inheritance will drive him to sue," replied Steve with a rueful grin.

"A quote–Niccolo Machiavelli–sort of," John replied with an actual smile.

"Steve drops a mangled one-liner and gets more out of you in five minutes than I get doing thirty years of standup," quipped Clyde. "I should have majored in English Literature."

"It's the delivery, Chuckles," John deadpanned. "Steve's delivery is better than yours."

"Speaking of delivery, this litigation babble is a downer, especially since we've come for fun," Clyde said, casting a grin at the Librarian. "Angi, did you bring Thing Two and Thing One?"

Angi had been fidgeting and reading her notes, waiting for her moment. "Fun? I've brought nothing but fun. Has Steve told you about our web traffic growth? We started the season with zero visits, and with each new sojourner blog, our web traffic has grown by five thousand additional active daily users."

Look what has become of our librarian wizard.

"For the past seven days, we have averaged over twenty thousand unique users per day. About three-quarters of those are accessing the public part of our site, which means they are from secondary sources. Additionally, logins to the private blog pages have not decreased. Users continue to visit for weeks, maybe even months, after their loved ones have passed away."

Clyde primed the pump. "May we ask what all this has done to FunBite donations?"

Angi beamed endearingly, like a . . . well, you know, as she said, "To the moon. Steve was right, most donations are ten dollars. In fact, over thirty thousand donations have been twenty dollars or less, some are recurring small donations by the same donors. However, we've also received over a hundred donations of over one thousand dollars, twenty-two donations of at least ten thousand dollars, seven donations exceeding one hundred thousand dollars, and one donation of four hundred fifty thousand dollars. So, the participation rate for donations has been a little better than expected, wouldn't you agree?"

✳ ✳ ✳

Clyde and John invited Angi to dinner near Pike Place Market and the three stayed behind to discuss funding for a Vancouver office. Ron, Meriwa, and Steve rode the elevator together.

"Where are you staying?" asked Steve.

Ron squeezed Meriwa by the waist and took his face out of her neck to say, "At the pool house with M."

Meriwa smiled in embarrassment. "What are you up to tonight, Steve?"

"Early to bed. I'm on the first flight out," replied Steve.

Ron released Meriwa. "No way. You're with us. We're heading to the Space Needle."

"No, next time," resisted Steve.

"Yo bro, not next time, this time," persisted Ron. "I've already bought you a ticket."

"I don't believe you," challenged Steve.

"Want to bet a dollar?" offered Ron.

"I'll bet two."

Ron reached into his pocket and extracted three tickets. "Pay up, loser."

The door opened. The beautiful couple walked out of the elevator ahead of Steve. Ron opened the door to exit the building and held it for them before taking Meriwa's arm. Steve fell in behind them. Ron looked over his shoulder. "Hey Steve, keep up." Meriwa extended her arm, and Steve took it. They walked three abreast like that, with Meriwa in the middle, all the way to the Space Needle.

50. Game On

Steve flew into Whitehorse in late March, both to miss the Rendezvous and to be near the river on April 1 for the second anniversary of Emily's passing. During his two-week visit, he also intended to finalize the contracts and interview new additions to the team.

All second-year sojourners had paid their fees, the schedule was set, and the initial MAID meetings were complete. Meriwa and John had been working out the final details for the visas.

Sitting by the glass door in Kind Café, Steve sliced slivers off his dirty chai cheesecake, sipped his latte and waited for Meriwa. His mourning for Emily offered no respite for the familiar sense of panic and longing that seized him as the Benz pulled to the curb.

Meriwa was the kaleidoscope-colored puzzle piece which some sophomoric gods, for sport, had somehow scavenged from another's puzzle box and snuck into his. Every time he encountered the unmatchable piece, the gods perched on high would laugh at his futile search for a solution, leaving him to writhe in anguish and unrequited longing.

Meriwa got out of the Benz, her long dark hair hanging down her back as she swayed and bounced up the walk in Kahului's black pearls, a tight black blouse, short gray skirt, black heels and Alamea's gold Cartier Tank watch. She smiled back at him, movie star makeup, movie star eyes. Whatever was happening today, Meriwa was definitely ready.

They had traded texts and spoken on the phone several times, but he hadn't seen her since August at the Space Needle in Seattle. He stood and gave her a hug. She took her seat across from him on the bench among the colorful floral pillows.

"Why do you walk like that?" he asked. "As though you are the most beautiful girl in the world."

"Why do you watch me like that, as though I am the most beautiful girl in the world?" She gifted him a delicious smile, complete in three dimensions with lashes, ivory, and dimples.

"Hello, Devil, long time no see," he said nonchalantly, trying to conceal the intensity of the currents pulsing through his veins.

"You like what you see?"

"Every little bit."

"What have you got for me?"

"Everything you need."

"Where you gonna put it?"

"Where do you want it?"

"I never said I did."

"I never said I would. Devil."

"A devil is a type of angel."

And so it begins.

"I missed you," he said in a sincere tone.

"I can tell," she said with a tilt of her head.

"What can I buy you?"

"Latte, skim, please."

Steve got up, ordered and returned. "What's happening today?"

"I have an interview with *CBC North News*," she replied. "They're featuring FunBite in a business piece promoting tourism in the Yukon."

"Aha, thus the getup. I was hoping all this was for me," he said as he made a show of appraising her.

She smiled. "It's always for you, Steve, always. I can tell that you missed me."

"Yes, it's called the law of attraction. Does it show?"

"It definitely shows. You look nervous, like you forgot your phone and lost your wallet someplace, and you're searching for them," she teased.

"So, you're still a biter, I see."

"I'm not a biter, Steve. Sometimes I bite, but I'm not a biter."

"Is this the whole thing? Because I can keep going like this forever," he said, as he got up to fetch her coffee.

When he returned, she had already covered the table in piles of paper. "Jessie is not in the office today, but she'll be in tomorrow. She knew I wanted to see you, so she asked me to give you tomorrow's itinerary. You have a full day of meetings and interviews.

"Here's the schedule for this year, by week, with Sojourner names. It's the latest. I just received it from Liz this morning. She also asked Jessie to print out the updated schedule for Rachel's debates."

Steve smiled as she handed him the page. He looked over the debate schedule as she paused to sip her latte. "Jesse has also printed you a copy of the sojourner schedule." She handed him the second page, but he set it aside and continued studying the debate schedule.

She continued as though he were listening, "As you can see, the first sojourner arrives on Friday, May 26, and then one per week until the last, who arrives on August 18. That's a total of thirteen sojourners over a span of fourteen weeks. Jessie has checked the list and accounted for all payments. Daisy has ensured that all the MAID stuff is in order. They want to go over this with you tomorrow."

"Uh huh." Steve set the debate schedule aside, picked up the sojourner schedule, and looked up at Meriwa.

"John and I have completed the visa process for all sojourners, except July 7 and August 11."

"What does this mark mean?" asked Steve.

"Here is the note about that," she said as she pointed it out. "Those are the two with incomplete visas. Don't worry, John and I will solve it this week. Here are the new contracts. We are renegotiating all the outfitter and supplier contracts. Please review them and if you have any questions, we can discuss them when I finish work for the day."

Steve shuffled through the vendor contracts. "Edward Pelly? We're hiring Uncle Ed again as the General Contractor after his performance last year? Have you discussed this with Ron?"

"Ron's not the boss, but yes, he knows. That's the way things work here. Unless you want to get crossways with Harold's entire family, we are going to have to hire one of the Pelly's as the General Contractor. You haven't met the other Pelly's, so believe me when I say, better the Pelly you know than the Pelly's you don't."

"I bet," Steve replied with a smirk.

"Here are the new FunBite lease agreements. These are mine, not yours, so I need them back. For the Therapy & Spa Center, Jessie is proposing the addition of two more therapy rooms and an additional wardrobe room."

"Has Harold agreed to the changes I suggested for the executive suite?" Steve asked.

"Harold hasn't agreed to any changes whatsoever. Any changes to the executive suite will result in Harold chiseling a new advantage. So, I hope you don't mind keeping your dinky little office."

"I love my office. It has a great view, and it's too small for meetings," Steve replied.

"Here is Harold's new contract. Of course, after the Jumping June mishap, he has a new burner company for APF. He has doubled the recovery fee and added a personal assistant for his son, Henry," Meriwa explained, handing over the contract.

"Henry has no need for a personal assistant. Now Harold's company is called *Autumn Flights*? Who came up with that?"

"Henry, not Angi. Harold doesn't listen to Angi. Here is the new contract for Whitehorse Cares. They've tripled the size of the company and doubled the fee per client. As you can see, Daisy and Lily have already signed the contract. I helped them prepare it. Please review it, and we can discuss it if necessary. I want this contract completed by tomorrow morning."

Steve nodded and finished his coffee.

"Angi's company has doubled in size. She has added new office space. Simon is hiring two more drivers. The therapists will be employed by Lily's sister Lucy so they won't be part of Whitehorse Cares this year. Lucy's new company is called Northern Lights Spa."

"Another FunBite company?" Steve asked, raising an eyebrow.

"Of course. Also, Jessie told me to remind you to wear a suit tomorrow. It's picture day for an article in the *Whitehorse Daily Star*, right?"

"Why did the newspaper select A Perfect Finish?" Steve asked.

"Because APF grew from zero revenue to four million US dollars in just one year. That makes it the fastest-growing new tourism company in the Yukon Territory. What other questions do you have?"

"Just one. Was that your picture I saw on a lamp post this morning? It said something about *Meriwa for Mayor*?"

She smiled. "Will I have your vote?"

"Will I have to become a sourdough in order to vote?"

She put her elbows on the table and leaned forward. Her words were soft and laced with concern. "Have they called you yet?"

"Not yet, but I'm sure they've been busy. I had hoped they would call for the holidays, but maybe their father didn't allow it. I still have their Christmas presents in my truck. Rachel usually asks me to help her rehearse for debates, but she hasn't yet. I missed Rachel's birthday and all of Michael's rugby games. Maybe they'll call during spring break."

"I'm sorry, Steve. Be patient. They are teenagers." Meriwa put her hand on his forearm, caught his eye, and gave him a squeeze before changing the subject. "Simon has a new driver he wants you to meet. He's going to bring him by your office at 10:30 this morning." She glanced at her watch. "Damn, I'm going to be late."

She took a quick sip of her latte and started gathering her things. She stood and posed, heel to instep, hands on her waist, thumbs forward, chest out.

"You're a whirlwind."

"Speaking of which, I have to whirl. Will you finish my latte?" She turned and grabbed a paper. Steve stood, grabbed her by her wrist, so he could feel the watch. She smiled then went up on her toes, as if to kiss his cheek, but instead she bit him hard on the left jaw.

"Ouch." He winced, released her wrist, and grabbed his jaw, before wiping away her saliva.

She grinned as he checked his hand for blood. "I'm so happy you're here, Steve. We're going to have so much fun."

Steve smiled back. "Yes, we are. Good luck with your interview, Honey Pie."

He opened the door for her. At the sidewalk, she looked back and waved. Simon opened the car door for her.

He made some notes about what she had said. As he sipped the latte, he noticed her lipstick mark. He turned the cup and licked it but there was no flavor. He continued sucking on the edge and sipping until the cup was drained. He carried the cup to the dish cart, returned, gathered the papers, and walked to his office in melancholy thought.

This time away from the children is forever gone. He's robbing all of us, maybe at a time when they need me most. If Emily knew, imagine how she would feel about this.

Is it possible the children actually blame me for their mother's death, and I'll never hear from them again?

He placed the papers on his empty desk, closed the door, flipped the lock, and hung his jacket. Crouching down, he turned the dial. Left three turns, right two turns, left, and opened the safe. There they were: two black soft-sided Harley-Davidson bags designed for a trike trunk.

What if I hadn't distracted Mark?

Mark Jr: "Also, the police sent me Alamea's rings, but what happened to the rest of her jewelry?" What if I hadn't taken the watch and jewelry?

Alamea: "Love prospers when a fault is forgiven." Whose fault? Her husband's or stepson's? What if I hadn't taken the letter? What if I had left Alamea's contraband? Would that have changed anything at all for anyone besides me?

He pulled the front bag out of the safe and set it aside. He reached into the back for the heavy one, opened it, pulled out a stack of hundred-dollar bills and fanned himself with it. He hadn't counted it since that night in the hotel room. It was exactly two hundred thousand dollars. Counting it had taken forever.

Clyde had said, "Just use it to start the company, like walk around money," but the fact that Alamea hadn't spent even one bill had made it hard to tap. Plus, it kind of seemed like Uncle Mountie would be on the lookout for somebody flashing big bills around town. Maybe as long as he didn't spend it, nobody could say he had stolen it.

I could count it again. Nah, too much work.

He returned the heavier bag to the safe, pushing it to the back. He stood, opened the other bag, pulled out Alamea's fancy Glock, checked the chamber, turned on the Trijicon red dot, assumed a draw position, and raised the pistol, holding it tight to his chest with both hands. He drove the gun forward, aiming at the target. It was the middle circle on the top of the right moccasin, part of the set of paintings Jessie had bought from a local artist. He repeated the procedure several times, turned off the Trijicon, and inspected the magazines.

The previous year he had brought with him on the motorcycle the twenty missing nine-millimeter shells to replace the ones he had used on the bear, plus an extra for the chamber. He picked up the gun and loaded it with the magazine containing the self-defense rounds and placed the gun in the bag. He put the other two magazines and the extra round in the bag beside the pistol. The chamber was empty, ready to rack and fire. He left the bag unzipped and placed it inside before locking the safe. He stood, went to the window, and watched the river rush by.

Lose a granny, save the planet? Really? How many times has life been wiped off Earth and resumed? What difference could any human make in saving a planet? How many Earths are there in the universe?

In five billion years, the sun will die and vaporize all life on Earth. When measured in billions, each life registers barely a flash in time. What difference would it make in the universe if seventeen flashes each ended a fraction of a flash sooner?

A couple pushed a baby stroller down the path. As they approached the food trucks, they stopped to discuss something. Litter was scattered across the riverwalk and around the hotdog stand that Eddie used to sell Feelin Yo Oats out of at night.

Wait until Akiko sees all those plastic spoons.

"Yo Stevo, we got a new product, ginger tea. You'll never guess the recipe."

Eddie is a sourdough now. I should check in on him. He's sleeping. It's too cold for kayaking and the trails will be icy. Maybe I should swing by The 98 Hotel later for some day drinking . . .

Steve sat at his desk. Jessie had prepared the list of FunBitten contractors. He spent forty-five minutes looking through them before texting Clyde. "Want to discuss new contracts?"

Clyde phoned and asked, "How's it hanging in Whitehorse?"

"Better. Everything looks better. Pictures of Meriwa on every corner, and her fingerprints on the page of every contract."

"From what I read, it seems like she's going to win."

"I haven't read anything about that."

"Yeah, that's because you read the *New York Times* and the *Wall Street Journal*."

"What is this about a new Whitehorse one hundred fifty thousand-dollar MAID for Tourists Tariff? Is that for real?" asked Steve.

"Yep. Meriwa's mother is a City Council hero for coming up with that. They expect it to become a revenue line item in Whitehorse General Hospital's income statement this year."

"Can Whitehorse create a specific municipal tax targeting just APF?" asked Steve. "And how is that a good thing?"

"They can, they did, and it's a great thing. The hospital is playing a critical role in APF's success, and this is a legit way for us to compensate them for services. Plus, it represents one more reason for the community to continue supporting us. You do remember the hassle the city endured after Jumping June, right? As long as the city is still looking for ways to exploit us, they won't be trying to exterminate us. As Eddie would say, 'Gotta ride the wave, Stevo.'"

"Yeah, never tried surfing before. I'm sure I'd be as good at that as I am at this commandant gig. Did you see the contract for Harold's new burner company?"

"Yes, but I found no surprises. He already warned you last year about doubling the recovery fee. Funding his son's personal assistant is annoying, but if that's the worst, we can deal with it, don't you think?"

"Sure, and today is not the right day to whack the hornets' nest. Simon is adding a car?" asked Steve.

"Yep, Eddie is flying into Seattle this week to fetch the second car and Akiko. I already have the replacement for it—the car, I mean." Clyde laughed.

"This afternoon I'm meeting make-up expert Lucy," said Steve. "She has a new FunBite company, Northern Lights Spa."

"Meriwa doesn't like mixing the therapists with the MAID professionals. She feels it's a chink in the armor in terms of nurses maintaining their independence," said Clyde.

"Did you see the increases for web marketing?" asked Steve.

"Yes. Angi is killing it," replied Clyde.

"She is but her fee per client will quadruple?" Steve asked, his voice escalating in volume. "Can you imagine how profitable Angi's company is going to be this year with thirteen sojourners? What were her words? 'To the moon.' Are we really going to fully fund Angi's second round of development?"

Clyde spoke calmly. "It's a pretty big strategic decision. Angi is sitting at the helm of the APF Therapy & Spa Center every day. If we lost her, what impact do you think that might have on APF?"

Steve raised his voice an octave. "I'm not sure we couldn't sit someone else to take her place."

"John says Angi is the only value-driver in the entire APF business proposition," replied Clyde in a soothing voice. "If it weren't for her Legacy Blog content, granny could just pop ten dollars' worth of pills from Walmart instead of paying two million dollars to stampede to the Klondike."

"When you put it that way, I have to agree. So, we'll pay Angi again," conceded Steve.

"Any other surprises?" asked Clyde.

"No, but I haven't met Eddie yet."

"You didn't mention the new lease agreements," prompted Clyde.

"I flipped through them but didn't notice any changes."

"The landlord is different," hinted Clyde.

"I didn't notice. Hmmm, I'm looking for it. You've got to be kidding. WH Main Street, a FunBite company? Meriwa bought the whole damn Bullet Hole Bagel building?"

Clyde laughed. "Yes, FunBite hit the jackpot last year—it raked in over two-point-five million dollars in donations. So Meriwa launched WH Main Street and arranged the financing to buy the entire building. She also added a property management company to the incubator. Now she's trying to get her baby sister to move from Toronto and run the whole shebang. FunBite is setting its sights on buying more Whitehorse retail properties."

Clyde paused for effect. "And speaking of Meriwa's baby sister, we had the pleasure of hosting the two at our pool house a few weeks ago. She works for Goldman Sachs in Toronto. She's another charming porcupine."

Steve raised an eyebrow. "Like a tag team? In pursuit of a First Nations Land Claims 2.0, but this time it's not just self-governance. Now they'll take over the heart of Whitehorse's tourist industry and the city government too."

"You don't read the local newspaper, but you do know something about the First Nations story. Good job, Steve. I'm impressed."

"Is she really like Meriwa?" asked Steve.

"They do share some remarkable traits," Clyde replied. "She and John got along great. The two spent all of Saturday working on a new trust agreement for Alamea's estate. Meanwhile, Meriwa was on the phone nonstop, juggling competing business deals. A joint venture with Princess Cruise Lines, a copper mine, and a bunch of local banks. This stuff is not just Clyde gossip, Steve. It's in the newspaper."

Steve shook his head in disbelief. "Those things don't really sound related, a cruise line and a copper mine."

"They're not. With the cruise line, Meriwa wants FunBite to control the buses that bring Skagway cruise ship tourists to Whitehorse. That way, she can determine which restaurants and shops the tourists visit, favoring FunBite spots, of course. As for the copper mine, Meriwa is negotiating on behalf of the tribe to purchase it via a FunBite mining cooperative. The miners who work at the copper mine would own it. Both concepts would be sponsored by FunBite but will require bank financing."

"Where does Meriwa get the bandwidth to do all this?"

"That's John's question," replied Clyde. "Is she still working as a public defender? She said she would resign soon."

"No idea. Why don't I ever ask Meriwa any real questions when I see her?"

Clyde laughed. "Akiko will be there next week. Why don't you discuss that with her?"

"Thanks, I can't wait. Has anyone done the math, based on higher fees, higher sales commissions, and these new contracts?" asked Steve.

"I've done a back-of-the-envelope analysis," replied Clyde. "Based on thirteen sojourners this season at two million a hop, minus fifteen percent sales commissions, I have APF up about fifteen million US dollars, pretax. Not too shabby, right?"

"That doesn't sound bad," said Steve.

"By the way have you heard the latest about the colonel?"

"No. Is that still a thing?" asked Steve.

"Very much so. With a little help from the colonel's half-sister Beth, John got the colonel's civil suit, along with a very angry colonel, literally tossed out of a Phoenix courtroom. The problem is Beth was the sole inheritor of the house and a pot of gold—everything except half the insurance policy proceeds. When the insurance company disallowed the double indemnity clause, due to Angi's video showing June willfully and of her own volition hopping out of the Zodiac, the colonel came unglued in the courtroom."

"Coming unglued is not supposed to happen if you're a colonel," exclaimed Steve.

"Yeah, or a US Army Ranger. Now Beth and the bat-shit colonel are not on speaking terms. In the colonel's words, "Beth and her bitch girlfriend had no right to sign my mother up for a trip to Auschwitz."

"The colonel said Auschwitz?" asked Steve.

"Yeah, bat-shit said it in court. It's part of the court record. You can imagine how John feels about that."

"What now?" asked Steve.

"We don't know. We haven't heard from the colonel since, but John said, 'Tell Stevo to watch his six'."

51. Yukon Stew

Following a hike and a shower, Steve indulged in some respite from Akiko by hanging out in his hotel room. He was on page five of the previous day's financial news when Clyde called.

"Did you hear about the donation for ten million dollars? It's from a private family office associated with Allison Brown. Does that name ring a bell?"

"Sure." Steve glanced at the list of sojourners. "From Memphis. She was Sojourner 2-2."

"The donation is in the bank," said Clyde. "Meriwa called to say her sister just put in her notice at Goldman."

"That must make Meriwa's mother very happy, getting both of her daughters back under her thumbs in the Yukon."

"No doubt. Mama's just butterflying the shit out of The Territory," replied Clyde with a chuckle.

Steve shared in the laugh, before inquiring, "Any news about the colonel?"

Clyde informed Steve that there had been nothing new since the colonel was thrown out of court. Steve told him Daisy had resigned, sold her company shares to Lily, and said she would have nothing to do with Eddie. This piqued Clyde's interest.

"That's strange," said Clyde. "Eddie called me last week. I wonder if it's related. He said he's been going above and beyond and deserves a raise."

"What does that even mean? What exactly are we talking about?" asked Steve.

"Eddie claims he is the key to our success rate, one hundred percent jumpers this year. He says he's been providing in-flight service and that his tea is the secret sauce. Without it, the grannies wouldn't have the nerve to jump."

"Nice. I don't know what to say."

"Maybe you should quiz Daisy about it, ask her why she quit. In addition, you could poll Lucy and the individual therapists to learn what Eddie has been up to. Also, is Eddie friends with Lily?"

"I don't know," Steve replied before asking, "Are you questioning the integrity of Top Gun's niece?"

"I don't want to put it that way, but if somebody is doping grannies without their consent before pushing them out the back of a plane, it seems like, as the CEO, you would need to learn about that, don't you think?"

"Microdosing grannies is old news, but actually shoving them out the back of a plane would definitely exceed my imagination."

"No doubt, and that precisely is the problem," Clyde admonished. "You do recall it was your idea to incentivize Harold with a recovery fee, right? Then it was Harold who kicked Daisy off his plane for bringing a granny back alive. At this point, you shouldn't need to drink Eddie's tea to imagine that one of our grannies, in her final moments, might be getting robbed of her final freedom of choice: *to be or not to be.*"

"I find that very hard to believe," said Steve. "And if it's actually true, it will be almost impossible to prove."

"Yeah. When the shit hits the fan, Harold will say, 'As God is my witness, I thought grannies could fly.'"

Steve chuckled. "If Harold gets arrested in Cincinnati, that might work, but I wouldn't bet on any judge in Whitehorse having ever watched an episode of WKRP. On the other hand, as long as Harold's in Whitehorse, he probably doesn't have much to worry about. He seems to have the inside track here. Anyway, I'll look into it."

Clyde described John's latest exploits. "He's been bragging about clobbering the twins and Mark Jr in court. It seems like Alamea's estate is now in the clear. We haven't touched a penny of it."

"Wow, that's great news. So now what?" asked Steve.

"Well, Alamea had planned to use the funds to finance the tsunami, but now that APF is cash flow positive, her estate can be used for the trust instead."

"What trust?" asked Steve.

"The trust is a beneficiary of the estate that invests in companies supporting Alamea's values, prior relationships, and interests," explained Clyde.

"You mean FunBite companies?" asked Steve.

"For example, yes," replied Clyde defensively.

Steve quipped, "Let me guess, the name of the trust is going to be ClydeBites."

"Ha, ha, very funny. In a word, no."

"And this trust is John's idea?" asked Steve.

"Somewhat. Also Meriwa's. It's all legal, of course. Seems to be something the two of them learned in shyster school. They have a term for it, deed of variation, or some such nonsense."

Clyde went on to confirm that it was already a done deal, and that Clyde himself was an outside donor. He mentioned something about Daisy's new business and that her new office was right down the hall from the executive suite, which surprised Steve.

"Maybe you should take a bliss break and just walk the hallways tomorrow," jibed Clyde. "You might discover the FunBite incubator is becoming an actual web."

"Yeah, with a pregnant black widow minding it from the corner."

"The fly from outer space awakens," quipped Clyde. "By the way, I noticed an article in the paper about a bear with a radio collar mauling some campers at Atlin Lake."

"Haven't heard a thing about that. Black or grizzly?" asked Steve.

"I think the article said male black bear. Does it matter?" asked Clyde.

"The grizzlies are territorial, less likely to roam."

"The victims were sleeping in a tent at a campground," Clyde continued. "Both were hospitalized. They were saved when another camper shot the bear. If it happened by Atlin Lake, is that near our drop zone?"

"Maybe. There is a lot of wilderness between the two lakes. It would depend on which side of Atlin Lake. At the nearest, it could be as little as fifty miles. That's an easy stroll for a roaming black bear."

"Are you worried?" asked Clyde.

"Maybe. Harold has been whining lately. He says next year he's going to charge five hundred thousand per recovery."

"That's bullshit!" exclaimed Clyde. "Why?"

"Harold doesn't want his men at the drop zone until the plane has cleared the area," Steve explained. "Putting beacons in skydiving helmets has decreased recovery times, but still, the bears are beating the recovery team to the sojourners' mangled corpses. The team has tranquilized a lot of bears lately. Harold says the recoveries are starting to become like running the gauntlet. The same male grizzly has been tranquilized for three weeks running. Last week they tranquilized the grizzly before getting stalked by a black bear sow and her cubs as they carried the body bag back to the Zodiac. That was one recovery, four tranquilized bears. Harold says all of the last five sojourner bodies have been seriously mauled."

"Mangled then mauled," replied Clyde. "I can't wait to read the headlines."

Steve continued, "The professor believes Harold's plane engine has become a dinner bell for some of the bears. In fact, he plans to incorporate the topic into his research paper."

"His research paper," repeated Clyde.

Steve pressed on. "Harold is now sending four men instead of three: two to carry the body bag, one to carry a tranquilizer rifle, and another with a rifle and real ammo to serve as an escort. They are trying to avoid killing a bear because then they would have to report the event to authorities."

"Sounds epic," deadpanned Clyde. "What are the chances the dead black bear was wearing one of the professor's trackers?"

"I would say quite high," replied Steve. "So far, they have put trackers on six black bears and one grizzly. There's no reason to invite the question though. The bad-boy black bear has already been shot, and hopefully the professor's research paper isn't going to blow us up when it comes out later this year. Let's just wait and see how it goes."

"Sure," replied Clyde. "So far, no freeloaders have died, a rogue bear has been killed, and the 'feeding the bears' research paper remains unpublished. What could possibly go wrong?"

52. Newsbreak

"Moonbeam, why is your desktop empty except for Alamea's journal? There's no sign that you're even in the death camp business. In fact, the only part of the business you seem to care about is the website. Doesn't that seem strange to you, being the CEO of a company and all?"

"Hi Akiko, I was just thinking about you and your mushroom boy."

"Those are two distinctly different matters, my little Mars Bar. Where's your phone? We've been trying to call you. You don't even have a computer in Space Mountain. Aside from the river, you're totally cut off from the outside world. No wonder you're always out to lunch."

"Did you have something in particular you wanted to say, Akiko, or did you just drop by to break my balls?"

"Sounds like fun, can't it be both? I have a message from Angi. She said to tell you the tsunami is here."

Steve's response–jumping from his seat with an open mouth and wild eyes–brought a grin to Akiko's face.

"What did Angi say, exactly?"

"Exactly? Well, first she asked, 'Why doesn't that sweetie pie, Stevie, ever answer his phone?' Then she said, 'Akiko, go get that charming, sexy spaceman. Tell him the tsunami is here.' Those were her words, well not exactly, but more or less."

"Angi said tsunami?"

"Tsooooooo-naaaaaaaa-miiiiiiiiiiii."

Steve entered the WWM offices where Angi and three others huddled around a desk with four monitors. On the center monitor, a reporter from *Fox News* was interviewing a very angry *Colonel Martin, Son of Murdered Pensioner*, according to the subtitle.

The colonel was saying, "It was Whitehorse Flights who were running the adventure tour. She paid them a million dollars. They tripped her out on magic mushrooms and loaded her aboard a rigid-hull inflatable boat, from which she plunged to her death in the Yukon River."

"Colonel, how do you know about the mushrooms?" asked the interviewer.

"It's in the autopsy. For three days, my mother was in the river. Once they recovered the body, the coroner found traces of psilocybin in her liver. You don't get that from drinking Kool-Aid. It's found in magic mushrooms, which means there's some shady business going on in Whitehorse."

"Shady business?" asked the interviewer. "So, you believe this company, Whitehorse Flights, took money to kill your mother?"

"They are the ones who killed her, but the company who took the money is called A Perfect Finish. You can see the pictures on their website. It's like a cult, a bunch of women chanting and singing around a campfire, preparing to die."

"Colonel, are you familiar with the Canadian law called Medical Assistance in Dying?"

"That's right, M - A - I - D. That's what my sister and her girlfriend signed my mother up for. It's like a modern-day Auschwitz located in the Yukon. They are preying upon our grandmothers, taking their money, snatching them from their homes, and murdering them on the Klondike Gold Rush trail."

"Retired Colonel and US Army Ranger, Lawrence G Martin, son of the late June Nelson who has allegedly been murdered for money in the Klondike by a radical cult. Thank you for coming on the program. Is this a case of elder abuse? When we return, we'll ask renowned elder abuse expert, Phoenix attorney Samuel Goldman."

Angi muted the sound. "The problem is too much traffic. It's going to crash our websites. I have four developers working on it right now as well as our CDN provider. In the past hour, we've doubled our resource allocation three times."

"You'll manage the traffic?"

"We'll manage but we've had to take down every external link to the FunBite companies because the traffic is crashing those websites too."

"We quit answering the phone. It's ringing nonstop," interjected Akiko.

"What does Meriwa say?" asked Steve.

"She's not available. She's been on the phone with John for the past hour," replied Akiko.

"What's happening with the blog conversations?"

"Everything on the private side is surprisingly positive," replied Angi. "On the public side, it's turning into a dumpster fire. Canada's MAID law is quite the polarizing topic in the United States."

"We already knew that," replied Steve. "That's why we're in the Yukon, right?"

"There are two more things I should mention," said Angi. "First, the number of donations less than one hundred dollars—we're getting almost two hundred per hour. Second, have you spoken to Liz yet? She informed me we've generated over six hundred leads in just two hours, before we disabled the website form. She said as many as twenty percent of the replies appear to be from qualified prospects. Steve, think about it—in terms of a tsunami, those numbers exceed our expectations, wouldn't you say?"

"I suppose they do," Steve replied, before addressing Angi directly. "I guess it's time for the inevitable. How do you feel about dusting off your meet-the-press plan? I'll give Clyde a call. In the meantime, do you think you could round up Jessie and Daisy and meet me in my office in an hour to go over our communication strategy?"

53. Meet the Press

Under cloudy skies in the mid-morning light of the Klondike summer, Steve stood on the wooden platform along the riverbank, on what had once been the loading dock for the White Pass and Yukon Route Railroad, staring into the cameras arranged along the railing, with the city of Whitehorse and the escarpment in his background. Nearby stood the CNN reporter, a tall handsome, blondish woman channeling Steve's aunt and bearing a familiar *no dessert until you eat your peas* manner. Around her neck, she wore a mauve wool scarf tucked stylishly into her long sage-green hooded coat with faux fur trim. Gathered around her was the CNN crew, including a sound technician, a makeup specialist and the cameraman. Steve watched as they fussed with her hair and prepared for the shoot.

The cameraman made his way to the railing and the sound technician addressed Steve. "Let's test the microphone, Mr Hamilton. We are creating a pre-recorded segment which we expect to be aired later this evening. When it is your turn to reply, Melissa will position the microphone a couple inches from your mouth. When she does that, be careful "not to move suddenly or bob your head towards the microphone. Just stand and speak naturally while looking into the camera. We will do a test run now, so let me begin." The sound technician spoke into the microphone. "With us today is Steve Hamilton, Chief Executive Officer of A Perfect Finish, in the City of Whitehorse, located in the Yukon Territory. Please give us a test, Mr Hamilton," he said as he pointed the microphone toward Steve.

"Testing, testing," Steve said, as he looked into the camera.

"That's perfect," said the sound technician as he handed the microphone back to the reporter. "Ready when you are, Melissa."

Melissa stepped beside Steve and offered a cursory smile and nod before looking toward the cameraman, who gave her a thumbs up. She began, "Good evening, I am Melissa Steward, and joining me tonight is Steve Hamilton, the Managing Director of A Perfect Finish, a company that has recently been at the center of a heated controversy surrounding Canada's Medical Assistance in Dying law and allegations of exploiting elderly Americans for profit. Steve, thank you for being here with us tonight. Can you begin by telling our viewers a bit about A Perfect Finish and the services you provide?"

"Thank you, Melissa. A Perfect Finish offers certified medical assistance-in-dying services to retired folks who wish to experience a final adventure in the beautiful setting of the Klondike wilderness. It is a two-week adventure that includes scenic aerial tours, nature hikes, stays at our luxury cabins and rejuvenating sessions in our luxury spa."

"Steve, the recent allegations made by Retired Colonel Lawrence G Martin have brought your company under intense scrutiny. He claims that A Perfect Finish is operating like a cult and preying on vulnerable Americans, exploiting Canada's MAID law for financial gain. Is that true? Are you, in fact, responsible for the deaths of retirees from America, including the Colonel's mother, and are you profiting from those deaths?"

"Melissa, I understand the concerns that have been raised, and I want to assure you and the viewers that A Perfect Finish is a legitimate and compassionate organization. We strictly adhere to Canada's Medical Assistance in Dying law and follow all the necessary protocols to ensure the safety and well-being of our clients. Our mission is to provide a unique and meaningful experience for those who choose to pursue medical assistance-in-dying in a serene and supportive environment.

"I assure you, our clients make a conscious and informed decision to seek end-of-life services. We work closely with medical professionals to assess each individual's eligibility and ensure they meet the legal requirements for Canada's Medical Assistance in Dying. Our team is dedicated to providing support, comfort, and care to our clients throughout the entire process. We are not preying on vulnerable individuals or exploiting the law for financial gain. Instead, we aim to offer an alternative option for those who choose a dignified and memorable end-of-life experience."

"Steve, while you emphasize the legality and compassionate nature of your services, critics argue that your company is not only commercializing death but also profiting from the suffering of others. Is it true that you charge clients millions in fees and still solicit them, and even their families, for donations? How do you respond to these accusations, and what safeguards do you have in place to ensure that your clients are not coerced or manipulated into making life-ending decisions?"

"Melissa, I appreciate the opportunity to address these concerns. At A Perfect Finish, we adhere to the strictest operating standards to ensure compliance with every detail of the law. We have no role in clients' end-of-life choices. Clients come to us for assistance only after they have made their own decisions. Furthermore, we do not solicit donations. However, we do offer clients the opportunity to donate to First Nations not-for-profit organizations supporting Whitehorse's local community. People admire the beauty of the Klondike and, naturally, they appreciate the warm hospitality of the people of the Yukon Territory. So, it's no surprise that some choose to donate.

"Our clients have lived extraordinary lives, and they trust us to provide an exceptional end-of-life experience. Our prices reflect the highest standard of care, support, and respect we provide our clients throughout their end-of-life journey." Steve straightened his tie and looked toward Melissa.

"Our research indicates that Canadians can typically access medical assistance-in-dying services in Canada for around fifteen-hundred Canadian dollars. However, your company charges American clients two million US dollars. How do you justify this significant price difference?"

"That is an excellent question, Melissa. It's important to recognize that while there are countless conventional ways to approach end-of-life experiences, no one should be criticized for their choice. Imagine I presented you with two options: a twenty-five-dollar two-week pass to visit the zoo, or a twenty-five-thousand-dollar, two-week safari in East Africa. Both experiences involve the viewing of lions and zebras, but that is where the similarities end. In the zoo, you would observe the animals relaxing in an artificial environment, whereas on the savannah, you would witness them in their habitat, interacting naturally. In the end, your choice would be based on personal preference, available resources, and affinity for zebras.

"To illustrate this further, two travelers starting from Honolulu, Hawaii and ending their journeys in Des Moines, Iowa have a wide variety of travel options. One may board a discount charter flight to Los Angeles and take a week-long bus ride overland, sustained along the way by bologna sandwiches and potato chips, while catching a wink of sleep here and there as best she can. Another travels by private jet, enjoying caviar and champagne and reclining for a restful night's sleep, before arriving early to precisely the same destination. For both such travelers in our example, the starting and end point are identical, it is only the journey and arrival times which are different.

"Similarly, a seventy-five-year-old who has just been diagnosed with early onset Alzheimer's can choose to invest millions for a long, predictable end-of-life experience in a memory care center, allowing her to continue well into her nineties, or use the same funds for a two-week breath-taking adventure tour in the Klondike. At A Perfect Finish, we believe individuals should have the right to choose their end-of-life experience according to their own philosophy and beliefs."

"Thank you for your explanation, Steve. However, another concern raised by your critics is the potential conflict between laws in some states which do not allow assistance-in-dying and your practice of transporting

American retirees to Canada for these services. Can you address this issue and explain how A Perfect Finish complies with both US and Canadian regulations?"

"Melissa, the fact that our clients choose to travel to Canada for their final adventure reflects their dissatisfaction with the laws of their own states. Once our clients arrive in Canada, they are subject to Canadian laws and regulations. A Perfect Finish operates entirely within the boundaries of Canada and we comply with the Canadian laws that govern medical assistance-in-dying."

"Your company has been accused of drugging clients with psilocybin and allowing them to jump to their deaths. Are those allegations true? Is that the method of dying you endorse for your clients?"

"First of all, psilocybin is a naturally-occurring hallucinogen that is found in species of mushrooms. We do not prescribe it to clients, but we do offer clients an anti-anxiety medication prior to flying. As for psilocybin mushrooms, they remain legal for medical use in the Yukon in cases of terminal illness, and have been endorsed by medical professionals as having the potential to enhance end-of-life experiences. While we do not explicitly endorse the use of psychedelics, we do understand the potential benefits. Should a client choose a psychedelic experience as part of her end-of-life choice, we would of course support such a choice.

"Regarding your question about the method of dying, clients choose their method of death. For a select few people, the exhilaration of jumping from an airplane, with or without a parachute, represents an extraordinary final experience.

"Think of it this way. Imagine you were terminally ill and decided to take your end-of-life experience into your own hands. What sort of announcement about your choice would you like to have posted in your home newspaper? The first option reports you died while skydiving in the Yukon; the second that you died on the bathroom floor by overdosing on pills; the third that you died in the ER, hooked up to machines after a long life in a nursing home. For my obituary, I would prefer the first option, wouldn't you? So, for any of your viewers who need information about our assistance-in-dying services, please visit our website at A Perfect Finish-dot-com. For discerning clients, we provide extraordinary end-of-life adventures."

"Thank you, Steve, for taking the time to answer these questions and address the public's concerns about A Perfect Finish and the services you provide. To our viewers, thank you for joining us for this exclusive interview. Stay tuned to CNN for further updates on this story and other important news developments. I am Melissa Steward reporting from Whitehorse, in Canada's Yukon Territory, signing off. Good night."

54. Sojourners from Outer Space

"Roving the moon without a phone again, are we? I've been meaning to ask you, Moonpie, what is it you see out there? Are you contemplating specks in the galaxy or drops in the river?"

Simon and Akiko . . . of all the things he could have told her about me. That figures.

Steve stood stone still, staring at the river.

"Moonpie, you crack me up. You're like an average Joe tourist, except you have an office window and a salary. What is it you do here? I forget. I mean aside from hiking and kayaking. Oh, and staring out your window."

"Hi, Akiko," replied Steve, without turning around. "I'm hiding, thanks for asking. How can I help you?"

"Hiding from the press? Why? I saw your interview. You were great. I mean, you could have tucked your shirt in a little better, but aside from that you were cool as a comet."

Steve turned to face his assailant. "Was that a compliment in disguise?"

"Yes, it was. I realize you are roving the dark side of the moon and I want to encourage you."

"Wow," said Steve as took a seat in his desk chair. "You came in just to be nice to me?"

"Wow, wow. Alas, no. I come bearing joyful news. Our little granny dropper just booked two new Sojourners directly over the top of your Sojourners 2-11 and 2-12. He's gotten permission from Eddie and Lily. Eddie said something like, 'No problemo, my Harry man.'"

"Sojourners from where?"

"From outer space. Who gives a shit? The point is, Harold booked them directly. Although, if you must know, I heard them speaking Japanese. That may be a clue for you, Mr Spock."

"Akiko, speak clearly. What are you trying to tell me?"

"I'm going to have to start bringing Angi with me to these little tête-à-têtes," Akiko said with a giggle. "A video of your little R2-D2 head swiveling around would be a priceless addition to your executive profile."

"Seriously, Akiko?"

"Listen to me, you Jabberwocky idiot. Watch my mouth move. Fuckface Flyboy just found a direct discount fucking booking. Two Japanese fossils want to die in the Yukon, and they've already paid Harold six hundred thousand US dollars each to hold hands for an eternity of blissful togetherness while they hop off the back of his fucking airplane. The icing on the cake is that your idiot employee already agreed to process them through the APF Therapy & Spa Center. One-way tickets with free tea service."

Steve stood, like he was about to take action, then he sat again, which caused Akiko to laugh and shake her head.

"Honestly, now that I think of it, what's the point of these little Space Mountain rides? Why do I even bother popping your space bubble with real information? I bet if I hadn't walked in here and mentioned it, you would have never even discovered what's happening right down the hall from you. You could just stare out your window for three more weeks of pure bliss, before heading off to fish in Alaska with Baby Kyle."

"Why would you refer to Eddie as *my* idiot employee, when he's *your* son?"

"Really? I tell you all that, and you quibble about Eddie's origins? How does Meriwa put up with your silly space balls? Oh, and speaking of the princess, maybe I should ask, my little Moonraker, why do you have lipstick on the side of your face?"

How can a woman this small and this old be this rapacious?

✱ ✱ ✱

Clyde called Steve and congratulated him on the new bookings. "I've discussed it with Meriwa, who just spoke to her cousin. Top Gun is bragging about direct access to a new pipeline. Somehow a Japanese businessman saw the colonel on national news and managed to contact Harold directly. Harold's plan has always been to try to cut out the middleman which, from his perspective, is you. It seems the opportunity has finally presented itself."

"What about the MAID forms?" Steve asked.

"Harold says that's the beauty of it," replied Clyde. "No MAID forms, no recoveries, Harold hands Eddie a few bills for snacks, and keeps the rest. At six hundred grand a pop, he's making triple what he would have made on our business, and he doesn't even have to do recoveries."

"I love it!" exclaimed Steve. "The bears are going to eat it up. The MAID murder police are going to have a field day. Eddie is going to be over the moon. The professor is going to win a Best Paper Award. The whole situation is uber priceless. It was especially great getting the news from your mom. Of course, for her, the entire ordeal was just one more hilarious entertainment opportunity."

"Do we have to call her my mom?"

"I could call her Dale Carnegie if that would make you feel better."

Clyde asked about Ron. Steve told him he was expecting him to ride in within a few days and that the fishing charters were already booked in Homer, Alaska. Clyde said it should be fun.

"Definitely more fun than being tortured by your Dale."

55. The Lone Ranger

It was 6:30 pm and after treading five trips up and down the Black Street Stairs, Steve returned to the executive suite to search for his phone. Bullet Hole Bagels had closed for the day and the outside door to the building was locked, so he used the code to unlock the tenant door and headed up the stairs. The executive suite was unlocked, and as he passed Jessie's empty desk, he heard voices and noticed Harold's door was ajar.

He found his phone sitting on the windowsill. As he walked out, he heard yelling. "Listen pal, I watched the tape, I heard *your* voice. You called her a cunt. You insulted her and then you killed her. Now I'm going to fucking kill you!"

"You don't understand," pleaded Harold. "I'm not even in charge."

Steve sneaked back to his office, quietly opened his safe, removed the soft-sided Harley bag, extracted Alamea's Glock 34, put an extra magazine in his front pocket, turned on the red dot optic, and stood outside Harold's door. He paused, took a breath, and rushed through the door as he racked the Glock and pointed it at the impostor. "Hands up!" he shouted.

The Ranger was quick. The moment Steve racked the pistol, the Ranger's right hand flashed behind his back. Steve took a breath and squeezed the trigger. The Ranger had already pointed his gun toward Harold as the bullet hit him in the chest. It knocked him back, but the Ranger still managed to get off a shot, hitting the moccasin picture hanging directly behind Harold. Steve hit him twice more, before the Ranger dropped the gun and collapsed to the floor.

The air reeked of gunpowder, and Steve's ears rang. He advanced in silence with the pistol pointed to the floor. He shook as adrenaline coursed through his veins. He knelt next to a pool of blood on the rug and checked for a pulse.

"He was going to kill me." Harold's words were weak. "Steve, you just saved my life."

"I know. I didn't want to kill him, but he seemed like an imminent threat, wouldn't you agree?" Steve sought confirmation.

"Well, he did intend to shoot me," offered Harold.

"How do you know that?" asked Steve.

"Think about it. He had a choice, draw or put his hands up. He chose to draw. When he drew, he didn't aim for the shooter, he aimed for his target–that's me. He came here to kill me and he cared more about that than living. You just saved my life. I honestly thought I was a goner. I was considering making a run for the door then you came in and shot him."

"I warned him. Why didn't he stop? He drew his gun and aimed it at you."

"Exactly. Honestly, I can't believe you just won a duel with a real US Army Ranger."

"I sort of surprised him, I guess, and he is retired, I mean was . . . is."

"He's definitely retired now. Sort of a dick too, don't you think?"

Harold almost got shot and suddenly sprouts a sense of humor.

Steve placed the gun in the waistband in the small of his back and rubbed the back of his neck. "Yeah, and anger issues–he seemed quite angry. I don't think it was going to be possible to reason with him."

"Right. So, that would make him a former angry, imminently threatening, retired US Army Ranger Dick," summarized Harold.

Steve's look of worry persisted. "Yeah, with bullet holes. He's not going to drip blood on the bagels, is he?"

"No, that would be the other side of the hall."

"What do we do now?"

"What do we do? You gotta get out of town, my friend. You saved my life, now it's my turn to save your ass."

"It was justified, right? Why would I leave? Why don't we just report it?"

"Steve, don't be an idiot. This is not America. If you really think you can explain that gun, feel free to stick around. Otherwise, I am telling you as a friend, you better get the fuck out."

"What about this Ranger Dick mess?"

"Today's Bullet Hole Ranger Dick mess is about to become tomorrow's smelly bear scat. By the time someone bothers to ask, Ranger Dick will be nothing more than just another stampeder lost in the Klondike." Harold was enjoying the moment. "Anyway, it's not your problem. This is the sort of thing I know how to manage. Give me the gun."

Steve extracted the magazine, unchambered the round, and checked the chamber before handing over the gun, the cartridge, and both magazines. He went to his office and got the black soft-side Harley bag made for a trike and returned.

Harold put it all in the Harley bag and zipped it shut. "Should I ask where you got this?"

"No."

"Uh huh. Don't worry, I'll take care of it. What about you, Steve, where are you off to?"

"I've been wanting to do a little fishing in Homer, Alaska. I hear the silvers are running. If I head out tonight, I can be there by the day after tomorrow."

"Perfect. Don't worry about any of this. Give me a call once you get there. Oh, and Steve, I mean this–thanks, buddy. I owe you."

56. Halibut Heaven

Steve had spent the day fishing with Ron in Homer and returned to his hotel. As he entered, he heard the phone ringing. He picked it up from the charger and called Clyde who informed him he was at an art show in Miami. Steve began the conversation by chatting about fishing, but Clyde interrupted him.

"John insisted that I tell you right out of the box, in the event you should ever require an attorney, you may contact him. He's really worried you're going to do something dumb, so I'm supposed to tell you to keep quiet. He did go on and on, gossip queen, loose lips sink ships, and so on. In shyster-speak, it all seems to translate roughly to 'shut the fuck up' about that matter, of which I've never heard."

"As I was saying, the fishing is fantastic. The silver salmon are in Kachemak Bay and today I landed the biggest halibut of my life. It weighed over two hundred pounds, four times the size of Ron's biggest catch."

"Sounds great, and really, I love listening to fishing stories, but Meriwa called this morning. She asked me to call you. She says she needs you in Whitehorse now. It's important."

"Tell her I said the fishing in Whitehorse sucks, on account of the dams."

"Funny, but really, we have an offer from someone to purchase the company. Meriwa recommends that we sell. She said we have already achieved Alamea's objectives, and now that we have an offer, we should take it. She said you took up Alamea's dying request and executed it like a real champion. She asked that you please return to Whitehorse now and help her sell the company. Those were her words."

"Why didn't she just call me herself?"

"John says if you need to speak to an attorney you have to call him. It's just too close to Meriwa's mayoral election to involve her. Also, Meriwa told me to tell you, thank you and that she admires your courage."

"Meriwa really said that?"

"Sure, and it's not the first time," replied Clyde. "She asks you to return now, and Harold agrees, too. You belong in Whitehorse."

"You do know we have fishing charters booked here for all of next week, right?" Steve resisted, half-heartedly.

"Leave Ron in Homer to fish out the charters." Clyde's words were fast and urgent. "Hop on your Harley tomorrow morning and make it to Whitehorse the following day. Really, Meriwa needs your help. You are the CEO. She cannot cut a deal without you."

57. Eddie is Polarizing

Steve was sitting in Space Mountain with Angi discussing website traffic when Akiko entered. Without knocking, she threw open the door and exclaimed, "Caught you!"

"Should I leave?" asked Angi.

"Yes, dear, unless you like threesomes."

Angi was already gone. Steve shook his head and asked, "Any word from Eddie?"

"What's the point, Space Jam? You know he's never coming back."

"Well, no, I'm still hoping we hear from him. Has he ever done something like this before?"

"Not exactly. I mean, he went to India."

"What makes you think this is a big deal?" asked Steve.

"The 98 Hotel let me see his room last night. His mushrooms are dying. Eddie would never abandon mushrooms, and he would never leave without saying goodbye to me. That means somebody took him."

"You really think so? What about his breakfast stand? Have you checked with his friend?"

"She said Eddie didn't show up last night. Simon is no longer speaking to me, but he told Ivonne he has no idea where Eddie is. Nobody has seen him."

"So, he just disappeared, and we have no idea what happened? Can you think of anyone who would want to harm Eddie?"

"Eddie makes friends wherever he goes. He also annoys some people wherever he goes."

"Eddie annoys some people? Akiko, Meriwa just told me Eddie infected the widowed sister of a chief elder with herpes."

"Yes, Moonpie, people find herpes annoying. That's why Eddie had to leave Hawaii. Relatives of his clients got annoyed. He had to close his business. Weren't you aware?"

"Aware? How could I be aware? He told me at the ball game he was taking this job so he could come to Canada to care for you."

"Yo, backspace, backspace. You bought that? Eddie has four Little Eddies running around the North Shore and he's never changed a diaper or raised a finger caring for even one Little Eddie. Do you know why? Because he can't. He's only capable of caring for mushrooms.

"You tell me, space case, how would you feel being all old and shit and having Eddie show up one day as your designated caregiver? Nightmare, right? So, if you bought Eddie's line about taking care of his dear old mother, you are a total backspace."

"Akiko, stop. You're getting off track here with all this Little Eddie bullshit. Let's talk about herpes. So, are you telling me Eddie knew he had herpes when he arrived, he came here anyway, he spread a communicable infectious disease in Whitehorse, and nobody thought that was worth mentioning to me?"

"Oh Chewy, don't be simple. You're the last person anybody would confide in about anything at all, let alone information about their breadstick and meatballs. What if Eddie had told you? You would have messed up the whole plan. Don't you see? This gig was a perfect fit for Eddie. A total win-win. Here, he could bang a bunch of old broads right before they hop out the back of a plane and nobody's ever even gonna know they died with herpes. It was brilliant, really."

"Yeah, brilliant. Obviously, someone agrees. I mean, it is possible somebody has actually disappeared him forever, and we may never find him."

Akiko's smile evaporated. "For Eddie, I think it was over once he was diagnosed. Before then he felt he had a lot to offer the world. I mean, not just as a surfer, a trip guide, or a guru. He used to talk to me before the diagnosis. Once, he told me he thought of himself as a sort of trip guiding guru with soul."

Steve folded his arms, shook his head, and looked down. Akiko continued, "Once he got diagnosed, he didn't express himself as much. He became withdrawn. I think the disease may have had an adverse impact on his self-esteem. Plus, it was bad for business, and he just needed some place to go. I mean, it's not like he could ever go back to Hawaii, and there's no way John was going to let him move into the pool house. So, where else was he going to find, you know, a final resting place?"

"Wow. Just wow."

"Wow, wow, wow, herpes. I tell you a bunch of really personal things and that's your reaction? Moonpie, you are definitely not guru material. More like a six-year-old kid in a planetarium, 'Wow, wow, wow, the cosmos, a whole big universe.' Why don't you look on the bright side? Now you can start letting old men hop out of planes."

"Old men? Why would Eddie's death change that?"

"Eddie . . . doesn't . . . rub . . . dudes. You know that, Moonpie."

"You're telling me Eddie doesn't rub dudes, and that's the reason Alamea targeted just old women, not old men?"

"You are such a cute little space bar. The business plan has nothing to do with Alamea. I tried to get Alamea to include Eddie in the plan. She said, 'No. Akiko, no. Absolutely no Eddie.' Those were her precise words. Then Clyde asked you to hire Eddie. You said, 'Well, okay.' See the difference, Moonpie?"

Steve shook his head.

"Don't worry, my little Space Jam, we all make mistakes. You wanna know the biggest mistake I ever made? Selling Asshole Sr that accidental death rider for double indemnity on his one million dollar life insurance policy. Big mistake . . . of course, you would be in jail today if I hadn't."

"That doesn't even make sense, Akiko. You're lobbing grenades faster than I can catch them. What are you trying to say about Mark?"

"After you had your little tea party with Asshole Jr in Seattle, he called me to inquire about the double indemnity clause, to confirm that it was going to pay out. I told him that if the Mounties got their hands on his dad's suicide note, he would definitely lose a million bucks. He told me he knew you were there that night but decided not to attack you to recover the Munchkin's jewelry and cash, because he didn't want you speaking to the Mounties or the life insurance company about anything you saw, or mentioning the suicide note from his dad."

"Wow. Really?"

"Wow, wow, wow. You look so fucking stupid right now. In the future, I'm going to start wearing a GoPro for all my Space Mountain rides. This is content Angi can't afford to miss."

"Do you mind explaining what you just said?"

"You're kidding? Where do you keep your Etch-A-Sketch? Think about it. You were there. You said Asshole Sr sped up when he saw you doing jumping jacks. It happened right in front of your little Martian eyes. You don't think that is something the life insurance company might be interested in hearing about before paying double for accidental death? Why did you think Alamea asked you to hand the suicide note to Asshole Jr directly instead of just letting the Mounties find the note?"

"You think Alamea believed Mark wrecked on purpose?"

"You wrote her message in the journal yourself."

Steve retrieved the journal and read the passage aloud, "Love prospers when a fault is forgiven."

Akiko looked at him. "Whose fault? She forgave Mark for killing her, but why? Giving the suicide letter to Junior was her final gift to the little prick, a present. With your help, the Munchkin secured an extra million in life insurance for Junior, but he could only collect it by going along with the accident story. He could not risk turning you in, because you knew about the suicide note and could become a potential witness to the murder. You see, without that final gift, APF never would have happened, and Junior would have taken the jewelry and the money. And maybe he would have contested Alamea's estate."

Mark wasn't just a crap rider; he was a murderer. Does Meriwa already know this? She told me they wasted the day in a pointless quarrel. She warned Alamea not to travel with Mark.

Maybe Clyde suspected it. That's another reason he hates the Mumfords so much.

I was the one who was there. How can I be the last to know?

Steve walked to the window and stared at the river, wondering whether Alamea could have been that aware and forward-thinking, especially given the chaos of the moment, her pain, and imminent death. Is it possible she had so intricately orchestrated everything? He thought back on the night of the accident.

Her first order of business was writing the codicil, obligating Clyde and Meriwa to proceed with her business. Second was securing a promise for the jewelry, ensuring that I would meet the team. Lastly, there was the suicide letter to Mark Jr, aimed at protecting the estate from attack.

Perhaps Meriwa was correct about Alamea always acting with intent. She arranged Meriwa's introduction to Ron and set me on a glide path to meet her as well. Did she anticipate the sorrow her death would cause and send me to alleviate Meriwa's grief? Alamea nursing her beloved, prescribing pain relief with the cure?

He turned and faced Akiko. "Let's go back to the part about targeting women. Why did Alamea plan to target only women?"

Akiko grinned as if it was Christmas. "She didn't. I did."

"Are you saying you changed Alamea's business plan to target only women just so APF would hire Eddie?"

"No, Master Luke. I would never do such a low-down, dirty, rotten thing like changing someone else's plan, but that's where you have it wrong. It wasn't Alamea's plan, was it? It was OUR plan. See Chewy, it was a SHARED document. It was OUR document. That's what it means when you share a document. It's called coo-laaaa-booo-raaa-shun. Since Alamea didn't object, we targeted only women, and then *you* hired Eddie." Akiko giggled with glee.

Steve glared. "Hold it, backspace, backspace. Are you telling me you changed the plan, and Alamea didn't notice?"

"Moonpie, I just told you that. The Munchkin didn't notice and she didn't mind because she was already dead. I wasn't the only one, you know? The business plan was also shared with Meriwa and Clyde. How do you think FunBite was added to the business plan? How do you think the million-dollar granny drops were added?"

"What? You're saying Meriwa and Clyde changed the plan?"

"Do you think Princess Leia coulda bought anything more than a hot dog stand by collecting pocket change from poor nursing home pill-poppers? See? The document belonged to all of us. It's not like we didn't have the right to change it, cowpie."

"You're telling me Alamea planned to target regular folks, not rich women, and that she never intended to drop them out of airplanes?"

"Finally, welcome back to planet Earth, Major Tom. Yes, Alamea intended to waste her fortune on a bunch of poor old gits, offering pill-popping deaths at bargain-basement prices. You've got to agree, our high-octane adventure deaths at stratospheric prices are better, right? You said it yourself, ten bucks per donation. That would have netted FunBite a hundred bucks per poor bastard MAID murder, versus half a million in donations from offing each of the rich bitches in style."

"You know, Moonpie, you could have discovered all this yourself. When you're ready for a little Keystone Kop adventure, sit yourself down with some milk and cookies and check the change history for the Business Plan document." Akiko literally giggled herself to tears. She barely managed to finish the sentence.

This is what my sister would have looked like if she had gotten that pony for Christmas.

"It's not funny, Akiko. Let's focus, so we can end this Gallipoli of a conversation. Are you saying Alamea never planned to drop grannies from planes?"

"Moonpie, you are so fucking cuddly. That point was never even mentioned in the plan. That's something Flyboy Dipshit came up with on the fly to get more fees, and because he needed a new boat to bribe Uncle Mountie. Meriwa and Clyde decided to let it happen because they needed Dipshit's support. They said it would intensify the tsunami. Alamea planned for the old bags to die at the Therapy & Spa Center, thereby avoiding all the bullshit drama that Dipshit orchestrated. And guess what? Everybody sat around eating popcorn, watching you swallow Flyboy's ridiculous proposal like a guppy. Clyde and I even bet a dollar on it. I won, of course."

This sent Steve back to his window. He stared at the river for a moment before turning around. "What about Eddie?"

"Quit worrying about Eddie. They took him at night. That means he was definitely tripping when they killed him. However they did it, knowing Eddie, I'm sure it was just one last happy trip. Don't you see, Moonpie? In his own way, Eddie managed to orchestrate his own Perfect Finish."

"Orchestrate . . . Perfect . . . Eddie? Yeah, great."

"That brings me around to my final point, Moonpie. I'm done here."

"What? All this, and now you're quitting?"

"Yes, Mister Spock, you could say that. In fact, let's just call this my formal notice of *final* resignation."

Steve placed the journal on the desk and stood up straight. "Ah, I see." He paused. "You think that without Eddie, your work is done. What about starting a Greenpeace chapter in Whitehorse? Isn't Ivonne depending on you for that?"

"Greenpeace, my ass," Akiko said, her jovial mood lost in the rear-view mirror. "I've spent the past forty years trying to save oblivious climate-deniers from oblivion and I haven't made a damn bit of progress." She paced back and forth, her voice rising. "Forget about the planet, Moonpie. It's not in peril. Earth has already experienced five mass extinctions. Humans will fry with the fucking baboons, but the planet will keep orbiting the sun long after we're gone. The Munchkin is gone, Eddie is dead, humanity is doomed, and now I'm done."

"I see. So, are you on the sojourner schedule?"

"Slow down, Rocket Man, I'm not paying anybody two million fucking dollars. This one's on the Munchkin. Got that? Harold already agreed. It's gonna be the ride that never happened, Japanese style. No flight plan. No recovery. Bear food."

Akiko spoke slowly. "Now it's time for you to listen, Steve. For once, pay attention. I have a request for you. A real request. Steve, are you listening? I want you to be the one."

Steve? I didn't think she knew my name.

Steve crossed his arms in front. "What do you mean?"

Akiko replied, "You little Ewok, I need you on that plane with me tomorrow, 2 pm take-off."

"Why me?" asked Steve.

"Now that the Munchkin and Eddie are gone, you're the closest thing to family I have."

Mercury, closest to the sun, first to vaporize when the sun dies.

"Look, my little Sox kitten, it's not like the choice was mine. I mean, out of five living men from Pluto, you would be like my . . . my third choice. You were the Munchkin's choice. That's our bond, you and me, our bond together. Friends forever, see?"

Steve pulled Akiko into a hug, whispering, "Okay, I'll do it." Akiko hugged him back . . . and squeezed his ass.

58. Get Outta Dodge

Steve made the phone call to Clyde from the Confession Bench, at the top of the escarpment to discuss Eddie infecting the widowed sister of an elder. Clyde said he didn't know Eddie had herpes and asked Steve if he had known.

"It's not on my regular list of interview questions," said Steve. "I was kind of wondering why you never told me about it when you asked me to hire him."

"This is the first I've heard of it," Clyde said.

"Then why did your mother tell me Eddie got run out of Hawaii by some relatives of former clients?"

"That sort of thing wouldn't surprise me, but it doesn't mean I've heard about it before today. Think about it Steve, if somebody gave your mom herpes, you're not going to hang posters around the North Shore: *Wanted Dead or Alive–This man gave my mom herpes.* Right?"

"Yeah, when you put it that way, I see your point. Your little brother told me an awful lot of personal information, but somehow, he managed to leave out this one little factoid."

"Yeah, Eddie has an ingenious way of disarming people by making them think he's a moron," said Clyde. "Are you worried about him?"

"Like how worried? Like someone already killed him before I could find him and kill him myself?"

"Yeah, something like that, for example."

Steve hesitated. "Meriwa said to me this morning, 'Steve, this is a big fucking deal.' Those were her exact words. I've never heard Meriwa say *fuck* before."

"Yeah, it seems like a big deal then. If somebody killed Eddie, it makes one wonder what could happen next."

"Before calling you, I decided I'd better interview our favorite little trash-talker," said Steve.

"Akiko? You actually initiated a conversation with her? Don't ever do that. About Eddie? I can't even imagine the rant."

"Yeah, but a geyser of information. She confirmed Eddie was diagnosed several years ago. And to think we could have discovered it from the get-go by simply asking the witch why Eddie was quitting his business in Hawaii."

Clyde said, "She confirmed it? Well then, that is conclusive."

"Akiko also said that Meriwa changed the business plan after Alamea's death to include FunBite."

"Oh yes, I helped her do that. That was just Meriwa making the changes to the plan that she and Alamea had previously discussed and then modifying the target clients so the business would be economically viable. As the administrator of Alamea's estate, I was for it. I could never have permitted the squandering of the estate for the pursuit of a foolish business idea. Now we have saved the estate for the benefit of the trust while also carrying out Alamea's wishes. You do see how that is fulfilling her final request, right?"

Steve hesitated. "I'm not sure. You're telling me that what we just did wasn't really Alamea's plan? She was planning to help poor people in nursing homes, and instead we targeted rich old women?"

"I know, I know, but it's really not what you think. Before you judge us too harshly, I want you to meet with Angi, Daisy, and Jessie. I'll arrange the meeting. Allow them to describe their incredible work outside of APF, and the brilliance of what Meriwa has orchestrated over the past year. You see, Meriwa managed to keep her promise to Alamea while also pursuing her own passion for advancing the rights and interests of First Nations in the Yukon. Ask the three ladies the same questions you're asking me now, and they will confirm that Alamea could not have asked for a more loyal friend than Meriwa."

"I don't know what to say," Steve replied in exasperation. "You showed me a business plan that had been radically altered without including me in the process."

"Steve, let's not get lost in the weeds. Alamea asked you to evaluate her plan and decide. Her business plan was always weak in terms of marketing and pricing, and it was still evolving. The fact that we continued to refine and improve the plan to make it economically viable doesn't change the result; we all just hit a homerun in terms of creating and exploiting a tsunami, which was the purpose of the company. Had anyone proposed that you pursue a business plan which had no economic merit, what are the chances A Perfect Finish ever would have gotten off the ground?"

"Yeah, I see what you mean," Steve conceded. "I would have rejected it. There was another alarming detail your Dale mentioned. She said Alamea didn't plan to drop grannies from planes."

"As far as I know, it wasn't a point Alamea specified in the plan," replied Clyde. "Harold had the idea, and we went along with it. Does it matter?"

"Actually, I'm stunned. It seems like we've gone to great lengths to orchestrate the most outrageous method of helping grannies die, and I don't see the benefit."

"The benefit is the sensationalism of the method in order to amplify the tsunami. It was an improvisation, and it worked, don't you think?" Steve didn't reply. Clyde continued, "Look, why don't you meet with the ladies to understand how APF fits into the larger overall effort, and then we can revisit the matter? For now, can we get back to the crisis at hand? Who is the infected widow? Is it a relative of Meriwa's?"

"She's First Nations. They're all relatives. As far as the clan, she's Wolf."

"Really?" Clyde replied. "I don't know if that's better or worse for us."

"When it comes to Eddie spreading an infectious disease in Whitehorse, there isn't a better. The Mountie is a Wolf. That's why I think it's time we try to speed up the sale."

"Where are we in negotiations with Kenichi?" asked Clyde.

"About ten minutes away from signing or maybe ten weeks, hard to say."

"Steve, can I call you back in ten? Where are you?"

"I'm sitting atop the escarpment and sure, I'll sit tight."

Steve sat on the Confession Bench and analyzed how all of this had come to pass.

Did Alamea really agree to FunBite raking the donations? Was Alamea trying to help desperate people in nursing homes find dignity in death only for us to target an entirely different market segment? Did we really drop grannies from an airplane to sensationalize press coverage and amplify the tsunami?

A butterfly flapped her wings and caused a tsunami. The outcome didn't unfold exactly as intended, but does it truly matter? Isn't this precisely the essence of chaos theory?

Steve's phone rang. It was Clyde, together with John. Clyde apologized for forcing Eddie on Steve and John added that they could discuss it further in person. Steve didn't reply.

In the background, John beat a *rat-a-tat-tat*. "In the meantime, we spoke to Meriwa. All of us agree it's time for you to abandon the sale and walk away from APF. Steve, it's time for you to leave the Yukon Territory."

"Abandon the sale?" asked Steve. "Are you serious? How about if I try to accelerate the negotiations and drop the price? We can complete the transaction as a fire sale."

"The company was always temporary," explained John. "We never intended for it to outlast the tsunami, and we never expected you to save it. What we need now is for you to meet Angi for a transitional meeting. She has an offer for you and needs your ongoing assistance. Her proposal is something we've been working on for a while. Obviously, the new developments are accelerating the timeline."

"I see. Let me discuss it with Meriwa, then I'll decide."

"Think of it this way," explained Clyde. "A Perfect Finish has already netted fourteen million dollars before tax. Your share of that will be over a million dollars after tax. Don't you think it's about time to cash in your chips? You could return to Denver with a nice stash and resume teaching, right?"

"Okay, let me see how much time I have and weigh my options."

Steve stared down the path as he signed off with Clyde and John. Meriwa appeared, walking through the trees with her hands on her hips and breathing heavily. As she passed the Kissing Tree, she zigged a little to touch it then zagged back to the trail.

She had run to reach him. Her arms glistened and her lavender t-shirt clung to her skin down to her navel. She smiled sweetly, dimples and ivory, as she approached. She hugged him hard. He hugged her back as though it might be the last time. Finally, he released her and as he did, she nipped his jaw, tilted her head, and grinned. The snipe left a mark on his chin, and her sweat left marks on his shirt. He smiled and breathed deeply to calm his racing heart.

They sat in the usual way, Meriwa on one end of the Confession Bench, Steve to her left with the imaginary picnic pack between them. Meriwa began, "Clyde told me I might find you here."

"You always do have the inside scoop," Steve said.

"Yep."

"What do you think, my little native?"

"The natives are angry."

"What should I do?" asked Steve.

"It's time for you, my cheechako friend, to get out of Dodge."

"If you say it, it must be so. How much time do I have?"

"You will ride out tomorrow morning."

"Tomorrow is Wednesday. How about I ride out Thursday morning instead? I will be gone by 8 am. Do you think you can buy me that much time?"

"What do you imagine you will achieve by delaying a day?"

"I have a commitment. To Akiko."

"I see. Of course. Let me call my father."

Meriwa made the call, mentioning Akiko's name and asking for the extra day. After hanging up and reading a text message, she said, "Jessie suggested dinner tonight at Wayfarer Oyster House, 8 pm with Daisy and Angi."

Steve nodded and gave her a thumbs up. Meriwa texted Jessie his reply and reached for his hand. They waited in silence. Steve stared far away at the top of Mount Lorne and thought of when he was a senior in high school and played gangster Sky Masterson in the spring musical production of *Guys & Dolls*. For a brief time, he shared an intense experience with the girl who played missionary Sarah Brown and they became quite close. Before the third and final performance, they sat and discussed the play. Following the final production, he never spoke with her again, leaving a void in his soul. They had graduated shortly thereafter and went their separate ways. Before he met Emily, he thought of her often.

Meriwa's phone rang. "Don't worry, it's done. Yes, yes, he understands." She pocketed her phone. "They agree. Thursday, you are on your bike and gone by 8 am. They want to know if you are westbound or eastbound?"

"Homeward bound."

"Then they'll be watching for you at Watson Lake."

59. Fire Sale

Before the Eddie news, Steve had agreed to meet Harold at 6 pm. He arrived ten minutes early, walked through the empty reception area, and knocked on Harold's half-open door.

Harold greeted him with a charming lilt in his booming voice. "Steve, welcome. Come in, come in."

Harold could have been a diplomat if he was just forty-two percent more reasonable.

Steve shook hands with Harold, who ushered him to a chair next to Kenichi.

Steve smiled. "Hello, Kenichi." Kenichi failed to acknowledge him, staring straight ahead.

"Thank you for coming," said Harold. "We have been discussing the transaction. Kenichi is prepared to make you a final offer for the purchase of A Perfect Finish."

Steve nodded to Kenichi and waited in silence.

"One dollar," Kenichi said, as he stared straight ahead.

"Canadian or American?" asked Steve.

Kenichi and Harold glared at him in unison.

"Does Meriwa know about this?" asked Steve.

"Meriwa is Crow," Harold boomed as he got to his feet. "Look, Steve, this offer requires no acceptance." Spittle appeared on his lower lip as he placed both palms on his desk and leaned forward. "All your options have expired. Some elders want you arrested, and some elders want you dead." He pointed his finger at Steve as he spewed droplets. "The only reason you are still sitting here is that you saved my life, but the clock is ticking. Do you understand?"

"The offer is one dollar," repeated Kenichi from the periphery.

Harold led Steve to the door with a smirk, taunting him all the way. "We can get our own clients now," he said. "As your late great friend would say, 'You're expendable, you know what I mean, Stevo?' It must really suck being an English teacher, wandering through life in a fog, always the last to comprehend."

Steve put his hands in his pockets and looked down as he pushed through the door and walked down the hall. Harold taunted him loudly from behind, his baritone voice escalating in a sing-song opera style. "That's our boy, Steve Hamilton, the cheechako from outer space."

Steve exited the Bullet Hole building, headed straight to Sheep Camp, trudged resolutely up the steep stairs, and took a seat at the bar. "Kurt, two Vespers, please."

60. Meriwa's Photons

After two drinks at Sheep Camp, Steve finished the first leg of the One Mile River Walk. It was a beautiful late summer evening and the path was teeming with residents and tourists. Even though it was just past 7 pm, the long daylight hours of the north made it feel as though it was mid-afternoon. Near the SS Klondike, he paused at the riverbank, to reflect on events of the day and his purpose in life. As he stared at the rapids, he said aloud, "Don't forget about me, sweet Emily." She heard him but did not reply.

Steve retraced his steps on the river path and turned up Main Street, heading toward Mac's Fireweed Bookstore. After browsing through books for half an hour, he checked the time before purchasing a final memento, a small notebook made for tourists. It included a hologram of a fierce grizzly bear on the cover and was labeled 'Whitehorse Yukon' in gold lettering.

He walked sullenly cross-town toward Wayfarer Oyster House. As he ascended the stairs of the restaurant, he reminisced about the first time he'd met Jessie. All the qualities he had noticed in her during their first meeting were still evident, but how confident and capable she had become!

Jessie, Daisy, and Angi were seated with drinks. "I hope I'm not interrupting."

Jessie and Angi hugged him, while Daisy nodded her greeting and offered the skeleton of a smile. Steve ordered a Yukon Gold and the others another round. Once the drinks arrived, Angi recapped their latest business developments, including the creation of a new Canadian company called *A Well MAID Plan*, which would have three offices.

As Angi launched into her description, it reminded Steve of the first time he had met her at Burnt Toast Café with Meriwa. He listened to her rapid-fire machine gun volley and watched her mouth move. He heard some of the words: her brother would be in the Toronto office, Daisy's cousin in Montreal, some nurses, American clients, Canadian clients. On and on she went. Steve nodded, remembering the glances he had exchanged with Meriwa during that first performance.

There was a second company in Seattle, Angi was moving into the pool house. They were selling franchises in the US. They already had bookings for January, and so on. It was another Angi performance, the sprinter killing it on the debate team.

Angi continued talking about the developments in the US and Canada, passage of more euthanasia laws by five more states and revision to Canada's MAID laws in some provinces. Steve had heard rumblings about the business developments, but this was the first he had heard about John and Meriwa's successes in lobbying states and provinces to revise or implement new laws.

Just when I thought the tsunami had abated and the wind had died, we discover that the breeze is actually growing.

"I can guess, but I'd rather ask, where did you get the money to start all these companies?" asked Steve. He looked at Jessie and Daisy who both looked toward Angi.

Angi laughed before confirming, "Clyde reinvested one hundred percent of his dividends from APF into the new ventures. Also, John created the trust from Alamea's estate, right? Together, that is over ten million dollars to fund the new endeavors." Angi slid a document across the table to Steve.

"You managed to complete all that since the tsunami?" Steve asked as he flipped through the pages.

Daisy and Jessie nodded, but Angi said, "No. As I said during our initial conference call, we have been preparing for the tsunami since day one. All of these initiatives were already in progress before the tsunami."

Steve nodded before redirecting the discussion. "What are the implications for APF?"

"Obviously, APF is dead," Angi replied. "The model was never sustainable or scalable. Imagine if ten percent of Americans and Canadians chose MAID as their final solution. That would be almost one thousand MAID deaths per day. We have been dropping one MAID customer per week out of a plane and fighting bears to retrieve their bodies. Clearly, that is not scalable. The company fulfilled its purpose, and now it is finished."

Daisy spoke up. "After Alamea's death, Harold came up with the idea of adding an adventure death to the wilderness experience. He needed clients and the RCMP needed a new rescue boat. See Steve, when Mark Jr first spoke to the RCMP, before you met him in Seattle, he asked them about Alamea's cash, so the RCMP guessed you were hiding the dough and planned to arrest you and seize it. Harold convinced his uncle to have APF pay him for a rescue boat outright as part of the contract and then donate the Zodiac to the RCMP. It was cleaner than seizing the money from you and trying to convert it for their own benefit."

"Akiko said the Zodiac was a bribe for the RCMP. So that part is actually true?"

Daisy replied with a pained expression, "Yes, Steve. Harold already had a Zodiac and didn't need another one. It is no secret. There was an article on the front page of the *Whitehorse Daily Star* featuring a big picture of Harold and the RCMP Chief with the Zodiac during the donation ceremony."

"How did Meriwa let all of this happen?" Steve asked, as he shook his head and fanned himself with the document.

Angi replied, "First of all, Meriwa made a lot of compromises with her uncle and cousin just to keep you out of jail. As for targeting wealthy clients and adventure deaths, everybody, including John and Clyde, agreed that as long as we were targeting wealthy clients, the drama of falling from an airplane would maximize fundraising results. It worked; we raised millions."

Daisy scowled in obvious dissent. Jessie hid a smirk behind her glass. Steve looked genuinely puzzled. Angi continued explaining, "Alamea always meant to handle deaths at the therapy center, but to a man with a skydiving plane, everyone looks like a jumper. Harold made a killing off the fees for airdrops and recoveries. We didn't really think you'd go for it, but once Meriwa's mother decided that you were trustworthy, they let Harold give it a shot. To our surprise, it worked."

"Worked? What do you mean, worked?" asked Steve. "Eddie said we only convinced those old ladies to jump by tripping them out."

"That's the point, Steve." Daisy scolded as though he were a child. "You are the one who agreed to Harold's proposal. None of it would have happened if you had stood up to him. And once he kicked me off his plane, we had no idea what was happening on those plane flights."

Steve shook his head, wiped his forehead with his napkin and removed his jacket. Jessie tried to soften the blow with a compliment. "Don't worry, Steve, microdosing clients allowed them to die peacefully. According to Harold, that is what they paid for, right?"

Steve took a long drink, pursed his lips and looked down.

Angi added another twist to the knife, "We still need your help, Steve. You heard about the professor's paper?"

Steve shook his head. "I know he's doing bear research."

"Next week, he is publishing a paper titled, *Conditioning Klondike Bears to Eat Human Flesh*. The press will go nuts and we need you to help us ride the wave. That is the point of this meeting. John prepared that redundancy agreement for you to sign," explained Angi as she pointed to the pages in front of Steve. "It terminates your employment agreement with APF and offers severance pay on the condition that you hold a press conference with the professor in Denver next week."

Angi paused to give Steve a chance to object. "Clyde is offering you a year's salary for redundancy, and ten cents for your ten percent stake in APF and letter of resignation, but you'll still get your share of the dividends, which is estimated to be over a million dollars."

Steve leafed through the papers and shook his head. "The dividend sounds great, and I guess a person might suffer through the nightmare of press conferences for a year's salary, but why would I give up my ten percent stake in a profitable company for ten cents?"

"Once the professor's paper is published, nobody in Canada, including you, will want anything to do with the original APF company," explained Angi. "It will be worthless. Contractors are abandoning the company like rats leaving a sinking ship."

"What was Meriwa's decision about her ten percent stake?" Steve asked.

"She has already forfeited her shares and received her dividend. Also, she appointed her sister CEO of FunBite. It will be easier for you to manage the press conference next week if you've already quit and sold your stake to Kenichi too, right?"

"I understand. Tell me, what happened to all the leads from the tsunami?" Steve asked.

Angi sat back and took a sip of her drink. "Since the tsunami, thousands of MAID service prospects have contacted us through the APF website. As part of the APF sales agreement Kenichi signed over all rights to the APF name to the new APF US company. Kenichi doesn't need APF to get new clients, so he doesn't value the brand, the website, or the leads. We already have more leads than we could process in three years and they continue just piling up, so we don't need Liz for sales anymore. And after the press conference, we will no longer need you, so you will be free to go back to teaching English."

A butterfly flaps her wings in the Yukon, fueling Meriwa's photons and creating a cosmic wind.

Steve continued shuffling through the papers. He wanted a little more time to understand the offer, so he kept her talking. "What is your proposition for your new companies? How will it differ from APF?"

He was reading and half listening as Angi continued, "We'll charge between five and fifty thousand dollars for clients to spend anywhere from a week to a month at our spas and production centers, where we will capture and publish videos and video calls like we did for APF. The difference is that now the focus won't be on impressing friends. The videos will be more personalized and down-to-earth, including messages directed at specific people, family and friends. For example, a video with a final message for your sister, or maybe an actual video conference, with both you and your sister together, recorded in our studio."

Medical assistance-in-dying for the average Joe? Just as Alamea had planned. Meriwa kept her promise to a friend, without compromising her own mission to help her people.

Steve pulled out his pen, signed the termination agreement and absentmindedly tugged on his wedding band.

Angi continued, "For the new companies, we will follow the method advocated by Dr Ira Byock." He placed the signed papers on the table in front of Angi as she continued, "Final messages to loved ones will be based on the *Four Things That Matter Most*: Please forgive me; I forgive you; Thank you; and I love you. Plus: Goodbye."

Angi's final words evoked a vision of Emily's final moments and eclipsed all he had just learned. He panicked at the realization that, in two days, he would be saying farewell to the Yukon River forever. Never again would he stand on the riverbank, listen to the surging current, smell the earthy pine, and pay tribute to the eternity of drops as they rushed to the Bering Sea.

61. A Perfect Finish

It was a beautiful clear day for a plane ride in the Yukon. At 1:30 pm, Simon picked up Steve in front of the Edgewater Hotel. Akiko was already in the car, wearing blue scrubs. She had styled her hair and applied her makeup. Despite the scrubs and lack of jewelry, she looked as stunning as ever, better than anyone could have expected a seventy-three-year-old woman to look. As Steve gazed at her, Akiko smiled at him, which caused him to catch his breath for an instant, worrying she might launch into a rant. In relief that she didn't, he smiled back. As they drove up Two Mile Hill, he offered his hand and she squeezed it, reminding him of the first time she had held it hostage at the ballgame.

Simon drove the Benz across the taxiway to the waiting plane. They boarded without a word. Henry helped Akiko to her seat, and they buckled up. Before takeoff, Henry served the tea. "Don't worry," said Akiko before taking a sip. "It's just a microdose."

Steve followed her lead. It tasted like unsweetened tea, a bit bitter and with a hint of ginger. Once Henry collected their empty teacups, Steve offered his hand again. Akiko held it and smiled sweetly at him. They held hands on the tarmac in silence for twenty minutes waiting for takeoff, or maybe they were waiting for the tea to take effect.

As Steve concentrated on his own breathing, he noticed Henry studying them. Henry seemed skeptical, maybe even judgmental. Steve looked around the cabin of the plane, and as he stared at the blue bulkhead, it seemed as if they were already flying, but the plane had not moved.

The plane engine started. Akiko patted his hand. "Relax and enjoy. This is going to be a fabulous trip."

Steve felt a rush of euphoria wash over him as the plane gained speed and pressed him backward into the seat. As it lifted off, he put his arms out as though he himself was flying. As the plane tilted eastward, he banked his own arms, turning the plane toward Grey Mountain, so he could get a better look at the Yukon River.

He put his arms down and looked out the window. There was the river, snaking through the city. From horizon to horizon, the river flowed as though God had left a faucet running and the city was about to be flooded. Steve worried about it overflowing for a moment, but then remembered the dams. He thought of how he had balanced on the bridge above the swirly currents, suspended between the blue and the black, and communed with Emily.

Aloud, he said, "The children don't need me anymore. It's time for us to be together again."

The plane leveled off and began tracing the path of the river toward Tagish Lake. Mount Lorne appeared in the distance. Akiko gave him a dreamy smile and said, "Who are you talking to, Chewy?"

"It's Emily. She's in the river. When I'm with the river, she understands me. She's waiting for me. That's why I'm here."

"No, you're here to sing to me," replied Akiko sternly.

Steve furrowed his brow in confusion. "Sing what?"

"Come on, Space Cowboy," she said with a giggle. "Sing me the song you sang for the Munchkin while you held *her* hand."

Steve nodded as the meaning dawned on him. He took a deep breath and sang the opening lines of *Beyond the Sea*.

As the plane soared over the Taku Arm of Tagish Lake, Akiko leaned her head back. Her smile grew as Steve sang softly in her ear. She squeezed his hand as he finished the third verse.

Steve leaned back in his seat and closed his eyes. Rachel appeared. When she saw the bearskin with the huge grizzly head pinned to the bulkhead, she scolded Steve. "It wasn't the bear's fault. Bears get hungry, too. You have no reason to fear them."

"Do you blame me for your mother's death?" he asked.

"Of course not," replied Rachel. "She had cancer. But did you remember to buy chocolate raspberry truffle ice cream?" It was Rachel's favorite, and Emily's too, and he had not purchased any since Emily's death.

"Do you still want me to buy it?" asked Steve.

"Just because a girl paints her nails doesn't mean she doesn't like ice cream," Rachel replied with a playful lilt.

As he searched his pockets for his stolen Goodenough pen so he could add the ice cream to his grocery list, Harold made an announcement. Henry stood up to go to the door controls. The plane leveled off as they flew along the base of Jubilee Mountain. The yellow light came on, casting a strange glow over them, and chaos enveloped the cabin as the door began to open.

Harold made another announcement, but it was drowned out by the noise from the open door. Akiko was lost in the moment and didn't seem to notice the mayhem of wind and light and noise which had descended upon them. Only Steve noticed it–this must be how Saturn feels. He was lost in a swirling cloud of mosquitoes which were refracting light strangely in loud patterns across the bearskin pinned to the bulkhead. Through the frenzy he heard Emily's voice. "I will always love you, Steve. Don't worry, someday we'll be together forever." Her words brought him back to Pioneer Cemetery, to the tombstone.

How long is forever?

He heard his name. Akiko called to him, "Steve, Steve. It's me."

He blinked and looked at her. Akiko was right–it was her. She was sitting right beside him. He looked around the cabin for Emily and Rachel. There was only Henry who gave Steve a very judging look before signaling to Akiko. She let go of Steve's hand and undid her seatbelt. Steve undid his seatbelt too, but Akiko stopped him and put her mouth to his ear. "Stay where you are, dear. I've earned this. This is my time, not yours."

He looked into her eyes, and she looked sternly back. For a moment, it wasn't Akiko–it was his grandmother, except without the whiskey smell. She was back and she wanted him to buckle up. God, he missed that woman. He had never said goodbye to her. He re-buckled his seat belt. Akiko kissed his cheek and stood. She seized the railing and lurched her way to the plane's rear door. Her scrubs flapped in the wind as she grabbed the handle by the door and turned to face him. The light changed from yellow to exotic green. Henry gave a thumbs up.

Akiko smiled at Steve, gave him a four-finger wave, and mouthed the words *bye-bye*, like a grandmother would do to a five-year-old as she stood by the mailbox and put him on the school bus for the first time. Steve blew a kiss to her and returned the four-finger wave, as though he was looking out the bus window at her. She let go of the handle and put both hands over her head like a diver. Gracefully, Akiko turned and dove straight out the door.

Akiko didn't invite me along on this trip to help her. She invited me so I could bid farewell from the precipice. It was her final gift to me.

"Emily is gone, my little Mars Bar. It's time to move on. Tomorrow begins your new forever."

A skeleton resembling Henry closed the door and spoke into his headset to the pilot. If the skeleton noticed Steve weeping, he gave no indication of it. The chaos, including the strange green glow and wind, subsided, leaving the cabin eerily still. The bearskin was gone. In its place, perched on the bulkhead, was a giant butterfly with purple dots, flapping its wings at a slow and easy pace. Steve raised his face higher so he could feel the breeze. The giant butterfly fluttered away, leaving Steve to weep alone as the plane banked hard to the west for its return to Whitehorse, without Akiko.

We first met at the Rockies versus Mariners game. "Hi, handsome, what are you doing over here all by yourself?"

"Sorry, just spacing out."

I could have replied, "Just watching the baseball game." Then, for the past two years, I could have been Joe DiMaggio hanging out in the Dugout instead of Jabberwocky lost in Space Mountain.

Damn, I'm going to miss those taunts from outer space.

When the plane landed, the Benz pulled out onto the taxiway. Steve climbed unsteadily down the plane stairs, and Henry opened the back car door for him and helped him take a seat beside Meriwa. She was wearing Kahului's pearl necklace and earrings, a teal silk blouse, checked skirt, and the three-inch black Prada heels. He touched the watch and then took her hand. She wiped a tear off his face, moved closer to him, held his arm, leaned her head against his shoulder and pressed her bare leg against his jeans. They drove down Two Mile Hill toward town like that in silence. Simon pulled up in front of the Edgewater Hotel and they walked next door to the Dirty Northern Bastard. They chose a booth and ordered dinner.

As the server came for their plates, Steve ordered more wine. From his seat in the Benz, Simon waved as they snuck the open bottle out of the bar and into the hotel.

Meriwa followed Steve up the stairs and to his room. He pulled one of his Harley side saddle bags out of the wardrobe and began removing shirts and jackets from hangers, folding them, and placing them in the bag.

Meriwa kicked off her heels, served the wine, and sat in bed with her legs up. She sipped and watched Steve pack. As he walked past the foot of the bed he stopped and looked at her.

"Honey Pie, you look quite fetching," he said.

"Do you really think so?" she asked with a smile.

"Do you ever think you're taking this too far?"

She uncrossed her ankles and raised her left knee a little. Peeking over the top of her glass, she took a sip. "What do you mean?"

Closing his eyes, he shook his head. He opened his eyes and smiled. "Uncle."

Meriwa giggled. Steve resumed packing.

They'd strung it out as long as possible, but the bottle was empty, and the packing was done. Meriwa texted Simon. He came to the room and helped her carry the extra stuff. Steve followed them out, and as they were filling the trunk, he put the single black, soft-sided Harley trike case into the trunk of the Benz.

"Meriwa, my sweet, can you please help me with this bag? I never found just the right spot for it." Steve said it as though there was no room on the bike, but given her smile, she knew it meant more.

When Simon turned, Steve took Simon's hands in his. They looked at each other in silence. Steve thought of the night they first met, and the river. "Goodbye, Simon."

"Steve, I'll be waiting for you at the Rendezvous. When is the Rendezvous?"

"The Rendezvous, in late February."

"Very good. The cheechako remembers."

Steve turned to face Meriwa. "Now, are you ready?"

Meriwa gave him a sober look. "I'm ready." She stepped back and with a smile, did the Hollywood pose.

Steve looked at her shoes, then slowly upwards, past her knees, hemline, small waist, blouse, Kahului's pearls, until he met her exotic eyes. He licked his lips. "Honey pie, you look delicious."

She put her arms around his neck, giving him a tight hug.

"Goodbye, Honey Pie, my love," he whispered.

"Goodbye, Mea Pie," she whispered, before biting his left earlobe and releasing him.

She took his hands and looked into his eyes. "Thank you, Steve."

"You're welcome, Meriwa," he replied, as she turned away.

Simon opened the rear door of the Benz. Meriwa got in, and they pulled away, leaving Steve feeling vapidly alone on the sidewalk in front of the Edgewater Hotel, in Whitehorse City, of the Yukon Territory.

What a Long Strange Trip It's Been.

Epilogue: Sunset on the Big Sur

They agreed to meet on the last Tuesday in September in Carmel-by-the-Sea. Steve rode in from Denver, arriving just past noon. Meriwa and Ron descended the stairs to meet him as he was unpacking his motorcycle in the courtyard of the Coachman's Inn.

"Nice shoes, Meriwa. Let me guess, Prada, size seven."

"How did you guess?"

"How was the ride?" asked Ron.

"Drop dead easy, eh? I would do it every Friday just to ride the Pacific Coast Highway, except for two little details: Utah and Nevada."

"Skipping school? Playing hooky, are we?" asked Meriwa.

"Yes, I have gone back to teaching. At this very moment, in Denver, a substitute teacher is grappling with the antics of my very own History of English Literature students."

Clyde was halfway through a drink. He rose and greeted them as they joined him at the restaurant bar. Meriwa exclaimed, "Steve, no wedding ring? Let me guess, you lost it playing poker."

"No, no. It turns out, it's not such a great conversation starter on first dates." Steve sensed his ears growing warm as he swiveled his glass on the counter. "The best news is about the kids. I have been teaching Rachel to drive and I am taking both of them fishing and camping next weekend with Cosmo."

"That's great news," replied Clyde. "They finally contacted you!"

"Michael told me that their father forbade them to contact me sooner. When they saw me on CNN, they insisted, and he finally gave in. They still love me!"

Clyde got up and spread his arms. "Great news, Steve. Good for you!" Steve stood and they embraced.

Steve took his seat. "So, what's new in Whitehorse?"

"Me!" exclaimed Ron. "I would like to announce that the new mayor and I are engaged to be married. I will be moving to Whitehorse next week to help with the new property development company. I'll be the first sourdough from Fremont, Indiana."

Steve joined Meriwa and Ron in a group hug. Clyde motioned to the bartender, who immediately brought them a bottle and began pouring champagne into flutes.

"You told Clyde in advance?" asked Steve.

"The engagement and election results were both announced Sunday in the *Whitehorse Daily Star*," Clyde said with a smile as he raised his glass. "Here's to the happy couple."

At 6 pm, they departed, convoying south on the Pacific Coast Highway. It was Kyle who, many years ago, had chosen the spot. Ron was the only one who knew it, so he led, riding two up with Meriwa on Alamea's Ducati. Steve followed on his Harley. Clyde brought up the rear in his Benz. The cliff was located less than an hour's ride from the hotel.

On that day, four people who had loved her watched Alamea's fluttering ashes join those of her parents, as the sun set on the Big Sur.

Author Bio

Christopher Lude is a writer and an entrepreneur with a background in investment banking, finance, and accounting. He has worked at Price Waterhouse, Bear Stearns, and AIG in New York City, Cairo, Moscow, Budapest, Vienna, and London. He holds a bachelor's degree in accounting from Manchester University and an MBA from Dartmouth's Tuck School of Business. He is a father of teenagers, avid motorcyclist, beekeeper, and chess coach, residing in Denver with his wife, Hanna. A Perfect Finish is his debut novel.

Online Index

Thank you for reading A Perfect Finish. Please see the online index which illustrates many aspects of the book, bringing the story alive and depicting scenes of Whitehorse, the Alaska Highway, and Klondike adventures.

www.APerfectFinish.info

Scan for Interactive Index

If you like this book,
please write a book review.

APF Casting

Visualize the characters through character representation. Learn more about the casting for A Perfect Finish by visiting the A Perfect Finish Casting page:

www.APerfectFinish.info

Scan to See APF Characters

If you like this book,
please write a book review.

Ride the ALCAN on a Harley

Are you interested in what it's like to ride the ALCAN on a Harley? Read the author's riding logs for actual road trips:

www.APerfectFinish.info

Scan to Read Riding Logs

If you like this book,
please write a book review.